THE CAPTIVE

Also by Bruce Grossman

Poetry
  We Go On Living

Memoirs
  No One Came To Taos To Be Jewish

THE CAPTIVE

A Novel

Bruce Grossman

PACOIMA PRESS

Printed in the United States of America
First Printing 2022

ISBN: 979-8-218-12097-9

Pacoima Press

THE CAPTIVE

A Novel

Bruce Grossman

PACOIMA PRESS

THE CAPTIVE

Cover Image Attribution: Sandy Koufax, Los Angeles Dodgers - Source Credit to "University of Southern California. Libraries" and "California Historical Society."

Cover Design: ZenithPublishingSolutions.com

Printed in the United States of America
First Printing 2022

ISBN: 979-8-218-12097-9

Pacoima Press

To our generation of captives, those who went and those who stayed and especially to those who did not come back.

He was a captive of baseball trapped by his talents and his instincts.

Jim Murray, *L.A. Times* Sports Columnist

Only two times in my life has the hair literally stood up on the back of my neck. Once was when I saw Michelangelo's work in the Sistine Chapel. The other time was when I first saw Sandy Koufax throw a fastball.

Al Campanis, Dodgers Director of Scouting

The only person you are destined to become is the person you decide to be.

Ralph Waldo Emerson

All we can do is breathe the air of the period we live in, carry with us the special burdens of the time, and grow up within those confines. That's just how things are.

Haruki Murakami

I devised a left-hander
Even more gifted
Than Whitey Ford: A Dodger
People were amazed by him.
Once, when he was young,
He refused to pitch on Yom Kippur

Robert Pinsky, "The Night Game"

CHAPTER ONE

Easter Sunday, April 18, 1965

What a game! Let me recap it for you, folks. First off, no one knew what to expect. It was cold this afternoon, and we are only six days into the season. It was no secret that Koufax had been diagnosed with arthritis in his left elbow after last season. I can't lie, there were some doubters out there. But on this day it only provided another challenge, another summit for the great pitcher. The Dodgers won six to two. It was an ordinary, perhaps even low-key, win for Koufax, a seven-strikeout complete game over Philadelphia; the kind of performance that has become his trademark. One of his nemeses, Dick Stuart, hit a two-run homer off him in the sixth inning, and he gave up five walks that indicated that his usual control was not yet on target. That probably had to do with his slow recovery from last season. But make no mistake, this Easter Sunday Koufax is back. His fastball sizzled, his curve had the big bite, and his delivery was smooth as silk.

It was the midsixties and times had changed. David Mandel didn't know it, but his life was about to tip out of balance.

Wednesday morning he woke early and walked outside. It was a crisp spring day in the San Fernando Valley with a hint of coolness in the air. The prevailing westerly winds had enough verve to push the smog through the canyons and over the forests of the Angeles Crest mountains into the vast abyss of the Mojave Desert. A scent of citrus wafted through the air from the wild fruit trees that lingered in the utility easements separating subdivisions. He was thinking about baseball.

From his earliest memories, David would go to sleep with box scores in his head. He replayed the games again and again, seeing the rectangular schema in black and white: at bats, hits, runs, RBIs. Then there were the pitcher's stats: innings pitched, hits allowed, runs, earned runs, bases on balls, and, finally, strikeouts. Sandy Koufax, a pitcher for the Los Angeles Dodgers, was starting his eleventh season, and David was more than a little interested. David pitched for the East Valley High School team. Koufax was his hero. They were both left-handed and Jewish. Koufax ended the 1964 season in August, failing to win his usual twenty-plus games. No one knew for sure what the '65 season would bring.

David was in love with Rita Cano. As a senior in high school, Vietnam loomed in front of him. He was waiting for Rita at their regular meeting place in the student government room. Rita, a cheerleader as well as class president, and David, a student athlete with excellent grades, had privileges and freedoms to be places without supervision or justification.

Full count, he thought as he paced around the room. Three balls, two strikes, no room for error. In this case, the next pitch was his rendezvous with Rita. He knew she would be walking in the door any minute. In David's mind, not only was the count full, the bases were loaded. He wanted to be with her, and at the same time, he knew it had to end. He needed to move on with his life, wherever that was going. Rita had made it clear she wanted marriage, or at least, a commitment beyond graduation.

They had arranged the meeting the previous night. David pulled the shades and sat down and imagined Rita. She had a rare, elegant presence that defied her age and upbringing. Sweetness pervaded all that she did; whether it was tending her father's garden or sharing lunch with her friends, she exuded warmth and integrity. At five foot eight, she was tall for an Asian woman, her body shaped and contoured in an athletic way; partly from running middle distances in track, partly from cheerleading, but mostly from the physical way she lived with her family—a daughter working like a man beside her father, in lieu of any sons.

David was excited when Rita entered. He liked what he saw. She was wearing her crimson cheerleading outfit—pleated skirt and sweater top with E.V. scrawled diagonally across the front. She had on white tennis shoes with tiny red pom-poms attached to the laces. Her outfit aroused him. He wasn't sure why. Maybe it was the vulnerability she conveyed. She confessed that she felt a twinge of embarrassment wearing the costume around campus. Once a game started, she said she didn't mind, but walking around campus looking so "cute" unnerved her.

"You're late," he said.

"I couldn't get out of Civics class until I turned in my report."

David moved toward her. He stood just over six feet, with long arms he worked regularly on the weight bench. His thick hair, dark eyes, and olive skin appealed to Rita's primal desires. At least that's what she had told him many times during the two years they had been together. David bent forward and kissed her. It was like diving into an ocean grotto. It was another world—green and blue fish, yellow coral, light coming in from all sides. He continued kissing her, pushing hard on her lips so he could taste the delicacy of her soft tongue against his. He grabbed his sweater and her coat and made a mattress of them atop the table, then he gently lowered her onto the bundle. Rita shuddered and pulled him closer. Just as he began to unbuckle his belt, Rita suddenly raised her hand and stepped away.

"I think we better stop," she said.

"Why?"

"I think you know the reason."

"You're afraid someone might come in? The door is locked."

"It's not the door. It's about our future."

"Future?" David replied.

"Don't play dumb. Don't insult me. You know what I mean."

Rita straightened her clothes and disappeared down the hall. He knew what she meant all right. He also knew that the "future" was plagued with uncertainty. As much as he loved Rita, he couldn't see any way they would stay together.

After practice David drove home with his best friend Lou. They were close. Both were pitchers, but there was more to it than that.

"Rita and I are fighting again."

"It figures," Lou said.

"Because?"

"Because you keep stringing her along and she knows it."

"I'm not ready."

"Like you always say, it's a full count. You got to do something."

David steered his Ford Galaxy toward Van Nuys Blvd. It was an artery along the eastern spur of the San Fernando Valley where his family lived. He knew it well. He knew the land around this neighborhood had once been graced with miles and miles of orange and lemon groves.

"Can you imagine how this place used to look," David said.

"I can. It must have been beautiful before they cut down the trees, flattened and flagged everything," Lou said.

David turned on the radio. The news was still reporting in vivid detail the execution of Perry Edward Smith and Richard Eugene Hickock that had occurred just after midnight. David had already heard the news that morning. Hickock was first at 12:41 a.m., and then Smith at 1:19 a.m.

"That whole business makes me sick," David said, "the way they described the last squirms and gasps." He had imagined the duo hanging all day. It was part of the reason he wanted to distract himself with Rita that afternoon. Sex had many benefits.

"You know," Lou said, "I saw an article in the *L.A. Times* this morning. Truman Capote was present at the execution. He's supposed to be writing a book about the whole affair."

Leave it to Lou to find some literary significance in the ghastly episode. It was part of what intrigued him about Lou. He'd not heard of Capote. David pictured the two men as they each stepped to the

4

gallows. Their heads twisted in what could only have been a cold, damning fear. Then pain and, finally, nothing.

"Okay," David said, "who is Truman Capote?"

David felt depressed after dropping Lou off at home. He wanted to see Rita, and at the same time, he wished he could just end it. They had planned to meet again at the library, but David wasn't sure if she'd show up.

He drove home through the familiar streets of the east San Fernando Valley. He passed the liquor store on Laurel Canyon where he and his classmates occasionally scored six packs of Coors and fifths of rum while waiting in the shadows and offering winos a couple bucks to make the purchase. He stopped for a moment at Flores Street, where Rita lived. He considered driving to her house but decided no. Her family would be around. He drove west past the Catholic church his friend CJ Agostino and his family attended every Sunday.

Greasy papers from the Tastee-Freez and local taco stands swirled in the spring winds and eventually found their home in the chain link fences of abandoned dirt lots. It was the sleazy part of the Valley, the piece no one desired; forgotten in the titillating, glitzy developments of Sherman Oaks, Encino, and the newer West Valley communities of Granada Hills and Canoga Park. The Hispanic culture had already been washed away, simonized, and flushed out. Any trace of Black culture was as absent as Santa Claus in July, except for the small enclave of Black families that lived east of the tracks on San Fernando Road.

There were the Asian families, mostly Japanese like Rita's, whose stories betrayed the golden-sunshine culture and, instead, represented the disenfranchised and forgotten. By 1965, everyone was ready to "unremember" the relocation camps where Rita's mother and father had met. Like so many proud American-Japanese families, they were still scratching out a living, having wasted their college years living between barbed wire fences in their own country, wondering what they did wrong other than be born Japanese.

David parked under a sycamore tree. Jacob, David's father, had planted several trees across the large corner lot where they lived, in one of the veteran's specials the government helped finance after the war. Jacob and his friend Phil ran a small auto parts store. They also rebuilt engines and transmissions. David worked with him in the summer, driving through the smoggy maze of L.A. freeways: The Golden State to the Santa Monica to the Santa Ana, then across the off-ramp to the Harbor Freeway and, finally, off at Bell Ave.

That night his father was working late to avoid the crunch at rush time. His sister Alex, short for Alexandra, six years his junior, had ballet lessons so she wouldn't be home either. It would just be him and his mother. David's thoughts were riveted on meeting Rita at the library. He braced himself as he walked in the door, determined to push through dinner and meet Rita. He hoped she wasn't still angry with him.

David sat down at the kitchen table and waited for his mother to begin the intractable war. Her annoyance and resentment spilled over whenever she suspected he was about to see Rita. It had been over a year since both Rita's and David's families forbad the relationship, but that hadn't stopped them. It just made it more complicated, and for David, until recently, more exciting. Lately he had doubts. Plenty of them.

"So what is tonight?" his mother scowled, putting a plate of breaded veal chops, mashed potatoes, and broccoli in front of him as soon as he sat down.

"The usual," he said as he crunched down on the crisp meat and snatched a bit of fried onion that had skirted off the top. "Studying at the library. I've got tests tomorrow in English and History, and then I'm going to meet the guys at the Highlander for a Coke or something."

"You're still seeing Rita, aren't you? That's what this library business is about. I've talked with you about this, it just isn't right. You know that her parents feel the same way."

"Ma, I told you what I'm doing, so just stop, okay? I've heard this crap a thousand times. I'm not seeing Rita."

"You're still seeing her. I know you. I can feel it, and you'll be sorry!"

"Thanks for dinner, Ma. I've got to go. I'll be home before ten."

David placed his dish in the sink and opened the refrigerator. He grabbed two of the chocolate and raspberry rugelach his mother had baked the night before.

"You're still the best baker in the Valley, Ma." He kissed her on the cheek, but it didn't reduce her disdain; her lips stretched taut, her eyes like a lioness about to attack.

"You're a liar, David. You are going to see her!"

He closed the door and walked into the twilight, wrapping the rugelach in wax paper and setting it carefully on the passenger seat. "Bitch," he murmured under his breath as he started the engine.

David knew his mother's story. He had heard it dozens of times. Her father, who drank too much, died when she was eight. His ice truck lost its brakes and smashed into a train in Chicago. The Great Depression was not a time to be raised by a single mother, even if she was as resourceful as his grandmother Judith. Her father's death opened a vein of torment that lasted through the years. Understanding didn't make living with her bitterness any easier. David was more than ready to leave home.

The San Fernando Public Library had a large parking lot that was never filled. He sat alone, waiting, still troubled by the executions that morning. The image of the two men flopping lifeless and spent was more than he could handle. His grandmother Judith had died the previous summer, and he quaked at the memory of her corpse lying stiff and sallow, looking like a mannequin from the wax museum. Death's immediacy lingered and disturbed him. David fixated on the image of one human being putting a noose around another. The executioner touching the freshly cut hair of the victim as he lowered the rope over the top of his ear, smelling the dread, the sharp musk of anxiety, then fastening the pleated cord around the neck and stepping back to witness. David could not let it go.

Rita drove her older sister's 1958 baby-blue Chevy. She wore her favorite black pleated skirt with a white frilled blouse, the first two buttons unfastened, revealing her tanned skin and the tiny gold cross she wore with quiet reverence. There she was with that smile, her lips moist, frosted with a pale-red gloss, and a thin wave of liner around her eyes. When he saw her getting out of the car, all his thoughts about Hickock and Smith, as well as a disturbing rumor that one of his friends might already be in Vietnam, vanished. He worried about what she had said earlier that afternoon.

Rita climbed into the Galaxy and kissed him on the lips. She slid close and snuggled up next to him.

"I'm sorry about this afternoon," she said. "Let's just forget about it for tonight."

"Music to my ears," he said.

"But David, we do have to figure this out."

"I know. Believe me. I know."

Rita put her hand on his thigh and he immediately reciprocated, so that they were both in full throttle as David left the parking lot and headed for the spot above Hansen Dam where they liked to park and look at the sprawling lights of the San Fernando Valley. Neither of them spoke about the future. They just let their passion have its way.

After dropping Rita back at the library parking lot, David turned on the radio. The Dodgers had won their second game of the season. Claude Osteen pitched a two-hitter against the Pirates. Ron Fairly hit a home run to seal the game, and Maury Wills stole three bases, giving him five in just two games. Koufax was scheduled for Sunday. David couldn't wait. The image of Koufax on the mound stayed with him and sustained something within him that he couldn't quite understand. He rounded the corner of his street and slowly eased into the parking space.

CHAPTER TWO

Thursday, April 22, 1965

It's a beautiful night here at Dodger Stadium, and Koufax just aced the New York Mets two to one for his second win of the season. In the bottom of the fourth inning, the Dodgers scored on singles by Maury Wills and Tommy Davis. The Mets came back in the fifth when Ron Swoboda singled home Roy McMillan after the aging shortstop, formerly of the Cincinnati Reds, got on base after an error by Wills. The game was tied until the bottom of the ninth when the Dodgers scored again to win it. Koufax struck out nine batters, gave up four hits and no earned runs. He complained that he felt off balance and out of his usual rhythm, and although he only walked one batter, he said that his control just wasn't there.

Monday morning David drove to Barney Kaufman's house to pick him up for school. They had been close friends since Little League. The "Barn" played catcher, and he knew every nuance of David's pitching repertoire.

As David pulled into the Kaufmans' driveway, the Dodgers game was still rolling around in his mind. Koufax! Koufax! What was it about him? The great pitcher never portrayed himself to be anything beyond a ball player. His sheer ability stirred and inspired David, but there was more. He wondered about the energy that pushed through Koufax's veins as he hurled a baseball. Where did it come from? As a pitcher, he could understand the thrill and passion of hurling an object through space, but when Koufax pitched, there emerged a concentrated motion, a balanced choreography that was soulful in its virtuosity and transcendent beyond words.

As usual, Barn was running late, so when David didn't see him outside, he parked and knocked on the Kaufmans' door. There was no response, so he opened the door and shouted, "Barn, come on, we're late!" Barn stormed passed David, his nostrils flaring like a gorilla, an unconscious tic that manifested when he was angry or nervous. Everything about Barn was expansive; his smile, his waist, his lust, all that along with his six-three and two-hundred-twenty-pound frame made him a force. What Barn had in size, he lacked in finesse. He threw his book bag and baseball gear into the back seat and started to rant.

"Did you hear about Rick Norris?" Barn blurted. "The crazy motherfucker! Can you believe it? He joined, and his asshole parents signed for him. He's already gone."

David started the car, put it in gear and took off.

"What are you talking about?" David quickly turned and looked at Barn's red-splotched face. "He did what?"

"He fuckin' joined the Navy three weeks ago, that's why he hasn't been in school. And he's already off to basic training. Jesus Christ, as nuts as he is he'll get his ass blown away. You know how he is, Christ All Mighty! Why didn't he tell anyone?"

David had known Rick since second grade. They had never been real close, yet he was still a friend. Always a little wild, always at the edge of things. Rick had disappeared. Now David knew why. He turned onto Van Nuys Blvd. It was a ten-minute drive to school. Traffic was light for the morning.

"You're sure?" David asked.

"Fuck yeah, I'm sure. He hasn't been in school, has he?"

There was a home game Friday, and David was slated to pitch, so he took it easy Thursday during practice. He jogged around the outfield with Bryce, Wiz, and Lou. Along with CJ Agostino and Barn, the six had been friends since the fifth grade. Bryce led the pack as they circled around the high chain link fence that divided the sheltered high school from the bedlam on the other side. Lou, Wiz, and David followed, with Barn trailing ten yards behind. They squawked about graduation, college, and Wiz and CJ's interest in joining before they got drafted, and of course, the recent news about Rick Norris. David couldn't shake the image of Rick in a uniform.

David found it difficult to imagine any kind of life that didn't include those five guys; they had shared their first drunk, their first sexual episodes, and at every initiation, they were there for each other. They stopped at the lone drinking fountain on the southeast corner of the field. Bryce shoved Barn when he attempted to sneak in before the others. They snarled at one another, then laughed and returned to the ball field. Lou now led the pack.

Driving home, David pressed his hands tightly around the steering wheel, as if the harder he squeezed, the more he could control his direction. There was the war, and there was Rita. David wasn't sure how it was going to end with her, but he knew it wouldn't last much longer. The war was making the front page of the *L.A. Times* as well as the six o'clock news almost every night. David learned a new lexicon of places; Da Nang, the DMZ, and the Mekong Delta. The Navy and Air Force had flown over fifty missions, some within sixty miles of Hanoi. The war was starting to boil over, and Rick was now headed into the steam.

After dinner David tried to find a place to listen to the Dodgers game where he wouldn't be disturbed. His father headed out to the garage where he had torn apart the guts of David's mother's 1960 Ford Falcon station wagon. Every year he swapped engines. The aluminum block couldn't take a lot of wear, but the good news was that the engines were easy to rebuild, if you had the right tools. His father was getting ready to remove and replace the old engine on Saturday, so he was just putting the finishing touches on the new version that required special wrenches with pressure gauges to be sure the seals were even and secure. David wanted to escape for the evening. He was about to set up his transistor radio with his books in front of him so it didn't look like he was just sitting around doing nothing, when his father said, "Hey David, could you give me a hand tonight?"

"Okay," David said. "Let me just finish up my homework and I'll be out in a minute."

"Don't take too long," Jacob said and walked out the side door to the patio that connected the house to the concrete pathway leading to the garage. David didn't really want to help until the game started. It bothered him that there was often a hermetic silence in the garage while he waited to pass a wrench or screwdriver to his father. The quiet didn't seem to bother his father, who had spent many years under the dark belly of large vehicles.

David put away his books and started into the garage. The radio was on to the pregame show; Vin Scully was talking about Koufax's last outing and how he didn't look like his old self. He had struggled and got the win, but Scully voiced concern about his "condition," and ruminated about the game that night, wondering which Koufax would show up. They were playing the Mets, and their lineup didn't have much punch, except for the right fielder Ron Swoboda, who had pretty good success against Koufax in the past.

The "Star-Spangled Banner" started to play. David disliked the melancholy drone and the accompanying sanctimonious patriotism the melody insinuated. Rick was going to Vietnam and the Ku Klux Klan was burning churches. The two events collided. Alabama State Troopers had killed Jimmie Lee Jackson, and marchers from "Bloody Sunday" were still recovering in Good Samaritan Hospital in Selma, Alabama. When the music ended David asked his father, "Do you need anything?"

From under the belly of the Falcon, his father said, "Hand me a 7/16 box wrench. It's in the first drawer on the right side."

"Sure, no problem," David answered. "Hey Dad?"

"Yes," his father replied as he started to leverage the wrench against a tight bolt.

"Does it ever bother you that the world is going to hell while we're adjusting valves and calibrating pistons."

There was a slight pause. "David, could you pass me that little can of penetrating oil. This bolt won't budge. David, the world is always going to hell one way or another. All any of us can do is make the repairs that are in front of us and hope for the best."

By the time that little exchange happened, Koufax had worked his way through the first inning. Scully said he looked like the old Koufax; both his pitches—the supersonic fast ball that seemed to leap over the bat as hitters swung and missed and his vicious overhand curve ball that broke straight down as if it were dropped from the top of an apartment building in Brooklyn. The announcer went on to laud how Koufax could also throw the curve at a much slower speed, making it virtually impossible to hit. It was such a pitch Koufax had used to decimate Mickey Mantle in the final inning of the 1963 World Series. A notorious off-speed hitter, Mantle looked paralyzed as Koufax stiffed him with his disappearing breaking ball, so that all he could do was stand in flat-footed amazement. Scully was full of those kinds of facts. The game dragged along. Each inning put David deeper and deeper into a trance. He no longer stood in the garage in the San Fernando Valley. He transported himself to another world where nothing existed beyond the mound, the chalk around the batter's box, the called strike, and the sound of the crowd.

"David, David, are you asleep?" his father called. "I need that torque angle indicator so I can set the valves. It's in the second drawer. It's that big tool with a gauge on it."

David jumped up and procured his father's request. Jacob deftly made the necessary modifications and called it an evening. By nine fifteen, David was back in his bedroom, listening to the final innings of Koufax's shutdown of the Mets.

The following day, all David wanted to do was discuss the game with Lou. Lou had a perspective that David wanted to hear, even if he didn't agree. They often shared lunch after Miss Swan's fourth-period English class. David needed a break from Rita. She was getting more restless as the end of the semester approached, and their future was anything but certain. Hanging out with Lou was a good diversion, although on this particular Friday, it turned into something more.

Lou and David gravitated to a particular bench between the Science Hall and the baseball fields. It required a bit of a walk, so most of the other students didn't bother with it. A lone pine tree provided just enough shade to keep the sun from hammering them as they ate. Lou Ash was a conundrum to David. He found himself both attracted and repelled. Lou was charismatic, impulsive, fearless, and at times very much a jerk, but he knew his baseball as well as David.

"Did you listen to the game last night?" David asked.

"No. I worked on that fucking paper for Swan's class," Lou said.

"Well, Koufax is two and 0 already. He didn't give up an earned run," David said.

"You really have a fixation on that guy. He's good, but so is Drysdale, in fact, Drysdale is more intimidating. There was an article in *Sports Illustrated* a few weeks ago where hitters talked about the pitchers they feared the most. Drysdale and Gibson were on the top of the list. Koufax wasn't even mentioned," Lou said.

"Yeah, that's probably because the hitters don't have time to really see the ball when he pitches. How can you ignore the number of strikeouts he has every season?"

"So what did you write about for Swan's class?" Lou changed the subject, yawning to emphasize his boredom in talking about baseball right now. David felt dismissed.

"That story, 'A Perfect Day for Bananafish,' was weird. All of a sudden Seymour blows himself away. I liked *Catcher in the Rye*, but this one was too strange for me."

"So what did you write about it?" Lou asked again.

Lou had a way of directing their conversations so he could demonstrate his superior knowledge and intellect. David hedged, knowing that whatever he said, Lou would refute it, but his curiosity outweighed his fear. David did want to get Lou's take on the story, so he blurted out, "Seymour kills himself because he can't relate to life after the war. He can't relate to his wife who is a shrew and a materialist. And he is attracted to the little girl because she is innocent, like the way Seymour probably was before the war. The bananafish are also innocent and naïve, thinking that life will have a happy future." David stopped and looked up to see Lou's smirk.

"That's the standard line. You'll probably get an A like you always do, but as usual, you really don't get the deeper meaning."

David sensed his face starting to flush and his muscles tensed. This was an old pattern. Lou, the know-it-all, offering David the privilege of his superior intellect. Reluctantly, David held his ground and listened.

"Salinger, like Hemingway, experienced war and came away profoundly wounded and discouraged about modern life. Seymour recognizes his limited choices; remain an alienated, tortured soul living in the superficial "phoniness" represented by his wife Muriel, a self-absorbed narcissist, or exit the scene completely, as he chose to do."

"Yeah, but suicide seems pretty extreme. He did it right in front of her while she was asleep!"

"Exactly! She is asleep, the whole society is asleep, meanwhile the bananafish gorge themselves and suffocate, drowning in their own gluttony. Does that sound familiar?" Lou asked.

David didn't know what to say, so he just sat there, looking at the ball field, thinking about the game that afternoon and wondering what Rita and he would do that evening. When he looked back, Lou was chewing on his sliced-turkey sandwich on wheat bread and staring at David with his icy blue eyes.

"Well?" he said.

"Well what?" David replied.

"Well, what the hell do you think about Seymour and the Bananafish? That's what we were talking about, wasn't it?"

"I guess I don't really care about Seymour or Salinger or your literary insights into the deeper meaning about things. I'll get my A and be on my way with Rita this weekend, and you'll be sitting around playing cards with the Wiz and Bryce or talking about books with your mom. That's what I think," David said.

"You know what's wrong with you, don't you, Mandel? It's not that you aren't bright, because you are. It's just that you are lazy and self-absorbed. It's always and only about you. It's really too bad that Rita doesn't see you for who you really are." Lou put down the sandwich he had been holding.

"Yeah, well, you know what's wrong with you, Ash? You have a two-by-four stuck up your ass all the way to your brain that makes you think you have some divine right to pontificate and judge all of us. But really, you are just a sad, lonely asshole who can't keep a girlfriend, never had a girlfriend, and wouldn't know what to do with a girlfriend even if you lucked into having one." David stopped for a moment. He heard Mick Jagger belting "Play with Fire" in his head. He gazed at Lou, realizing that things were getting worse, and as much as he wanted to stop and take back what he had said, it was too late. And then the dam burst.

Slowly, Lou put away the remains of his sandwich. David noticed the blond hair above his knuckles, his fair skin deeply tanned, and his crew cut, still fresh from last weekend. David saw that the sun started to melt the butch wax that held the curls straight up. Once, in a rare moment of vulnerability, Lou had told him how much he despised the thick curled shock of blond hair that made him look like Harpo Marx when he allowed it to grow out.

"You know, Mandel, she really doesn't care for you. It's just that she feels sorry for your ass and she believes you'd fall apart if she ever left you. She pities you, that's all, pure and simple pity. It's me she really opens up to, not you," he said.

"Right," David said. "You do the same thing with everyone's girlfriends. But you are the one they pity. You're still a virgin. You're the only one left, and it's not even because you think you're too good, it's really because you are just too scared. That's the truth."

Lou took a couple steps toward David. Neither flinched at first, then David snapped. He could smell the remains of turkey and mustard on Lou's breath, and he could detect the scent of his fear and and the musk of his anger. David looked straight into Lou's face. He stared and stared until all he wanted to do was obliterate what he saw, and at the same time, he wanted to embrace him and make Lou understand that their friendship was more important than any of this nonsense about books and society. Suddenly Lou's lips turned up ever so slightly, transforming his frown into a sneer, and that did it. It was a full count, and David delivered his pitch. His mind grew dark, then red, and then his arms exploded from his shoulders, pushing Lou hard once, and then again, and again. Finally David punched him hard in the chest. Lou stumbled and fell back, his face filled with disdain. Slowly Lou got up, brushed his pants off, all the while staring straight at David with his frosty eyes until, finally, he simply turned and walked away without a word.

Chapter Three

Monday, April 26, 1965

What a strange night here at Dodger Stadium. It drizzled on and off before the game. It was more like San Francisco than Los Angeles. Koufax lost his first game of the season. He must have had trouble warming up because of the damp weather. By the end of the first inning the game was pretty much over. Tony Taylor, the second basemen, led off with a single, but he was thrown out trying to steal. Johnny Callison followed with a home run, Richie Allen singled, Dick Stuart doubled him home. The left fielder, Cookie Rojas, tripled, and just like that it was three to zero. Koufax lasted six innings, gave up seven hits, including the home run, two doubles, and a triple. He only walked one and had six strikeouts. Although the Dodgers came up with three runs and nine hits, the Phillies scored once more in the top of the ninth to seal Koufax's fate, and he lost four to three.

David had trouble sleeping. The fight with Lou replayed again and again. He woke up at 5:00 a.m. Saturday and started writing down his thoughts. It was Lou; past, present, and future. The scuffle had flipped a switch inside him. It was as if his entire navigational system had disappeared. The more he wrote, the more he realized what a mistake he had made. They had shared so much.

CJ showed up at his house unannounced in the middle of the afternoon. David was surprised. It was unusual for any of his friends to visit before calling. They walked into the backyard and sat in lawn chairs.

"I heard about your fight with Lou. Sounds like you got the best of him," CJ said.

"I just lost it and smacked him once. That was it. He just walked away."

"Yeah, it's a good thing he did. You would have really messed him up."

"Probably. You never know," David replied. "Want some lemonade?"

"Sure," CJ said.

"What the hell are you doing here anyway? You in trouble or something?" David got up and CJ followed him into the kitchen. The house was empty.

"Naw, I just figured I'd come over because I know how you get when you and Lou get weird with each other," CJ said.

David stared at him as he poured the drinks. CJ, formerly Charles Joseph and until a couple years ago known as Charlie, was a close friend. Unlike Lou, CJ had no pretentions and very few inhibitions. He had hated the name Charlie. He told David it sounded like a taxi cab driver's name. One day he just upped and changed it. His parents, Tony and Dolores, didn't mind, in fact they liked it.

David handed CJ the glass and they adjourned to the backyard.

"Listen, the real reason I came over is because I want to go to this dance tonight in downtown San Fernando. They are doing a tribute to Ritchie Valens. It's going to be hot."

David sipped his drink and looked into CJ's bright blue eyes. His curly red hair and freckles made him look clownish, but there was a reckless wild tilt to his face. He appeared cocked and ready for action. "I've got two six-packs chilling on ice in the trunk. What do you say?"

"What time?" David asked.

"Seven fifteen. Be ready."

Rita was busy anyway. There was a birthday party for a cousin in East L.A. All girls. Hanging out with CJ would get his mind off Lou. He liked CJ. He had a soulful sweetness, an artistic perspective that was different from his other friends. The Agostinos were Italians, Roman Catholics. They were a handsome family. CJ's mother, Dolores, possessed a carnality that appealed to David and his friends. She never missed an opportunity to display her full cleavage that summoned comparisons to Sophia Loren and Ava Gardner. Trained as a soprano at Julliard, Dolores played and sang her favorite arias in the evening, wearing silk lounging gowns.

CJ honked at seven fifteen, and David sped out the door. He hadn't thought about Lou all afternoon. The scent of English Leather permeated the car as CJ peeled out, leaving just enough rubber to turn the heads of a couple of neighbors watering their lawns. The night was cool and open for business. David squeezed the edge of the seat as CJ purred through the street, teasing the speed limit.

"My dad nearly busted me because he found the beer when I was adding more ice," CJ said.

"Did he take it?" David asked.

"No. I told him I was bringing it for everyone at a party and he laughed. He said he used to do the same thing for his buddies. He said he was always the one who could score and told me to be careful." CJ said.

"Your dad is a good guy. And he sure knows his baseball," David said.

Of course Tony Agostino knew baseball. David had heard Tony's story many times. Before the Second World War, Tony played a season with the New York Giants. Then he joined the Marines. After he was discharged, he tried to get back, but he'd lost it by then. Still, he had played with the big boys and earned his glory and the credentials to be the resident baseball expert in the neighborhood.

"Well, I wouldn't say he's a *good* guy. Sometimes he's a real jerk," CJ said.

David knew what he meant. CJ inherited more of his mother's demure and musical traits. It was a part of CJ David admired and respected. When CJ dropped out of baseball at fourteen in favor of piano lessons, Tony was pissed. He wanted his son to finish what he couldn't because of the war. His rancor was multiplied because Tony managed and sponsored the youth team that CJ quit.

Ironically, it was CJ's older sister, Veronica, who was the athlete in the family. She ran sprints and starred on the basketball team. She was also beautiful, and each time David saw her, he couldn't help but wonder what a night with Veronica would be like.

CJ had related to David how awful his father had treated him after he stopped playing baseball. Finally, Dolores put an end to his hostility toward CJ by threatening to lock him out of the bedroom. CJ had joked about it at the time with David. Tony had backed off.

"Well, your dad is an intense guy, but he's helped me a lot with my curveball. He's old school," David said.

"Don't I know it. We're okay now. I've been talking to him about enlisting," CJ said.

"You're kidding."

"No, but let's not get into that now. It's party time, remember?"

David nodded and imagined "old school" Tony. David had heard the story from CJ. Tony came from New York and had fought his way to success, selling used cars, first in the Bronx and then in California. He switched to real estate in time to catch the first wave of development in the east Valley, and now he was riding high, at least from what David could see. Tony liked gold chains, opulent red wines, and good cigars.

They arrived at the San Fernando Community Center and found a parking space under a grove of eucalyptus trees. It was away from the crowd and street lights. CJ opened the trunk and yanked a six-pack of Colt 45 malt liquor. It wasn't David's favorite, but it packed a punch. They each popped a tab and chugged. The dance DJ was blasting "Summer Time Blues."

"Lou's a piece of work," CJ said and took another long draw of brew.

"Yeah. I can't really figure the guy out. He's a strange one. I wish I could have controlled my temper."

"He's a prick sometimes. I kind of stay clear of him. He deserved what you gave him."

"Maybe. It felt good at the time, but now I'm not sure what to do."

"Just keep chugging." CJ handed David another can.

They drank the first six-pack and staggered into the dance. The band was good. "Oh Donna," "We Belong Together," "That's My Little Suzie," were bouncing off the ceiling one right after another. There was no shortage of girls wanting to dance, and David and CJ accommodated. They partied hard until the music stopped and got phone numbers they each knew they'd never use. On the way home, CJ confessed his unwavering decision about enlisting. David listened and hoped it was just the beer talking, but feared his friend was deadly serious.

Sunday afternoon David called Rita. His head hurt and his mouth felt dry and rotten.

"Hi, I was wondering if you want to get together tonight."

"You've got to be kidding," she said. "You and CJ made quite a scene last night. You are an asshole as far as I'm concerned." She hung up.

He sat with the phone in his hand for a few seconds. He knew she was justified in being angry with him, but as he ruminated, he realized that he didn't care about anything right at that moment. It was going to end with Rita sooner or later. Maybe sooner was better.

Monday morning Rita came rushing up to him at the break.

"I'm so sorry," she said. "You were an asshole, but I shouldn't have hung up on you."

"Nothing happened at the dance," he said.

"I know. It's just that when I heard you were drunk it set me off. My Dad started drinking again, and then when I heard about you it put me over the edge."

"I'm sorry," he said. David realized his one night of debauchery, innocent as it was, reminded Rita of the times Tommy would stumble through the house, eventually finding his way to her bedroom. David felt badly, and at the same time, it was a welcome reprieve from the gloom he was carrying for Lou.

"Let's get together tonight. I miss you," he said. It was true, and at the same time he knew the end was near.

"Yes, I miss you too."

Nicky's Big Beef drive-in was the local favorite. Rita ordered the BLT with fries and a vanilla milkshake, David the double cheeseburger with onion rings and a cherry Coke. They both overdid the salt and ketchup. The soft comfort food went down easily and helped diffuse the quagmires they both faced. The future ceased for a few minutes as they sipped on straws and became stupefied with caloric madness, swaying in giddy delight to the tunes coming out of the jukebox—The Four Seasons singing "Dawn" and "Big Girls Don't Cry."

After David apologized to the point of tears, Rita forgave him again and allowed him to rationalize his transgression on the basis of his falling-out with Lou. They left the drive-in and headed to their favorite spot above Hansen Dam.

David drove home after an hour of fervent make-up sex with Rita. He turned on the light in his room, sat down on his bed, and immediately started to ruminate about Lou. They had been through this before, and it pained him that Lou could act as if David had fallen off the earth. Now it was the same. When they passed each other in the hallway or the locker room, Lou's eyes never drifted in David's direction. For Lou, it was a complete erasure of David's identity. Even on the ball field, when a random toss was required, Lou did it in such a perfunctory way that David was reduced to a stationary phantom.

David got up, grabbed some ice water, and walked outside on the patio while everyone in the house slept. It was quiet, and the calmness of the night added to his confusion and angst. Koufax had lost his first game of the year, but it was only April, and there were plenty of games left to play. Try as he might, the only constancy he saw in the days and weeks ahead had to do with a baseball player and a season that was just beginning. He could see thousands of stars and noticed the dots of satellites racing across the sky, orbiting with predictability, night after night, until they crashed.

CHAPTER FOUR

Friday, April 30, 1965

Dodger Stadium was packed tonight, as it usually is when Koufax is pitching. Over forty-eight thousand fans got to see Sandy battle the Giants. Here's a quick recap. In the second inning, Jack Hiatt, the Giants catcher, hit a home run and gave the Giants a brief lead. The Dodgers tied it in the bottom of the third, and then took the lead in the fifth on hits by the Davis brothers, Willie and Tommy. In the top of the sixth, Koufax didn't get anyone out; he gave up hits to Harvey Kuenn, Jesus Alou, and Willie Mays. That was it for the night. He was charged with six hits, three runs, only two earned. He didn't walk anyone and struck out seven. The Dodgers managed to score three more times in the seventh and eighth innings, pulling out a six-to-three victory. Stu Miller finished the game. As it turned out, Koufax had strained his thigh muscle. The trainer reported it was nothing serious, but it was a scare and he didn't get the win. It was an atypical Dodgers game; they committed five errors but had twelve hits. Hopefully, Koufax will be on the mound again Wednesday when he takes on the Cincinnati Reds at Crosley Field.

All week, David and Rita had burrowed into the *What are we going to do after graduation?* trance. David received his letter of acceptance to UCLA. Rita had applied to Berkeley but was placed on the wait list. She wanted desperately to get out of Los Angeles and was still crusading for David to go with her. Meanwhile, Rita enrolled at L.A. Valley College where everyone was admitted as long as you had a high school diploma. Earlier that month she had let it slip that her fantasy was that they would get married after graduation. It didn't surprise him, but in his mind there was just no way, yet he went along with it for awhile. He didn't say yes or no, but the last thing he wanted was a wife.

Avoidance proved to be the best tactic with Rita. He mastered that technique by listening attentively, letting her know he understood what she said and how it made sense for her, but saying that he just didn't know right now. Time was running out, and David realized that he would have to break it off with Rita soon. He didn't want to stretch it out over the summer, giving her any hope. Imagining a life without Rita both excited and terrified him. He romanticized that there would be a steady stream of new women at college that would keep him from being depressed and heartsick.

Walking toward the gym on Friday to prepare for the game against Laurel Hills, David looked around for Lou. He was nowhere to be seen. They still had not talked. David was slated to start, and he knew that Lou might be called for relief duties if he failed to complete the game.

David and Bryce sat next to each other in the locker room before the game. Both were nursing injuries. David had strained his left oblique the previous week. Bryce had turned his ankle during the same game, so they went together after lunch to the trainer to tend to their wounds. That gave them enough time to stretch, warm up, and be ready to play at three thirty. The grim concrete room had the stench of bleach and salted sweat mixed with the fragrance of unwashed laundry. David looked at Bryce silently, aware that in less than three weeks, when the season ended, nothing would ever be the same.

As they sat there, Bryce confided that he was thinking of terminating his relationship with Shanti. They had been together about the same length of time as Rita and David. As they talked David realized they both needed to find a way out. It wouldn't be easy.

Here's that full count again, David thought. The game was just a couple hours away. More than pride, David sensed a righteous determination, a desire to demonstrate his prowess to himself, and as much as he hated to admit it, to Lou as well. He wondered if Koufax had ever thought about having to prove himself. Surely, he must have had those moments. Lou would probably be sitting at the end of the bench ignoring and judging him at the same time. David slammed his locker closed and headed toward the field.

In the first inning David had his fastball working. He struck out the first batter on three pitches; two fast balls and then a wipe-out curve. He thought he heard Lou yell out in support, but he wasn't sure and didn't want to get distracted. The next hitter hit a line drive to Wiz at shortstop. He leaped and made a brilliant catch. Two outs. Next up was Laurel Hills' first baseman. He was a tall lanky kid, well over six feet, with a generous strike zone and a serious scowl on his face. Barn pumped his large meaty fist in his catcher's mitt and set a target. David rocked into his windup and fired a strike on the outside corner at the knees, exactly where Barn wanted it. David turned his back to home plate and rubbed the ball, wondering what to throw next. Although surrounded by his teammates, he felt alone. He swiveled back to see Barn with one finger down and his mitt high, indicating he wanted the fastball up. Another strike. This time the big guy swung and missed. Why fool around and waste a pitch? Barn read his mind. He wanted it low on the inside corner of the plate. David could feel adrenaline surging from his chest to his shoulder and down his arm. He wound and delivered. The bat didn't move. Strike three!

David slowly walked toward the dugout, searching for Lou's eyes. He wanted to sit down next to him as if nothing had happened between. He wanted to hear a little praise from Lou for his first-inning performance. Barn and Wiz followed David to the bench and slapped his back.

"You've got it today, Doc," Barn said.

"Way to fire," said Coach Martin.

David glanced toward the end of the bench where Lou sat with a couple of other players. They were talking, but David couldn't hear what they were saying.

There were only a few games left in the season, and David wanted to leave his mark. Maybe there would be baseball after high school, but he doubted it, so every moment on the mound gripped him with a sense of urgency. Today his stuff was electric. He was loving it. In the second inning, the Laurel Hills team went down in order. David sat down next to Barn and waited for his turn to hit. Bryce lined a single to center, and Barn followed with a thundering home run, giving David and East Valley a two-to-0 lead. David hit a looping single to right, but was stranded when the next hitter struck out and ended the inning.

David walked the first batter in the third inning and then gave up a double to the Laurel Hills' center fielder that scored the runner. It was now two to one. David managed to strike out the next two batters and got the third out on a pop-up to Wiz. The next inning David settled into a rhythm and got the side out in order, although he noticed a pinching sensation in his oblique. Between innings he stretched and the pain went away. Lou walked by, heading toward the drinking fountain as David was exercising, but didn't say a word. "Asshole," David murmured under his breath.

David eased off his fastball the last two innings, fearing that if he threw with his full velocity, he would tweak his back again. Instead, he spotted his pitches on the corners and moved the ball from low to high in the zone to keep the batters guessing. His curveball still had a good bite. With two outs in the last inning and the score still two to one, David walked two batters after a single by the tall first baseman. The bases were loaded and Coach Martin sauntered to the mound.

"David, you've pitched a great game, but I think your tank is empty."

"I've got this," David replied. "I know I can get this last out."

"Lou is ready to finish this for you," the coach said.

"No. I'm okay. I want to finish it myself!" He slammed his fist into his glove. "Come on, coach."

Coach Martin looked at David and then at Barn and Wiz who had joined the huddle.

"What do you think, Barn? How's his stuff?" the coach asked.

"Let him have this last guy. He's already struck him out twice." Barn grinned at David.

Coach Martin padded David on the shoulder and trotted back to the dugout. Lou, who had been warming up, returned to his seat at the end of the bench. Barn squatted behind the plate and flashed two fingers. David nodded and released his curveball, which clipped the outside part of the plate. Strike one. Barn pounded his mitt hard, encouraging David to keep it going. Once again Barn put down two fingers and David responded with the same result. Strike two. One pitch away and David noticed a tightness in his chest. He shrugged and rolled his shoulders back and took a long slow breath. One pitch. He focused on the sign from Barn. One finger and Barn lifted his mitt high toward the shoulders of the hitter. High fastball. One more pitch. His oblique started to pinch again. David thought about Lou, wondering if he cared about the outcome. Wondering when and/or how all this nonsense would end. But it wasn't nonsense. One more pitch. David wound up and released. The batter swung and missed. Strike three. David punched the air. Barn sprinted out and wrapped him up a bear hug.

David gave Bryce a ride home. Bryce was solid and compassionate, and their situations were not so dissimilar. Both were probably headed to UCLA, although Bryce still had some other options. David trusted him and confided his ambivalence about when to break it off with Rita as well as his angst about Lou.

"I want to cruise by Lou's house before I drop you off. You all right with that?" David said.

"Why? It's dinner time and I want to get home."

"I don't know. I just want to drive by and maybe knock on the door."

"For what? And besides, your deal with Lou doesn't have anything to do with me."

David didn't reply. He was sick of the situation with Lou and didn't have an answer. He dropped Bryce off at his house and wheeled the car back toward Lou's house. Night had taken hold, and David parked around the block from the house and started walking. He turned the corner onto Lou's street and was relieved to see that there wasn't anyone outside watering or hanging around. He walked slowly toward the Ash house, not sure what he was going to do or say. When he was three houses away, he decided to turn around. Then he changed his mind and kept walking toward the house. He still wasn't sure what he was going to do. Lou's bedroom was off a side yard filled with bushes and a maple tree with a healthy head of leaves. He considered again a direct approach—knock on the door and just confront Lou. But what to say? I'm sorry? It felt trite, and his courage escaped him.

In the darkness, it was easy for David to creep into the yard unnoticed and peek into Lou's window. There he was, sitting at his small writing table, twisting a pencil in his right hand. He was reading something David couldn't make out. Lou looked calm and engaged. David felt the urge to tap on the window. The branches of the maple tree started to poke his back. He didn't know what to do next. Suddenly, Lou came over toward the window, and David ducked, holding his breath, afraid to move. He waited for what seemed like a long time and then slowly slid back toward the street.

When he got back to the car, he opened the door quickly and sped away. *What a fool*, he thought, and then turned on the Dodgers game. He hoped that Lou had not seen him. And if he had, what would he say? He didn't have an answer. It was the bottom of the third inning and the Dodgers had just taken the lead. David kept driving toward a park in Van Nuys where he knew there wouldn't be a crowd of people. He wanted to just listen to the game for awhile until he figured out what do next. In the sixth inning, Koufax left the game with a strained thigh muscle. David started the engine and let it idle for a few seconds, then shifted into gear and drove home.

Chapter Five

Wednesday, May 5, 1965

Well, here we are at Crosley Field. Our fears about the strained thigh muscle were nothing more than that, fears. Before the game, Sandy said that he was ready to go, and he was. The Dodgers prevailed over the Cincinnati Reds four to two. For most pitchers, the victory tonight would have been stellar, but after the game Koufax downplayed his performance. He said that he didn't have his best stuff, but was able to make the pitches when he needed them. He didn't make any excuses about the muscle strain. He paid homage to the Reds sluggers Pete Rose, Vida Pinson, and Tony Perez. He said he was fortunate to not give up any big hits. In fact, the only extra base hit was a double by Tommy Harper. Koufax scattered nine hits, walked a batter, and allowed only a single earned run while striking out eight batters. After five starts, his record is now three wins against one loss with three complete games. And what's encouraging is it's the second consecutive win since Tommy Davis broke his ankle on Saturday. Losing our top hitter and last year's batting champion looked dire, but the Dodgers continue to find ways to win.

David called Rita from a phone booth next to Vons market on Saturday morning.

"You did what?" she said.

"I told you. I snuck around the side of Lou's house and looked in the window. I think he saw me."

"So what?"

"So I feel like an idiot. What do I say if he saw me and says something?"

"I don't know?" she said. "Tell him you are sorry and you weren't brave enough to just knock on the door. That's the truth of it."

David figured she was right, but that didn't change the situation. He wished he hadn't done it, but he did.

"Yeah, well, if he weren't such a jerk, it would be a lot easier," David said.

"David, is this why you called? I've got things to do."

"No, no. I wanted to get together tonight. I'm missing you."

"Really? It sounds like you are missing Lou."

"Hey, come on. I want to take you out for dinner, and there's a band at Ciro's I want you to hear." There was a long pause.

Then Rita said, "What time?"

"How does seven sound?"

"Just perfect," she said.

The traffic over Coldwater Canyon was light. Rita looked particularly beautiful. He wanted to forget dinner and the music and find a place to have her.

"Keep your eyes on the road," Rita squealed as David swerved a little too close to the edge of the steep road.

They got to the restaurant near the Sunset Strip—Amore, a little Italian place. It was surprisingly quiet for a Saturday night. David looked across the table and started to laugh.

"What's so funny?"

"I just can't believe how much I adore you," he said.

"How much?"

"More than my imagination can conjure."

"Well, we both know about your imagination," she laughed. "But how does that translate to what happens after we graduate?" Her smile transformed into a *You better take me seriously* grimace. She looked into David's eyes.

"Don't think I'm not thinking about it," he said.

"I'm sure you are just thinking about it. But that isn't getting us anywhere."

David froze. He wasn't ready to make a decision, not now, not sitting here at this restaurant before they had even ordered dinner. He wanted to stay with Rita as long as possible and move on after graduation. A part of him desired to be with her for the rest of his life. *OK, just say the truth.* His face thawed and he reached across the table for her hand.

"You deserve an answer. I really don't know what I want to do after graduation, and if you can't wait . . . well, I guess it's over."

The waiter arrived and they ordered.

"Well, it's not over as far as I'm concerned," she said. "I just wanted you to know I'm stressed, I'm scared, and I love you."

"Me too," David said. He didn't know how much longer Rita would put up with him. He had never felt so close to anyone. He suddenly thought about Lou, but that was different.

The waitress arrived with fresh hot bread and two dinner salads. The conversation turned to the evening's event. A band called the Bryds was playing at Ciro's. David had read a review in the *Times* and was excited. He hoped Rita would dig the music and the night would spin into a romantic and sexual tryst.

After dinner they strolled to the nightclub and got there before the line was too long. David bought tickets, and they found seats toward the front of the stage. Rita reached over and took his hand. It was warm, and she inched her shoulder close to his. David knew how she was. She'd get upset and irritated with him, but then she would relent, forgive or forget, or do something inside that made the moment right again.

They ordered drinks just before the band took the stage. The group took their instruments and started to play. David had heard of two of the guys in the band, Jim McGuinn and David Crosby. McGuinn had been around as a folk musician with the Chad Mitchell Trio, and David had seen him once before with Judy Collins. But tonight, as Crosby joined McGuinn on vocals, the band was totally electrified.

"They are fantastic," Rita whispered into David's ear.

He nodded and put his arm around her, swaying with the tunes. The band finished the first set with "Mr. Tambourine Man." David had heard Dylan's original folk version, but this was incredible. The lyrics rolled around inside David's head and he resonated with every word. Especially the ending:

Yes, to dance beneath the diamond sky with one hand waving free
Silhouetted by the sea, circled by the circus sands
With all memory and fate driven deep beneath the waves
Let me forget about today until tomorrow.

When the music ended, David was fired up and wanted to keep the night rolling. They drove back to the Valley, talking about the band. David turned left on Ventura Blvd. toward the freeway that lead to their special parking spot overlooking the west Valley.

"David, I'm pretty tired, can we just call it a night? It's been wonderful," Rita said.

"Really, after all the fun you don't want to?"

"It's not that I don't want you or want sex. I'm tired, but more truthfully, I've had it with car sex."

"Okay. I just thought."

"I know what you thought, David."

"All right then," he said, absorbing the rejection and realizing that things were rapidly changing.

David started the car and turned left onto Ventura Blvd. Rita snuggled close to him.

"You deserve an answer and I promise I'll let you know soon," he said. He frowned and turned toward Rita as she replied.

"Tonight was wonderful. I love you. I'll see if I can arrange to use my cousin's place this Wednesday. She usually works a late shift."

"That would be great," he said, relieved that no decision would be necessary until after Wednesday.

Tuesday afternoon at practice, David was warming up with Wiz and Barn. They played pepper, taking turns bunting the ball back to each other.

"Any word about Rick?" David asked Wiz. Wiz was closer to the Norris family than David. Barn had the bat in his hand.

"Crazy Ricky, no telling what he'll do," Barn said.

"This whole war thing stinks. What are we doing over there?" David said.

"Not for us to decide," Wiz said as he tossed the ball back toward Barn.

"Shit yes, it's for us to decide," David said.

Wiz looked at David, his face smeared with indignation. Coach Martin blew his whistle, and they ran in for batting practice.

Running alongside David, Barn said, "You might want to tone it down with Wiz. You know he and CJ have been talking about enlisting after graduation."

"I know," David said. "Believe me, I know."

Lou was the first to throw at batting practice and he chatted up all the hitters, making sly comments except when David stepped up, then he went dumb. David swung and missed at the first three pitches Lou threw. Lou sneered as he wound up for another pitch. David swung and clobbered the fastball deep into the shadows of left-center field. "Bring it on," David shouted. They were the first words he'd uttered directly to Lou since he smashed him in the chest.

Lou said nothing. The next pitch curved down and away from David, but he stayed with it and lined it into left field. Lou flung a high inside fastball that brushed David away from the plate and sent a clear message. It went back and forth between them for awhile. David barreling up a mass of balls while occasionally missing badly and making Lou look like he got the better of the encounter. The duel finally ended when Coach Martin yelled out, "That's enough, Mandel, let's get another hitter in there." David walked off, clutching his thirty-three-ounce bat and feeling satisfied, even though what he really wanted still remained very much elusive.

When practice finished on Wednesday, David drove to meet Rita. Tonight was the night. They were set for a rendezvous at Dina's. Rita's cousin lived alone in a small one-bedroom apartment off Chandler Blvd. in one of the many courtyard-like complexes that lined the busy streets of the north Valley. On the way over to the apartment, David thought about Dina. He not only liked her, he greatly appreciated her generosity. She was an affable young woman, only a couple years older than Rita, who always made her place available whenever Rita asked. "I understand," she'd say. "I've been there."

Desire filled David's pores as he cruised into the parking space at Dina's apartment. He walked up the steel staircase and looked out at the sky with its thick, lugubrious, almost-beautiful clouds. He knocked.

"Anybody home?"

Rita rushed him with open arms and almost bowled him over.

"Wow, I'm happy to see you too." They kissed for a long while.

Rita had already started on dinner. David could smell the oil simmering and saw that Rita had sliced and diced scallions, mushrooms, and carrots for fried rice. The jumbo shrimp lay idle, still encased in their shells. After their embrace Rita ran back through the maze of cluttered furniture into the galley kitchen and plunked the veggies into the sizzling oil, then she ran back to David. They started to kiss again until David gently pushed her back.

"At this rate, everything will burn and we will starve tonight," he said.

"It's okay with me," she smiled and laughed and made a noise in the middle of her throat like a mini hiccup. It was cute and seductive. Suddenly, David felt more ardent and less hungry.

"Well then, turn off the oil and take off your clothes."

Without a blink, she dashed to the kitchen, turned off the stove, and dropped her clothes in a pile right on the floor. She stood naked beside the green vinyl kitchen chairs, poised akimbo. David stripped as fast as he could. They stared at each other as if meditating on the image before them. David looked tenderly at Rita's body—the slight disproportion of her breasts, the right one just a little larger, her slender, elongated neck arched just to the left, her shoulders jetted back, and the little mole on her right shoulder beside the dimple on her bicep. He glanced down at her knees, round and perfect, and recalled how he had often massaged her smooth sculpted legs. Finally, out of embarrassment more than anything else, David stepped closer and wrapped her in his arms.

He danced Rita's naked body near the window and felt her ease into his chest. The sky filled the panes with an array of burnt-orange and crimson hues, so he could see the shape of the wispy clouds and the saturation of colors slowly dissolve into the night. The aroma of the vegetables lingered. David cupped her breasts; each nipple perfectly alert and nimble as he felt her quiver against his stomach. She was ready. David lifted her. She wrapped her legs around him, and they rocked and swayed, ending up on the table.

Exhausted, Rita whispered, "I bet you are hungry now." She smiled.

"A little," he said as he stared at her body. They got up.

"Listen," He continued, "let's not get dressed at all tonight, let's have a naked dinner."

"That sounds marvelous. Why don't you crank up the heat on the stove?" she said.

David did what she asked, all the while wondering at what point they would climb into the sheets and have another go at it. Meanwhile, Rita directed him to peel and devein the shrimp. They stood hip to hip, their bare feet nestled against one another. His shoulders rubbed hers while she heated the rice and veggies. He finished the shrimp and made a salad.

David scooped a dollop of salad dressing on his finger and nursed it into Rita's mouth as she gingerly moved the fried rice from the pan to the platter she had waiting next to the sink. As she turned away from him, David grabbed her shoulders and spun her around, kissing her and rolling his hands down her smooth hairless back, then inched his fingers up against the soft folds under her buttocks. He nudged her toward the bedroom. He faced her and looked deep into her dark, dark irises, into the pools without end, as they moved, unaware of anything but the delicate, subtle rhythm of their bodies. He saw her smile and, for a moment, felt the weightlessness of their life together. He loved Rita and remembered the nagging torment that ached within him, thinking it was just a matter of time until he had to let her go.

"My God, what has gotten into you tonight?" She sighed and returned to the kitchen and relit the frying pan for the shrimp. "Can we eat now?"

After dinner they pretended to watch television for awhile but got bored quickly with the new comedy *Get Smart*, so they each started to read. They burrowed into their copies of *The Great Gatsby* they were reading in preparation for an exam on Friday. Rita put her feet up on David's lap. They were both still naked. David began to massage Rita's feet as he read the part in the book where Daisy tells her husband Tom that she and Gatsby are in love, that they have loved each other for five years. Incredulously, Tom wants to deny the truth, but Gatsby insists that Daisy repudiate her love for Tom. Poor Gatsby, David thought as he moved his hands up along Rita's perfect legs. Poor everyone who loses in love.

"Let's go to the bed," he whispered. "We'll take a little nap before it's time to go. Under the light blankets their bodies folded and cupped effortlessly against one another. They lay together for a long time, dozing in and out of reverie and sleep. David couldn't imagine giving up this kind of pleasure. He loved her and found himself wanting to say, "I want to be with you forever," but he remained silent.

Rita turned to face him. "I hope you are at least giving us a chance. This is so extraordinary, you know. We'll never have this with anyone else."

"You're right," he agreed. "Yes, a chance."

"That's all I ask," she said, "thank you." She squeezed him tightly.

It was after midnight when David opened the Galaxy door and fell into the soft cushioned seat. Rita had just driven off, and he sat for a moment listening to the rhythms of his heart as he gazed into the inky L.A. sky. The stars glistened and blinked. He wished there was a simple map to get him through the next couple months, a way to pilot through the dark night, but nothing appeared except a distant flash from an ambulance.

He turned onto Chandler Street and flipped on the radio. It was Koufax recounting the evening's game. Sports radio was rebroadcasting his postgame interview. Sandy Koufax's voice was soft and understated. He sounded tired but confident, and as was often the case, there was just a twinge of apology. The Dodgers beat Cincinnati. Koufax's calm demeanor filled David with a sense of wonder as he drove past the Budweiser Brewery on Roscoe Blvd. The Brewery smelled of roasting hops. It reminded David of the aroma of the swirling beer that swayed and dripped as the hawkers plied the crowds at Dodger Stadium.

David knew that, somehow, everything would work out, even though he could not envision a clear path. He knew Koufax had come back from his minor muscle pull. He knew Koufax's next start was just four days away, against San Francisco, and that was enough to keep him going, at least for now.

CHAPTER SIX

Sunday, May 9, 1965

Well, it was a big crowd today at Candlestick Park. Koufax was matched up against Gaylord Perry. Over 40,000 fans got to see their Giants beat the Dodgers six to three. In the bottom of the fourth, Jesus Alou nailed Koufax for a homerun, his second of the year, and it gave the Giants a two-to-0 lead. The Giants' starter sailed through the first five innings before Willie Davis tied the game with a two-run blast in the top of the sixth to make it a two-to-two game. The Dodgers took the lead in the top of the seventh when Wally Moon drove in Wes Parker to give Koufax a brief lead. But Koufax was off; his control was terrible. He walked four batters, threw two wild pitches, and although his fastball was electric—striking out eleven in just seven innings—he didn't make it through the eighth. The Giants scored four runs in the bottom of the eighth. Jesus Alou had two more hits and the third baseman, Jim Hart, smashed two doubles and scored two runs. Koufax lost and his record now stands at three and two. It's too early to tell how the rest of the season will unfold for Sandy. Let's hope this is just a little bump in the road. His next start is against Houston on Thursday at Dodger Stadium. Hopefully, he'll turn it around against the Astros.

Thursday David dragged himself out of bed and just made it to school in time for his first class. Rita was already sitting in the second aisle, second row. She had placed a couple of books on the seat across from her in the first row, saving a seat for David. He nodded as he made his way to the desk and reached across, touching her shoulder and whispering, "Thanks." Before the bell rang, David craned his neck around to see if Lou had arrived. Lou sat solemnly in the back of the room, reading a book David could not make out. When the class ended, David glanced furtively toward where Lou had been sitting, but he was gone.

"You just can't let go of him, can you?" Rita said. She took his hand as they walked out of the room.

"He's a jerk," David said.

"Maybe. But you are a little pathetic. Just face it. He doesn't want anything to do with you."

"Well, that's pretty obvious. Hey listen, let's get together this Friday. Dinner and movie?"

"And talk about the future?"

"Yes, that too."

"Really?"

"Yes, really. Oh, I told CJ I wanted to meet him for lunch. Just wanted you to know."

"You aren't going to talk him out of going, you know."

"Maybe not. But I can't just do nothing either."

Rita shook her head and went off to class.

"Everyone is going to go sooner or later," CJ said as they ate lunch under the large outdoor canopy where everyone had gathered for the past three years. While CJ chewed on a double cheeseburger, his red hair glistening in the sun, an innocent smirk slapped on his face, he said, "You'll see, David, all of us will be there. They aren't going to allow anyone to escape, the best you can do is join and at least have a choice. Maybe I'll be lucky and get sent to Alaska or Germany."

"I know you don't believe that," David said. He imagined CJ in a uniform carrying an M-14 and a cigarette hanging out of the corner of his mouth, stalking through the jungle. He shivered.

"I heard Jackie Reyes' brother got sent to Germany last year, and now it looks like he'll get out next year with all kinds of perks and never have to serve in Nam. So don't feel sorry for me. Besides, it's my ticket out of here. College isn't an option. I'm sick of school, sick of my family, and sick of being stuck. I'm ready. And you know what? I want to go to Nam. That's where the action is!"

He took a long sip of his vanilla shake and pulled Lydia Ramirez, his girlfriend, closer to him. She was slim with long black hair and wore lots of eyeliner and deep-rose lipstick. Lydia was perky, intelligent, and she looked particularly sexy today in her tight cashmere sweater. David knew that even though she supported CJ, she didn't want him to go any more than Claudia wanted Wiz to go. Lydia's brother was already in Vietnam, a Green Beret, so she understood firsthand what was going on over there.

"Tell you what," David said. "Let me take you out for breakfast at Tito's Sunday. Give me a chance to talk some sense into that thick Italian skull of yours. You don't have to do this."

"You aren't going to talk me out of it, but I'll take your breakfast offer."

"Okay, I'll pick you up around nine."

Rita and David went to dinner Friday night, then to a movie, *The Pawnbroker* with Rod Steiger. It depressed them, and afterwards he drove to their special spot overlooking the Valley.

"God, what a downer," Rita said, staring straight ahead. "That war was so horrible."

"Sorry, I guess that was a lousy choice," he said.

"But, it was a powerful movie. It's just a discouraging story."

"Yeah. Maybe it's why I can't stand the thought of CJ and Wiz going off to war."

"It makes me think about my parents and how they were moved to that Manzanar relocation camp. It was horrible."

It was a tragic, hypocritical, and racist story. The only good thing about the experience was that her father Tommy had pitched and played first base for the San Fernando Aces, the internment team. He was good, according to Rita.

After the armistice, her family moved back to the east Valley and tried to start over, but Tommy never let go of his rancor. Japanese ballplayers weren't welcome in baseball after the war. One failed job after another led him right to the bar. By the time Betty and Rita came along, he was already a broken shell of a man with rough edges that needed to be dodged as much as possible.

"I know it was awful," David said. He knew she had to get away from home, and soon.

"David, let's go. I know you wanted to talk, but I'm just done."

"Next time," he said and started the car. He felt like he'd made it through the minefield once again.

As he planned, Sunday morning David drove over to CJ's to pick him up for breakfast and take him to Tito's Pancake House on San Fernando Road. Tito's, a classic spot, had been around for thirty years; it served as a local family place as well as a truckers' hangout. While Tito had all the American specialties, including pancakes, CJ and David always targeted the cheap Mexican fare: the huevos and enchiladas filled with the hottest salsa in Southern California.

"You ready?" David knocked and opened the door to CJ's house.

"Be right there, I'm just shaving. Say hello to Veronica, she's in the den."

David walked through the living room, decorated with Italian ceramic figurines of saints and classical Romans and plates and cups from Tuscany. Down the three steps of the split-level sprawling home, there was a cavernous den filled with baseball trophies and a large elk head over the bar. Tony had shot it in the Tetons in 1956. Veronica sat on the end of one of the two large leather couches that filled the room. She was reading *Vogue*, her legs crossed, her red hair draped and flowing over her green silk blouse. She didn't notice him until he called her name.

"Hi Ronnie, when did you get in?"

"I drove in Friday from Phoenix."

David walked over and sat on the couch across from her. She put down her magazine, leaned over and touched his knee. David smelled the Chanel mixed with the scent of her lipstick. Veronica was a real looker, now a senior at Arizona State studying political science, she was headed to law school and life in the fast lane."

"David," she whispered, "I'm really worried about CJ. Isn't there anything you can do? He's hell-bent on joining and going to Vietnam."

"I know," David replied, as she removed her hand from his knee.

"Believe me, I've tried and continue to try, that's why I invited him to breakfast. From what he and Wiz have told me, they are planning on leaving the week after graduation. I know. It sounds pretty crazy," David said.

"Crazy. It sounds suicidal. CJ isn't any more ready for combat than I am. He'll never be ready. He is running away from his father and trying to prove something that doesn't need to be proven. David, when I think of him over there, I . . . I . . . "

Veronica's eyes started to flood with tears, and she reached over and put her hand on David's knee again.

"David, please promise me you'll try and talk him out of this, please." David felt her fingers squeeze.

"Yes, yes, I promise," he said, staring into her doleful eyes.

"Hey, what's going on?" CJ shouted from the top of the stairs. "You trying to hit on my sister?"

"CJ, you always take it right to the street level, don't you? I'm just telling David how upset I am about my friend Jane at school who just lost her baby."

"Hey, Ronnie, I was just joking. I know my buddy David would never try anything with you, and besides, he's already got his babe," he said as he walked down the stairs and over to the piano.

David knew otherwise. He would like to "try" almost anything with Veronica.

"CJ, just stop it," Veronica said, raising her voice just enough to let CJ know she'd had it, wiping her eyes with a tissue at the same time.

"Well, are you going to buy me breakfast or what?" CJ said while running his hands across the keys, playing a little riff from Mozart's Piano Sonata No. 14.

"We are out of here," David said and nodded toward Veronica.

"Have fun," she said, looking up at David, pleading with her eyes.

On the way to Tito's, they passed the turnoff to Rita's street. David wondered what she had planned for the day. They hadn't talked. Lydia lived in the same neighborhood, and CJ wanted David to cruise past her house so they could snoop on her. David declined, since he was hungry and knew that if they did stop, CJ would want to drag her along, and David didn't want any distractions that morning.

"Veronica's looking pretty fine, isn't she?" CJ said.

"She always looks good. You know she is really worried about you, don't you?"

"I suppose so. She's afraid her little brother is going to go down in Vietnam." CJ yawned as he pushed the power-window button and let in the fresh air. "Do you mind if I smoke?"

"Yes, I mind. For Christ's sake, the air smells so good, why foul it up with those cancer sticks?" He knew once CJ started, he'd chain-smoke the entire morning.

"Man, you're irritable today," CJ said as he stuffed his pack of Marlboros back in his shirt pocket.

"Maybe so. Right now it's rough for everyone, even if you don't think so," David said.

"I can see that. I stay up nights wondering what the hell's going to happen. Hey, you just missed the entrance!"

Inside, Tito's was a little smoky, but they were seated quickly despite all the people. Spanish music played on the jukebox, with an occasional song by the local hero, Ritchie Valens, a Pacoima boy who died in an airplane crash in 1959 with Buddy Holley. Ritchie's big hit "La Bamba" started to play as David and CJ sat down at a booth with a red-and-white-checkered vinyl tablecloth. A curly haired, smiling waitress named Kathy greeted them, "Buenos dias, hombres, what would you like?"

They ordered without looking at the menu. Kathy disappeared into the kitchen.

"This place is great, isn't it? You'll miss shit like this if you go over there," David said.

"What, you think I'll go over there and not come back. Thanks bro," he said, rubbernecking around for single girls.

"No, of course I don't mean that. You could be hanging out with the rest of us, that's what I mean, instead of . . ."

CJ cut him off. "Instead of what? You think this is my choice? Hey, I didn't start this war, I didn't start this draft, I don't have anything against the Viet Cong or communists or whoever. I just don't want to sit in some dumbass classroom reading books that make no sense just so I can run away from the draft. It sucks either way, but at least this way I'm making it my decision, and they say I'll get the training I want." CJ put three teaspoons of sugar in his coffee, stirred it and looked at David. "What!"

"That's a shitload of sugar," he said.

"Yeah, it is. So what? Anything else you want to criticize while you're at it?"

"I'm sorry. Look, I just . . . I . . . I don't know, it bugs me, that's all. It just doesn't seem right," David said.

"It isn't right. And there isn't anything we can do about it. Here's breakfast, do you think we can just enjoy it and not talk about this anymore for now?"

"Hijos, here it is!" Kathy said and lowered the steaming plates.

They didn't talk about it. They slurped and dipped their tortillas in the sultry sauce, and savored their friendship alongside the smell of chili and eggs while the music played. Things were still good, at least for that morning. After he dropped off CJ, David stopped by to see if Bryce was home, but he had gone out with Shanti.

At home, David sat alone on the patio. Lou still had not said a word to him. He began to feel like an idiot. He wanted to talk with someone, anyone. He needed to give Rita an answer. Wiz and CJ were determined to get themselves killed. Everything felt insurmountable.

He turned on his transistor radio and listened to the last three innings. He felt desolate. The Dodgers and Koufax were not going anywhere, and neither was David. His life dangled in a precarious web. Whenever he got into a conundrum like this, he started looking at the sports section of the *L.A. Times*, especially at the box scores. The statistics momentarily eased his burden. He knew that he wanted to get away, anywhere, but there was no place to go. Full count.

CHAPTER SEVEN

Thursday, May 13, 1965

Oh my, oh my, what a game! Koufax simply decimated the Houston Astros. It was his first real masterpiece of the season; a thirteen-strikeout, three-hit shutout. All the Astros could accomplish were a couple of singles by shortstop Eddie Kasko—who for some inexplicable reason, consistently hit Koufax better than most players in the league—and an eighth inning double by Jim Wynn. In the second inning, "Sweet" Lou Johnson hit a home run and that was all Koufax needed, although the Dodgers scored again in the sixth and seventh. The big news was that Johnson had been beaned in the sixth inning and had to leave the game. Lou's batting helmet had a dent as big as a baseball; fortunately for Johnson, the Dodgers, and Koufax, he was determined to be free of any serious injury after being examined at Daniel Freeman Hospital.

Maury Wills stole two more bases and scored when Wes Parker doubled him home. Speed and control dominated the game. Koufax did not walk a batter; neither team made an error. Koufax notched another shutout, the twenty-eighth of his career in his 320th start. Koufax has already set the record for shutouts by a left-handed pitcher with eleven in 1963. Events in the world might be heating up, but here at Dodger Stadium, Sandy Koufax has cooled off the Astros three to 0.

David talked with CJ at lunch on Monday. Same conversation. Same result. David figured Wiz might be more open and reasonable, although it appeared that they were both dead set on leaving right after graduation. Before the end of lunch, David asked Wiz if he would be around that evening.

"I'm busy with school shit the next couple nights. How about Thursday?"

"Thursday it is," said David.

"What's this about anyway?"

"Nothing. Just end-of-the-year stuff."

"Right. Just so you know, I've talked with CJ, so I know what you are trying to do."

"Can you blame me? You are being a fool."

"No blame. Just that you are the fool. Let's just have some fun. See you Thursday."

It was a little after eight o'clock when David parked in front of Wiz's house. Wiz was sitting on his front porch, smoking a cigarette. The Dodgers game had just started and the moon had sprouted over the dark hills with a brown smudge on its crown. David listened as Koufax disposed of the first Astro batters.

"Yo, Wiz," he said. "Koufax is pitching tonight. Scully says his fastball is really popping."

"Money in the bank." He exhaled.

"You still wrestling with that history paper?" David patted him on the back.

"I'm good. The paper is done. You can look it over. It will pass and that's all I need right now." He took another drag of his cigarette.

"Yeah, great, let's check it out. Your folks home?" David asked as they walked inside the house.

"No, they went out to dinner at Chris & Pitts."

"Are they giving you a hard time about joining up?"

"Mom is kind of flipped out, and Dad understands but doesn't like it. It's just the way it is," he said.

"It doesn't have to be." David picked up Wiz's essay from the living room table. The title was The Role of Diplomacy During the Cuban Missile Crisis.

"Good topic," David said. He glanced through the three-page report. It looked like Wiz had copied most of it out of the World Book Encyclopedia but changed it around enough so it couldn't be called plagiarism.

"Hey, this is ready to go as far as I'm concerned," David said, not wanting to confront him like Lou would have done. "Too bad we aren't using diplomacy in Vietnam."

"This whole communist thing disgusts me. Why don't they just back off and let things be?" Wiz jumped up from the couch and started pacing around the room.

"And you could say the same thing about us. Why don't we just back off? China and Russia are a lot closer to Vietnam than we are," David said, realizing things were about to escalate.

Wiz walked out the door. David followed him. "Where you going?"

"I thought we were going out," Wiz said. He got in the Galaxy and slammed the door.

"Want to go to Bob's?" David asked.

"Not yet. Let's go cruise Van Nuys. Maybe we can pick up a few chicks."

David started the car.

"Wait, I'll be right back." Wiz jumped out of the car.

"Right." David cringed. Cruising was about his least favorite thing to do, the inane ogling up and down crowded streets, windows down, radios up, tongues sharp, everyone trying to out- cool the other. For what? But, it was what Wiz wanted so why torpedo his idea?

In a couple of minutes Wiz returned, reeking of English Leather cologne and wearing a pressed white long-sleeved shirt, opened to his chest, with a polished gold chain dangling from his neck. He looked at David. "What are you waiting for?"

David took off. "Got your hunting clothes on, I see," he snickered.

"Hey, got to play the part. If you want to fish, you need the right bait."

Wiz reached down and turned on the radio. Roy Orbison sang "Oh, Pretty Woman." That's real cruising music," Wiz said.

David turned left onto Van Nuys. The traffic was thick, but he didn't mind.

You know they have an agenda," Wiz said.

"Huh?"

"The commies. They want all of Asia. Then they'll keep moving west."

The Drifters were singing "Under the Boardwalk." *Just let it go. Don't get into it with him*, David thought.

They were stopped at the light and there was a Pontiac Bonneville revving up next to them. A guy with a black T-shirt, sleeves rolled up with a pack of camels, looked over at David and revved his horses again. "Come on man, let's do it."

"Fuck you," David said and rolled up his window.

The light changed and the Pontiac laid out a trail of burned rubber.

"You could have taken him," Wiz said.

"Yeah, probably, but so what? I thought you wanted to cruise, not drag race."

"And I thought you wanted to talk me out of signing up."

"Of course I do. Why get your balls blown off for nothing? We've got no business getting involved over there. Let the Vietnamese settle it."

"You mean the Chinese and the rest of the commies. Can't you see what's happening?"

"You don't really believe that crap do you?" *This is going badly*, David thought. "Hey, let's just have some fun like you suggested. Sorry. You are going to do what you want anyway," David said, but hoped that wasn't the case.

"You got that right."

They drove south on Van Nuys past the Broadway department store, past the large banks and small bakeries, until they arrived in Sherman Oaks, where the traffic started to back up and the music growled and wailed so that it sounded like a hundred different parties all happening at the same time. Wiz hung out the window and leered at the coeds, who were basically doing the same thing. David tuned to

KFWB. They were playing the latest Beach Boys' album *Today*. It started with "Do You Wanna Dance," followed by "When I Grow Up (To Be A Man)" and "Help Me Rhonda." The more David listened the more he loosened up. He chimed in with Wiz as they checked out the passing cars. The entire scene was like a caravan of steel and rubber, each car a cage filled with hungry, sex-starved teens, all of them wanting nothing more than a quick lick of excitement. Just as they approached Bob's Big Boy, Wiz got a strike from a white Mustang convertible with two blonds and a redhead. Hard to say what the real hair color was, but Wiz hooked in for a block-long conversation, and they set up a rendezvous at Bob's for a round of cherry Cokes.

Wiz and David lucked out and scored a six-top just as they walked through the door, a small miracle because Bob's on Van Nuys was always jammed once the weather started to turn balmy. David experienced himself sliding into testosterone-laden quicksand. *Abort, abort*, he thought, but there was no way out. The girls were all wearing tight blue jeans and sleeveless blouses, and their hair was popped out in various hair-sprayed poses.

Wiz jumped out of his seat in a priapic frenzy, gesticulating and whistling like he had just struck oil and couldn't wait to tell the world.

"Calm down," David said. "They'll think you want take them to the Hollywood Bowl this weekend. Slow down. What's the matter with you?"

"Here they come. What do you want to do?"

"I want to go home and listen to the ball game with you. Try to talk you into making the right decision."

"David, can't you ever lighten up? Here they are." Wiz started his spiel. "Hi ladies, I think there's enough room for us all."

David lowered his head and slumped.

"Girls, this is David and I'm Wiz, and you are?"

In order they chimed "Leah," "Becky," "Rachel."

It was easy to see that Becky led the pack. She was tall and blond, with a perfect surfer tan, high cheekbones, and crystal-blue eyes that made her physically stunning, but it was her straight posture and poise that made it clear she called the shots.

"We'll join you guys for a little refreshment, but don't get the wrong idea," Becky said.

"Hey, that's great," Wiz said. "Just wanting to enjoy the company of you attractive ladies."

"Thanks for joining us," David said.

They curled together in the booth, exchanging stories about concerts they'd attended and the best beach spots and local bad-boy car gangs. Wiz trumpeted his plan to join the Army and save America from the red plague. David noticed the three girls glance at each other after his disclosure.

"Excuse us," Becky said. "We need to freshen up a little." The three headed for the bathroom.

"I don't think they're supporters of the war, Wiz," David said.

"We'll see."

After a few minutes, Becky and the other two returned to the table. "Thanks for the conversation guys. I think it's time for us to go."

"But we haven't even ordered," Wiz protested.

"No, aren't you lucky? We saved you some cash. Good luck over in Vietnam."

They disappeared out the door, Becky leading.

"Great job, Wiz, nothing like shooting your wad too soon. You want to order something or should we just bolt?"

"Hey, no pain, no gain. I'm not going to pretend to be anyone other than who I am. Yeah, let's order some food. Maybe we can entice some other chicks needing a table."

David recalibrated his focus on Wiz. "So, don't you think you'll miss this kind of *action* being in the Army?"

"You just won't give up, will you?"

"Anything wrong with that? I mean this isn't a fairy tale. They're dropping real bombs and spraying real bullets over there."

"Hell yes, we better be using real bullets, I don't want to be stuck in some fox hole with a white flag and a peace sign. You can dodge it all you want, but eventually they will knock on your door, and unless you run to Canada or go to prison, you'll end up in Nam just like me and CJ."

"I doubt it," David said, although what Wiz was saying might be true. No one knew what was going to happen. They were bombing North Vietnam with more regularity every day. David had just read that the Viet Cong had overrun South Vietnamese troops in Phuoc Long Province north of Saigon. More and more guys were being drafted. The war protests were gathering steam; a few radicals had already burned their draft cards on national television.

"Remember, knucklehead, right now they are issuing deferments for college students. All you have to do is stay in school until this blows over."

"I'm not a coward," Wiz said.

"No, you are an idiot," David said. As soon as the words came out of his mouth, David realized he'd blown it. He felt stifled and wished he could take back his words. Wiz scowled at him.

"Sorry, you are not an idiot."

The food and drinks arrived. For awhile they said nothing. David looked up and noticed Wiz scanning the restaurant for more girls. Wiz wouldn't make eye contact with him.

"Wiz, you just really got me pissed off. I don't want you to do something you'll regret. You've seen the shit that is happening over there."

Wiz poured ketchup onto his plate, dipped an onion ring into the puddle, and ate it. He glanced back at David and took a large bite of his burger and chewed it. Wiz shook his head and sipped on his Coke.

"Not your problem, David. Just back off and we'll be square again."

David nodded. *Back off,* that was a fastball, hard and inside. It wasn't his style to back off, except maybe with Rita. He pitched. He backed batters off the plate. He needed to be at the center of the action and now the count was full once again. He felt edgy. Still, he realized conversations about Vietnam and being a solider were useless. *Fuck it,* he thought. *Fuck this whole mess. Fuck the booby traps filled with snakes and bamboo spikes, fuck the hidden grenades.* Wiz didn't want to hear about any of it.

They finished their meal without finding any other female company, although Wiz did make a few attempts. David picked up the check.

Wiz looked over to him. "Thanks for the food," he said. He shook his head and winked at David. "You worry too much, pal. Take me home."

David left Wiz at his doorstep and turned toward home, feeling hollow and isolated. He considered heading over to the pay phone next to Vons and calling Rita, but as he approached the market, he realized he didn't want to talk to anyone, not even her. He pulled off into a short alley that dead-ended in an old lemon orchard preserved as an easement for the electric company, the last remnant of agriculture within the vacuous sprawl of 1950's tract homes. The quiet, combined with the scent of lemon blossoms, softened him for the moment.

Sitting there, he thought about the game the next day. In all probability it would be his last, and he imagined himself standing on the little hill in the center of the diamond, the bases dusted—white and empty, the grass clipped tight, the plate edged in black, beckoning him to bring forth his pitches.

He recalled a conversation he'd with Lou last year about pitching. Lou said that pitching is an introspective activity. He asserted that every pitch carried the possibility of hope and despair. Like the placement of words in a sentence, a pitcher choses fastballs, curves, or change-ups in every at bat. The at bats turn into innings, the innings into games. "It's like writing a story," Lou said.

David drifted into his own fantasy about pitching: *At the center of the field, a pitcher is like the heart of the team's body, he creates the blood and circulates it around the veins of the basepaths that define the field.*

Isolated at every encounter, feeling the vulnerability of his mission, he screams and agonizes inside over the success or failure of each launch to the plate. There is the minor grievance of a walk or a single and the major humiliation of the home run, when the shame and embarrassment is unbearable. Balanced against all that is the triumphant glory of the strikeout. Nothing in baseball is so sweet and gratifying for a pitcher as when he has vanquished a batter with three strikes, and then he silently watches the dejected warrior return to his dugout—distraught, frustrated, and conquered. You become intoxicated with your own power, and then you have to learn the lesson; it doesn't mean he won't obliterate you next time. Without humility, a pitcher has no grace.

He stretched his arms above his head and started the car. It had been a long day. He turned on the radio and listened to the recap of Koufax's stellar performance as he drove home.

CHAPTER EIGHT

Monday, May 17, 1965

The Dodgers made quite a debut tonight here in the Astrodome. They got a gift from the Astros, who had a mechanical breakdown in the eleventh inning, giving the Dodgers a five-three victory. With the score tied one to one in the top of the eleventh inning, the Dodgers scored four runs. Koufax started the rally with a single; he galloped to second on a single by Maury Wills, and then Wes Parker walked to load the bases. All Star second baseman Joe Morgan took a perfect double-play ball and flung it into the Astros' dugout, allowing two runs to score. Remarkably, the sure-handed Morgan did the same thing on a groundball by John Roseboro, and just like that, the Dodgers had stolen four runs on the Astros. The base running must have worn Koufax down because he couldn't close out the Astros in the eleventh. Trying to redeem himself, Morgan singled, as did Bob Aspromonte, and Koufax was finished for the night. Bob Miller came in and recorded his fourth save of the season. Koufax gained his fifth victory against two losses. Through ten innings he allowed one run, three hits, and had again struck out thirteen batters. From where I sit, it looks like the left-hander has settled into his orbit.

Monday, as David drove to school, he realized that CJ and Wiz were definitely enlisting in the Army after graduation. He felt a growing distance from both friends. The talk with Wiz only served to reinforce his frustration in changing their minds.

He parked and took out his gym bag. In a few hours he would be playing the last game of the season. He wanted a win; it meant more than he wanted anyone to know. He wasn't sure how his life would be without suiting up for baseball. It had been so much a part of it for so long. He wanted this last game to be his best. Something he would remember for a long time.

Later that afternoon David tied his spikes and walked toward the field. Adams High School, the local rival, was in first place, and David's team had crawled up to third. He felt nervous about the encounter; his record stood at two wins and two losses. If he won, he would jump into the lush green pasture reserved for those with winning records. He wanted to go out a winner, especially against the top team. Barn, Wiz, and Bryce were pumped as well. This would be their last game together. David suspected that Lou felt resentful that he got the last start of the year, but no words had been spoken. Lou had pitched well the week before against Lincoln High. Lou and David had identical records.

As he warmed up, he noticed his fastball had good velocity. After the first two batters, Barn's fat lips spread into a mischievous grin as David's pitches rang with a *smack-pop* in his glove. In the second inning, Barn hit a magnificent home run over the center-field fence, staking David to a one-run lead. David was perfect for the first three innings: no hits, walks, or errors.

The first Adams High hitter in the top of the fourth was their shortstop, a kid named Skip Petlin. He had a .425 batting average. David had struck him out on three pitches in the first inning, so he decided to shake off Barn's call for a curve ball and started him with the heater. A screaming line drive exploded toward David's head, and he ducked just in time to see his no-hitter disappear onto the center-field grass. Bryce scooped it quickly and threw it to second, limiting Skip to a single. Now David had to work from a stretch, which he didn't mind, except that Skip loved to steal bases. Skip immediately jumped out ten feet, daring him to throw over to first base, hoping to get David's attention away from the batter. Nursing a one-run lead, David had no choice but to indulge Skip and see who would crack first. David tossed over to first base five times. Then he proceeded to walk the next batter on four straight pitches. With runners on first and second and power hitters coming to the plate, David was in trouble. Barn jogged out to the mound, mask in hand.

"What the fuck, David! Forget the runners and just concentrate on my glove."

"Okay," David said and nodded. Barn slapped him on the shoulder and ran back behind the plate. Barn set up his mitt as a target on the lower outside part of the plate, and David located his pitch exactly into his friend's glove. The batter, a muscular six-foot-two first baseman, could do nothing but watch the curve slide past him for a strike. He had expected a fastball. Barn called for a fastball on the next pitch but wanted it inside. David followed his direction and again found success. On the next pitch, David wasted a fastball high and outside, just as Barn wanted, and then finished the batter off with another curve ball. Barn pumped his arm in the air and pointed at David. "Yeah, see what happens if you listen to me!"

David zipped through the next two batters and headed back to the dugout. Barn followed him and said, "Don't worry. This one is in the bag. Just let me set you up, and we'll be fine."

David sat down next to Bryce and looked out across the field. He was surprised when Bryce suddenly started talking about the war. "Did you hear that the Navy stepped up their patrols in Vietnam? Cronkite talked about it last night. They're trying to disrupt the supplies coming in from the North by ship, so they've tripled the number of ships patrolling south of the 17th parallel. You heard anything more about Ricky?"

"No, have you?"

Bryce shook his head and walked to the on-deck circle.

David kept throwing curveballs through the fifth and sixth innings, and just as Barn predicted, he stayed out of trouble. He gave up a couple of meaningless singles in each inning, so by the top of the final inning, David had preserved a narrow one-to-nothing lead. The first batter was Skip Petlin. Barn called for the curve. David complied, but he felt something pull in his back as he released the ball. He knew right away something was wrong. The pitch had no snap, so Petlin murdered it for a double down the right-field line. David was afraid another curve ball would hurt his back, so he threw a fastball down the middle to the next hitter, who promptly whizzed into left field so fast that Skip couldn't advance to third. David walked the next batter on four pitches, and after each pitch he felt a burning sensation in his back. He had pulled his oblique again. After the walk he threw his glove down in disgust and turned out toward center field. He was finished.

Coach Martin, Barn, and Wiz all arrived at the mound at the same time.

"It's my oblique, I pulled it again."

"Shit," Barn yelled.

Coach Martin patted him on the back.

"You pitched a great game." The coach quickly signaled for Lou to come out to the mound and walked over to the umpire to explain David's injury. Lou would get all the time he needed to warm up.

David stood on the mound, waiting for his mute ex-friend to replace him. His arm felt like an iron beam. It was all David could muster to hand the ball over to Coach Martin and silently nod to Lou. To his chagrin, as he stepped off the mound, Lou said, "Don't worry, I got this covered."

David turned around and said, "Thanks." Then he slowly walked to the dugout. Those were the first words Lou had uttered to him in weeks! Suddenly the wall had come down.

Lou finished his warm-ups. The late afternoon sun started to fade. Languid clouds draped across right and center field. David smelled the flat dry scent of the chalk along the third baseline. He had crossed that line so many times, but this time was different. He knew something in his life was about to change. Fresh blooms of clover poked up in the grass outside the dugout. David felt the tension on the field as Barn settled back behind the plate, and Lou peered in for his first sign.

Lou wasted no time disposing of the last three hitters. Barn, Wiz, and David all arrived at the mound at the same moment. They hugged

Lou and each other and then danced around the infield until they finally fell over in a heap like in a rugby scrum.

They screamed "Number one, number one!" until they were hoarse. They weren't really number one, but that didn't matter. It was a game to remember and embellish, a spicy moment of triumph they would always savor.

David walked over to Lou as the other players were leaving the field. Lou was sitting at the end of the dugout bench, taking off his spikes and staring out toward center field.

"Thanks for the save, you were really hot today," David said.

"Yeah, you weren't too bad yourself. Six innings, nine Ks, three hits, no runs; I'd say that's a pretty good line. Not a bad way to end your season. You might even get a couple lines in the *Valley News*."

"I doubt it," David laughed.

"You never know. You deserved this game, and I wasn't going to let anyone take it away from you."

"I wish we could keep going. I think we just hit our stride, and you just needed a few more games to really show your stuff," David said. He wanted to keep the conversation flowing.

"Maybe, but I think I'm pretty much done with baseball. There are a lot more important things to deal with at this point. You know what I mean," Lou replied.

David looked at Lou as he packed his cleats into his gym bag. The rancor had melted away as if it never existed. That was it. David started to offer an apology and a version of his story about how he wanted to say something sooner. How foolish it was and what a jerk he had been to start the fight and say what he had said. But before David could say a word, Lou raised his hand and said, "Forget it. It doesn't matter, it's not worth it. Let's just move on."

It sounded good enough for David, so he took Lou at his word and vowed to never mention anything about it again. After showering they walked to their cars.

"Could you come over tonight?" Lou said. "I need to talk with you about something and I don't have time right now."

"No problem," David said. He wondered what Lou wanted. Suddenly they were friends again, and something was up. It was just like Lou to stir up some excitement.

When David got home, he immediately called Lou and told him he'd be over around seven o'clock. After dinner he drove over to Lou's house. Lou was sitting outside his front door, reading, as the last gasp of light faded from the sky. He closed the book and signaled that he needed to go inside for a second. David waited in the car. It amazed David how much information could be conveyed with simple hand gestures, like the signals between pitchers and catchers. Lou bounced into the front seat and said, "Let's go get some pie."

"Katie's?"

"Exactly. We need to do some serious talking and a little bit of celebrating."

David parked the car and they walked into Katie's Pie House— one of the last original places left in the Valley from before the Second World War. In addition to great pie, it was legendary because one of the first waitresses who worked there was Norma Jean Baker. There was a signed photograph of Miss Norma Jean, her perfect legs framed by her pleated pink skirt, hanging above the prized booth at the far end of the restaurant. It was auspicious that after all the years David had gone to Katie's, this was the first time he had the good fortune to sit under the legs of a young Marilyn Monroe. David slid into the booth and opened the menu. Lou did the same from the other end. Lou wore a white oxford-cloth button down shirt, new Levi jeans, and penny loafers; everything starched, pressed, and immaculate. With his short blond hair and azure eyes, he looked like a perfect poster boy for a UCLA promo magazine.

"Did you know she was Jewish?" Lou asked.

"Who?"

"Norma Jean. She did it for Arthur, converted I mean."

"I didn't think you cared about any of that Jewish stuff."

"I don't, but when it comes to Marilyn Monroe and Arthur Miller, it's a different story."

"Yeah, she was a piece of work. Hard to believe she actually went to Laurel High School," David said as Lou looked hard at the menu. "Great game today, you really saved my butt."

"It's okay. So listen, I'm thinking that we need to start searching for a place to live after graduation. We are both going to UCLA, and you're the only person I can imagine living with. I don't want any part of that bullshit with fraternities. So you're it, David."

"Yeah, I feel the same." This was all happening fast, David thought. One day he doesn't acknowledge my existence, the next we are intimate roomies. Yet it felt right, at least for the moment. There was something captivating, almost spellbinding, about his attraction to Lou. Whatever it was, he could feel it grip him once again.

Lou put his hands on the table; they were like a couple of cat paws and made David uncertain as to whether he wanted to pounce or make nice. The waitress brought their pie.

"There is something more immediate I wanted to talk with you about though, something that could be really remarkable if we can pull it off," Lou said. "My mother has a cousin with a cabin up north of San Francisco. She offered to let me use it as a kind of graduation present. If you can get away from Rita for the weekend, we could go up there together."

"Sounds fantastic. I'm sure I'll be able to get away. It could be that Rita and I will be goners by then away."

"Well, I'm not so sure about that, but that's your business. My plan is to check out North Beach, City Lights Bookstore, and maybe hear Ginsberg, Synder, or Corso read their poetry. Then head out to the cabin. It's right next to Point Reyes, a place called Mount Vision."

God, now he was into poetry, David thought. He had heard of Ginsberg, but not the others, and he immediately felt challenged and intimidated.

"That's my idea," Lou said.

"When do you need to know?"

"As soon as possible, because otherwise she'll rent it for that weekend."

They finished their pie, and David drove Lou home. He went to sleep that night, not thinking about his last victory, or Rita, or Koufax, but only of the impending news that he'd be living with Lou that fall and that they had a trip planned to a place in the redwoods called Mount Vision. It felt like the beginning of a new life filled with wonder and excitement. He dreamed of a long weekend laden with good talks, new insights, and hikes into the wilderness. Maybe some women too? It was all too thrilling and filled him with more possibility than his mind could contain.

Tuesday morning David saw CJ, Wiz, Barn, and Bryce gathered around the cafeteria table, sipping hot chocolate. He was thinking about Koufax and how they were both on a roll. As he got closer, he saw Wiz gesturing wildly about something. "What the fuck," Wiz was saying as David reached the group. "His old lady got the word last night. They're shipping out in three weeks."

"What are you talking about?" David said.

"Our boy Rick is assigned to a PT boat headed to the Mekong Delta, and that's not in Mississippi. Rick's mother had said he wasn't supposed to let anyone know, but he wrote that he wanted her to tell me and then share it with all of you. He said he's looking forward to kicking some ass. Yeah, Ricky, way to go!" Wiz said.

David didn't want to deal with this latest development, not that there was anything for him to do. CJ and Wiz were on the verge of signing up. Rick was already trained and about to be deployed. He was the first to leave, but certainly wouldn't be the last. It was a mess. There was mayhem and destruction flashing through the evening news every night. Wasn't that enough to dissuade anyone from wanting to join in the carnage? Apparently not. And then there was Rita.

CHAPTER NINE

Saturday, May 22, 1965

It's Chicago, and the temperature has been in the low fifties all afternoon with a cold wind blowing off the lake. Koufax's arm started to swell up in the sixth inning, but he pushed through the pain. Despite his swollen elbow, he pitched a complete game, allowing just six hits while striking out twelve Cubs. The Dodgers won three to one, and Koufax's dominance over the Cubs continues. Here's a recap of the scoring: in the second inning Ron Fairly singled and stole second. He scored on a base hit by third baseman Dick Tracewski, giving the Dodgers an early lead. In the bottom of the fourth inning, with no outs, Ron Santo hit a home run to tie the game, but Koufax remained in control. In the middle of the sixth inning, the Dodgers scored twice on a walk, a couple of infield hits, and a fielder's choice.

It was the sixty-fourth time he struck out ten or more batters. Koufax has amassed 309 strikeouts against the Cubs in only 257 innings. It's still early in the season, so there will be plenty more chances to fatten up his numbers against the Cubbies.

David woke up in a panic Saturday morning after dreaming about Rita. His throat was dry, and he had a headache. He had partied hard the previous night. He looked at the clock. It was 9:25. The dream, thankfully, dissolved as he started toward the kitchen for a glass of water. The house was empty. He remembered his mother telling him that everyone was going shopping in the morning. CJ and his father were picking him up at ten to go shooting.

Tony Agostino didn't like to be kept waiting. David shook his head as he buttered a piece of toast and chewed it quickly. He finished the glass of water and poured another. He wondered why he had agreed to the target shooting. His thoughts then turned to Rita, and he felt a twinge of guilt and shame. He had strung things out for too long. He still had not ended it. Maybe tonight he'd have the courage. Another full count.

He looked at the clock: 9:40. He finished his toast and his second glass of water, then marched back to the bedroom and got dressed.

Precisely at 10:00 a.m., David heard honking outside. He was out the door before a second round of noise commenced. Tony and CJ Agostino waited in the "Black Monster," a four-wheel-drive, double-cab F-250 Ford truck. David hopped into the back seat.

"I like a man who is on time," Tony said.

"Morning, Tony," David said.

"I didn't know if you'd be ready after last night," CJ snickered.

David didn't answer. Tony passed a bag of donuts into the back seat.

"Thanks, Tony," David said.

"Coffee?" Tony asked, passing a thermos.

"Sure."

"By the way, congratulations on your win the other day. Sorry I wasn't able to make the game. I really wanted to see you guys go out with a win, and I'm glad you did. CJ told me all about it."

Tony pulled the Ford onto the road and gunned the engine. The last time David had been in the Black Monster was the fall of 1963 when they had all gone hunting.

CJ turned around and punched David in the shoulder. "You ready for some fireworks?"

"You bet," David said, not really certain if his headache was ready.

They drove north and east toward the foothills. There was a brief silence, and then David knew what was next. Tony had a deep and abiding reverence for his "weapons." He needed to make a little speech about safety and proper terminology. Everyone who participated in his outings never referred to rifles or pistols as "guns." Guns were what people used on television and the movies. Guns were what children used in their games. If you have a weapon in your hand, Tony said, you either refer to it by its proper name, a Browning Automatic, a Glock .38 caliber, or you call it what it is; a weapon, a tool, an instrument designed for lethal situations, and you better know how and when to use it. He gave his talk, and that was that.

They arrived at a private eighty-acre plot of land that Tony had purchased ten years earlier. David remembered how Tony had bragged about the deal the last time they went shooting. The story involved an old man in a nursing home who needed some money for surgery. Tony learned about the unfortunate senior from one of the secretaries at the nursing home. Agnes had once worked for Tony, and they were close.

One day, Tony showed up at the nursing home with his check book. Agnes accompanied him. The two *Samaritans* entered with flowers and avarice and left with a quit-claim deed to the 120-acre tract and a lot of promise for the future. After giving Agnes five acres and selling another thirty-five to one his partners for twice the price he paid, Tony walked away with eighty acres and several thousand dollars in his pocket. Now the land provided a little refuge where Tony could shoot his weapons.

Tony parked the Ford under the shade of an oak that dominated the rolling grasslands. The landscape had started to turn from green to tawny, a shade that would continue throughout the summer until the rains came again in the late fall. Tony was wearing all camo. David and CJ were dressed in their usual jeans and T-shirts. They got out of the truck, and Tony stopped and looked at the boys.

"David, I'm sure you remember the protocols that I have regarding these weapons. You've always been good at following the rules, and that's one reason CJ and I feel secure about inviting you whenever we go hunting or shooting. Do you have any questions?"

"No, sir," David said.

In the back of the truck was a plastic bag CJ had filled with tin cans. He told David he'd really wanted to bring bottles, but Tony despised the look of broken glass. He said it made him feel like he was in the ghetto; a place, he said, that should just be wiped off the face of the earth.

David's job was to set up the targets along the northern edge of the range while Tony and CJ loaded and checked the weapons. David slung the plastic bag over his shoulder and started walking. As he moved through the grass he remembered their last hunting trip.

It was in October, in the coastal mountains just east of Santa Barbara in the Los Padres National Forest, with a few pairs of resident condors. David remembered being more excited about the possibility of seeing the giant prehistoric birds than shooting a deer, which wasn't going to happen anyway, because only Tony, Wiz, and CJ had tags. David was brought along to help lug things and as a HIT man, a "hunter in training," the guy who did all the grunt work and provided another pair of hands to applaud when Tony brought down a trophy buck.

Finally, on that last hunting trip, CJ bagged his first deer. It was an early Sunday morning. The temperature hovered right at twenty-eight degrees, David noted, looking at the mini-thermometer on the zipper of his worn-out red down parka, thinking that this wasn't a sport he would ever to do with his own father. Not that his father didn't know how to shoot guns, or rather *weapons*. He had been an infantryman during the invasion of Italy, but he spent most of his time in the motor pool. Still, he brought home several sharpshooter medals that he kept buried under his socks. He had shown them to David when he was a young boy.

CJ and David had stumbled upon some tracks that morning, then CJ spotted fresh scat a little off the trail. As they inched along through the dark pine trees, they flushed out an eight-point buck. David saw it before CJ and nudged him a little. CJ rose quickly, without a breath of hesitation. He fired and brought the buck down right where he stood. They sprinted over. The large mammal still had steam erupting from his nostrils. It gasped heavily. There were vapors forming around his face as he quivered, realizing it was over, but the elegance of the animal was such that it never gave a hint of surrender, just an acceptance that all living things know when their time has come. Even though he hadn't fired the shot, David felt sick and awestruck at the same time. He was an accomplice as well as a conspirator in the death that now lay before him.

"Holy Shit!" CJ said and stared down at the dying animal. David saw CJ's eyes well up with tears. He quickly wiped them away and looked at David in silence.

"What have we done?" David whispered to himself. The big creature exhaled for the final time. Before another minute passed, Tony and Wiz appeared. Tony bore an expression of ego-driven mortification, his uncontested role as tribal leader had been usurped for the moment. David read it like a banner headline across his forehead. At first Tony looked startled, but then he relaxed, wrapped his large glove-covered hand around his progeny, his only son, and for a single baleful moment, allowed himself to get choked up. He said, "Oh my God, look at the size of him! Great shot, CJ." Tony kneeled down and stained his new gloves with the fresh blood oozing from the animal's wound. The buck's vacant stare captivated the father and son. It linked them in a timeless moment of repose that David never forgot.

That was year and a half ago, David recollected as he finished setting up the targets. Tony and CJ already had their weapons ready to fire. David's choice was a simple .22 caliber rifle, the standard beginner *gun*, the only firearm with which he had reasonable accuracy. Tony had selected a sinister pistol; a long reprehensible monster that he claimed had enough kick to bring down a grizzly bear. Grizzlies had long been extinct in California, but that didn't matter to Tony. CJ wanted to use a pistol as well, but Tony insisted that he use the hunting rifle. He said something about needing to get ready for real combat.

Late morning sunshine spread across the low foothills like butter on warm bread. Apart from the reports of their guns, nothing but silence filled the countryside. The birds disappeared once they started firing, the nearest car was several miles away, and even the wind decided to evacuate the scene. After the crack of a bullet entered the hollow skeleton of a stewed-tomatoes can, a remnant of one of Dolores' lasagnas Tony put his magnum in the large holster he wore across his chest and under his arm like the ones David had seen on the TV series *The Untouchables.* Tony walked over and stood behind CJ. He watched him drill target after target into the heart of each cylinder, dead center every time, without a quiver or hesitation. David watched Tony smile and nod. He poked CJ on the shoulder. "Son, with that kind of shooting you'll have nothing to worry about. You just stay alert, stay focused, and everything will be just fine. Believe me, you've got what it takes to be a good soldier."

David's thoughts suddenly turned in another direction. He saw his friend sitting at his piano and recalled the delicacy of his strokes across the keyboard, not on the trigger. He felt a peculiar closeness to CJ as he fired off a few more rounds. He was relieved when Tony turned to the boys and reported they had exhausted most of the ammo. "Sorry, guys, I guess we should have brought a few more boxes, let's pack it up for now."

CJ and David returned the rifles to the backseat of the truck, and as they did, Tony thanked David for coming along. David nodded.

"You going to Shanti's party tonight?" CJ asked as they hopped into the truck.

"Oh shit. I totally forgot. Thanks for reminding me. Yeah, of course, I told Rita I'd meet her there around eight. What time are you going?"

"Right around then," he said as he secured and locked the rifles in the rack right behind David's head.

It was after two o'clock by the time David got home. He listened to the last part of the game. Koufax won again. Imagining the great pitcher soothed him. He showered to get the acrid smell of the gun powder out of his hair and skin. Alex and his parents had returned from shopping and were now off visiting cousins who lived in Long Beach. At a little after six, he left a note about the party at Shanti's house; he wouldn't get home until after midnight. Now that he was eighteen, his parents had relaxed any kind of curfew. They settled upon being reasonable with each other. As long as David let them know what was going on, they tolerated it, even if they didn't like it.

Rita wasn't at the party when David arrived, but everyone else was. Of course Bryce had been there since six thirty, helping pick out the music, set up the chairs, arrange the food, and move all the furniture back against the windows so they had plenty of room on the dance floor. Wiz and Claudia, CJ and Lydia, and Barney and Maxine were all mixing around with another dozen friends. He noticed Lou's blond curls in the distance. CJ nudged David as he walked in and revealed a pint of Bacardi rum inside his coat pocket; it was already half empty. "Don't worry," he said as he read David's mind, "I've got plenty more in the car, get yourself a Coke and some ice, and I'll load you up." He rocked along to the beat of the Rolling Stones' "The Last Time." CJ swung and swirled his arms, bopping from one foot to another while David found a large yellow plastic cup and filled it halfway with ice and Coke. CJ waltzed over to the food table and loaded the remainder of David's cup with rum and then hustled back to Lydia, slathering her with kisses as he dragged her out on the dance floor. Lou came over with his yellow cup filled with the Puerto Rican high test and joined David as he pawed through the miniature-triangle tuna sandwiches Bryce had cut up. David wasn't hungry, but the party made him nervous, and after a couple of sips of the Coke-rum mix, he started to get agitated, especially since Rita hadn't arrived. Lou was now hovering beside the food table.

"What do you think?" Lou asked, while crunching on chips and dip.

"Think about what?"

"Our trip. I haven't heard from you since we talked the other night. Are you still up for it?"

David hadn't thought about it for the last twenty-four hours. He had been worrying about Rita. Lou was starting to irritate him.

"Yeah, of course I'm up for it. Are you feeling the rum yet?"

"Yeah, I am. Fucking CJ, I think he's got ten bottles stashed under his front seat. I hope he doesn't go driving around tonight," Lou said.

"I don't think he'll be able to go anywhere. Look at him. He must have started a couple of hours ago, right after we got back from shooting," David said.

"Huh?"

"Me and CJ and Tony went out shooting at his place above the dam. Tony owns some property up there, and he asked me if I wanted to go shoot. It was pretty cool, except it feels like Tony is setting up CJ to be the perfect little soldier boy. Gives me the creeps."

Rita walked in, wearing a short black skirt and a new flowered sleeveless top that looked like it came from Hawaii. She had a gardenia in her hair.

"Hey, Lou, listen, I've cleared it with my folks and I'll have the Galaxy ready to roll, so I'm all set for the trip. Let's just keep this between the two of us for now. At least until I figure out when I'm going to break it off with Rita. I'm not sure why that matters, but it does."

"Don't worry. I just wanted to be sure you were on it."

"It's a done deal. I'm on it, but right now I gotta go."

David caught Rita's eye. She gave David a little hand signal, meaning that she wanted a few more seconds with Shanti, so he sipped his rum and Coke and watched her, admiring the way her ass curved in the tight black skirt. Someone put on "You Belong to Me" by The Duprees. It was their song, and he decided not to wait another second. The breakup would have to wait. Soon, he thought, soon, but not tonight.

"Excuse me, but might I have this dance?" David wrapped her up in his arms and started to dance. There was mild applause from Shanti and Bryce and a few others.

"Why the applause?" David whispered.

"We're the historic couple. Shanti and Lydia think we were made for each other."

"Really? That's swell," he said, feeling the rum and the roundness of her hips.

"You look gorgeous tonight," he whispered and took a long whiff of her gardenia. "Where'd you get the flower?"

"Trade secret," she laughed.

"God, I love you, I love everything about you—the way you walk into a room, so relaxed and honest, the way your eyes laugh when I talk with you, the way you are in the world, so forgiving and open. How could I be so fortunate?"

"Just dumb luck. That's all I can give you credit for at this point. I'll reassess my opinion in a few weeks," she said.

David didn't say anything after that. He knew she was joking and not joking. They danced and held each other through the song, feeling the years between them. It was terrific and frozen at the same time, the present and the future wedded as they held each other and slid between the lines of time. Their friends soared with their own memories, dancing around them, all of them floating on rum and Coke as they sang, "I'd be so alone without you."

CHAPTER TEN

Wednesday, May 26, 1965

Sometimes, no matter how hard you try, it just doesn't go your way. And that's how it was tonight for Sandy Koufax and the Dodgers. It must have been frustrating for Koufax to have given up just two runs and lost. But the worst part is still to come. Here is how it went down tonight at Dodger Stadium. Lou Brock singled in the first inning and immediately stole second. Curt Flood beat out an infield hit, and suddenly the Cardinals were threatening. With one out and Ken Boyer at the plate, the two fleet-footed Cardinals pulled off a double steal. Boyer promptly launched a long fly ball that produced a run, and just like that, Koufax was down one to zero. The Dodgers tied the game in the bottom of the second. The game rolled along with the score tied one to one. Koufax wasn't so sharp, but he managed to keep the Cardinals from scoring through the sixth inning. In the seventh inning, the Cardinals had a runner on first with Curt Simmons, the thirty-six-year-old pitcher at the plate. Simmons had not had a hit all year and was overmatched against Koufax, yet somehow he made contact and singled to right field, moving reserve catcher Bob Uecker to second base. Next up was Julian Javier, the lead-off hitter. Javier was batting .379 against left-handed pitchers, and he promptly crunched a single to right. Uecker somehow evaded Torborg's tag after a pinpoint throw by Ron Fairly and scored. That was all the Cardinals needed. Koufax allowed seven hits, one walk, and struck out six batters in eight innings, but Simmons had given up just five hits and one run. Koufax and the Dodgers lost two to one. Sometimes you just can't win. That's it for tonight.

It was Monday and classes had virtually ended. There were no finals or papers or even deadlines, still David was a bit overwhelmed about the future. He opened the front door and stared into the morning light, then took a long deep breath and felt a tinge of smog and coughed. Rita, graduation, the trip with Lou, Wiz and CJ, Rick Norris, the *future*. *Fuck it*, he thought, *just let it go*. He got into the Galaxy and headed to Barn's house. He smiled as he drifted into the Kaufmans' driveway. The yellow hibiscus was in bloom, and that meant that Barn's father would be in a good mood; he adored those flowers as well as his one grapefruit and three orange trees. They were the treasures that affirmed his escape from New York City.

Barn was David's social weather vane, constantly pointing in the direction of the next party or potential female encounter. Barn craved money, fancy clothes, a Cadillac, and a house on the beach in Malibu. What made him so appealing was that he had no illusions about his desires or goals; he challenged and goaded everyone to refute his dream of success. His avarice was an open book. He always smelled freshly showered and deodorized, his clothes were crisp and fashionable; his fully developed guise made him look robust as well as giving him a presence that was much older and more complete than the rest of the gang.

"Good morning, Sam, I suppose Barn is still preening," David said as Sam opened the door before he even knocked.

"Of course, of course. He's making himself beautiful for the world that he plans to conquer. The suckers are already lining up to empty their pockets so my son Barney can make a killing and buy his home in Malibu."

"It's not such a bad plan, is it? Most of us don't have a clue as to what we want to do."

"So what's wrong with that? My God, the worlds going to shit again, so how could you know or even think about any real future with this war about to explode. The only good news on the horizon is that it looks like LBJ is about to get this voting rights bill finally passed. Did you see the Senate passed its version seventy-seven to nineteen? It's only Strom Thurmond and his bunch that voted against it. It's 1965, and those assholes still want segregation. I'm telling you, there is going to be a race war the likes of which you and I have never seen unless something gets done, and done fast."

"Race war, you really think so? I think the whole thing is moving toward what Martin Luther King is trying to do—nonviolence, marches, and sit-ins," David said.

"It's about violence, David, mark my words. I know what it is like downtown, I see the guys on the street corners and they're not talking about Dr. King. And do you think my Barney listens or cares about any of that? Not a chance. Have some toast, a little coffee. I just made it fresh, come and sit."

Sam's hands looked like David's first baseball mitt, a flat stomped piece of dark leather with wide puffed fingers. In one paw, Sam held a large nickel-colored serrated knife with a worn wooden handle, his other hand caressed a loaf of pumpernickel, the size of a football. David sat down on the strawberry-colored vinyl kitchen chair and clasped his hands on the Formica tabletop.

"Dark or light toast? David, are they still teaching Kafka in school?"

"Dark please. Kafka? I think we read something last year in English, a short story or maybe a novella? I know I've read Metamorphosis, so that must have been it, the one where the guy wakes up and discovers he has become a cockroach. So yeah, they still teach Kafka. Why?"

The toast popped up and the kitchen filled with a comforting smell.

"Just wondering, that's all. What he wrote still has punch. All this government double talk; the way they are conducting this war without really identifying any real enemy, other than the creeping communist menace. And what does that really mean? It's just another fear tactic to get us to take our eye off the ball. Butter or cream cheese?"

"A little butter is fine." Sam laid the toast on a white plate and lowered it in front of David with a steaming mug of coffee. "I remember Lou and I talked about Metamorphosis. One day you wake up and your whole world has changed," David said.

He crunched a few warm bites of the pumpernickel and sipped his coffee.

"Exactly. Wake up or we'll all be living this nightmare and we'll think it is just a dream. Kafka, you need to keep reading him, David," Sam said.

"I'll take a look next time I'm at the library."

"No, no I have all his books. There aren't too many. I'll get them for you."

"Please, no, Sam. There is just too much going on and I don't want to be responsible for your books. I'm moving in a couple of months or maybe sooner, if Lou and I can find a place."

"Okay, but if you ever want to borrow any of my books, it would be my pleasure. Don't be a stranger, David. You're a seeker like me. And that won't change."

Just then Barn appeared. He and David walked out the door and drove off toward school.

"My dad chewing your ear off again?" Barn said as he checked his hair in the rear view mirror.

"No, he was just asking me about some books."

Barn ignored his answer and opened the window. "Freedom, David, freedom. Two more weeks and we're finally liberated."

Barn was right. The time was approaching, and he had plenty on his mind. Kafka would have to wait.

Rita greeted David as he walked into the cafeteria, filled with all their friends. She looked sad and defeated.

"What's wrong? You look like someone just died, is everything okay?"

"Nothing is okay, David. And you, better than anyone, knows that. What could be okay? Graduation is a week from Friday, and not only do we not have any plans for that weekend, but more importantly, what is going to happen after that? You've dodged and dodged and all I hear is what you are doing, what *your* plans are. I don't hear anything about 'us,' about 'our' plans."

"Rita, you know I'm trying. This isn't easy for me either. I think about you and me all the time," David said.

Everyone was looking at them as Rita continued. "That's not good enough. Why don't you just come right out and say it, you coward! Just say it straight out that you are going to break up with me right after graduation. Or, are you planning on stringing me along for the summer, so you don't have to worry about who you're going to screw until you start college? Just say it and get it over with, don't drag this out anymore, David. I can't take it. That's the least you can do after all the time we've spent together."

The gears in David's mind locked. He stared at Rita and his body stiffened, his muscles and bones froze in a virtual vise. He was aware of nothing except standing in complete catatonia. He scanned the borders of Rita's body as she stood before him, tears of anger and grief streaming down her cheeks. Their friends looked on like a Greek chorus, waiting for David's lines to be delivered. After a few seconds, moved more by fear than any rational plan, David tried to gather Rita into his arms, but she protested, screaming, "Don't touch me, just don't touch me."

"You're right, you're right. But can we go somewhere and talk alone?"

Rita turned and stomped outside to an empty glade and sat down under the shade of a large elm tree. David joined her.

"I'm sorry I haven't talked to you about graduation, but I wanted it to be a surprise." David sidestepped the greater accusation about *after graduation,* hoping that his *surprise* about a special graduation evening would temporarily assuage Rita's wrath. He kept whispering, "I'm sorry, it will be all right," he said. Then finally, he felt her release into his arms.

"So here's what I have planned, I'll pick you up early, I don't care what your parents say or do. This is graduation, we're both eighteen and they can't stop us!"

Rita nodded. "I already told them we were going out. I hope that was all right." She laughed slightly and then started to cry. "David, I'm sorry. I'm just so scared that this won't work out, that you'll leave me and all this will just fall apart."

"Look Rita, let's just keep this in perspective and stay with graduation, that much I really know, I want to be with you, just you. I don't care about the party."

"But I care about the party, David. I want to be with our friends."

"Okay, all right, that's what I was saying about picking you up early, because I know that's important to you. We'll go out to dinner early, but it's a surprise so you just need to be really dressed to the nines, heels, the whole shmear, you got it?"

"Yeah, I got it. I love you."

"I love you too."

David felt his emotions thaw as he smiled and held Rita and noticed the usual stirring below his waist, a guarantee that his wiring was still intact. He wasn't sure how the rest was going to work out, except that he had bought himself another couple weeks. He knew his relief would be short-lived, his destiny with Rita would soon unfold.

By Wednesday he knew the inescapable was approaching. The trip to Mount Vision served as a fulcrum, a platform to launch a new part of his life as well as a time for shelter and disappearance. It felt cowardly and appealing to become invisible for a few days after the severance; no phones, no chance of a sighting, no fallout from Rita's friends. It would be perfect. So as David walked with Rita to their American History class with Mr. Smith, who looked like a grown-up version of Tab Hunter, he decided that his next step was to start getting his stuff ready for Mt. Vision.

Later, as Rita went off to French class, David stood at the edge of a grassy glade near the entrance to the English building. Whatever escape routes remained were temporary, the trip north and the knowledge that he would have Lou as a roommate mollified him for a moment, but he knew that Lou could still be an asshole on any given day. It irritated him that he seemed to need Lou more than Lou needed him.

David walked around in a fog the rest of the day. His actions were unforgiveable, guilty with intent. He prejudged himself responsible for the pain and suffering that Rita would experience within a couple of short weeks and felt sentenced to remember his lies, his sins of omission, his plots and deceptions. He hoped Rita would be okay. With all she had going for her, she'd find someone else. The thought took his breath away for a moment. He knew that she wanted to get married and that that was her ticket out of the Valley and away from her family.

During lunchtime he disappeared into the far corner of the grassy field that bordered the school along Laurel Canyon Blvd. What David wanted and needed more than anything was just to settle his mind and thoughts. His brain was like a broken machine, cycling and cycling but never arriving at a stop. He didn't talk to anyone the rest of the day. An eight-foot chain-link fence above a four-foot concrete foundation kept the student body corralled. The fence netted all the wayward paper that blew west on the back of the prevailing Santa Ana winds. He huddled down, wondering when he'd find his bearings. He knew he would, he just didn't know how or when.

After dinner David decided he'd better make this *surprise* really happen. It took him the better part of thirty minutes to get through Topanga Canyon. He was headed to Fred's by the Sea in Malibu. He flicked on the radio. The game was tied at one to one. The glory of the Pacific abounded through his windshield, the surf glistened with an iridescent sheen and the red tide composed of microscopic sea creatures created a brilliant, astounding effect.

David pulled straight into the first parking area across the highway in Malibu and turned off the engine. It was the end of the road. The territory across the Pacific Coast Highway from Santa Monica to Ventura County Line was his refuge. Despite the smog, the jammed freeways, and the interminable subdivisions, once his feet hit the sand and his nostrils opened to the sea, he was liberated. The ocean was the one pure element left in the decayed basin of fallen angels. David got out of the car, took off his shoes and socks, tied them together and strung them over his shoulder, rolled up his pants, and kicked through the surf, sauntering north along the wet cool sand. The moon was half full. He felt his despondency wash out to sea as he walked and realized that as long as he could connect with the wild part of himself, somehow, everything would be all right.

He kept walking until he reached his destination a mile down the beach, a large white sign with red and blue flashing bulbs. Fred's was just ahead. He sat down below the outdoor patio, rubbing the caked and crumbled sand from his feet with his black cotton socks, and then put on his shoes. He hopped up the steps past the sax and piano players, across the bar to the high desk where a gorgeous, young blond hostess, who looked like Sandra Dee, stood in front of a large leather book. She blinked, smiled, and raised her overly tanned shoulders. "May I help you?"

"Yes, yes." David looked straight at her movie-star face. "Yes, I want to make a reservation for Friday, June 4, a little before sunset. So let's see, do you think seven thirty would work, or should I make it earlier?" He glanced up at the Sandra-look-alike eyes, and she nodded.

"I think that would be perfect, the sun should be setting close to eight, so that will give you time to settle in and get comfortable. You want to dine on the patio, I assume?"

"That would be fantastic. By the way, what's your name?" he asked.

"I'm Amy, but I'm not sure if I'll be here that night, it's graduation you know . . . I guess, of course, you know. And your name is?"

"David, David Mandel, a pleasure to meet you, Amy."

Aroused and enthused, his walk back to the car was filled with fantasies about life after Rita. There were so many possibilities he could hardly contain himself, but those fantasies didn't help with the fact that he still needed to complete what he had started. It wouldn't be easy, or fun, or anything he wanted to think about any longer that night. He had accomplished what he had set out to do.

When he climbed back into the car, he immediately turned on the game. Koufax had already exited and Miller was pitching in the top of the ninth. Scully recapped what happened in the seventh, and David couldn't believe what he heard, except it seemed to fit into the craziness of the week. Koufax lost two to one. He was six-three for the season. Later, David fell asleep with a sense of uncertainty. His world was like a sand castle about to crumble.

CHAPTER ELEVEN

Sunday, May 30, 1965

It's Memorial Day here at Dodger Stadium, but the only mourning taking place is in the Cincinnati dugout. By the bottom of the third inning, the Dodgers were already ahead eight to one. It is rare that the Dodgers score so many runs when Koufax pitches. Really, the game was over by the time Koufax took the mound in the top of the fourth inning. In the top of the sixth, with the Dodgers leading ten to one, Koufax must have stepped off the gas a little and the Reds managed four runs off the lefty. But it didn't matter by then, and the Dodgers scored two more in the bottom of the eighth to close out the grieving with a twelve-to-five victory.

Koufax struck out thirteen batters in claiming his seventh victory. He's now struck out ten or more batters sixty-six times in his career. That's all we've got from Dodger Stadium today. Enjoy the rest of your Memorial Day holiday.

David and his friends were still talking about the *mystery punch* Friday morning. David had seen the punch Muhammad Ali delivered to Sonny Liston's jaw so many times on television he had lost count. The fight had been Wednesday night. He and Lou had seen the broadcast in a restaurant with a direct feed. David and the guys were deconstructing the bout before classes started. They gathered around a picnic table outside the English building.

"Did you hear that Congress is talking about an investigation? They think Sonny took a dive," Barn said.

"It wasn't a dive. He walked right into Ali's compact cannon, that's what happened," Wiz said.

"Yeah, I saw Liston's head snap back a dozen times. The politicians and the big boys in boxing can't believe Ali is the real thing," David said.

"It's because he's smart, he's poetic, he's Muslim, and he's not afraid to speak his mind. That's what everyone is scared of," Lou asserted.

"Hey, guys, tell you what. Why don't you come over after school? I'll set up the ring like we used to do, and we can each go a couple rounds. It will be fun," Bryce said.

They all agreed. David wasn't sure that it sounded like fun, but he had to admit that Muhammad Ali had renewed his interest in the pugilist sport.

By four o'clock Bryce, with the help of the others, had roped off a small ring in his backyard. When they were fourteen, it had been a regular event to come over in the summer evenings and spar with one another. Bryce's father Brent had boxed in the Army and enjoyed coaching the boys to the point where they each had a solid grasp of the fundamentals.

Wiz and David matched up first. Wiz donned the red gloves and David took the black. With the others hooting and guffawing, Wiz and David circled each other, slowly at first, then Wiz started to dance and prance, imitating Ali. "Come on, Mandel, give me your best shot."

David measured the distance between them, reaching out with his right arm and tapping Wiz on the shoulder as he moved to his right.

"Smack him," Barn shouted.

Wiz threw a couple of quick jabs that David blocked with his glove. David countered with a quick left that hit Wiz on the ear.

"Sorry," David said.

"Don't be sorry, Mandel, you'll get in trouble," Wiz yelled. He snorted and moved back to his left, and as he did, he popped David in the nose, stunning him slightly.

"Yo, Wiz. Give it to the peacenik," CJ shouted.

"Ding, Ding," Bryce said. "End of round one."

David and Wiz retreated to opposite corners of the improvised ring. They glared at each other and then laughed.

"You like my mystery punch, Mandel?" Wiz said.

David could feel a trickle of blood flowing from his right nostril. He took off one glove and pinched his nose to stave off the bleeding. Barn walked over and handed David a paper napkin.

"Tear off a piece and stick it up in your nose. That will take care of the bleeding. Don't let that little bug poke you again or you'll be seeing double the rest of the evening. Keep your gloves high," Barn said.

"Don't worry. It was a lucky punch," David shouted. He looked over at Wiz, who was still grinning ear to ear.

"Ding, ding," Bryce said. "Round two."

David moved slowly toward Wiz. He tested his distance to him with his right glove poking him in the face, but not with any force. Wiz slapped his gloves together and waltzed right, and then left.

"Come on, Mandel, give me your best shot, but you can't hit what you don't see," Wiz taunted. He was bouncing on his toes, bobbing his head from side to side, then leaning in toward David quickly, then backpedaling out of reach.

David plodded after him. He tried to dance like Ali as well, but Wiz was clearly quicker. He hit Wiz with a short right jab to the side of his head. It slowed Wiz down for a second, but then he continued weaving and ducking. David suddenly dropped his gloves and stared at Wiz.

"Let's just stop now before either of us gets hurt," David said. "You're the better boxer."

"You aren't going to wimp out on me, Mandel, just because your nose got a little bloody. The peacenik concedes after the first round. You are more pitiful than Liston," Wiz said. He popped David in the right eye so quickly that his head snapped back.

"Come on," Wiz whispered. "You couldn't talk me out of Vietnam, and you aren't going to talk me out of giving you a licking."

David raised his gloves and skipped right, then left. Knocking sense into or out of Wiz was not going to happen. Someone was going to get hurt, and no one was going to be crowned anything. David clenched his fists inside the gloves. There wasn't a good way out of this. He wished Wiz would be reasonable, not just now but in what he was about to do with his life. Wiz was on him, moving more quickly than before, so fast that David thought he would tip over. Too much thinking. He felt a sharp blow to his nose again. The wad of napkin popped out and he tasted blood on his upper lip.

"Come on, Mandel, come on," Wiz said, his eyes lit up with anger. "Show me what you've got!"

How do I get through to this guy? Wiz threw a left that David deflected, but it landed hard on his shoulder. Then he came back with a right that hit David squarely in the stomach.

"Ninety seconds left," Bryce chimed.

Wiz came forward again with a quick left-right combination, but David parried both strikes. If he didn't do something, Wiz would keep attacking. David could see the rage in his face. Fear. Kill or be killed, he was preparing for what he'd be encountering in a few months. Full count. He needed to respond, and quickly.

Wiz came in again, feigning with his right and hooking with his left. The glove was headed toward David's already bloodied nose. David blocked the left and quickly responded with his own left. The blow hit Wiz straight and true as David stepped forward the same way he followed through on the pitching mound. There was a loud thud. Wiz dropped to the ground.

David looked down. Wiz's eyes were closed, and he wasn't moving. CJ ran over first and bent down where Wiz was sprawled.

"You okay, Wiz? Talk to me," CJ said.

"Wiz, sorry. I didn't mean to . . . ," David said.

Just then Wiz opened his eyes and shook his head. Groggily, he stood up with CJ's help. He looked at David.

"Sorry? Why be sorry, motherfucker. Your left is like a flying anvil. You need to harness that rage and enlist with me and CJ. Who's up next? Barn, why don't you take on Bryce. I'm done for now."

David tried to apologize again, but Wiz didn't want any part of it. They fought hard, and now it was over. Wiz was going to Vietnam regardless of who got the last punch.

The boys continued boxing until each had their fill, then they adjourned inside where they continued to talk about the fight and speculate on the future of Muhammad Ali.

On Memorial Day David woke up startled. The previous night had been extraordinary. He and Rita met at her cousin's apartment. The promise of a *special* graduation dinner at Fred's place had done the trick. Rita had been even more amorous than usual. So David was surprised to wake up with such a fright. He quickly remembered dreaming about death, his own. In the dream he had been in a fatal car accident driving home from Rita's house. At the moment of impact, he woke up, but he knew he had died.

He got dressed quickly and walked into the kitchen. His mother had already prepared breakfast. Everyone was starting to eat. The plan was to go to the cemetery and visit his grandmother's gravesite. It was the first Memorial Day since she had died. Grandma Judith had been a sweet and generous woman. David was fond of her, and her death was his first encounter with any significant loss. Jacob's parents were still alive. Judith's husband, Grandpa Abe, had died when David was two. He had missed the unveiling of Judith's headstone three months earlier because he had a spring baseball tournament. It had been over a year since the funeral.

His mother had wanted an open casket viewing before the formal proceedings. It was his first ringside seat to death. At the time he didn't think he had a choice as to whether to take a look or not. The sight of sweet Judith, draped in white—but looking yellow, waxed, and utterly stolid—plagued him for several months. What was worse was the incongruity of the theme-park atmosphere at the funeral *park* and the solemnity of the event.

David, Rose, Jacob, and Alex all piled into the Ford Fairlane 500 in route to Hillside Memorial Park. This would be David's inaugural viewing of the granite headstone with the vital statistics that lie in wait for everyone. A date with death, David thought as the car pulled away. David and Alex each pulled out their transistor radios and put in their single ear plugs.

"David, I can't tell you how happy this makes me. You have no idea, no idea," Rose said as Jacob turned the corner.

"Thanks, Mom."

"What about me?" Alex squeaked. "The star of the family graces us with his presence, and suddenly everything is about how wonderful he is."

"Alex, don't get your mother aggravated. The trip hasn't even started, and you're already causing grief. Don't start," Jacob interceded.

"Start what? We are going to visit Grandma's grave. Isn't that special enough? Just because *you know who is with us*, it's special."

"Alex, just shut your mouth or I'll shut it for you," Rose fumed.

"Physical violence? Threats? That's not going to work anymore, Mom," Alex said.

"Everyone needs to just calm down. Alex, that will be enough," Jacob said, trying to assert his patriarchal authority.

His sister had guts and brains, and he loved her spunk, but she'd riled the tiger. He leaned over toward her and whispered in her ear, "Just let it go for now. Save it for another day." He wrapped his arm around her shoulder and gave her a squeeze. Alex smiled and turned up the volume on her radio.

They entered the cemetery. There was music playing and flags waving. A huge mural of Al Jolson, Eddie Cantor, and George Jessel loomed just inside the entrance. David took out his ear plug as the Dodgers game was starting.

"This place is evolving into a Disneyland for dead people," David snickered and put his ear plug back.

"Don't be disrespectful," Rose murmured.

"I'm not. They are," David said, pointing to the mural.

Just as they rolled past the chapel, David heard the Dodgers score two runs in the bottom of the first inning. Koufax had breezed through the top of the lineup, his fastball sizzling again, according to Vin Scully.

His father drove directly to Grandma Judith's grave, avoiding the ordeal of the chapel, the gift store, and the Star Hall of Fame photos that lined the walls inside. At the intersection of Isaac and Rebecca Streets, Jacob parked the Fairlane, and the family climbed out into the dense Los Angeles air. Cars were lined up along the curbside in every direction, as if it were a gathering place for a perennial block party.

The cemetery filled David with thoughts of death. The grass, the asphalt, the clouds all subsumed into a lingering memory of Grandma Judith's coffin being lowered slowly, his mother weeping, his father solemn and steadfast, his arm tight around Rose's shoulder. It was foreign and powerful. David recalled the wretched stillness and permanence of her interment. Hillside, with its ultra-green, perennially cut lawns remained a spiritually contaminated dumpsite, not because of the dead, but because of the mendacity of the living.

They walked out to where Judith's stone rested, a flat slab of granite that could have easily once been a chunk of the Sierra Nevada. It was now polished and etched with her name and the relevant dates, her life reduced to these simple statistical relevancies, a very deconstructed box score that tugged at David's sense of proportion in the world.

Suddenly David started coughing. Perhaps it was the smog, or dust, or the pollen, but he felt like he was gagging.

"David, are you all right?" Alex said, seeing his wan condition.

He tried to speak, but nothing came out. Finally, he said, "No, I'm fine, I think maybe I'm a little carsick."

"It's the smog," Jacob replied. "It gets pretty thick during the afternoon."

"Try not to breathe too hard. Just take little breaths and blow your nose. Little breaths, take little breaths," Rose chimed. Blowing your nose always solved the problem, regardless of the circumstances. Rose walked over to her mother's grave and took a stone from her purse and placed it on the corner of the rectangular block. "Try not to breathe too hard, darling."

Good advice for the ghosts, David thought. His eyes were starting to burn like they had been doused with acid, and while the avoidance of aspiration might have worked for his mother, it had little effect on David. His eyes started to drip, and he began coughing again.

"Could we drive out to the beach and get some fresh air?" David asked. "This is literally killing me."

"Yeah, and it's no place to die," Alex chortled. "Let's go to the beach, there's time."

"Kaddish, Kaddish before anything. Then the beach," Rose said.

The four of them huddled around the newly installed headstone. Jacob passed out small blue prayer books that he had kept from Judith's funeral service. Together they recited the mourner's prayer for Judith. Rose started to cry. Jacob put his arms around her, and they stood silently for a few moments. David gazed around at the sea of grievers. He coughed and wiped his eyes. This was just the beginning, he thought.

CHAPTER TWELVE

Thursday, June 3, 1965

There were lots of fireworks at Busch Stadium tonight, and it is still a month away from the Fourth of July. In the end the Dodgers beat the Cardinals eleven to ten. The Cardinals started red hot, exploding for seven runs in the first three innings. Koufax has usually dominated here at Busch Stadium, but not tonight. In the second inning, Junior Gilliam and Willie Davis both made errors, and that opened the gates for five unearned runs. Koufax struggled to regain his momentum, but couldn't retire anyone in the top of the third inning and was pulled after giving up six hits, including a home run to Ken Boyer. He walked one and only had one strikeout.

The game continued to be a slugfest, both teams stacking up runs and hits. In the top of the eighth inning, Ron Fairly hit a two-run homer to nudge the Dodgers ahead.

It's been quite a day. First Edward White takes a walk in space, and then the Dodgers come roaring back to win a thriller. And Koufax? Well, maybe the stars just weren't aligned for him tonight. That's it from Busch Stadium in St. Louis.

By the time Thursday rolled around, the cemetery episode was fading from David's consciousness. He hoped he wouldn't be visiting the dead again anytime soon. Friday was graduation, and today was the last official day of classes.

David spotted Rita as soon as he got out of the car. She was wearing a pair of hip-hugging, thigh-snapping black pants that gave life to every sinew of her perfectly shaped legs. Her peach silky blouse traced the tight wiry lines of her bra, enough to suggest what didn't need any clarification at all. She looked more gorgeous than ever. She leaped into his arms and kissed him full on the lips, as always so delectable and free. David reciprocated.

"I love you so much. I'm so happy this is the last day. I've been ready for so long," Rita said.

"Yeah, me too. I won't miss this place. God, you look beautiful. You ought to wear those pants all the time." David gave her the once-over.

"Well, if you live with me maybe I will."

David laughed nervously and kissed her. Fortunately for him, the bell for first period rang, and throngs of students surrounded them, allowing him to dodge her entreaty. They joined hands. David nudged his shoulder against her silky blouse and caught a trace of plumeria perfume. They walked through the rows of lockers. They nodded to each other silently, smiling as they entered Mr. Nash's Contemporary Life Skills Class, *for the last time.*

Of all the classes, this was the only one David would actually miss. More than anything, Nash taught that every person needed to think for himself and make decisions that had integrity. Every class began with a reading of the newspaper, and he expounded on the heresies, inanities, and hypocrisies of the Johnson administration as well as the deadly encounters that were taking place in the south as Martin Luther King's civil rights movement continued to expand and gain strength. When Malcom X was gunned down in February, the contemporary issues class was the only place students could go to deal with their grief, anger, and confusion. Nash had an uncanny gift for unraveling difficult, complex issues and emotions. He reminded them about the graduation ceremony that was scheduled to start at 1:00 p.m. the next afternoon.

"Let's cut the rest of the day," Rita whispered.

"Don't you want to say goodbye to your teachers?"

She stared at David and shook her head. He hesitated for a moment, not wanting to get busted the last day of school, then said, "All right, wait till after second period when the parking lot is a little quieter. Where do you want to go?"

"Let's grab Lou and head out to Manzanita Creek. It's always cool up there this time of year," Rita said.

"Great, you get Lou and I'll get my stuff from my locker and meet you at the car."

The trailhead to Manzanita Creek was fifteen miles northeast of the school. David had taken Rita there last year at the beginning of trout season. He had lucked out and caught four rainbows that Rita brought home to her mother.

David found it odd that Rita wanted Lou to come along, but it worked for him because there wouldn't be talk about the *future*. Maybe she secretly pined for him and thought about a threesome out in the woods on a soft patch of grass, under a canopy of willows. Perhaps Rita wanted to live out one final fantasy before she was cast into the swirl of adulthood. The idea of a ménage troubled him. Leaning against the Galaxy, David took a long drink of water, trying to flush away the image. Just then Rita and Lou passed through the chain-link gate, laughing about something he couldn't hear.

"Do you believe that he didn't want to join us? Lou said he felt like he'd be intruding!"

"We wanted you to join us on this last important day," David said. He laughed, hoping that his anxieties weren't spilling out on the ground for Rita and Lou to see.

"Hey, let's get going before they decide to lock the gates on us," Rita said.

David climbed in, started the car, and flicked on the radio. They were playing "Oh Donna." Rita piled in next to David and slid up against his thigh. Lou started to get into the backseat, but Rita motioned for him to sit next to her in the front. They all squeezed close together, hip to hip, as David turned onto Van Nuys Blvd., all of them singing,

I had a girl and Donna was her name . . .

When David reached Foothill Blvd., he turned right to Osborne, and made a left going east, in the direction of Little Tujunga Canyon, where a gravel road led into the Angeles Forest and the trailhead for

Manzanita Creek. David had his right hand resting on top of Rita's left leg. Lou had his window open, his arm draped out the side of the car. They had stopped at a little Mexican grocery store and picked up some orange juice and Mexican sweet breads, which they passed back and forth as they drove slowly up the forest service road. Lou knew enough not to say anything about them looking for a place to room together at school.

"Why don't you turn off the radio and I'll read you something," Lou said.

"I like the radio," David said.

"David, just turn off the radio and let Lou read us something," Rita said.

David shrugged and turned off. As always, Lou had his own idea about what was important and meaningful. David slid down a bit in the seat.

"I've been reading this new poet, a guy named Jack Gilbert. I read some of his stuff in *Harper's*. He's pretty good, David. I'll lend you his book sometime, it's called *Views of Jeopardy*. I like the title. Jeopardy, like what is happening every day."

"Well, maybe I can read it later, because here we are at the trailhead," David said.

"You're a jerk, David," Rita said.

"I agree, sometimes I'm a jerk and sometimes I get us to the place where we are supposed to be. So why don't you and Lou grab the snacks and water and whatever else and let's start hiking."

When David opened the door, Rita gave him a look that said *You really are an asshole sometimes.* But her acrimony didn't last but a few seconds, and as soon as they crossed the little footbridge that led to the trailhead, Rita grabbed both David's and Lou's hands and started up the path.

Rita plopped down on a flat moss-covered rock and peered into a pool, looking for fish.

"Hey, look at these tadpoles." She pointed at the murky black circles with feather-thin tails, darting in every direction. "Lou, come check it out, they're really cool."

Lou leaped across the steam and sat next to Rita. He moved in close so he could see the larvae zooming around. The sun penetrated through the alders and willows, warming the trio. Rita arched her back like a feline about to strike, and then stretched her lips into a smile.

"This is so beautiful, David. Thanks for sharing this place."

She turned quickly and kissed him long and hard on the lips, and then said, "You don't mind if I kiss Lou as well, do you? Just a kiss, just to make this right, make it special? I don't know why. I just want to do. It's okay, isn't it?"

What the fuck, does she want a ménage? David thought. *But it's going to be over between us soon anyway.*

"Yeah, sure, kiss him."

"Wait, wait. What if I don't want to be kissed?" Lou said. "It feels weird."

"What's weird?" Rita said. "Am I weird because I want to kiss you? We've been friends for all these years, and maybe I won't see you again for a long time, or maybe I will. Who knows? But it's one of those times when I feel like just being free. And if you don't want me to kiss you, I understand."

"It's not that," Lou protested.

"Yeah, Rita's not that great a kisser anyway," David said. Rita gave David a killer glance.

This whole thing was starting to make David feel uneasy. Suddenly, Rita turned and stared straight into Lou's blue eyes and wrapped her fingers around his blond hair, lowered her lips onto his, and gave him a tender kiss that lingered just long enough to get Lou's full attention.

It all happened so fast that David didn't have time to say a word. In a voyeuristic way, he enjoyed watching Rita's sexuality in action, even though it was just a kiss. In the aching silence that followed the smooch, they all looked in different directions, their eyes plowed into the scrub oak, through the pines and rocks that extended upward toward the bald peaks of the Angeles Crest. Somewhere upstream a canyon wren warbled its descending mating song. David looked at Rita. She gazed up at the sky, and he saw a tiny wisp of perspiration form on the downy part of her neck, a place familiar to his senses. His love for her at that moment abounded without restraint, and had Lou not been there, he certainly would have taken her like he had so many times, lapping up the salty tastes that lingered around her flesh.

"Are we hiking or what?" Lou stood up and stretched his hamstrings, pushing against a laurel tree and looking back at Rita and David.

"You see how energizing a little kiss can be? Imagine what would happen if you got more than that," David said.

"Fuck you, David. Come on, let's go."

David turned and looked at Rita.

"I'm ready," Rita said. "I just want to be sure to pick some wildflowers on the way back to take home to my mom. I think there's a lot of wild lupine out right now, I can smell them." She brushed the dirt off the bottom of her black pants and started walking up the trail behind Lou. David followed, occasionally slapping away tangled remnants of moss and lichen that still clung to the fibers of her pants. She kept pushing his hand away as he pleaded that he was only trying to help.

They walked for an hour. Lou and David checked for trout in the shadowy pools and found quite a few rainbows. They planned on returning sometime in the next week if they could. No one else said anything about the kiss, not on that hike or anytime afterwards. Rita wasn't going to make a play for Lou. David was certain he would not have allowed it, even if she had. Rita needed someone who was ready to take on the day-to-day making of a life together. That was not Lou. Nor was it him.

As they walked back down the trail, the conversation went silent. David, oddly, thought about Koufax. It allowed him to bury the dreary truth of what he needed to do and dodge what fate might have in store for him. It was bad enough that CJ and Wiz were about to sign their names in blood, but what the hell was he going to do after Rita?

Back at the school parking lot, Lou took off quickly. David walked Rita to her car. She started to open the door and then turned to David. He kissed her and started to walk away.

"Is that it? Nothing else?" she said.

"I love you."

"You do? It's hard to tell. You seem totally distracted. The only time I noticed your full attention was after I kissed Lou. Maybe I need to do that more often. I know you have a lot going on, but I need a little more from you right now. I'm pretty freaked out myself, and it doesn't seem like you're going to be of much help. What am I to do?"

"What you're supposed to do is go home, take a shower, make yourself beautiful for tomorrow. Meanwhile, I'll pick up the flowers I ordered for you at Bell's Pharmacy and get back here before the final countdown at 1:00 p.m. tomorrow. Oh, and remember that I'm taking you to Fred's."

"Sweet words, but I know you're actually just a well-disguised coward. One beautiful night and then you disappear into the ether."

"I'm not vanishing from you Rita, it's just . . ."

"Just what? Please don't insult me, David. I know perfectly well what is about to happen. Part of me has known since the beginning, and you know what? It's really all right with me."

"What is *all right* with you?" David said.

"What we've had has been precious. I don't regret a minute of it. I just want the same honesty that we have always had. No lies."

"Fair enough, no lies," he said.

"I don't believe you. See you at the goddamn graduation." Rita fumed. She got in her car and drove off.

David drove home, engulfed in depression and shame. Rita had seemed so loving on the hike and all week, for that matter. Hopefully, she'd relent and they'd have another night together.

At home he listened to the entire Dodgers game. Not even Koufax could lift him from his sadness, and he wallowed throughout the night, nibbling on sunflower seeds, potato chips, slices of orange, and drinking ice water. Several times he ignored his mother's calls to come inside and watch *I Love Lucy*, and then *Get Smart*, but he knew the inane laughter that characterized the sitcoms would only make him feel more miserable. As he sat in the chaise lounge, looking out across the red-topped cinder block fences that handcuffed the yards together, over the shingled roofs and onto the burnt horizon, he imagined a time when he would be gone and free of the gravitational chains of the Valley life. Between innings, on the Dodgers broadcast, news commentators talked about the "remarkable" spacewalk that had taken place earlier in the day. Edward White spent twenty minutes walking around in the cosmos and refused to return to the Gemini space capsule. He was so intoxicated with the view and experience that he disobeyed Captain James McDivitt's order to return, simply saying, "This is fun." When he finally returned, he mournfully said, "It's the saddest moment of my life."

David gazed out into the dark Valley sky. White didn't want the weightlessness of space to end. David could understand the sentiment. He didn't want to return to the gravity of his life. He knew his life with Rita would soon be over, but he wasn't totally sure he wanted to let it go.

Meanwhile, "Koufax the Invincible" had been betrayed by his fielders and yielded more runs, albeit mostly unearned, than at any time in the past two years. Even the great Sandy Koufax got thrashed tonight. David knew that Koufax would soon return to his stellar form. He always did. Tonight he didn't make it beyond the third inning, but David knew his inner resolve would carry him deep into the season. He hoped he could do the same.

CHAPTER THIRTEEN

Monday, June 7, 1965

Tonight at Connie Mack Stadium, the Dodgers trounced the Phillies fourteen to three. The Dodgers came out swinging, scoring three runs in the top of the first on a Ron Fairly home run. Maybe Koufax got giddy with that lead, because in the bottom of the inning he served up a fat one to Dick Stuart, the Phillies' first baseman, and suddenly it became a one-run game. In the top of the third, a Maury Wills single and a Willie Davis double netted another score, making it four to two. Meanwhile, Koufax found his groove and mowed down the Phillies like dry stalks of corn. No telling what got into the Dodgers in the top of the fourth, because they erupted; four singles, a double, a triple, a hit batter, and one Philadelphia error brought in seven Dodgers runs. The game was over at that point, but they continued play, and when Koufax struck out the final batter (with the bases loaded) in the ninth, it gave him thirteen for the night. Not only did he pick up his eighth win against only three losses, but he collected two base hits, a minor miracle. That's it for tonight from the City of Independence.

It was graduation day. Rita ignored David before the ceremonies. Her rebuff stunned him so thoroughly that he almost forgot what to do as he crossed the stage to receive his diploma. In the pandemonium afterwards, with the hundreds of family members milling around, David pushed his way toward Rita and forced himself into her presence. Before he could say a word, she gave him a perfunctory nod, followed by "Congratulations, David, I wish you well at college."

Every cell in his body screamed *No wait. Don't leave. Not yet. Not now.* But his voice uttered, "Rita, you don't understand, please . . ."

"David, it's over, we're finished, that's it. I've got to be with my family."

"But what about our dinner at Fred's?"

"You must be kidding," Rita said. She turned and disappeared into the crowd.

David spent the evening with Lou. It was Friday. They hopped from party to party, but David was too downhearted to enjoy any part of the festivities. Lou did his best to mollify his friend, but David was inconsolable. As much as he had anticipated the end of the relationship, it didn't approach the emptiness he felt. Graduation night without Rita was like an ocean without water. Incomprehensible.

Wiz and CJ were having a party Saturday night to celebrate graduation and their final days as civilians. At first David considered not going. He was still pining about Rita, but that wasn't going to go away anytime soon. Not going was just not an option, but he refused to think of it as a farewell party or a going-away party, and the notion of festivities that honored the continuation of the war made him angry. Somehow, he still held a thread of hope that the two would change their minds at the last minute.

The gathering was at CJ's house. Tony bought a side of ribs, two dozen sirloin steaks, several vats of potato salad and coleslaw, along with generous amounts of liquor. Tony believed if you were old enough to serve you were old enough to be served. While it seemed inevitable that Rita would make an appearance, David prayed she wouldn't show up.

When David arrived at CJ's house, Veronica greeted him at the door, her eyes full of doubt and fear. She threw her arms around David in a silent embrace.

"David, I'm so happy you came. CJ told me about you and Rita. I'm sorry, but I suppose you knew this was going to happen. Are you okay?"

"I think so. It's all happening so fast. How are you doing with CJ's leaving on Monday?"

"Insanity, it is pure insanity," she whispered. "My father is nuts. This is his life's work finally coming true, his warrior son is off to war. I can barely stand to be in this house."

David nodded and admired Veronica's eyes. They looked inviting and sad, a place to perhaps rest his soul and forget about the immediacy of the dreadful send-off as well as the deep ache from his breakup with Rita.

"Is Rita here?" David asked.

"I haven't seen her." She touched his arm and David sprang to attention. "Come have a beer. I want to talk with you."

Veronica disappeared into the kitchen, and David heard Tony blurt out his name.

"David, David, come back here and have some ribs. Come on, boy, let's celebrate. These tigers are about to roar out into battle."

"Be right there, Tony, you can make me a plate."

"It's ready when you are."

Veronica returned and handed David a Heineken. David popped it open. Veronica moved over to a green velvet loveseat in the corner of the living room. She pointed to the chair next to her, and he sat down.

"So what's next?" David asked.

"Nothing, I've run out of ideas. I'm working on prayers, and when that happens, I start to feel like a hypocrite because I don't have faith anymore."

"Faith in what?"

"Faith in anything. Tell me how to reconcile the fact that we can send men into space, they walk around with suits that insulate them from freezing and boiling at the same time, we can talk with them while they are a hundred miles up in space, but we can't figure out how to get along with people who have different political ideas."

David gazed at Veronica; her perfectly trimmed auburn eyebrows, with just a hint of dark liner, were haunting. She had her hair pulled back and wrapped with a jade-colored silk scarf so that it draped over the nape of her neck.

"There is no changing their minds now," David said.

"I can't believe it."

"Neither can I." He put his hand on her shoulder, and she placed her palm across his wrist. They looked hopelessly into each other's eyes.

"I have to go join the party. Maybe we can talk later," David said sheepishly. Veronica nodded and he jetted away toward the crowd.

Lou, Barn, Bryce, Lydia, Maxine, and a few others surrounded CJ and Wiz. The music was loud and raucous. "Shake" by Sam Cooke blasted across the backyard, mixed with the fragrance of barbeque ribs and steaks.

"Shake, Shake, Shake,
Listen while I talk to you,
I tell you what we're gonna do,
Shake, Shake, Shake . . . ,

"Shake, shake shake!" David said. He clambered up to Wiz and CJ and slapped them heartily on the back, feigning drunkenness in order to slide into the prevailing mood of *Fuck the world, I'm off to Nam.* David drained his Heineken and reached for another in a large galvanized wash bucket filled with ice and beer.

"Yo, David, our long-lost pacifist friend, Wiz and I want you to join us, come on, we'll go down as a threesome, or is it a trio? Who cares, you'll join us," CJ said.

"Hey, you guys don't need my help, two tough dudes like you . . . you'll take care of business."

"He's just yellow," Wiz belched and staggered against David, his eyelids flapping in disarray as if he had smacked into a wall.

"He's no coward, he's just smarter than we are, Wiz. You know we don't have a clue," CJ belched.

David noticed Veronica standing at the back door, looking fretful, and he saw why in another second. Rita walked right past her and made her way to where Shanti, Lydia, and Maxine where sitting.

She wore a crimson dress, a summer version with spaghetti straps and just enough dip to reveal a shadow of cleavage. David felt a stab in his heart. He wanted desperately to stay and finish the evening with CJ and Wiz. His umbrage wasn't with Rita, it was with the whole the situation; the war, his friends, his future. He figured the best solution lay in his hand, so he opened the Heineken and poured it down the hatch. The beer gave him a buzz, so instead of fear, he felt a guileless bale of courage as he approached Rita.

"Hi, Rita," David plugged his face into the circle of women who were equally intoxicated except, of course, Rita, who had just arrived.

"What about us, don't we get a Hi and a pretty little smile?" Maxine cackled.

"But of course, ladies, aren't we all having such the great time tonight. How wonderful to be liberated from the bonds of mediocrity."

"You don't mean me, do you?" Rita and the others laughed as they watched David squirm in response to Rita's barb.

"But of course not, I think you know I meant our endearing alma mater."

"Not a problem, David. Do you think it's safe to crash the stud circle over there? I really want to talk with CJ and Wiz."

"Yeah, Barn gave a toast and blessed us all with good cheer, safe passage, and a little 'I Will Follow Him,' number. Everyone is free to wander."

"Well, great you've seen to that again. Thanks," Rita said.

"Wait!" he said, but she disappeared toward the back corner of the yard where the guys had regrouped in a tight cluster. David thought he discerned the sweet syrupy fragrance of burning leaves, but realized the only incinerating that was taking place were brain cells going up in cannabis smoke. He retreated inside to relieve himself. There were photos hanging on the walls above the rose marbled floors of Tony and Dolores's home. David checked his eyes in the mirror to see if they were already bloodstained. They looked alright. As he opened the door he practically fell into Veronica.

"How'd it go?" she asked.

"Short and awful. I got about five words out before she dashed off to get stoned with your brother."

"So you're liberated, isn't that what you wanted?"

"I thought so, but things don't always work out the way you think they will."

"I suppose not. You going back to the party?"

"Actually, I'm hiding out, hoping Rita will leave soon, and if not, I'll probably just head home."

"Come with me," she said.

David followed Veronica to the end of the stone hallway where her bedroom was located. She closed the door and sat down on the bed, looking at David longingly as she leaned back into a mass of scalloped pillows. The entire room was done in shades of green and yellow, the bedspread was aqua, the walls were painted pale lemon. Veronica wore a straight black skirt, cut just above the knee, and a sleeveless mauve blouse that accented her long silky arms. She could have been wearing a beige housecoat and a pair of floppy slippers. It wouldn't have mattered.

"Don't even think about it," she said.

"About what?" he laughed.

"Look, it's not that I don't find you attractive, because I do. And it's not that I haven't noticed the way you look at me."

"Okay," David said, "so what am I doing here?"

"I want you to promise me two things. First, that you'll write to CJ. He cares about you, I would say that he loves you, except I know you don't talk like that with each other, but more importantly, he respects you and I know that he'll write you. And secondly, I want you to call me when you hear from him because I'm not so sure he'll correspond with me. It's just one of those things; either he doesn't take me seriously or he doesn't want me to worry, so even if he does write, it won't be very truthful."

"I can agree to that," David replied.

Veronica leaned over to the night table and opened the top drawer. Her skirt slid up a couple of inches, exposing the side of her thigh. David looked while she grabbed a pen and pad of paper.

"Here is my address and phone number. Call me collect and I'll call you back, or if you can't reach me, drop me a postcard." David nodded as she handed him the paper.

"Now come here." She pulled him onto the bed beside her and wrapped her arms around him. "I'm so damn scared for both of them. CJ has this thing about him that is fearless or reckless, I don't know, it just makes me crazy."

She pulled David in tight and he could feel moisture on her face. He smelled the musty fragrance of fear, love, and worry. Their clothes crumpled as they held fast, and when he couldn't help himself any longer, he kissed her on the cheek and stroked her long hair.

"Don't worry, he'll come back safe," he said, not believing any part of it.

Fortunately for David, Rita had left by the time he returned to the party. CJ and Wiz were ripped and decided to cruise Van Nuys Blvd. one more time. They wanted David to drive the Galaxy, but he opted out, feigning nausea and a headache. They gave him a hard time. Finally, he insisted and left as their noisy complaints faded into the night. David needed to get home and somehow unravel the feelings he had about Rita. His anxiety spiked as he walked out the door, knowing he had agreed to take Wiz and CJ to the induction center Monday morning. It was all happening too fast.

Monday morning David awoke early with a start. Both sets of parents wanted to drive their respective sons to the site, but the boys didn't want the emotional scene that would have accompanied the goodbyes. They wanted David to be their chauffeur. On one level, it was all so ordinary. Simple logistics, pick up his friends from point A and drive them to point B. David racked his brain, trying to find words or an excuse, a reason for them to cancel the whole deal. But all possibilities had been exhausted. There would be no stay of execution.

It was dawn. David walked outside just as the sun rose in its infinite glory, unfettered and filled with demands and responses. The Galaxy was trim and clean, the way he liked it. He had emptied the trunk in anticipation that his friends might have a lot of stuff, but when the time came, each one had just one small suitcase, enough for their toiletries and personal gear.

He picked up CJ first. When he opened the car door, his large round, ruddy face reminded David of a clown, with a strong aroma of stale beer and potato chips. "Did you sleep at all?" He asked.

"Hell no. I just got home an hour ago. Thank goodness my mom packed everything last night. We drove out to the county line and made a huge bonfire. Barn filled his car with a bunch of old furniture he bought at the Salvation Army on San Fernando Road. You should have seen it; it was bitchin', old chairs and little dressers all exploding with the waves crashing in the background. We had a great time. Lydia broke down when I said goodbye a couple hours ago, but what the hell. I expected that."

"I suppose so. Sorry I didn't make it, but I just felt like I was getting the flu or something. I'm fine now," he lied.

"That's good, we needed one sober solider to make sure we made our appointment with destiny." CJ hopped into the front seat, and David drove a couple blocks to pick up Wiz.

"Hey look, there's Wiz all ready for battle. He looks like shit, doesn't he?" CJ said.

Wiz was slumped down on the steps of his white porch, half asleep, half drunk, his black satchel in front of his freshly shined shoes.

When David lowered the window, CJ shouted, "Wake up, pussy cat, the day has arrived, get your ass in gear!"

Wiz climbed into the back seat, shut his eyes, and went to sleep.

Monday morning, like any weekday, had traffic. Even though it was less than twenty miles to the induction center on Broadway in downtown L.A., David had allowed an hour and a half for the journey. Wiz remained crashed out in the backseat. David turned on the radio; the DJ was playing a new release by the Rolling Stones, "Satisfaction." David amped it up as they passed the Osborne exit, and CJ started to sing along. His voice was clear, bold, and free of inhibition. They cruised past Lankershim Boulevard and heard the news that the astronauts, McDivitt and White, had returned safely to Houston. They reported that while Ed White did well in space, he did get seasick waiting to get picked up in the choppy Atlantic, four hundred miles off the coast of Florida. The newscaster announced that traffic southbound on the Golden State might be delayed due to an overturned car in the left lane near the Griffith Park exit.

"Well, maybe we won't make it today and I'll have to join the Navy like little Rickie Norris," CJ mused.

"We've got plenty of time, and if it looks bad, I know the back way down San Fernando Road. My dad and I take it whenever it gets really bottled up. Have you heard anything about Norris."

"Not a thing, but Wiz and I were talking about finding out once we get squared away. Apparently, when you are part of the starched brotherhood you can get a lot more inside dope about what's going on with other guys in the military. I'll let you know as soon as I hear something. I'm sure that little shit is up to no good, probably doing something outrageous like hanging from trees and offing gook boats with his machine gun."

"Well, any news about him would be good, it's been about a month since we heard anything," David replied.

"Not a lot of deliveries in the bush," CJ said.

"I suppose not. Did you have a chance to say goodbye to Veronica? She's really worried about you," David said.

"She was sound asleep, and I didn't want to wake her. I figured I'd call everyone as soon as I get through this first hurdle. They even give guys in jail a chance to make a phone call, I suppose we're at least on that level," CJ said.

"I'd hope so."

Traffic was still moving pretty well as they approached the Olive Street exit in Burbank. They humped along at sixty-five, which meant they might have time to grab a quick bite before the induction circus began. David saw the beginning of Griffith Park off to his right, a vestige of the natural world gasping for breath between the throngs of automobiles and the sprawl of industry. The park was a place where he and Rita had strolled and picnicked, spread a blanket, made out, drank lemonade, read, and occasionally went to the zoo. He drifted back in time and failed to notice that traffic had started to slow down; suddenly he had to brake hard, waking up Wiz.

"What the heck, Mandel, you trying to kill us before we get a chance to do it ourselves?"

"Relax, Wiz, you needed to get up anyway, we'll be there soon."

"Not the way it's starting to look." CJ said as he pointed to the lines of cars now parked in front of them.

"Don't worry, I'll get you there on time. This always happens as you get close to the Glendale Freeway. They said there'd be a slowdown near Griffith Park, so here it is. The radio prophets are the diviners of our world."

"I think you better get us out of here. I don't want to start my Army career being declared AWOL and spend my first day facing some irate master sergeant."

"Wiz, I said I'd get you there on time, it's seven fifteen, and we've only got about six miles before the Broadway exit. If things don't clear up, I'll get off at Stadium Way and zip around Chavez Ravine."

Just as David had said, the traffic started to move again after they passed the overturned vehicle that had now been loaded on a tow truck. Two black and whites edged into the right lane, and once they passed, everything loosened up. David sailed past Stadium Way, where the Dodgers would not return for another week. They were still in Philadelphia; Koufax was slated to pitch against the Phillies tonight.

It was seven thirty by the time David turned onto Broadway and headed southwest toward the induction center. The narrow dark streets of downtown Los Angeles were crowded with cars and shadows. David powered down his window and inhaled the acrid stinging air that had already warmed and began irritating his throat and lungs. People were bustling toward the revolving doors that led to the courthouse and office buildings, but there was no defining center to the area; just a series of asphalt channels, each with gray unmarked buildings. Only the scattered winos that peeked out from the alleys gave the place any distinctive character. It was into these cluttered streets that David was about to deposit his two close friends.

Before parking they cruised the nondescript induction center, a steel-and-glass storefront, and saw that it was closed tight, no lights or crews waiting around outside. It was 7:35. There was a Winchell's Donuts shop on the corner. David pulled into a metered parking spot and deposited a quarter. Wiz and CJ tumbled out, stretching their arms straight up in defiance of the granite building that dwarfed them.

"I'll buy you your last civilian meal before you become privates and start dressing in all green."

"God, I can't believe this is really happening," CJ yawned. "It happened so quick."

"What?" David mused.

"I don't know, school, playing around, Lydia, all of it."

"Well, maybe you can still change your mind."

"Right. Go back and face everyone, say that I chicken-shitted out."

"No, just that you changed your mind."

They walked into the donut shop and Wiz stepped up to the counter. "I'll have a jelly-filled sugar donut and a large coffee. CJ what do you want?"

"I'll have a cinnamon roll and a hot chocolate." Turning back to David, CJ said, "Thanks for the sweets and the cocoa, but I'm not shifting anything. I'm just letting you know what's going on. I hope that's okay."

"Of course. We've been over all that shit. I just thought . . . ," David stammered.

"I know what you thought, and it isn't what I'm thinking. You didn't order yet. We better get going."

"Right." David was next in line. He ordered a large coffee and a glazed donut. They sat down and chewed the dough and sugar slowly, glancing back and forth at each other, smiling and searching each other's eyes as they downed the coffee and cocoa. By the time they finished, it was five to eight, just enough time to walk the short block to the induction center.

"Time to go, David. Let's get the suitcases out of the trunk," Wiz said, wiping a crumb of sugar from his top lip.

David walked outside and opened the trunk. Wiz and CJ grabbed their bags and each gave him a tense shoulder hug. When he locked the car and started to walk beside them, CJ turned and said, "Thanks for everything, David. Wiz and I can handle it from here. Keep in touch and stay away from my sister." He laughed and turned down the street.

CHAPTER FOURTEEN

Saturday, June 12, 1965

Shea Stadium rocked tonight as Koufax beat the Mets five to 0. The Dodgers were smacking the ball with authority. They had eight hits, including three doubles that produced five runs. But really, the way Koufax pitched he only needed a single run. He was close to perfect— giving up only five hits while striking out eight, and raising his record to nine wins and three losses. It was his eighth complete game in just fourteen starts. It's hard to say what it is about watching Koufax that is so extraordinary. He simply goes about his business, and in doing so, he leaves an historic wake of decimated batters. I can't help but tell you that we are witnessing a kind of heroic greatness in this man's performances night after night. It's miraculous. That raps it up for tonight; Dodgers five, the Mets zero.

CJ called David later that night and told him that he and Wiz signed up as "buddies," meaning they were guaranteed to be together at least for basic training and, hopefully, be deployed together as well. That was the promise, so at least the recruiters kept the first part of the pledge. They shipped out the next day to Fort Ord.

By Thursday night David had everything he needed for his trip with Lou. He took a final inventory of his gear: sleeping bag, two changes of underwear, three T-shirts, a five-gallon water container, a rain poncho, a legal pad, hiking boots, an extra pair of jeans, his favorite black wool sweater, one long-sleeved blue oxford shirt, and his faded and patched jean jacket. In a separate bag there were enough groceries for the weekend. He had a hundred dollars in his pocket.

As David carried his clothes and food into the garage, his father was still tinkering with the Galaxy, taping wires and securing bolts.

David saw that he had taken the time to shine the chrome around the wheels and polish the entire car.

"Dad, you didn't have to do that. It's only going to get dirty on the road."

"It will be easier to scrape off the road kill with a little wax on the front end."

"Well, thanks for everything. I'm just going to arrange things in the trunk and then get some sleep. Will you wake me in the morning? I told Lou I'd pick him up at six thirty."

"Yes. I checked the pressure in your spare and it's fine. You know how to work the jack?"

"Of course."

"Just checking. I'll wake you in the morning."

"Thanks."

Lou stood next to the curb where a white rectangular box had numerals 6 5 4 9 stenciled in black letters. Basic, easily identified for the meter readers, trash collectors, paper boys, and other service providers that tended the suburban asphalt lanes of the San Fernando Valley. As he eased the car into the driveway, he noticed Lou had begun to let his hair grow so that his tight curls were now displayed as a short cropped Afro. Lou wore a navy-blue T-shirt, just tight enough to highlight his pectoral muscles, and jeans that were a little too short. His white crew socks were revealed at the ankle above his black loafers. He looked ready and vibrant. He greeted David with a sardonic smile that said he knew something that David yearned for, but still could not grasp. He stood beside his red backpack with a bag of groceries. His hands dangled from his pockets, thumbs anchored inside. David felt his adrenaline heighten as he stopped and opened the door.

"Ready?" David asked.

"Yeah, I brought some coffee and donuts. Have you eaten?"

"No, I don't have much appetite in the morning, but the coffee sounds good."

"How about the maps?"

"Maps, of course, you know my dad, the car is totally outfitted."

"Where should we stash the pot?"

Lou had scored some pot from a friend at UCLA who graduated from East Valley last year. He had invited Lou to a couple of parties earlier in the spring, and had turned him onto a bag of marijuana that now resided inside the red backpack. David had smoked a few times with Lou during their senior year. It helped mellow the sharp edges of their friendship.

"Do you have anything already rolled?"

"One fat joint that should last all the way to San Francisco."

"Perfecto! I've got a little stash spot under the carpet against the back seat on your side."

Lou reached down and hid the bag. He opened his hard black sunglasses case and pulled out a wheat-colored cigarette that looked like a miniature burrito with its ends twisted into tight little points.

"Shall we christen the trip?" Lou said.

"Not quite yet, let's celebrate once we get out of the Valley," David said.

David started the car and tuned in KRLA. They were playing "Only the Lonely" by Roy Orbison. The wind was blowing west, the sky looked open and translucent. David felt liberated but a bit disconnected. No more Rita. He missed her. A part of him wanted to hit the brakes on his life as he climbed the on-ramp of the San Diego Freeway at Roscoe and accelerated south toward Route 101.

They headed straight out of the Valley toward Oxnard and Santa Barbara. The miles started to strip away, and once they passed Topanga Canyon and slid into Calabasas, David felt an enormous relief. Lou talked about the trails around Mount Vision and what cafés and bookstores he wanted to see in San Francisco. It all sounded good. David was ready to get away. As they approached the sign to Camarillo State Mental Hospital, David turned to Lou and said, "Now's a good time to light up."

"I was thinking the same thing."

Lou opened the pocket of his tan chambray shirt that he wore over his blue tee and took out his glasses case, flipped it open, and took out the joint. David pushed in the lighter, and when it sprung out he handed it to Lou, who fired up the grass and took a long slow toke. David opened the window and felt a tinge of salt air as Lou passed the joint to him.

"This tastes incredible," David said and passed the joint back to Lou.

"Yeah, ole Gilbert came through again, one of the fringe benefits of being at university."

"Well, I'm ready. I'm glad we're doing this together, you know what I mean? I can't imagine taking this journey with anyone else," David said.

"Nope, me either."

David looked out the window. The hollow monotony of the San Fernando Valley had melted away as they approached the beaches of Oxnard. David wondered how many more years he would have to wade through the muck of suburban life before he might really make the break.

"Do you think part of why Wiz and CJ enlisted was to get away from all this?" David gestured behind him.

"No. I think they'll come back and hunker down right here. They'll get married and live the dream."

"I hope they do come back," David said.

They left Ventura and followed the 101 as it joined Highway 1 and blended with the bright crystalline Pacific. The colors blasted through David's sunglasses. Flocks of shorebirds glided along the ocean edge. The smell of the surf cleansed David's mind of the despair he felt about his friends.

Just outside the beach town of Carpentaria, a pretty little hitchhiker with a tattered backpack smiled and wiggled her thumb in their direction. Before Lou could protest, David stopped twenty yards north of where she stood. She gamboled toward the Galaxy, her short brunette hair wrapped in a lime paisley scarf. She wore a pair of dangling beaded earrings, tight-tight jeans, and a black sleeveless jersey blouse. And she was braless.

"Hey, thanks man. I couldn't believe it; I've been standing there for more than two hours. All these morons with their kids going to the beach just ogled and pointed at me like I was some sort of freak. My name is Ginger, and I really appreciate you stopping. Boy, smells really good in here."

"Hi, I'm David and this is Lou." Lou raised his eyebrows in Ginger's direction.

Make yourself comfortable," David said as Ginger climbed into the backseat. Then he pulled back on the highway.

"You guys wouldn't want to share a little of what you were smoking?"

"Well, I don't know. You might be a narc disguised as a cute little hippie girl. You're not a narc are you?" David said laughingly.

"Not hardly. Does your friend talk?" Ginger said.

"Yes, I talk. Happy we could give you a lift. Where are you headed?" Lou answered. David could tell Lou wanted to get rid of her as soon as possible. The intrusion rubbed him the wrong way. David didn't begrudge him, but Ginger looked too good to pass up.

"Morro Bay, just north of San Luis Obispo, some friends of mine rented a place there. It's on an acre of perfect farmland. We plan to do an organic garden and sell the stuff down in Santa Barbara," Ginger said.

"Well, we're going to San Francisco, straight up 101, so we can drop you in San Luis Obispo. How is that?" David said.

"That would be incredible, especially if we can get high together on the way."

"I'm sure that can be arranged," David chimed.

Ginger's face was soft and round with reddish cheeks. Her eyes lit up when she talked and her smile was full and genuine. When David looked back at her, he saw her lips were full and looked moist with icy-pink lipstick. The scent of her patchouli oil wafted into the front seat. The pot, the ocean air, and his new-found freedom stirred his fantasies. He pulled the car over to the edge of the road near the entrance to Carpentaria State Beach and turned off the engine.

"What are you doing?" Lou asked.

"We're making a driving change," he said. "Do you mind? I'm going to take a little breather. I've been up since 5:00 a.m." But sleep wasn't what he had in mind. Lou glared at David as they switched roles. Lou started the car and sped onto the on-ramp.

"What do you guys do?" Ginger squeaked as she stretched out in the back seat and started to unlace her high-top converse tennis shoes.

"Nothing," David said, "We're about to start UCLA and duck out of the war."

"Sounds cool. My friends never registered for the draft, they just dropped out, and so far nothing has happened."

"More power to them," Lou sniped.

"What's your problem?" David chided.

"No problem. I'm just the driver; don't mind me."

"Hey, Lou, lighten up. It's a beautiful day and we have our whole life ahead of us."

"Right, beautiful day along the cheery Pacific Coast, while we're bombing the shit out of North Vietnam and our friends are getting ready to go over there," Lou said.

"What's got into you?" David said.

"I'm just driving. You were the one who was just talking about Wiz and CJ."

The joint had gone out, and David relit it and handed it to Lou. "Have another toke, you need it," David said.

Lou inhaled and passed the joint back to David, who took a puff, then handed it back to Ginger.

"God, your friend is a real downer. We are in California, not Vietnam," Ginger said. Then she stretched out across the palatial back seat.

"I know where we are!" Lou retorted, his eyes now glued to the freeway.

"Hey Lou, I'm going to hop into the back seat and keep Ginger company. I hope you don't mind."

"No, fuck no. Why should I mind?"

"Well, we can change off. But I think it's rude to leave Ginger back there all my herself."

"I don't mind squeezing up front with both of you."

"No thanks," Lou said.

David climbed into the back. Ginger raised her legs and then plopped them down on his lap.

"Do you mind?" She laughed.

"Not in the least."

Lou cranked up the radio. They were playing "Ring of Fire" by Johnny Cash. David took out the remainder of the joint and fitted it onto Lou's roach clip, struck a stick match with his thumb, and fired it. After one long slow toke he passed it to Ginger, who was propped up against the two car pillows and plaid blanket that adorned his backseat. She leaned forward and whispered, "Thank you," and then settled back and sucked deeply on the marijuana. Between her drags, she looked at David with glittery eyes. She had a thin one-inch scar above her right cheekbone that marred what would have been a perfect face. Lou powered open all the windows from his master control and blasted the radio. He didn't say another word for the next hour. That was just fine with David.

"So, are you spoken for?" Ginger asked.

"Not anymore. My girlfriend broke it off a couple weeks ago. The time had come."

"You sad about it?"

"Sometimes. Other times, like now, I don't really think about it. How about you?" David said.

"I don't really believe in getting serious. I'm too young, you know what I mean? I want an old man sometime, but not now. Are you sure you are comfortable with my legs up on your lap?"

"It's fine. But you can't really see the ocean. Look, there're some dolphins."

Ginger shot up and twisted around just in time to see a pod of bottlenose dolphins break the calm sapphire surface with their black bodies. They ripped through the ocean fabric, then splashed back in an aquatic ballet. David leaned in close to Ginger as she watched the dolphins. He felt the sultry temperature of her skin. They laughed.

"They're so sensual, aren't they?" she said.

"Yeah, they are real sexual creatures," David said.

She laughed again and turned her face toward him. He kissed her. She tasted like the dope they had smoked, and she kissed him back with eagerness and intention.

"You are a delicious boy, well maybe boy isn't the right word." She grinned and looked down at his jeans and then she kissed him again. Her hands climbed under his shirt and before another moment passed, he followed suit, probing her bare breasts. The crisp air rushed around them and the sound of the speeding highway added to the thrill. David propped up the pillows against the seat and eased Ginger down, framing her face in his hands.

David covered them with the red-and-yellow-plaid blanket. For a brief moment he thought of Rita. Lou never looked back or wavered, his foot planted on the accelerator. It was a smooth ride in the Galaxy. They fell asleep somewhere south of Santa Maria.

When the car stopped, they sat up. Their arms were wrapped around each other, smiling like a pair of happy drunks. Lou turned around and said, "I need to pee and get some coffee. Are you lovebirds hungry or thirsty?"

"I could use the bathroom," Ginger said.

"I'm down for some coffee. You want any?" David asked.

"Yeah," she said.

Ginger busted out of the car first and headed to the restroom. Lou flipped the keys back to David.

"Your turn."

"Sure. Are you pissed?"

"No, how could I be pissed at someone who is just a flaming asshole?"

"Hey, what was I supposed to do? You weren't interested," David said.

"That's not the point. We just started this trip and what's the first thing you do?" Lou said.

"She's pretty and kind of smart."

"So what? This is about us, isn't it? Wasn't that the point of this little adventure?"

"I'm just trying to go with the *flow*—forget the past and have a good time," David said.

"Well, I'm not trying to forget anything, David. Life is too short." Then he wheeled around and headed into the store. David followed him inside and bought three coffees.

David took the wheel and offered Ginger a seat between him and Lou. *Yeah, life is too short,* he thought. But what difference did it make if he had some fun? Lou would get over it. At least he hoped so.

"You guys should check out our place. It's just beautiful. They call it Los Osos, the bears. You'd like it," Ginger said.

"What do you think, professor?" David turned to Lou. "Do we have time for a short detour?"

"I think you already took your detour, Davey boy. I want to get up to the cabin while we still have a little light."

"Well, there's your answer, Ginger. Maybe on our way back or another time."

"You're always welcome," she said.

As they approached the turnoff to Morro Bay, David put his hand on Ginger's knee. There was a burger stand on the north side of the street and a Shell gas station on the south side. David pulled into the gas station and hopped out of the car. Lou didn't move. Ginger grabbed her pack from the back seat and walked over to David and gave him a kiss. She scribbled a set of numbers on a piece of crumpled paper.

"Hope to see you again soon, and thanks for everything." She winked and started walking down the road with her thumb waving in the breeze.

David got back in the car and steered north. There was dead silence for the next thirty miles until Lou said, "Do you want to hear some poems I've been writing?"

"Sure," David replied, relieved that the quiet had ended.

There wasn't much David could say about Lou's poetry. He didn't know whether the poems were good or not, the fact that Lou was writing them was enough to impress him. He found himself once again fascinated by Lou. Of all his friends, Lou had the most verve and creative juice. There were times when Lou's self-righteous attitude pissed him off, but mostly David found himself comporting with Lou's ideas and beliefs. Lou stopped reading after a few minutes.

"Hey man. You've really got some talent. I liked them. And I'm sorry about the Ginger thing," David said.

"What did you like about the poems?" Lou asked.

"I'm not sure. The imagery I guess. The way you jump from idea to idea. With poetry, I just like it or I don't. But you are good."

"Thanks. Ginger was cute. I just didn't want the distraction, but I get it. But from here on in, it's just you and me."

"Absolutely," David said.

They continued north through the wide costal valleys of central California. David was awestruck by the beauty of Steinbeck's country and the mystical trails that led into the redwoods and the Tassajara Hot Springs, where he'd heard that monks and poets chanted, split wood, and discussed the nature of consciousness. He'd read that supplicants sat for long hours in prayer, attempting to bring harmony to a world that was rapidly falling apart.

By five o'clock, they were headed toward the Golden Gate Bridge. Driving through Golden Gate Park, David saw throngs of hippies gathered in small groups playing music, tossing frisbees, and dancing. He felt a twinge in his left arm and imagined flinging a plastic saucer with the group. It wasn't the same as baseball. He missed the game and wondered about Koufax.

Driving across the bridge, David marveled at the fact that Koufax's opaque character served to create an almost mystical spirit for his fans. There was a fearlessness and a capacity to endure pain without complaining or making excuses that David venerated. The prosaic quality of the man, compared to his intrepid exploits, accentuated his appeal. It was the ordinariness of his being that made his greatness even more prominent.

"Hey David, you haven't said anything since we passed the park. You getting tired?" Lou said. "Look out there. It's beautiful." Lou pointed to the vastness of the Pacific as it flowed into the bay.

"Gorgeous, just perfect," David said. "I'm fine, just pondering, that's all."

"Well stop *pondering* and start enjoying the view," Lou said.

"Right on," David said. He honked the horn as they crossed into Marin County.

CHAPTER FIFTEEN

Wednesday, June 16, 1965

Summer isn't officially here, but tonight sure felt like a perfect summer night at Dodger Stadium. The Dodgers beat the Giants two to one behind the incomparable Sandy Koufax. It was the Wills-and-Koufax show tonight. Wills stole two bases, giving him forty-one. In the fifth inning, he beat out a bunt, stole second, and scored on a Jim Gilliam single. In the seventh they followed that same script and broke a one-to-one tie. Koufax threw a complete game, giving up six hits and only one run in winning his tenth game of the season. It's only June 16, and Koufax has reached double digits in wins. Who knows how far he'll go once summer really begins. That's it for tonight, enjoy the rest of this beautiful evening.

Everything worked out as planned once they crossed the bridge. Lou had good directions. They took the turnoff to Highway One in Mill Valley and swirled around, then over Mount Tamalpais, a once-active volcano that dominated the Marin County landscape. Past the turnoff to Muir Woods, the road divided and then topped off on a saddle that afforded a spectacular view of the Pacific. David pulled off, even though the sun was getting low in the sky.

"Just for a minute," David said. "I want to take in this view."

Lou followed him to the edge of the cliff where they saw sea lions lounging on the rocks below.

"It's incredible," David said, looking out over the endless Pacific.

"I'm glad you stopped. I think I was getting carsick or something, my head started to throb as soon as we started up the mountain. This air feels good."

"You're right about that."

"I'm sorry about that scene with Ginger. She was really all right, you know. I guess sometimes I just get uptight," Lou said.

"Roger on that," David said.

"It's just sometimes I really like being alone with you."

"Is it serious?'

"Fuck you, Mandel. You're the only one who actually takes any interest in what I'm trying to do."

"And what exactly is that?"

Lou ignored the question and said, "What do you say we push on? I'm still wanting to get to the cabin before nightfall."

They stopped in Stinson Beach, the last town before the road narrowed and climbed up to Mount Vision. Lou wanted to pick up some fresh food at the one small grocery store in town. The grocer, who looked to be in his forties, had shoulder-length salt-and-pepper hair and a handlebar moustache. He wore a neatly pressed crimson bandana around his neck. On his red T-shirt, beside a white silk-screened pelican, he had a little blue nametag—Frank Whiting.

"So where you going to camp?" Frank asked.

David started to respond, but Lou bumped him with his elbow. The groceries were now bagged and sitting on the counter beside a stack of *San Francisco Chronicles*. David noticed the banner "BOMBS BLAST OUTSKIRTS OF HANOI!" Frank saw David looking at the paper and snatched one up and put it in the bag.

"It's on me," he said. "It's good to read the paper, you never know what you'll find between the lines. You guys dodging the draft? Lots of people heading to the hills these days. I don't blame any of them. I mean, what the hell are we doing in that peaceful little country, who cares if they try communism for a decade or two? God knows they tried the colonial and feudal methods long enough to know that it doesn't work. Where'd you guys say you're headed anyway?"

"We didn't," Lou said.

Lou looked irritated and David knew he'd better not extend the conversation, so he simply said, "Mt. Vision."

"Hey, wait a second," Frank said. "Are you Lou Ash?"

Lou stared at Frank for a second, looking surprised and a little miffed.

"Yeah, how do you my name?"

"Your cousins, Abe and Margo, are old friends of mine. They told me you were coming this weekend and asked me to stop by and make sure everything was all right at the cabin. I was going to head up there as soon as I closed the store."

"They didn't mention it to me," Lou said.

"Well, you're welcome to call them up and check for yourself. Abe and I went to high school together in the city. Good people, Abe and Margo. Too bad they moved up to Portland. Now I only see them when they come down to visit. You want to give them a ring?"

"No, I believe you," Lou said. "But, I think we can manage on our own."

"Suit yourself, but I promised Abe I'd stop by. How about I check with you guys in the morning? If you have any trouble tonight, I live just down the street, 803 Meadowlark Lane. Just stop by."

"Okay, Frank, but I don't think we'll need anything," Lou said.

"Have a good night, and keep an eye out for those white deer," Frank said. He smiled and waved goodbye. "See you tomorrow."

The turnoff to Mount Vision was only a short way down the highway, so they had enough light to weave their way up the fire road to the top where the small redwood cabin awaited them. Lou unlocked the old iron padlock, freed it from the hasp, swung open the door, and shouted with jubilation as if he had just been laid for the first time. David wasted no time unloading the car trunk. They quickly ordered and sorted the foodstuffs and their sleeping gear. Lou filled the kerosene lamps from a red gas can that was stored beside the outhouse, about a hundred feet west of the cabin.

By sunset they were on the porch, sitting on a couple of pine chairs, obviously made with hand tools and lashed together with some type of animal gut. Lou sighed a breath of relief. It was quiet except for a few lingering jays and a great horned owl that had a residence in an old laurel tree to the right of the outhouse.

"What you think about that guy Frank?" David said.

"I'm not sure. He's seems a little weird, but if he's a friend of my cousins, he's probably all right."

"Okay, but there is something about him that makes me a little uneasy," David said.

"Hey man, it's going to be fine."

Lou leaned back on the chair, arching his shoulders, so David could see his taut muscles as he dug into his tight jeans and teased out a small remnant of foil. He held it up as if he had just pulled out a prize trout. Carefully, he unfolded the joint, then dipped again into his pocket for a couple of wooden matches. David watched as he gracefully struck the match along the rough deck wood and swept the fire up to the joint that rested between his lips.

"Here," Lou said and passed the joint to David.

"What an incredible sunset, this view is outrageous," David mused.

"I told you this place was amazing. Wait till you see it in the morning."

"I'm worried about CJ and Wiz. The whole thing seems unreal. They're really gone," David said.

"I know what you mean, but they made that choice and there's nothing to do now except try to stop the war."

Saturday morning David woke before Lou and stumbled outside. He was still groggy from the marijuana. His head felt heavy and disconnected from the rest of his body. He grabbed his jacket and made his way to the outhouse. David heard a couple of sharp shrieks and turned just in time to see a dozen fallow-white deer break through the rabbit bush and scrub oak. They bounded into the shadowy patches of light, then disappeared into the redwood and Douglas fir forest that spread up toward the top of Mt. Vision.

"They're really something, aren't they?"

David jumped up and spun around. Walking up the road, wearing a red-and-black wool jacket and a pair of tattered khaki shorts, was Frank Whiting.

"Yeah, they are really beautiful. You are sure up early," David said, not knowing exactly how to respond to the intrusion.

"I'm up at sunrise. I wanted see if you two were interested in a little guided tour."

"Well, let's check with Lou, but I think he's still asleep."

"I'll make some coffee that will wake him up. You probably never worked that little propane stove in the cabin."

Frank walked straight past David into the cabin and turned a couple of levers below the single-burner propane stove, flicked his lighter, and shoved a teakettle on the burner. He poured the water from a red plastic container, opened his backpack and removed a coffee filter and a small bag of ground coffee.

"Bring three mugs, would you? They're stacked in that old footlocker behind you. You'll find dishes and silverware in there as well, and a few spoons while you're at it."

Within a few minutes Frank had boiled the water and produced three steaming mugs of fresh Italian roast coffee. The aroma woke Lou. He opened his eyes, his blond ringlets matted and compressed on the left side. He looked dazed as he saw Frank Whiting towering above him with a cup of strong coffee. Reaching out, Lou looked up into the man's face.

"Thanks," Lou said, "but you really didn't need to come up here."

"I know, but like I said, I promised your cousins. How's the coffee?"

"Fantastic," Lou said.

Lou sipped the coffee and struggled into consciousness, every so often looking up at Frank, who busied himself outside, pulling off tarps that hid stacks of firewood.

"This will make your visit a lot warmer. I don't suppose either of you thought of bringing an ax or a saw? Doesn't matter, this will be plenty of fuel for the few days you're up here."

"Thanks," David said. "You've been great, but I think we're really going to be okay." David wasn't sure about that, and something still bothered him about Frank.

"Listen, guys. I know you'll be fine. I just wanted to show you a trail that will lead to that big herd of deer. It's pretty amazing, and you might stumble into them or you might not. What do you say?"

David was silent as he looked at Lou.

"All right. Let's check it out together," Lou said.

"And one more thing," Frank said. "I thought you'd want to meet my friend Rene Lacombe. He runs a coffee house in the Mission District. He's a writer, but more to the point, Wednesday night he's hosting a poetry reading that I think you'll want to attend."

"I'm listening," Lou said.

"Rene wants to host you. It's going to be a big night. Ginsburg, Corso, Synder—that group. Rene knows them all," Frank said.

"Why?" Lou said.

"Hey, like I said, your cousins are my people."

Lou stood on the porch, transfixed. David couldn't quite believe what he was seeing. Lou nodded toward Frank as if he were in a trance. He looked humbled.

"So, do I tell him you'll be there?"

"Hell yes," Lou said. "We'll definitely be there! Thanks."

"All right then. Let's have some breakfast and then hit the trail," Frank said.

"Hey, Lou, I thought we were leaving Monday," David said.

"What and miss a *reading* like that. I told you I wanted to hear those guys, and now it just drops into our laps. We'll just call home and tell them we're staying a few more days. Is that a problem for you?"

David thought for a few seconds. "No. It should be fine."

After eating they filled up water bottles and threw some nuts and raisins into their day packs along with a map that Frank said they wouldn't need.

They hiked up an old animal trail that Frank said was made by a herd of tule elk. That led to the intersection of the Bolinas Ridge trail where, thanks to Frank's trained eye, they spotted a gray fox as it slashed between a stand of redwoods, then disappeared in the dark foliage of wild blackberry and thick brooms.

Frank moved deliberately along the path, pointing out differences between the scat of coyotes, bobcats, and the hair pellets of a great horned owl. He picked each apart with detached candor, using his lean leathered fingers and a twig to detail the habits and haunts of each creature and their discreet idiosyncrasies. David watched how Lou stopped and scribbled notes as Frank pointed out things along the hike.

After walking north for a few hours, they rested. Frank darted off the trail every so often to look into the woods. He'd tilt his head back as if to get a better read on the wind across his cheeks, and then he would bounce back and continue telling stories about Rene and his friendship with Kerouac and the other beat writers. Lou was mesmerized by the names and the history.

Suddenly, Frank stopped as they approached another opening toward the sea. He put his large hands back behind him and spread his fingers open, wiggling them to get David and Lou's attention. Slowly, he bent his knees and moved into a crouch, beckoned that they do the same, and pointed to a clearing in the northwest.

"There, there. What do you think of those incredible deer, my boys? Aren't they something?"

"They are. They look magical, like a herd of phantoms," David said.

Lou looked over at David like he had just seen the sky open up. They gazed at each other in amazement. "Truly awesome," Lou said. Frank grinned at them. Then they hiked back to the cabin.

Frank said they'd probably covered a little more than fifteen miles by the time they returned. Lou and David collapsed onto the old steel bunks, kicked off their boots, and became silent in their weariness while Frank boiled up water for ramen noodles. After filling their bowls, he took a long slow pull from his water bottle and started to reorganize his pack.

"I think you two can handle it from this point on," Frank said and disappeared into the night.

They spent the next three days exploring other trails, reading, and Lou did a lot of writing. David kept track of his thoughts on his legal pad. They went to town Monday afternoon and visited Frank. They treated themselves to dinner at the local café after walking along the beach.

On Wednesday they packed and headed into the city. Frank had given them directions to Rene's place and said Rene had offered to put them up for the night. Lou seemed a little off. He complained about a headache again, so they stopped at a drugstore and bought some aspirin. Lou quickly downed a couple, and after a half hour, the pain subsided.

The poetry reading was going to start at eight.

"Why don't we drive down to the Mission and check it out before the reading? Find out what's going on and maybe meet Rene?" Lou said.

"Sound's good to me. How you feeling anyway?"

"Pretty good. Let's go," Lou answered.

They started back toward the city, and then drove through the old Presidio, where the Army was stationed during the Second World War in anticipation of a Japanese invasion after Pearl Harbor. The streets were quiet and laced with tall eucalyptus and laurel trees. David followed Lou's directions, and they stopped for awhile at Baker Beach, where they walked along the shore and shared a joint. They admired the elegant spans of the of the Golden Gate Bridge. Lou pulled out his notebook and read a poem he had written while they were on Mount

Vision. He had imagined the seventh century Chinese poet, Wang Wei, driving across the famous bridge, stopping in the middle of traffic to admire the view while a flock of pelicans flew across the sky.

Short squat crazy man
Sits atop his red Chevy
Crazed with love,
They honk from every side

While he stops traffic.
Wang Wei does not care
He admires pelicans as
They fly, seven strong

Beneath the bridge, nothing
But wind and sea for six
Thousand miles. They make
His poem strong.

"How did you come up with that?"

"I just did. I've been reading a collection of Chinese poetry. They knew what they were doing."

"You should read that tonight."

"We'll see."

"I've been thinking about CJ and Wiz again. I wish I'd been able to convince them to come up here before they took off. Maybe it would have made a difference. Look at this place, I mean it's just so unbelievable. Maybe . . . ," David trailed off.

"Give it up, David. You just need to let it go. They'll be all right. It makes me sick to think about where they're going and what's going on over there too. But you know there was no changing their minds. CJ and Wiz always saw things different from you and me. Do you think they'd be interested in going with us tonight?"

"No."

"Right, they'd want to be looking at the titty bars on Broadway or trying to pick up stranded flower children at the Wharf."

"It still freaks me out."

"Well, there's a lot to get freaked out about these days. Let's go meet Mr. Lacombe."

Rene Lacombe greeted them at the door. He was well over six feet, an imposing figure with his broad shoulders and long blond hair pulled back into a ponytail, his face red from the sun and edged with lines that amplified his character. Frank had told them Rene's story. Lacombe had written a novel about Gandhi that had become a cult classic. The son of a French diplomat, Rene grew up in New York City and attended several prep schools during the war years, never lasting more than a semester. He advocated a pacifist philosophy with a hedonistic lifestyle, mixed with a strong dose of Eastern mysticism. In early 1947, before it was fashionable to travel to the East, Rene took a freighter to India and somehow was able to gain access to Gandhi for several months, or so the story went. Rene witnessed the revolution while studying in an ashram in northern India, then returned to the States and entered Harvard Divinity School and wrote his thesis on how Gandhi used Christ's teachings to create a revolution. As soon as he received his degree, he disappeared somewhere in Mexico, and spent the two years writing his novel and hanging out with the *beats*.

"Welcome the to Garden of Light. I recognized you both from Frank's description. Thanks for coming. Can I get you something to eat, some coffee or tea?"

"We just ate, but coffee would be great," David said.

"Espresso or regular?"

"Espresso."

"Make it two," Lou added.

"Fine. Then I'll be right back. Find yourself a table."

The Garden of Light Cafe was unlike anything David had ever seen in L.A. Old couches and stuffed chairs lined the walls and corners; bookshelves crammed with weathered paperbacks covered much of the wall space; photographs of writers, actors, poets, and rock stars occupied the remaining walls. It looked like someone's living room, but not anyone David had ever known.

"Two espressos and a couple of fresh chocolate chip cookies I made for tonight. How was your stay on the mountain? Did you get much writing done?" He looked at Lou.

"Yeah, I finished a few poems."

"Frank has an uncanny sense of people. If I believed in such things, I'd call him a seer, but someone might think I'm crazy, and I've got a respectable business to run here," he laughed.

They sat and sipped espresso while Rene busied himself for the night's reading. David wasn't sure what to make of the scene around him. He began ruminating about Koufax as game time approached. The Dodgers were playing the Giants in Los Angeles, but David stared out the window and wondered what it would be like to live in San Francisco and watch Koufax pitch against Mays and McCovey at Candlestick Park. Then his thoughts drifted back to the reading as the crowd slowly filed through the door.

"Look," Lou said, "there they are." He pointed to the three men entering the room. "Ginsberg, Corso, and Gary Snyder." Rene was at the door to hug them and direct them to a table near the mini stage at the back of the café. After providing the poets with refreshments, Rene waltzed over to Lou and whispered, "I want you to read some of your poems. It's part of our tradition here, and the guys wouldn't have it any other way. There are a couple of other local poets reading first, but I'd like to introduce you as our guest from Los Angeles. Maybe you'll be the next Bukowski. He was up here a couple of months ago. It was quite a hit."

"That's fine. Just give me a nod and I'll go up. So maybe three short pieces? "Lou said.

"Perfect." Rene disappeared back into the kitchen.

"I can't believe you're really doing this," David said.

"Why not? What's there to wait for? Don't you think I'm good enough?"

"No, of course not. I mean you're good—at least as far as I know. It's just getting up there and doing it."

"If you write it, you might as well read it," Lou said.

Lou noticed that Ginsberg was glancing over at them. Rene must have told him that Lou was one of the poets who was going to read. David watched Ginsberg zero in on Lou, his eyes riveted on his friend's blond curls and intense eyes. Ginsberg waved for them to join him.

Lou got up and headed over. "Are you coming?"

"No. It's your show. I'll wait here," David said.

David sat alone in search of a lonely woman who might want company for the evening. He watched Lou laughing and gesturing as he was conversing. Ginsberg and the others looked enthused. Lou sat at their table until it was his turn. He read the three new pieces that were clean and etched with a sneering commentary about war, against a backdrop of the white deer that roamed in the mountains across the bay.

After the reading they stayed and talked with the poets until after midnight. Rene provided them a small room behind the café he had designed for special guests. In the morning David and Lou had more espresso with granola and bananas and fresh-baked muffins.

"You were magnificent last night, a triumph!" Rene said. My God, you really had their attention, and the connection to the deer in Point Reyes was masterful. Keep writing and come back whenever you want. Don't hesitate to send me your work, I'll show it to Ferlinghetti, and who knows?"

"Well, thanks Rene, that is really generous of you. I think I will take you up on your offer. David, are you about ready?"

"Yeah, I'm ready." Setting down the sports section of the *Chronicle*, David got up and shook Rene's hand. He didn't say a word to Lou about Koufax beating the Giants. He knew Lou wouldn't be interested. They got into the car and headed south. As they passed San Jose, Lou started to complain about his headaches again. David pointed to the aspirin in the glove box, and Lou took two as the sun angled upward.

CHAPTER SIXTEEN

Sunday, June 20, 1965

It's Father's Day at Dodger Stadium, and Koufax has just mowed down the Mets in the ninth. The 52,000 fans, many of them fathers, have been treated to a one-hitter. Today the Time's banner had a headline about it being "Bachelor's Day," not "Father's Day," to honor Koufax's status as Mr. Eligible in the baseball world. He may not be a father, but he had plenty to celebrate today. The only hit was a home run in the fifth by first baseman Jim Hickman. To make it more delicious, he outpitched another legendary lefty, Warren Spahn. Koufax's record is now eleven wins against three losses. He leads the league with 147 strikeouts in only 128 innings, and by striking out twelve Mets, he now has sixty-eight double-digit performances in his career. As usual, the ever enigmatic Koufax didn't leave much of a contrail for personal publicity today. His private life is more a Rorschach, an opportunity for writers and fans to project their own dreams onto his celebrity. But today's game was a great performance to add to his body of work.

Don't forget, we've got another game today. Don Drysdale will try for his twelfth win of the season in the nightcap.

Lou's headache dissipated by the time they were in Los Robles. He slept for the next hundred miles and David glanced at him from time to time. He looked peaceful and uncomplicated. No torment, no animus, the perplexing pall that sometimes engulfed him was replaced by an angelic glow that felt safe and approachable. Whatever it was that percolated inside Lou's consciousness, it fascinated David. He envied his disdain for the conventional and the frivolous. Their friendship was at times mercurial and often made David feel conflicted and confused. But for the moment, everything seemed to be all right.

David started thinking about Ginger as they crept closer to San Luis Obispo.

"Good nap?" David asked.

"I think so." Lou squeezed his spine up along the red upholstered seat, cleared the scratch out of his slumbered throat, opened the window, and took a blast of the warm, fecund costal air.

"The headache's gone for now, but that was a rough one. They seem to be getting worse and a little more frequent."

"Maybe it's this batch of pot. My head has been pretty groggy in the morning."

"Could be. So did you really think I held my own last night?"

"Fuck yeah, big Lou. You kicked some literary ass, like a regular Ezra Pound."

"Pound was a fascist and a madman. Don't compare me to him."

"Sorry, I just thought."

"You didn't think, Mandel, you just pulled a name out of your American Literature textbook."

"That's not true, I didn't say Wallace Stevens or Hart Crane," David said.

"You could have said Baudelaire or Rimbaud."

"I could have said any number of names, but instead I said Pound. You are right, Pound is kind of an asshole. I stand corrected. But you're like a prickly bitch sometimes." David turned up the radio, now playing a medley of the best of Motown; "My Girl" by the Miracles, "The Way You Do the Things You Do" by the Temptations, and "Stop in the Name of Love" by the Supremes. The music seemed to calm Lou down,

"Sorry, David, you're a good friend. I guess I'm still feeling out of sorts."

David was amazed and relieved, because with Lou, it could have exploded in a split second. Maybe something shifted, the reading might have been a turning point for him. All these new characters in his life must be exciting. Perhaps Lou's dreams of being a writer would come to fruition.

As they approached San Luis Obispo, David started thinking about Ginger again.

"So I was thinking of making a little detour in San Luis Obispo," David said.

"That's cool, just leave me off and I'll hitch home."

"It's fine. I'll go back another time." The petulant bastard had returned.

There was silence for the next sixty miles except for the Motown medley that kept on playing. David stopped for gas in the cutesy town of Solvang north of Santa Barbara. After filling up, he drove down the street to a Danish bakery.

"I'm getting some coffee," David said. "You want anything?"

"Yes. sounds good." Lou followed him inside.

They sat down at the counter and ordered coffee and pastry.

"Listen, David, I have been thinking. We have to find a place to rent pretty soon. I saw something in the papers last week. With everything else going on, I forgot to follow up on it."

"Where is it?"

"Santa Monica, just across from the beach. From the ad, it sounded perfect. I called the landlady and she said to come by anytime. Just call first."

Driving back to the Valley, the amiable Lou was back again. They decided to check out the apartment the next day. David dropped Lou off around 7:00 p.m. and headed straight home.

Thursday morning Lou called just after nine o'clock.

"The landlady said she'd be around all day and to come by."

The boys didn't waste any time. David picked Lou up at ten, and they were touring the apartment by eleven. It wasn't big, but they agreed it was doable. The best part was its proximity to the beach. Friday they returned to make sure they wanted it. The landlady said she'd take a fifty-dollar deposit and hold it for a few days until they had the full amount for July's rent. They signed a month-to-month lease and celebrated by taking a run on the beach. Afterward they dove into the waves and swam as far out as they could. Things were looking up.

Sunday was Father's Day and the Dodgers had a doubleheader against the Mets. David perused the morning paper. The press was making a big deal about the two Dodgers dominators pitching back to back. Game one was Koufax. Game two was Drysdale. It wasn't often that the Dodger stars pitched together in a doubleheader, and to top off the festivities, Koufax was pitching against the incomparable forty-four-year-old, Warren Spahn.

He put down the paper and went outside. He had promised his father he'd mow and edge the lawn one more time. Everything was finished by eight thirty. He had raked and swept all the clippings and turned on the sprinklers before going inside to shower. He and Alex decided they'd make their father's favorite breakfast: lox, onions, and eggs with fried potatoes and a bagel. The sizzle of the onion wafted into the living room, and soon their father joined them in the kitchen. A smile beamed across his face.

"Happy Father's Day!" Alex rushed up against his chest and swept her arms around him.

"Hey, how did I get so lucky?" Jacob Mandel laughed.

"Just good genes, I hope," David said as he flipped the omelet in the cast-iron frying pan.

After breakfast David looked around his room, taking an inventory of what he wanted to bring to the apartment. He scanned the posters: Jon Arnett, halfback on the proverbial losing L.A. Rams; Koufax; Jackie Robinson; the Lettermen; and a recent blow-up of Joan Baez. Her new album *Joan Baez/5* had become one of his favorites. He decided on Joan. He'd leave the rest.

While David was organizing the books he'd take, Alex traipsed into the room.

"Hey, by the way, this came for you yesterday. I told Mom I'd give it to you, but you didn't get back until late. Anyway, here."

It was a letter from CJ. It hadn't been quite two weeks since he enlisted. David opened it quickly while Alex stood in the doorway watching him, her right foot tucked up against her left knee forming a perfect triangle, her back arched. She slowly licked the remains of the fried potatoes from around her lips.

Dear David,

Just a quick note. We don't have much free time. We're shaved and uniformed, no guns yet. Wiz and I are in the same unit, that's a plus. Most of the NCOs are southerners and don't like anyone from California, they call us "pussies." Well they call everyone "pussies," so I guess I shouldn't take it too personally. Right now it's pretty awful, but that's basic training. I can see that they're trying to just break us down enough so we won't resist all the Army bullshit. Nothing I can't handle. I just want to get on with it and get over to Vietnam.

Having Wiz here keeps me sane. Sometimes we just look at each other when the corporals start one of their tirades about our beds not being made correctly or our shoes not being shined so we can see our face on the tips.

I wanted to thank you for driving us down to the enlistment center. You're a solid friend and I'll miss hanging out with you. When I get back I'll teach you how to really shoot. Give Veronica a call every once in a while and let her know that everything is going to be fine. Got to go. Lights out.

> *CJ*

David stuck the letter in the top drawer of his bureau under a layer of black and navy socks and turned back toward Alex.

"Everything is all right so far. He's just making contact."

"That's good," Alex said.

"You're worried, aren't you?"

"Of course, I'm a worrier just like you. I guess it's a family trait, at least on Mom's side. While you were gone I heard Mom talking to

Wiz's mother, trying to calm her down. She's really upset. All the news keeps getting darker and darker. Do you need any help packing?"

"Not really. There isn't very much."

"I'm so sick of this war. They made a big deal on the TV morning news about having shot down three Red MiGs. They were either North Vietnamese or Chinese. It's all so disgusting. And it's just getting started, isn't it? It's not going to stop anytime soon, I know it."

"For once you might be right. It doesn't look good."

"Thanks a lot, David. Promise you won't abandon me here in this trap. You'll come visit and get me out of here sometimes, won't you?"

"I will. I'll bring you to all the violent antiwar rallies where women burn their bras and guys incinerate their draft cards. I promise."

"You better."

The day turned hot. By noon it was languid and stifling. Bees and wasps buzzed around the yard, lapping up the nectar from their father's plum and apricot trees. After lunch, David shuttled Alex over to Sav-on drugstore for an ice cream cone.

Driving home David thought about CJ's and Wiz's fathers. He wondered what they were thinking right now, while he was licking frozen treats and sweating incessantly in the afternoon froth above the asphalt landscape.

Suddenly he pulled into a driveway and turned around. He pointed the car straight east, toward the Angeles National Forest.

"Where we going?" Alex asked as she slowly sculpted the edges of her ice cream into a cylindrical mound.

"Up."

"Well great, but don't you think you should ask me first. You know, I might have other things to do besides drive all over the Valley. Besides, it's Father's Day. Don't you want to hang out with Dad?"

"Want me to take you home?"

"I didn't say I wanted to go home. I just said I'd like to be consulted."

"You are consulted. We're going up into the hills above Hansen Dam, up past the old Polo Club where you used to ride horses with your friend, what's her name, Lisa Marie."

"Fine. Drive me wherever you want. Kidnap me, hold me for ransom if you want."

"Lexie, we're going to the top of the mountain to cool off for a little while."

They passed the trailhead where he, Rita, and Lou had hiked the last day of school. He remembered the way she had kissed him and how heated he felt. He realized, on some level, he wasn't close to being finished with Rita.

He parked at the top of the mountain. He and Alex walked out to the edge of the bluff where the afternoon smog lit upon the Valley like a thin piece of toast, making a pollution sandwich for the dismal residents. Above them the sky peaked silver blue, enough so it felt a bit cathartic. David spread out the plaid blanket from the back of the car and shook out the memories over the lupine and California poppies. Alex flopped down and pulled out a pair of oversized sunglasses from her little purse, making her look like a mini version of Audrey Hepburn. David sat down beside her and stared up and away from the sun.

"Look, David, I think that's an eagle."

"Maybe," David said. "It's pretty huge."

An enormous bird glided away from the sun, and as it did, David noticed it didn't have the crested noble head of an eagle; instead, it flashed a hint of red. Its wing span looked to be over six feet, larger than the common turkey vultures that cruised the thermals in these mountains.

"Could it be a condor?" Alex mused. "I heard there's just a few pairs left, but no one has ever spotted one around here."

"You're right. I don't know what else it might be."

"Oh, David, this is so cool. No one will believe us."

"Who cares? Look at the damn thing soar."

"We studied them in school last year. They're like loons and swans; they mate for life. Can you believe it? And they share the nest responsibilities, they take turns scavenging. When one returns, the other goes back out to conserve energy."

"You learn all that stuff in school?"

"Yeah, and the most extraordinary thing is that they blush when they get upset or excited. Their whole head turns almost purple. Isn't that amazing?"

David nodded. Then the condor was gone as quickly as it had appeared. Alex and David stayed for another hour, hoping it might return. It didn't.

On the way home David turned on the game as they crossed Foothill Blvd., heading west toward San Fernando Road. Koufax had just finished the fifth inning against the Mets. The Dodgers trailed one to zero in the top of the sixth. Jim Hickman had the only hit against Koufax, a home run into the left-field stands.

"Are you hungry?" David asked.

"Sort of, what do you have in mind?"

"I was thinking tacos at the stand on Van Nuys."

The Dodgers first baseman, Wes Parker, walked as David pulled into Sophie's Taqueria, and before he could open the car door, Ron Fairly doubled down the right-field line and scored Parker and Gilliam. That made it two to one going into the bottom of the sixth.

"What do you think is going to happen?" Alex said.

"I think Koufax will win like he usually does."

"No. What is going happen to you?"

"After college, I'm going join the Merchant Marine, sail the world and eventually settle down somewhere in the Pacific Northwest, where I'll live alone just at the edge of the city in a forested little community near a trout stream. How is that for an answer?"

"Ridiculous, I'm sorry I asked."

"Good, that was the idea."

"I'm going to miss you."

"I haven't left yet. I told you I'd invite you over as much as my landlady will allow."

"Right, like you are going to ask your landlady. What a crock!"

By the time they got home, their father had retired to the back patio, sipping iced tea and nibbling on a piece of mandel bread his mother had made for Father's Day. Alex disappeared into her room. Rose was preparing dinner. David sat down next to his father and smiled. "Happy Father's Day," he said.

CHAPTER SEVENTEEN

Friday, June 25, 1965

Well, Koufax did it again. Tonight at Dodger Stadium, Koufax beat the Pirates four to one, striking out twelve and bringing his record to twelve-three. In the fourth inning, Koufax singled home his batterymate John Roseboro to take the lead. That was all he needed. The Pirates managed only six hits and never really threatened after the fourth inning when the Dodgers took the lead. From the way he pitched this evening, it doesn't appear like he will ever lose another ball game. It was a nine-inning gem. During his post-game interview, Koufax criticized himself, complaining about missing a few spots here and there while grousing about the one run he gave up in the second inning on a couple of singles to Don Clendenon and Bill Mazeroski. The man seeks perfection every time he takes the mound.

Summer is here, and we've got a lot more baseball to play. Thanks for tuning in and that's it for tonight.

Lou called Monday morning.

"Hey, sorry to bother you, but I can't go with you to the apartment. Those headaches have come back. I'm going to the doctor this morning to see what's going on."

"Oh man, I'm sorry," David said. "I'm sure it's nothing, but it's good you are going to get it checked out. Don't worry, I'll take care of the apartment. I've got enough for the rent."

Lou thanked him and hung up. David was worried, but felt it would all work out. Nothing could happen to Lou, not now. After a few minutes, he called Bryce and asked him if he wanted to go and see the apartment and then spend the day at the beach. Bryce agreed.

David hadn't heard anymore from Wiz or CJ, except Wiz's mother called Rose again and reported that Wiz had called her a few days earlier and wanted her to send some "real food." He had complained about the bland cafeteria junk the Army was putting out every day. Otherwise, there wasn't any news.

David picked up Bryce and they drove to Santa Monica. Bryce still hadn't decided whether he was going to live in the dorms or join a fraternity. His coach wanted him to stay clear of the fraternity scene, but Bryce liked the instant perks fraternities offered; friends, women, and shortcuts through school. It would have been great if he, Bryce, and Lou could have lived together, but with all the training, practices, and games, it didn't make sense to live so far from campus.

They arrived at the apartment. Bryce got out of the car first and stretched his long muscular arms back over his head, yawning as he pushed forward and took in a deep breath.

"Smell the surf, man, this will be great for you two, being so close to the ocean. What is it, two blocks?"

"Short blocks. Definitely close enough to walk. Yeah it will be fantastic, a dream really," David said.

"So which place is it?" Bryce said.

"Right over there on the left, the little bungalow, number 2A."

The complex consisted of three tiny duplexes with a small brick-lined courtyard in the middle and hibiscus bushes on either side of the doors. Bryce walked right up to the window and peeked inside.

"Cozy. You sure there's enough room for both of you? I mean the way you two get along?"

"You can't see the bedroom. It's decent sized, enough space for a couple of beds and dressers, and it has a large walk-in closet. It's plenty big. You'll see. I'll get the key and you can check it out."

The manager of the place lived in 3B, Grace Yamamoto, an obese woman who looked to be somewhere in her twenties. She smoked long dark cigarettes and had stringy dark hair with just a fringe of bleached blond. The two times David had met Grace, she was never dressed in anything but a frayed pink-and-purple-flowered tent dress. This morning it was no different. She opened the door with a nervous laugh as she puffed away on her cigarette and welcomed David like he was her long-lost brother.

"It's good to see you. Is everything all right? You and Lou are still planning to move in, right? I've had so many inquiries, I hope you're not backing out."

"No, Grace, everything is cool, I just wanted to show my friend Bryce the place. I wondered if I could get the keys now so we don't have to bother you again on the first. I can give you the rent today."

"Oh, darling, that would be fine. Yes, of course." Grace turned her head and hacked for a few seconds, then took another drag. "Let me get you both sets of keys."

David took the rent check out of his wallet and traded Grace for the keys. She invited them inside and, as she did, her kimono opened to bare her cleavage. When Lou and David signed the lease she had pulled the same routine, as well as sporting a little leg as they sat at her Formica kitchen table, her robe open top and bottom. Her entire apartment reeked of nicotine. David peeked inside while Grace grabbed the keys. There were several paintings of beautiful pastoral scenes of wild birds and Japanese gardens and two statues of the Buddha. She returned with the keys and asked if they wanted a cup of tea and some cookies.

"Maybe another time," David said.

David walked Bryce through the apartment. It was musty but had enough windows to light up the place. David cracked open a couple of them to let in some fresh air.

"Plenty of room. You're right," Bryce said.

"Yeah, it will be great. I've got furniture lined up and so does Lou. We'll have you over as soon as we move in."

David locked up and they drove off to Sorrento Beach, just south of Santa Monica. David gave the attendant a dollar for the day and popped the trunk. Chairs, blankets, cooler, Frisbee, football, surf riders, and radio. California dreaming was about to start. It was a perfect Pacific day: cloudless and serene with mixed smells of fresh-washed sand, grilled burgers, fries, and hot dogs, all sweetened by the syrupy fragrance of Coppertone sun screen and Hershey's cocoa butter. The beach was flat and clear of trash, the volleyball games had already begun. The surf was up, but the water was smooth between the rollers.

Bryce and David picked a spot of equal distance between the grill, the girls' volleyball game, and the surf; it didn't get any better. David was feeling smug, blessed, and liberated. They spread the blanket, unfolded the chairs, stripped to their swimsuits, and hunkered down for the day. He turned on his black transistor radio with its new batteries and extended the antenna for maximum reception to 1110 KRLA, where he knew he'd find Dick Hull, The Hullabalooer.

The sun's rays delicately started to crisp his skin. The dull swat of the volleyballs thumped as they bounded and floated over the nets. Bikini-clad coeds with beads of sweat trailing down their bodies ran and jumped like goddesses, racing through the sand. David couldn't quite believe it. It was an impeccable day, almost too good to be true.

"Yo, Bryce. We did it. Can you believe this?" David said, stretching his arms out.

"Yeah, I'm going out to the water as soon as I inflate this surf rider."

Their heavy-duty neoprene boards allowed them to zoom across the waves. They rushed out to the water, splashed through the surf and were catching breakers within minutes.

David remembered the last time he had been here with Rita. It was late August last year, and it was just the two of them. The day had been a scorcher and they spent most of it in the water, riding wave after wave in abandon, stopping only to kiss, eat, and listen to a few tunes. Time had evaporated like the water on her flesh. David missed her and felt a longing like a cold undertow while he navigated through the wild water, imagining her lying with someone else, uttering the same refrains of adoration that until recently were only for him. His distraction caused him to miss an enormous wave that crushed him down into the brine. He gulped a mouthful of water and felt the sting of the salt pulse through his sinuses. When he came up, Bryce was beside him, guffawing as he spit out the sea.

"You took it straight on. What happened?"

"Thinking of Rita and didn't pay attention. Love's revenge, I suppose."

"Well, keep it up and you'll drown. Watch out, here comes another biggy."

They paddled out just in time to catch another swell as it crested and lifted them clear off the water, then pushed them home to shore.

"Nothing like it. You still thinking about her?"

"It's hard not to on such a gorgeous day."

"I heard she's hanging out with someone."

"Who?"

"I don't know. I just heard it from Lydia, but she didn't say who it was."

David was silent. They paddled out and caught half a dozen more rides. Then they headed for their blanket. The thought of Rita being with someone else soaked his brain.

Bryce slapped David on the shoulder, seeing him wobble as they walked back through the sand. David flicked the radio on to KRLA, "Huggy Boy" was spinning the Beach Boys' "Fun, Fun, Fun." David turned over and caked his chest and legs with cocoa butter.

The sound of the waves plunged against the sand. His eyes shut, the sound rocked him back and forth between thoughts of Rita and the immediate bliss of the day. The radio blasted "Walk On By," by Dionne Warwick, followed by the Rolling Stones' "Time Is on My Side." He was losing himself in the music when he felt the plunk of a volleyball on his chest. He opened his eyes and saw a pair of muscular female legs above him. She wore a crimson bikini. Her beauty immediately stunned him.

"Sorry," she said while she reached down and retrieved the volleyball. She laughed as she stretched her perfectly bronzed arms down to the sand. Then she pranced back to the game, displaying an equally perfect backside.

"Eight serving nine," David heard her bark as she tossed and then cranked a wicked serve across the net.

"Nine serving nine," another ace serve splashed just within the back rope line for a point.

The next serve resulted in a desperate return and the girl in the crimson bikini surged to the net, leaped and rammed the ball down so hard it ricocheted off the shoulder of the girl trying to defend and zoomed directly back at David again. He caught the ball just as she ran over.

"Sorry. We'll try to keep it in play."

"I hope so, you're ruining my perfect day at the beach."

"You don't look like you're suffering too much."

"You'll never know," David laughed and tossed the ball up toward her.

She winked at him and scampered back to play. David wished he had a quicker comeback. Everything about her twinkled. She looked like a cover girl, full of bounce and verve, with a disarming smile that melted him.

"I guess it's your lucky day," Bryce said.

"You think so?"

"Yeah man, what do you think that wink was about?"

"I doubt it. That doesn't happen to me."

"Hey, that's the medicine you need to pull yourself past Rita. Look at her abs!"

At fourteen serving twelve, the ball miraculously sailed into his hands again. She came bounding up with a big grin, but before she could say anything, David said, "Sorry, but this will cost you two things."

"Oh really?"

"Your name and you join us for a Coke."

"Melanie and I prefer lemonade."

"You got it."

After the game, the two girls sauntered over, towels draped around their necks, dabbing rivulets of perspiration from their faces and torsos. They introduced themselves. Melanie Saltzman and her teammate Angie Smith had just graduated Beverly Hills High School and were both recruited by USC to play freshman volleyball. Melanie stood right at six feet, and her friend, the setter, was a couple inches shorter, but equally gorgeous with firebird-red hair and sky-blue eyes.

"Where are those lemonades?"

"Coming right up. Bryce, please entertain the ladies."

"My pleasure."

David was back in a flash with fries and four lemonades stuffed with ice and fresh lemons. Bryce kept the girls laughing and engaged. David snuggled down in the sand beside Melanie and offered the drinks to her and Angie.

"Thanks, David. I like a man who keeps his word."

"Well that's good, because if there is one thing about me you can count on, it's trusting my word."

Melanie's aquamarine eyes held him captive the rest of the day. The conversation flowed easily. Bryce and Angie went back in the water long enough for David to secure a date that Friday. Nothing like good old-fashioned luck. Melanie had just broken up with her boyfriend a couple of weeks earlier, and she was looking for the same kind of escape as David. He couldn't believe she'd go out with him, but she didn't even hesitate.

Friday night David picked up Melanie at her home on Roxbury Drive in Beverly Hills. When he walked through the door he figured he would just grab her and go. It was a small house by Beverly Hills standards, but thick with the smell of money and appointed with enough marble and gold to let David know he'd entered another world. Marilyn Saltzman was tall and good looking, handsome more than beautiful, with short auburn hair, an elongated neck, and vitreous silky skin that hadn't seen the sun in a long time. Her lips were painted a deep vermillion, and she had diamonds on three of her fingers, around her neck, and on her ankle.

"Mother, this is David Mandel, the boy I told you about a few days ago."

"Such a pleasure. Dear me, I do see why you would be interested. David, what are your plans; not tonight, I mean for the future?"

"Mother, I told you."

"No, it's fine Melanie," David said. "I start UCLA this fall and I'm not sure after that. I think I might major in English, but I want to keep my options open."

David didn't have a clue beyond that. He regarded the interrogation as a necessary step to get out the door with Melanie. Marilyn's pretense and phony eastern or British accent just came with the territory. David and Melanie started for the door.

"Don't be too late, darling, you know how I worry."

"Before midnight, Mother, and if not, I'll call. Good night."

"Oh David, one more thing. You aren't one of those war protestors are you?"

"Mother!"

David wasn't sure how to respond. He hesitated. War protestor? Not yet. Against the goddamn stupid war? Yes. Worried about his friends? Hell yes.

"No. But, I've got one friend over there already, and two more on the way, so it's personal and it's troubling."

"Yes, it certainly is," Marilyn said.

Melanie took David's hand and practically pulled him out the door.

"Sorry about that," Melanie said while she slid into the front seat. She wore white pants with black flats and a salmon-colored silk blouse that dipped low enough to entice his interest. Around her neck she had a very delicate single pearl with a grayish hue to it and a pair of earrings to match. "Mother is just like that."

"Not a problem. Moms are just moms," David said.

"I didn't know you had friends over there already."

"I tried to get the two of them to change their minds, the other guy didn't even tell anyone. He just joined one day back in March and that's been pretty much all anyone has heard about him."

"I thought you had to at least finish high school," Melanie said.

"Or be over eighteen. My friend Rick was held back in fourth grade and was nineteen when he joined. It makes me sick."

"I'm so sorry. What's the plan for dinner?"

"Bryce told me about a place on Santa Monica, Vic's. Is Italian okay?"

"Love it. I've been there a couple times and it's always great. Romantic too. If that's what you had in mind."

"Why not? You look beautiful, by the way."

Everything went well, better than David could have imagined. A perfect quiet dinner and a chance to delve into Melanie's life. Her parents had divorced when she was thirteen. She said it was a vile, acrimonious event that left everyone bloodied, blind, and bitter. Her older sister Janet extricated herself within the first six months, demanding to be moved to a boarding school in Santa Barbara, where she immediately gained twenty-five pounds and started a serious relationship with marijuana. Janet had come home one weekend a month to help shepherd Melanie through the emotional minefield of the divorce.

Her father, Benjamin, was president and CEO of Beverly Hills National Trust. According to Melanie, he was a three-piece-suit, pin-stripe, no-nonsense, bottom-line, only-the-facts type of guy who strayed from the straight and narrow only when it came to tawdry affairs of the night. The divorce was precipitated by one of his affairs. One night Janet caught her father at his office apartment with his secretary, in a seriously compromising position. Benjamin tried to bribe her out of disclosing the affair, but to no avail.

After dinner David parked down the street from Melanie's house. They kissed between sweeps of the Beverly Hills cops. After their first pass one of the patrols actually stopped and asked David to roll down his window. Melanie laughed and called out the window, "Jeff, everything is fine. This is my friend David. We're just talking about the Dodgers. How'd they do tonight?"

"Hi Melanie, sorry, I didn't see you and didn't recognize this car. Oh, by the way, they won."

"Jeff, let the guys know this car will be around here for awhile, will you? No need to hassle a couple of aspiring college students."

"No problem. How's your Mother?"

"Very well, thank you. I'll tell her you inquired."

"Nice meeting you, officer," David said. Jeff pulled away in his sleek patrol car. "Do you know all the police in Beverly Hills?" he asked.

"Only the important ones. You get used to it growing up here. They're like innocent uncles, just doing what they were hired to do, protect the rich and famous and their progeny."

"Do you like the Dodgers?"

"More than the Angels." She laughed and they kissed again. Her kisses were deep and loose, filled with promise and generosity he hoped would soon bloom into summer fruit.

David felt dreamy as he pulled away from Melanie's house and headed west on Wilshire toward the San Diego Freeway. There were faster ways back home, but he wanted to drive through the empty streets of L.A.'s finest fashion-laden windows. He tried to imagine what it must be like to live in such a place, where money was so disposable. All the mannequins looked like variations of Marilyn Saltzman—lean, stiff, vacant, and impenetrable. David passed the dark granite walls of Beverly Hills National Trust and noticed the lights on the third floor.

Driving home, he wondered where Rita was at the moment. In the strong arms of a new love? Home watching old movies with her mother? Maybe she was at a party in East L.A.

He tried to imagine what CJ and Wiz were doing. The war was going badly. Johnson was trying to get some intervention from the U.N., but everyone knew where things were headed, and it wasn't good.

David wheeled onto the San Diego Freeway at Wilshire and automatically dialed in one of the late-night sports shows. Koufax had won another game. David felt a sense of comfort, knowing all was well in that part of his world. And then there was Melanie.

CHAPTER EIGHTEEN

Tuesday, June 29, 1965

Koufax breezed through the Giants nine to three today at Candlestick Park, where the Pacific winds always blow. It was another complete game. He struck out ten Giants. It is only June 29 and Maury Wills stole his forty-sixth base. Wills is on track to steal a hundred bases, and Koufax looked like he wouldn't ever lose again. His record bumps up to thirteen wins against only three losses. It seems like there isn't much you can count on in this fickle world except Koufax winning baseball games.

Both John Roseboro and Jim Gilliam went deep. Roseboro finished with five RBIs for the day. The usually anemic-hitting Dodgers looked more like Giants than the Giants tonight, slamming eleven hits.

And we haven't see the last of the wind, because we're off to Chicago next.

David's mother knocked loudly on his bedroom door. He turned over on his pillow—sleep sweet sleep, but he knew he had to get up. It was Tuesday and he had promised his father he'd go to work to help stock a new order that had arrived the previous day. David's cash was running low. Melanie had more expensive tastes than Rita.

"David, get up. I need to talk with you right away."

"Just let me get dressed."

"Right away, David, it's important."

David dragged himself down the hallway to the kitchen, where his mother sat slumped in the chair next to the phone. Her eyes looked blank and vacuous. She was fiddling with a pencil, tapping it up and down, and biting her lower lip.

"David, I just got a call from Molly Ash. Lou is in the hospital at Kaiser Permanente. He collapsed last night. He lost his balance and fell. When he tried to get up, he said he couldn't walk. They rushed him to the hospital, did some X-rays, and found a tumor in his brain. This morning they did a biopsy, and now they're waiting for the results."

"What? Wait! Is he going to be okay? This can't be!"

"They don't know anything more than what I told you. I'm sorry."

"Can I see him?"

"Probably not today, he's still recovering from the biopsy and they want to run a few more tests. Molly said he'll probably be able to see visitors tomorrow."

"I just talked to him yesterday. He sounded fine. We were planning on moving in Friday. This is ridiculous, impossible. No!"

David walked out the side door past the washer and drier and slammed the door behind him.

"David!" Rose hated the sound of doors slamming. David didn't care. He walked out into the yard and started pacing around. His father's roses were glorious, but their beauty was incongruous to the news he had just received. He wanted to drive over to the hospital and drag Lou out of the room, shake him into the person he was just yesterday. This could not really be happening. What about their plans? He'd recover. They'd remove this tumor and he'd be back in a week or two.

The grass was still damp from the sprinklers. It smelled fresh and fragrant. He remembered playing catch with Lou before their games. He could feel the sting of Lou's fastball on his palm and see the glint of his smile, knowing that he had caught the pitch in the thin center of his glove, where all that protected his hand were a couple of layers of cow flesh. It was enough to absorb the initial shock, enough to keep the bruise to a minimum, but not nearly enough to mollify the pain. He'd take that physical pain compared to what he now felt.

He heard his mother call from the kitchen but didn't answer right away. After a few seconds, he called back that he was fine. He just needed to be alone for awhile.

"Okay. I'll let you know if I hear anything else. Lou's father is there at the hospital with Molly," his mother shouted back.

"Great."

Chester, Lou's father, wouldn't do Lou any good. Maybe he'd be okay for Molly, but Lou couldn't relate to his father. Lou had told David that he realized early in his life that his father had limitations when it came to being a dad. Chester worked for an advertising firm that specialized in food and fine-restaurants, and he was their top salesman. While Lou played his heart out in Little League, Chester was usually at home smoking Paul Malls and watching golf while sipping gin and tonics.

David decided to go to work, but he called first and let his father know what was happening and that he'd be late. He wanted to drive by the hospital before he went to work. Kaiser Permanente Hospital was a multi-storied monstrosity that loomed over the flat valley landscape. After circling around Roscoe Blvd. a few times and imagining Lou lying alone in a cubicle with a white turban wrapped around his head, he parked in the lot. He felt helpless and alone. He looked up at the bank of faceless square windows and wished he could erase the truth of what was happening. *Full count and I've got no idea what to throw.* David sat there for a couple minutes, then started the car and drove toward the Golden State Freeway. He felt nauseous, frightened, and disconnected.

There was a lot of stock to put away, so David made arrangements with his father to work late and finish up so he didn't have to come back the next day. He also wanted to miss the traffic, but more than that, he wanted to see Melanie. He had called her at lunch and told her about Lou.

By seven o'clock, he was ready to leave. There was a small shower stall in the back of the store. David cleaned up and then called Bryce to see if he had heard anything. Lou was stable for now, but the pathologist's report still had not come back. There probably wouldn't be any more news until the morning. David jumped on the Santa

Monica Freeway and headed west. Fortunately, the traffic had dissipated, and he knocked on Melanie's door while there was still a bit of daylight.

She looked beautiful and sexy, wearing a pair of white shorts and a green silk blouse. Before he could say anything, she wrapped her strong arms around him and squeezed him close to her bosom. "You can relax, we're alone. Mom's out with some friends."

For the first time since he had heard the news about Lou, he allowed himself to feel vulnerable to the point of tears, but he held back and simply enjoyed the warmth that Melanie offered.

"I'm so sorry about your friend," she said. "Is there anything I can do?"

"Just seeing you helps for right now."

She kissed him gently on the lips.

"Let's get you something to eat," she said. "I know just the place."

Melanie directed him to Cantor's Deli on Fairfax. As they cruised down Wilshire Blvd., David told her he was scared that Lou would die. She tried to reassure him and put her hand on his thigh.

"David, it's terrible. You sure you want to go out tonight?"

"What else can I do? I'd rather be with you than anyone else right now."

"Okay, but just tell me if you want to bail at any point."

David found a parking space without too much trouble, and the line for a table was short. A chunky, cheery waitress showed them to a tight booth and left a couple of foot-long menus. David ordered chicken soup and they decided to split a corned beef sandwich. It felt good to share food with Melanie. Her appetite matched his bite for bite, and he knew as he looked at her bronzed face, high cheekbones, and blue eyes that their other appetites would be similar as well. For a few precious moments, as he slurped down the last of the soup, he forgot about Lou and felt soothed.

"What now?" Melanie blinked and wiped a trace of mustard from her lips.

"How about a movie? I heard *A Thousand Clowns* is playing in Westwood. It's supposed to be great."

"Is that what you really want to do?"

"What I really want to do is find a secluded place to be with you," David said.

"Then let's do that. What about the beach?"

David took Santa Monica Blvd. to Pacific Coast Highway and turned north till he found a stretch of dark beach and parked beside the seawall. The stars beat back against the moonless sky, the darkness accentuated the fluorescence of the red tide as the waves crashed in front of them.

David took a blanket from the car, and they walked down to the beach. He started thinking about Lou lying in the hospital room, alone and afraid. How could anything like this happen? Lou had more strength and passion than anyone David knew. He was primed and loaded for the future, hopefully this tumor would just be a blip on his screen. David found himself shaking off images of death and trying to spill his negativity into the tide, hoping to drown it in the "algal bloom," as Melanie called it.

David put his arm around her shoulder and felt the softness of her blouse dissolve into his skin. She leaned against him as they drifted along. He stopped a few times to kiss her. She responded with openness and desire, so that each time he pressed his lips to hers, it released a bit of the gloom he felt.

Finally, they couldn't take another step, and they lay down on the blanket. No lights in sight. They were alone. Sweetness surrounded them inside and out. Melanie took off her blouse and folded it on the blanket. Then she unhooked her bra and let her breasts loose in the warm night air. The magic of the evening unleashed itself. The stinking world of Southern California, Lou's tumor, the bloody, stupid war that swept away CJ, Wiz, and Ricky disappeared. In front of him, the red tide illuminated excitement with every wave that pounded into the forgiving and undemanding sand. Now with

Melanie's bare chest against his, and knowing that it would be only a matter of minutes before they plunged into lovemaking, his somber mood lifted. Melanie was ravishing, but more, she willingly embraced his dread and uncertainty like an angel steeped in wisdom.

They floated back to the car, sated and enveloped in the rapture of their budding romance. It was close to eleven, and David figured they ought to start back. The freeway was empty and they were back in Beverly Hills in less than thirty minutes. They were listening to KRLA and singing along with Roy Orbison and the Rolling Stones.

"How about some coffee before you drop me home?"

"Sounds great."

"I know a place on Rodeo Drive that's open all night. They have great pies, I think we earned it."

All the radio news was off by the time David started home, so he didn't find out about the game until the next morning when he opened the paper. Koufax had won again. He didn't spend much time reading details. He wanted to get to the hospital and see Lou. As far as David knew, the pathology report still had not come back.

Molly and Chester were sitting in the room with Lou when David arrived. Fortunately, the second bed was empty so the space was large enough for all of them to sit. There was a vase with lilies, carnations, and sunflowers on the shelf next to the window. Lou had a thin smile on his lips. His head was crystal-white, the rest of him still looked ripe with life. The television was blasting news about Vietnam. Lou turned it down as David walked closer to the bed.

"Moving day?" he asked before David could get a word out.

"Tomorrow. How you doing?"

"I feel like shit."

"Thanks so much for coming," Molly said. "If you don't mind, Chester and I need to grab some breakfast and I think Lou wants to talk with you alone."

Lou didn't acknowledge what his mother had said. He just stared straight at David with his fiery eyes and waited until he heard his parents' footsteps leave the room.

"I can't believe this, I'm really sorry," David said.

"Yeah, well here's the deal. The pathologist's report just came back this morning and it's cancer. Big time cancer. I've got what's called an anaplastic astrocytoma tumor. It's a nasty, horrible cancer. They're going to operate Friday morning, some super-high-powered surgeon that just comes here once a week. My doctor said he's done hundreds of these operations and he's the *best*. Like that's supposed to make me feel better. Now I know what all those headaches were from. I've got a whole tribe of little cells having a party inside my brain."

"Jesus Christ, that sucks. I mean it really sucks, it stinks, what can I do?"

"I don't have a clue. I'm really bummed because I can't even read. My brain won't cooperate, my concentration is gone. Doctor Snider, my hospital doc, says that once they remove the tumor I should be able to read again. It will take the pressure off the brain. That's if they don't bust up anything inside and start me hemorrhaging."

"Barn and Bryce want to come over. Are you okay with more visitors?"

"Definitely. Let's party until I drop. Rita and Shanti called too and they want to see me. You're not jealous are you?"

"No way. I think she always preferred you anyway. I'm over her."

"No, you're not. Who are you kidding?" Lou said.

"Listen man, it's really fine, let's have a party today. Should I call them?"

"No need. My mom has already taken care of it. They'll all be stopping by tonight. What are your plans?"

"Nothing. Just to hang with you. I'll finish up packing later today. I think I'll pass on the party. I think it will be more than enough for you to see those four."

"How's your new girlfriend? Bryce told me you scored with some hot chick from Beverly Hills, a volleyball queen?"

David didn't want to talk about Melanie and what might or might not be happening. Before he could say anything, Lou got tired and asked David to leave for awhile so he could close his eyes.

David walked out and stood in the hall, watching the gurneys move up and down the sterile aisles. Emaciated white-and-blue-clad patients with tubes dangling above their heads were being carted in all directions. There was an eerie silence broken only by the sound of doctors and nurses being paged.

He gazed out the lone window at the terminus of the corridor where the sun broke its defining light through the glass. At some point the thought of Lou's death broke through and David felt himself cave in and collapse. He looked for somewhere to sit. There were no chairs to be found, so he leaned against the wall and slowly slid to the ground, realizing as he descended how much Lou meant to him. It was only a couple of weeks ago that Lou was breaking out with his poetry and beginning a new life as a writer, and now this horror show.

As David sat crumpled in a heap ten yards from Lou's door, he realized he needed to call Frank and Rene and let them know. Without questioning himself, he rushed down to the first floor lobby, got five dollars' worth of quarters, and charged into the phone booth. David still had the phone number for the Garden of Light Café in his wallet. He dialed and Rene answered. He explained the whole ordeal from the start to the surgery on Friday. Rene listened and didn't say a word until David finished.

"So, David, I have a plan. I'm going to check with Frank, but be prepared to see us tomorrow."

"What are you talking about, tomorrow?"

"Well, the operation is Friday right and we need to see him before the surgeon does his thing. We need to talk with him, he'll understand. Trust me. Let him know we're coming tomorrow. We'll see you then."

"Wait."

"Can't wait, David. See you tomorrow."

Now what have I started? David thought. He took the elevator back to the third floor and peeked into the room to see if Lou had his eyes open. He was sitting up, looking out the window. The back of his head looked like a peeled potato.

"Lou?" He turned and Lou's face was smeared with a wizardly, sly smile, as if he had just come back from a conversation with his "maker." David noticed that he had several notebooks on his nightstand.

"I'm here. Did you think I'd bolted from this place?"

"I was kind of hoping that maybe you'd make a break for it. Let's put on a hat and get your jeans and scoot you out the door to the beach. What do you think?"

David stared at Lou's stubbly cheeks. He wore the standard blue hospital gown and was framed by the bland pastel colors of the walls. Everything was muted and void of imagination, so when he looked at Lou, embedded in his lifeless cell, he stood out like a diamond cast in a pool of sand.

"I think I'd faint half way down the hall, so you'll have to hijack me in a wheelchair and disguise me as a new mother with a little bundle in my lap. That might work if you put a scarf over my head." He laughed and then turned away and glared out the window again, as if to reconnect with a force outside himself.

"Listen, I spoke to Rene while you were resting, and he said that he and Frank will be here tomorrow morning. I hope that's okay. I told him I needed to check with you, but he said it didn't matter, that they'd be here regardless. I'm sorry."

David held his breath, hoping that Lou wouldn't protest and insist that they lock the doors or make him stand guard downstairs to keep them at bay. At first Lou didn't say a thing, but continued his meditation with the clouds, and then after a couple of seconds, he turned to David.

"Of course they're coming. What did you expect?"

CHAPTER NINETEEN

Saturday, July 3, 1965

We are here at the Astrodome, the day before we celebrate our independence, and Sandy Koufax liberated any doubts about the Dodgers remaining in first place. He posted a resounding three-to-one victory. The game had special significance because a rookie pitcher named Larry Dierker was starting against Koufax. Dierker, a local kid from Taft High School in the San Fernando Valley, was signed by the Astros right out of high school at seventeen. He made his major league debut on his eighteenth birthday and struck out Willie Mays. Koufax and Dierker, the legend and the rookie, battled evenly for the first two innings. But in the third inning, the kid walked Koufax, who was then forced out by Maury Wills. Willie Davis singled Wills home and that was the start of Dierker's demise. Koufax needed only the slightest edge to bear down against his opponent and put the game out of reach. In the fourth frame, John Roseboro led off with a double and scored on Lou Johnson's single. Johnson made it to third on Jim Wynn's error and scored on a sacrifice fly by Jim Lefebvre. Koufax followed with a solid double that crushed his young rival. With a three-run lead, Koufax simply turned on the after burners and coasted to a three-to-one victory. Joe Morgan popped a solo home run off Koufax in the bottom of the eighth to take away the shutout, but that was the only extra base hit he surrendered. That's it now, enjoy your holiday tomorrow.

It had been hard getting to sleep on Wednesday, so David opened the window to the backyard. The coolness and the aroma of the night-blooming jasmine wafted inside. He imagined the box score from Tuesday's game; nine innings, eight hits, three runs, one base on ball, and ten strikeouts. David ran the line of numbers twice more in his mind, multiplying the strikeouts by the estimated number of starts remaining for Koufax. Koufax had already amassed 167 strikeouts in his first eighteen starts, and David figured he had at least another twenty starts before the end of the season. He fell asleep predicting that he'd have well over 350 strikeouts by the end of September.

Frank and Rene were hovered around Lou's bed on Thursday morning when David arrived. They were talking and leafing through the steno notebooks that Lou had stashed beside his bed. Frank had a red-and-white kerchief strapped around his blond-gray hair, and Rene wore a navy blue beret titled slightly to the right. Rene's face was old and young at the same time, but what characterized him more than anything was his constant "Mona Lisa" smile. He looked like he knew the answer to the question of eternal life, but would only offer you an occasional obtuse clue. Frank, on the other hand, behaved more like a mystical motorcycle mechanic; his agenda was more serious and direct.

"Aha, Master David arrives," Rene punctuated the M in Master. "You just missed Molly and Chester, sorry. You might have informed them that we were coming. It took Lou and me a little while to convince them that we weren't drug smugglers. But we're all clear now. I just needed to recite some Wordsworth for Molly and had to invite Chester up to San Francisco for a Basque dinner to ease their trepidation. Of course, it helped that Lou finally just told them to get the hell out, but in a tasteful manner. So come forth, Mr. Mandel, we don't have a lot of time to finish this project."

"What project?" David walked over and nudged Lou's foot as it wiggled under the white cotton blanket. "What's going on?"

"Frank and Rene are going through my notebooks and we're deciding what poems to use for the book."

"If Ferlinghetti won't publish it, I have a friend in Mill Valley with a small press, and we'll get a first edition printed and go from there. Maybe two hundred copies? What do you think Rene?" Frank looked across the bed to Rene.

"I think Ferlinghetti would be a fool not to publish it, but then we've seen him pass up this kind of opportunity before. Here, David, look through these and see what you think," Rene said.

Rene handed David a couple of Lou's notebooks, scribbled with blue ink where Frank or Rene had made comments about the poems. "Keeper, Strong, Definitely, Yes . . ."

David started reading the poems. Every few moments, he looked up and gazed at Lou, who was adding his comments to the notebooks as they passed them in a circular motion, creating a communal experience.

"He is our next Rimbaud," Frank said.

"No, I don't think so. I think Lou's voice is unique; it's his own, not really like anyone, I'd say." Rene looked at Lou intensely with his cosmic smile that relaxed and elevated simultaneously.

By one o'clock they were finished. Frank and Rene gathered the notebooks and put them in their respective day packs, all the while reassuring Lou they'd have them back to him within a week. Lou offered no resistance.

"Those loonies left yet?" Chester walked into the room while Lou and David were talking about their next trip to San Francisco. They planned to drive straight up Pacific Coast Highway this time. Lou offered to stop the first night and stay with Ginger and her friends. Evidently, the tumor had activated a new sentimentality that David couldn't take seriously.

"Yeah, Dad, they're gone. You can come in and be your usual obnoxious self."

"Lou don't talk that way to your father. You know he means well."

"Of course he means well. He's just obnoxious and judgmental. He knows that and appreciates it as well. Right Dad?"

"Goddamn right, son. What would the world be without a few assholes like me?"

"Chester!"

"Molly, if it doesn't bother Lou, then why the hell should it ruffle your feathers. Right, son!"

Molly turned her attention to Lou. "You haven't eaten, have you? The surgeon doesn't want anything in your stomach, something about the anesthesia."

"Nothing in my stomach, Mom, just the hospital air and a lot of metaphors that Frank and Rene left behind."

"Lou, I brought you a *Sports Illustrated* and a *Playboy*," Chester said.

He gave Lou a little nudge and handed him the brown paper bag with the two magazines. He turned to Molly, shrugged his shoulders, reached into his shirt pocket and nervously pulled out his pack of Paul Malls, tapped it in his palm, then placed it back in his pocket before Molly could protest his smoking. Chester looked at his son, then walked over to the window and stood with his hands wedded behind his back. He moved his feet apart like a solider standing at ease, and drifted away.

"Is there anything else you'd like right now?" Molly asked.

"Mom, I'm fine. I'd just like to have some time to rest. Maybe you and Dad could come back a little later. I'm really okay. I just want to talk with David for a little while."

"You're sure? There is nothing we can get for you?"

"I'm sure."

"Molly, let's go. Let the boy be. You asked him and he told you. Let's go. See you later, son."

Chester squeezed Lou's shoulder and latched onto Molly's hand as she remained transfixed on Lou, her eyes filled with terror. They shuffled out the door. Molly looked back once more, then they disappeared down the blank corridor, leaving Lou and David alone.

"Sometimes she's just too much for me to take. She looks at me like I'm already dead."

"It must be hard for her," David responded.

"It's hard for me. I don't want to think about this surgery, but there isn't anything else to think about, and just thinking is an effort sometimes."

David didn't know what to say or do. He stared at Lou in his pale-blue gown. The hospital intercom was incessantly calling and directing surgeons and nurses to operating rooms and recovery stations, requests for Doctor Goldberg on line 5321 and Dr. Albert on line 6237. A tall Black nurse with a blue name tag stenciled with "Rowena" came in the room before David regained his tongue.

"Hey, darling, anything I can get you? How you feeling, sweetheart?"

"I'm okay for now. You know I don't have many choices." Lou's voice was soft and endearing.

"I'm sorry, honey, but those doctors are real fussy before an operation," she said.

Rowena had an incredible body. David thought it would be great if she leaned over and let Lou have just a little squeeze. He could see that Lou was delighting in her attention. He wished Lou could just tumble onto Rowena and have one great fuck before the operation.

David watched as she checked his friend's pulse and blood pressure. Lou was joking with her as she reached behind him with her stethoscope to check his lungs. She whispered something in his ear. David turned and started to walk out, but Lou called him back.

"Where you going, Mandel?"

"I thought I'd go get a Pepsi." Rowena looked at David blankly.

"Mandel, you don't need to sneak out of here. Rowena's just telling me about her paintings and wanted to know if I was interested in seeing them. Can you conceive of the kind of colors a woman like Rowena might have on her palette?"

"Oh, yeah. I can imagine."

"And what do you mean by that?" she laughed.

"I mean, I imagine a lot of greens, and red earth tones, and soft yellows, that's what."

"Well, David, if you're going to go, then go," Rowena said and smiled. Her eyes lit up like fireworks as she pulled the drapes around Lou's bed. "I need to draw some blood."

David walked down to the end of the hall where the phone was and called Melanie. She wasn't home. He wanted to call Rita, but that was ridiculous. He sat down and looked around at the corridors filled with empty gurneys and busy medical people deeply involved in doing good in the world. He wondered if Lou would make it through tomorrow's operation.

When David returned, Rowena was gone. Lou had propped himself up in bed, his head titled forward as he tried to read a book of poems by Jack Gilbert. He looked up at David.

"Hey, Mandel, I thought you dropped off the earth."

"It looked like you wanted some time with Rowena, so I just starting talking to a guy down the hall whose kid is in the hospital. How'd it go?"

"Huh?"

"With Rowena?"

"What the hell do you mean?"

"Never mind," David said.

"Hey, check out this poem I found. I can't concentrate for too long, so reading poems works for me."

Lou pointed to a poem called "Between Poems." It started out:

A lady asked me
what poets do
between poems.
Between passions
and visions. I said
that between poems
I provided for death.

"I've been thinking about that," Lou said.

"Yeah." David could see that he wanted to talk about it. And why not? It wasn't anything David was ready to *provide* for himself. He wanted to run out of the room and scream in the bright sunlight. He wanted to call Melanie and meet her at the beach and watch the waves roll onto the forgiving sands. He wanted to be anywhere but here. He gazed around the room at the heart monitor, the stainless steel trays, the forty-five-degree hospital bed that propped Lou up into his book and *provided* for his thoughts about death.

"I could die tomorrow. I know that and no one wants to talk about it except Rene and Frank. They asked me if I was afraid of death, and I said I hadn't really thought about it. Rene said it might be a good idea to talk and we did. It's always just been an abstraction, not that I haven't tried to imagine it from time to time. I'm pretty scared when I consider it. It's like the end of the story. Period."

"I'm glad you are talking to me about 'it.' But, you are going to come through this and we're going to have one hell of a time living together."

"That's a great thought, Mandel. But it's like a punch in the stomach. Death? *No!* Not now. Not me! After Rowena left, I started thinking, how do I provide for death? I don't. Death provides for me. It's just waiting outside in the hall reading the newspaper. Really, it's fucked, just fucked."

"It is fucked. I don't know what I'd do without you. That's all I know." As the words came out of David's mouth he looked at Lou, and he didn't move or flinch or say a word. They played catch back and forth with their hearts, silently acknowledging what they both realized and witnessed.

Lou reached over and took David's hand. "Hey, would you please get me a copy of the *Times*? You can read to me about how screwed up the world is before they cut into my brain."

Molly and Chester were hovering around Lou when David returned with the paper. Lou looked at David with a crunched face of resignation, sandwiched with absolution. His mother straightened the single sheet that covered his gown, and every few moments, she waved her hand softly over Lou's head. Chester unabashedly pursued the *Playboy* that he had bought for Lou, his thick glasses barely hiding the dark bags under his glassy brown eyes. David didn't want to disturb the family scene, and at the same time, he felt compelled to at least attempt a rescue of his friend. The thought of leaving him in this masquerade irked David. He thought about Lou's mortality and the insanity of life's meager choices. In the background, Walter Cronkite droned on about the recent attack on Da Nang.

"Here's the paper." David walked over to Lou's bedside and plopped the *Times* next to his thigh, brushing his muscular leg with his knuckles and pushing slightly as if to say, *I know you want them to leave.*

"David, that's so sweet. You must be tired. I start to fall asleep after just a couple of hours and you've been here all day," Molly said.

"Thanks," David said. "I'm going to leave soon. I just wanted to share one more thing with Lou." He pulled a chair close to the bed and opened the sports page of the paper.

"Look at this." David pointed to a story at the bottom of the page: *Dierker vs. Koufax Fireworks Start Early.*

"You remember that guy? He pitched for Taft," David said.

"Of course I do. You think he can beat Koufax?" Lou asked.

"I don't know. Dierker beat Spahn the other day. It's hard to believe he's in the *big's*. I guess it could have been us."

"Not a chance, Mandel, you never had the velocity or the control."

David laughed and nodded. He put his hand on Lou's shoulder and said goodbye.

"Thanks, man." Lou rolled his eyes, letting David know he'd relinquished his body to his mother for the night.

David walked around the bed and gave Molly a hug. She looked like someone who had been out in the rain for a long time without protection. David shook Chester's soft salesman's hand and gazed into his bloodshot eyes as he said good night.

Sleep was the last thing on David's mind when he got back to his parents' house. It was still July 1, and technically he had another place to live. He had already packed most of his clothes. Bryce was set to pick him up in the morning with his father's pickup truck so David could move his bed and dresser over to the apartment. He didn't remember falling asleep. The last thing he recalled was thinking about Alex.

When David awoke, he found a letter from CJ stuffed under the door. He must have walked right over it last night. He stuffed it into his pocket and squirted out of the bedroom. It was eight thirty. Alex was still asleep and his mother was sitting in the kitchen looking at *Better Homes and Gardens*, probably wishing they lived in the hills above Ventura Blvd.

"Can I make you some breakfast before you leave? How was Lou last night?"

"He was about the same. No thanks. I'm not very hungry. I think I'll just have some Rice Krispies and grapes."

"You'll be hungry again in an hour, that's not a breakfast. You've got a big day today. What did you decide about the apartment? About Lou, you know what I mean."

"Yeah, of course I know what you mean. There's nothing to decide. I'm moving in and hopefully Lou will move in as soon as he's able. That's all."

Bryce picked him up and they quickly loaded the truck and the Galaxy. The bed, table, and chairs in the truck, and the rest in his car. David pulled over once when they were in Santa Monica to call the hospital and see how the surgery went. Bryce stood beside him as he talked to Molly. All she was able to tell him was that he was still in surgery.

They unloaded the truck and the car and were finished before noon. David called again after they had lunch from the Dog House on Ocean Blvd. Molly said that he was in the recovery room but was still unconscious. The surgeon said that it was too early to make any predictions. His vitals were stable, and the surgery had gone well. They hoped they had removed all of the cancer.

Bryce and David went to the beach just across the street from the apartment. It was quiet compared to Sorrento Beach because there weren't any food joints on the water, just long stretches of sand with lifeguard towers every hundred yards. They body surfed for a couple of hours, and then Bryce drove back home before the rush-hour traffic.

David showered for the first time at his new place. He got dressed and realized that CJ's letter was still in his back pocket. He took it out and opened it.

Dear David,

At least we're still in California. Ford Ord is close to the ocean and that's a plus. After a couple of weeks of being kicked around, Wiz and I seem to have this figured out. We're in the same platoon but in different squads. It's all right, we're in the same barracks and endure the same D.I.s (drill instructors). Sgt. Lane and Sgt. Margolis are equally sadistic, but Lane has a shorter fuse, and last week he stuffed me in a footlocker and rolled it across the floor because I left my boots in front of my bed instead of putting them away. He likes to make life lessons out of us. Starting last week, we have Sundays off and play poker till lights out.

Both Lane and Margolis tolerate me because I am a better marksman than either of them. All that practice Father made me do with the "weapon" has paid off. At least for now. Wiz is pretty good as well. The Army is lame, no one takes the training seriously except for the hot stuff: bullets, grenades, and bayonets. It's all about survival.

Sometimes I worry about what's next, but usually I'm fine with the decision I made. I really want to get to Nam. Rumor has it there is going to be a big buildup soon and they might be asking for volunteers. I'm thinking about it. Sooner rather than later, that's what I want. Get it on, get it over with, and get home.

Give everyone a squeeze from Wiz and me.

Always,

CJ

P.S. Have you called Veronica?

David hadn't called Veronica. It wasn't a bad idea, but at the moment he needed to sort out what was happening. David folded CJ's letter and put it in his blue canvas rucksack. For the next three hours, he unpacked his new life. By five o'clock he needed a break and walked down Pacific Ave. to a phone booth. His phone wouldn't be hooked up until Monday. He called the hospital and Molly said that Lou would probably be sedated for the next forty-eight hours. His brain needed time to recover.

Saturday night he and Melanie ate at a small Italian restaurant on Pico Blvd. Seeing her helped get his mind off Lou. When he got home the Dodgers game had just ended. It was July 3 and the fireworks hadn't started, but Koufax had just won his fourteenth game and the season wasn't quite half over. David pondered the possibility of him winning thirty games. Something that had not been done since the depression. But what of it? David looked around the new place; the paint looked tired on the faded beige walls, the big rug had several dark stains. At least there were new lace curtains hanging crisply across the windows. They were like beacons welcoming the light. His books were stacked in wooden orange crates. David looked out into the night. The lights from Ocean Ave. spilled in through the open window. Koufax sailed through his consciousness. He added another win in the harbor of victories. For the moment, his fears were slaked, his uncertainty smoothed. It didn't matter why. David knew that he'd be able to sleep soundly for the first time in many days.

CHAPTER TWENTY

Wednesday, July 7, 1965

Tonight at Crosley Field it was all Reds. They beat the Dodgers seven to six. Sandy Koufax lasted just four and two-thirds innings. It was supposed to be a battle between the two winningest pitchers, Koufax and Sammy Ellis, who has the second best record in baseball at twelve-three. But Ellis was knocked out after five and a third innings, after giving up three runs on six hits.

Frank Robinson rocked Koufax in the first with a two-run homer, and Pete Rose drove in two more in the second inning. By the top of the third, it was five to nothing, and when Koufax left with two outs in the fifth, he had surrendered nine hits, five runs, and three walks—a crushing experience, softened only by the fact that second baseman Jim Lefebvre tied the game in the eighth inning, thereby saving Koufax from his fourth loss. Leo Cardenas, the skinny shortstop, ended the game with two outs in the bottom of the ninth with a home run off Bob Miller. The win put Cincinnati in first place, tied with the Dodgers.

On the Fourth of July, David decided to walk the beach before making any decisions about the day. Melanie wouldn't be home until late. He longed to see her again. The world didn't feel welcoming or safe. Not according to the news. Brezhnev honored the day by announcing the Soviets had orbiting nuclear missiles that could easily overwhelm any technologies the U.S. had in place. At the same time, the East German government decided to tighten the reins on shipments into West Berlin. The forces of good and evil lapped against each other like smoke and fire; indiscernible, combustible, and unrelenting in their dance across the swollen media desert.

Before going to the beach, he walked to the phone booth and called the hospital. He talked with Molly and heard that Lou had emerged from the sedation, but he had been moved to intensive care and no one was allowed to see him except the immediate family. David felt relieved but frustrated that he'd have to wait another day or two before seeing his friend.

He arrived back at the apartment and found Alex sitting on the stoop, decked out in a red polka-dot sundress and a way-too-large straw hat that drooped halfway down her forehead. Her forearms draped on her legs, and her back slumped down so she looked like she was in crash position on a sinking airliner.

"Whoa, how'd you get here?"

"On the wings of angels, can't you see the glow around my brow?"

"Come on, Alex, what's up? Are Mom and Dad here checking on me after two days or what?"

"Always imagining that it's about you. Some things never change."

"Right. Like your banter. How do you fit that big brain on your pillow every night?"

"Yes, I'm so happy to see you as well. Did it ever occur to you that I might miss you? Mom doesn't stop talking about how wonderful you are and why don't I get my act together or I'll never get into college like the great David?"

"That's baloney. Just blow her off like you always do. So come on, how'd you get here?"

"I told Dad I was missing you terribly last night. He offered to drive me out to see you, but I knew if he did, it would have infuriated Mom, or at the very least she would have insisted on coming along. Just what you need, right? An invasion from the dysfunctional home team."

"Well you got that right, so what happened?"

"Nothing, I just took the bus, or I should say I took the buses. I keep the schedule under my mattress for emergencies, you never know when you'll have to evacuate."

"God, it never crossed my mind to take a bus to the beach. Christ, how long did it take you?"

"Two hours and twenty-three minutes, including the initial walk to Woodman and Van Nuys. My loyalty to you is remarkable, don't you think?"

"Alex I think you're out of your head to spend two and a half hours on a bus just to get out here."

"How quickly you forget the age of complete dependency, as if you made it through the seasons of acne without blemish or embarrassment!"

"My phone isn't hooked up yet. Let's walk over to Skip's Diner and you can call home and let them know you made it alive in your polka-dot dress. How many buses did it take to get here anyway?"

"Just three, but it was the wait on Wilshire that slowed things down. So what are we going to do to celebrate this auspicious day in our history?"

"Well, until you arrived I didn't have a clue, but now I guess I'm doomed to spend the day with you."

"And night! This commitment needs to include fireworks or I'll never leave your domicile."

"A threat duly noted and sufficient to accomplish your goal. So call and let the folks know you arrived and you will be delivered home safe and sound after the festivities."

Alex raised a large flowered satchel that Grandma Judith had used to lug fruits and vegetables from the little markets on Fairfax Avenue. The bag had what appeared to be several soft lumps that David was sure contained all she needed for the day.

It was a sultry cloudless day, with all of Los Angeles looking for diversions. The beach was the logical place to escape. David put all the beach stuff in the back seat and drove till he found a parking spot not too far from the pier. They walked to the sand and set down their towels and blankets, then took to the water and played in the surf until they had sufficiently cooled off.

Walking back to their spot through the Frisbees, volleyball games, kites, and surf riders, two lobster-red, beer-bellied guys staggered toward them. The fatter of the two bloated drunks stumbled into Alex, almost knocking her down. He could have been twenty or thirty, but David couldn't tell because his face was already squished and wrinkled with a mixture of sleeplessness, sun, and alcohol.

"Oh, I'm sorry, didn't even see you lit-lil girl. Let me help you." The fat guy stumbled toward Alex while his friend just gazed, drooled, and nipped on his bottle, veiled in a paper bag.

"Hey, just back off," David snarled. "She's fine, just move away and don't touch her."

"No, no, I just want to help her up."

"She's already up, so just move on."

"What's your problem, man? It's Fourth of July, we're having a party and the lit-lil girl falls down and I'm being a gentle . . . man and helping her up."

"She didn't fall, you bumped into her because you're plastered, that's what happened."

"David, let's go, I'm fine. Let's just go," Alex said.

"Yeah, David, you just go and shut your big-ass mouth," the second guy finally spoke. He was sporting a pair of lime-green trunks that sagged well below his navel. He had patches of wet sand on his right knee and elbow, and his eyebrows were crusted with salt as he squinted at David.

"You don't want no problem, David, just do what the kid said, and just go."

A small crowd of onlookers started to gather and formed a circle around the four. The fat guy stopped moving toward Alex and directed his full drunken countenance at David, while his provoking friend pinned David with his drunken glare. Fighting on a public beach wasn't what David had in mind for the day. He could see Alex becoming more and more frightened and embarrassed.

"David, let's go, come on."

"Right, David, just move on like a good little boy," the second jerk taunted as he put down his bottle and took a step toward David.

David looked at Alex. She looked pale as a peeled cucumber, her arms shaking and waving hysterically. "David, come on!"

Trapped in the moment, David's nerve endings pulsed and whirred, and he stared back toward the distant horizon where a catamaran bobbed in the freedom of the open Pacific. David turned toward Alex in hopes of a simple solution. He shrugged and was about to answer when Alex screamed, "David!"

David turned to see the mouthy guy with the lime-green trunks charging him like a middle linebacker, his arms jetted back to get maximum acceleration, his matted, sweaty bucket of hair steamed toward him like a wildcat. Quickly, David twisted around to see if the first jerk, the one with more girth, was also attacking, but he looked stiff and bewildered as David shifted back in time to dodge and push the human train down into the sand. Instantly, he popped back up and attacked, this time fully erect as if he were trying to skip a few rungs on the evolutionary ladder. Without thinking David unloaded his fist into his soft belly. The drunk gasped and collapsed on the ground. At the same moment, David heard a whistle and a scream. "Hey! Hey! Break it up, that's enough."

A larger circle of fireworks seekers had formed, and Alex stood frozen at the sight of the guy writhing on the ground. Prancing to the rescue was a tall, muscular lifeguard, his nose completely white with zinc oxide, an official black plastic whistle bouncing between slabs of his gargantuan pectorals.

"I saw what happened! I've already warned this guy and his friend once this morning. He had it coming. I'll get them both off the beach. Are you all right?"

"I'm fine," David replied.

"Okay, everyone, the excitement is over. You can all go back to enjoying your holiday. Sorry for this disturbance."

Mr. Lifeguard escorted the two guys off the beach, and they disappeared into the over-gorged parking lot. David stared down at the spot where the second jerk's knee landed, and for a second, wished Lou had been with him. They would have really taken care of business.

"Whoa, you really decked that guy. Are you all right?"

"Of course I'm all right. Haven't I always told you that I'd protect you?"

"Yeah, but you didn't have to show off like that, you could have just walked away and ignored him. He wouldn't have followed you."

"Right, I forgot you are the expert on male aggression."

"I just think drunk guys are too stupid to be really dangerous. You could have just tucked your ego into your pocket and escorted me down the beach."

"Alex, I'm hungry. Why don't we get some lunch?"

They devoured a couple of burgers and shared a bag of fries from the grill while lounging on the blankets. They each had a root beer, then settled down for an hour of serious tanning. David had trouble keeping Lou out of his mind. The image of him lying dazed in the ICU unnerved him. He needed to do something to get out of his head. Finally, he said, "Hey, you want to walk to the pier?"

"I thought you'd never ask," Alex replied.

It didn't take long to get to the pier and all its amusements.

"David, please, let's do the Blue Streak, please." Alex tugged him under the portal that announced "Yacht Harbor * Sport Fishing * Boating * Cafes. They squeezed through the crowd. The Beach Boys' "Fourth of July" was blasting through the speakers. The smell of corn dogs, french fries, and soft-serve ice cream slammed them as they wound their way through the frenzy to the ticket booth. After two rounds of the roller coaster, three spins on the carousel inside the Hippodrome, one long-delayed revolution around the ferris wheel, and a couple of whipping-car near accidents, they retreated back to the beach with two quart-sized plastic glasses of lemonade drenched with fresh-cut lemons.

By five o'clock, the beach began to clear up enough so you could see more sand than beach towels, but the remaining crowd appeared entrenched for the remainder of the day and the sunset that would be followed by Mayor Yorty's Independence Day fireworks celebration. David promised Alex they'd stay for it. They sat watching the sun slowly edge toward the horizon.

"Do you think Lou is going to die?" Alex asked.

"No, but the whole ordeal is terrible. I have a hard time thinking about him the way he is."

"Brain cancer. It's really bad, isn't it?"

"Yeah, it is."

When the fireworks ended, David drove Alex home. She slept from the time he got on the San Diego Freeway at Wilshire until he got off at Nordoff. It was ten thirty by the time he parked under the sycamore tree and walked inside. He knew his father would be asleep. He knew his mother would be up waiting.

"How was it?" his mother asked.

"Great, we had a fantastic time. Thanks for letting her come out to see me."

"I didn't let her come out, your father did."

"Well, thank Dad for me."

David remained very much awake as he drove home. His thoughts slammed against the walls of his mind like a rubber ball. What's next for Lou? He needed to find a way to get through the coming days. In the morning, he'd go to the hospital. He knew that and only that.

Lou's head was wrapped and taped, three tubes descended into his arm from plastic bags above his bed. He lay still and quiet. Molly whispered something into his ear. David stood frozen in the doorway, his mind incapable of registering the person on the bed as being his friend. The scene looked like a television set from *Dr. Kildare*. David imagined Richard Chamberlain down the hall consulting with Ben Casey. Molly looked up and greeted David with a pantomime, her lips forming the words "Come in," and then she gestured to the chair beside Chester, who was busy inside *Sports Illustrated.*

"Molly, why are you whispering and making yourself look ridiculous. The nurses were just in here talking to Lou in a normal voice. He's not asleep. He told you the noise doesn't bother him," Chester said.

"He's been through a lot and I think he needs his rest."

"Molly, please say hello to David. Hi David, thanks for stopping by."

"Thanks, Chester."

Lou didn't move when David spoke. His eyes were fixed on the window. David walked around the foot of the bed and saw his crunched, exhausted face; a ring of purple outlined his right eye. He blinked at David with his left eye and tried to squeeze a smile.

"They messed me up," he stammered, and then closed his eyes and breathed quietly. Molly reached for a glass of ice water with a flex straw and wedded it to his lips.

"Here, honey, try to drink a little."

Lou lifted his head just enough to create sufficient gravity for the water to descend. He puckered his lips and pulled in the liquid. He coughed lightly, then put his head back down. David kept searching for a vocabulary for the moment. Every phrase that entered his mind seemed trite. *How's it going? How are you feeling? Can I get you anything? It must have been rough. You should have seen the fireworks.*

He said nothing. Instead, he touched Lou's leg and gave it a squeeze, and then walked over to the top of the bed and whispered, "I'm here for you." Lou moved his head slightly up and down and opened his eyes. David stared at him, the eyes glazed over with drugs, pain, and confusion, and certainly fear. Fear. David felt his stomach wrench and twist. His throat grew dry and tight. He sat down next to Chester who handed him the *Sports Illustrated* with a lead story about Mickey Mantle and the Yankees. David stared at Mantle's wistful, boyish face, the ex-lead minor from Spavinaw, Oklahoma. He recalled the '63 World Series when Koufax caught the switch-hitting superstar flat-footed on a called third strike in the ninth inning. The flamboyant Yankee and the taciturn Dodger could not have been more different. It was like choosing between cotton candy and a bowl of lentil soup.

Lou went back to sleep. David sat quietly next to Chester, who now flipped through the gloss of the *Playboy*, his hands trembling slightly as he held each page in a detached trance. Chester reached up and scratched the stubble on his right cheek with little burrs of grey, then cleared his throat and said, "You really like baseball?"

"Yeah, I do."

"That's what Lou told me. He likes it too. I wish I'd seen him play more often. He was pretty good."

"I think so, he's still good."

"That's right," he said. "That's right. We'll get through this. I'm sure of it. He'll be out of here before long and then I can do something about my regret."

"Chester, don't talk that way," Molly piped. "We have only one mission and we need to keep our attention focused."

"I'm attuned Molly, very much attuned to a positive outcome. I will be here until Lou is completely and totally recovered. I just wanted to express my gratitude to David."

"Of course, Chester, of course!"

Turning away from Molly, Chester tapped David on the knee and then placed his hand on his bicep and said, "Come on, I'll buy you a drink. I need some company."

Chester gripped the arms of the chair and launched himself into the room. Lou stirred in bed and moaned, turned and moaned some more, and then he was silent again. David looked at him. The architecture of his body appeared disconnected from the friend-person that David had known all his life.

David and Chester found an empty table in the cafeteria. They drank iced tea.

"I tried to be a good father. I tried. But I don't think I did a very good job."

"I'm sure you did okay. Lou never said anything bad about you," David lied.

"How can you know what's right? You have to provide. You have to make a life for your family. That's all I have tried to do."

"You did what you had to do," David replied. There wasn't more he could add.

David spent Tuesday and Wednesday at the hospital. Lou started to recover slowly. They talked quietly for a few minutes at a time, but mostly watched television and sat in silence. Lou faded in and out, sleeping a lot, trying to get his brain working again.

Just before David left on Wednesday, the oncologist came in and talked with Lou, Molly, and Chester. David was asked to leave. When he came back, Lou told him the oncologist had said they were not sure if they got all the cancer. Lou looked frightened. The doctor had recommended a course of chemotherapy. It was tough to leave him in that state, but Lou said he just wanted to sleep.

David got home and collapsed on the bed. It was hot, and the smog hammered him with its acerbic grip; his eyes burned and his throat felt like someone had clawed it to pieces. He called Melanie, but she was busy with her friends. For dinner, he made a couple of leathery minute steaks paired with frozen french fries and half a head of lettuce and sliced tomatoes. After dinner, he walked along the mostly empty beach and lost himself in the breaking waves that crashed and crashed without respite. He listened to the game, but even Koufax had been vanquished and offered no solace tonight.

CHAPTER TWENTY-ONE

Sunday, July 11, 1965

Forbes Field is just beautiful today. Partly because of the weather, partly because Koufax held on to win game number one of a double header against the Pirates. It started out disastrously. A loss would have knocked the Dodgers out of first place. The boys in blue went down quietly in the top of the first. In the bottom of the first inning, Bob Bailey led off with a home run against Koufax. It's rare that Koufax gives up a lead off a home run. Two batters later, Donn Clendenon clobbered another hanging curveball into the right-field stands for the second homer of the inning. It didn't look good for Mr. K.

In the bottom of the third, the Dodgers reserve catcher, Jeff Torborg, tripled. Koufax singled him home and the Dodgers were only down by a run. Koufax blitzed through the Pirates in the bottom of the third, and in the Dodger half of fourth inning, a couple of singles by Ron Fairly and Jim Lefebvre, a passed ball, and an error by the third baseman netted three unearned runs and gave the Dodgers a three-to-two lead. The Dodgers scored another unearned run in the eighth, but it wasn't necessary, because Koufax shut Pittsburg down after that first inning barrage, allowing just three more hits and no runs. The win moved him to fifteen-three, and he struck out ten Pirates, running his total to seventy-two times in his career that he has struck out ten or more batters.

Baseball is a funny game. Koufax started by giving up two home runs and ended the game getting a four-to-two win. Sometimes, you just never know how things are going to turn out.

Bryce showed up at David's apartment on Thursday morning, ready for work. Jacob's partner Pete had torn his ACL playing softball and was going to need surgery. It was busy at the store with several large orders of parts to be unloaded and put into the inventory. Bryce needed some work and David's father need the help, so David asked Jacob if they could work together. He was fine with it.

David put some juice and coffee on the table.

"Did you see Lou?" Bryce asked.

"Yeah, I saw him but he didn't say much, except that his doctor wants him to start chemotherapy today. Now they're not sure if they got all the cancer, so they have to give him drugs. Molly said the tumor was in a spot that made it impossible to use radiation. All that's left is the poison. The whole thing is just fucked."

"How did Lou seem?"

"Seem? Seemed like he was scared and kind of out of it. They sliced into his brain. Damn, I just can't imagine," David said. He was getting distressed thinking it.

"So, are we ready to go?" David asked impatiently.

"Ready."

David took the Santa Monica Freeway straight east toward downtown. The big news on the radio was the arrival in Vietnam of the "Big Red One," a thousand infantrymen from the U.S. Army's first battalion out of Fort Riley, Kansas. Three thousand more troops were due to land later that week, and the newscasters were making a big deal about how *we* were going to get this war over as soon as *we* had enough troops. The question was how many were enough. It was just a matter of time before CJ and Wiz got their orders, and Rick Norris was probably already there.

"You think Lou's going to make it?" David asked Bryce as they crossed through the interchange onto the San Bernardino Freeway."

"Yeah, don't you?"

"I hope so."

Just as they pulled into the store, the Sunshine Food Wagon arrived. The wagon serviced all the nearby manufacturing businesses. Rosy and Simon were the proprietors, and David had cultivated a kindhearted relationship with them over the years when he helped his father in the summers. Simon had played tackle for USC in the fifties, and Rosy had run track. Their degrees, in business and education respectively, didn't guarantee any kind of decent job. Simon inherited the Sunshine Food Wagon from his father, Ron Taylor, an enterprising Black veteran. Simon had told David that his father realized early that making a living and being successful had more to do with ingenuity and hard work than education.

David walked through the back of the store and let his father know they were there. He asked him if he wanted anything from the cart. He said no. Bryce was close to the front of the line by the time David returned. He could smell the bacon, mixed with pepper and eggs, wafting in the air. The redolence of fresh coffee covered the cart like a cloud dropped down from a café in heaven.

Swarthy workmen were lined up from neighboring businesses, their greased knuckles twitching in anticipation. They jabbered and poked and joked about the pennant race and the horses from nearby Santa Anita. Bryce fit right in, he had already struck up a conversation about the upcoming basketball season at UCLA. The sports writers were buzzing about a seven-foot kid from New York City who could shoot like a six-foot guard. The name Lew Alcindor was dotting the sports pages. Bryce reached the front of the line and hollered over for David's order. David waved at Simon and gave him the thumbs up. That meant his regular bacon and egg sandwich on a kaiser roll. After the crowd dissipated and Bryce and David finished their meal, they went to visit Simon and Rosy as they cleaned up and readied for their next stop.

"Yo, David, man, how's it going? I haven't seen you in awhile," Simon said.

"Pretty good, except I've got a good friend in the hospital with brain cancer—that's not so good. I've moved into my own place in Santa Monica and that's sweet, and Bryce and I are starting UCLA in the fall."

"Sorry about your friend."

"Congratulations about UCLA," Rosy said. "It must be really rough right now with your friend so sick."

Rosy was attractive, warm, and had a special elegance that defied her choice of work. David couldn't understand why she didn't at least go into modeling or television. She was articulate and scintillating, tall with owlish eyes that radiated laughter and courage.

"Yeah, it's tough," David said.

"How long are you going to be working with your dad this summer?" Simon asked.

"I'm not sure. At least a few weeks for now."

"Good, so we'll see you tomorrow anyway."

David and Bryce sat down on a couple of steel milk crates as Rosy and Simon drove off. Everywhere the asphalt exuded heat like a hardened mass of lava. The sky reflected itself in the stale pools of water and oil. The streets and alleys were pitted and pocked from the heavy loads that passed daily. The Hostess bakery was around the corner. Its incessant hot cloud of wheat, yeast, and sugar poured into the smog.

"I don't know how to handle this thing with Lou," David said.

"What's to handle?" Bryce sipped down the last of his Coke.

"That's what I mean. It's like trying to wrestle a bird; I just can't grab onto it."

"What the crap is the "it" you keep talking about? Lou's sick, real sick, and we both know he might not make it. There isn't a damn thing we can do about it."

"Yeah, so that really stinks. I suppose the "it" is what do I say to him? How am I supposed to be with him? You know what I mean?"

"I don't know. I just go there and sit. Sometimes we watch TV, sometimes we talk, sometimes it's just being quiet or talking with Chester and Molly. That's it, David, that's all there is. What are you expecting?"

"I wish I knew. It just gnaws at me. I know there is something else; there must be. He can't just die. Not now."

"David, just give it a rest. Let's go over there after work and see him. Maybe he's better today."

They worked late. By 7:00 p.m. they had locked the doors and set up for the next day. Without any traffic, the drive back to the Valley went fast. It was only a thirty-five-minute dash to the hospital. It was still light outside when they entered.

Lou was sitting up on the side of his bed, looking out the window, his bald head slumped and tilted to the side, his shoulders sagged with a heaviness that David couldn't interpret. Was it defeat or pain or confusion? Whatever it was, it wasn't good.

"Look who's here." Molly sounded very bright and enthused for having been at the hospital for so long. Chester wasn't around. Molly told them he needed to go home and prepare for a road trip to San Diego tomorrow. Lou turned around and half smiled at them, then motioned for Bryce and David to come around to the side of the bed.

"He had a chemo treatment this morning and it wasn't very pleasant," Molly said as they walked around to face Lou. His eyes were floating out the window.

"Not pleasant isn't quite right, it was a total disaster. I've been shitting all day and feel like I swallowed a snake. I'm tired, guys. I don't know how long I'll be able to talk. They gave me some kind of medication about thirty minutes ago."

"It sounds awful," David said. He felt hopeless and inept as he looked at Lou.

"That doesn't do it, Mandel, awful isn't even close. Excuse me, I've got to go to the bathroom."

"You want some help?" Bryce reached over and grabbed his arm.

"Sure, just slide these bags along as I do my shuffle."

Bryce helped him balance on the left and David shored up the right. He could feel Lou's bones sag against his arm. His bicep was soft and fleshy. The same arm that had flung fastballs now could barely lift a glass of water. Lou disappeared into the bathroom, and Bryce and David looked at each other with terror and sorrow. Lou groaned behind the door. David winced as he heard coughing and then a flush of the toilet. Lou opened the door. He forced a smile.

"I'm okay," he strained as he grabbed onto David's arm and they worked their way back to his bed.

"I'm tired. I think I need to rest for awhile."

"Whatever you need," David said.

"We'll stop by tomorrow," Bryce said.

"That will be good." He closed his eyes.

Molly waved goodbye. They headed down the corridor and descended in the elevator.

David took Nordoff Street to the San Diego Freeway on-ramp and zoomed south. He missed Melanie, and yet, he found himself longing for Rita and wishing he could call her and just talk.

"It's crazy, but I'm missing Rita," David said. His years of love for Rita felt interminable. She knew Lou, and that made a difference right now.

"Of course you do. God, you were with her for all of high school. What did you expect?"

"I don't know," David answered. He wondered if it would take an equivalent amount of time to get over his heartache, as if love were some kind of basic algebraic equation. He hoped he was wrong.

"David, you all right?" Bryce asked. "You look like you just saw a ghost."

"No, I'm okay. It's Lou."

"Yeah, me too. But don't miss the turnoff. Santa Monica Blvd. is just a mile ahead."

"Right." David exited the freeway and was back at the apartment in fifteen minutes.

Just as he opened the door the phone rang. It was Veronica. Bryce followed him in the door and collapsed on the couch.

"Hi, David, how are you?" Veronica sounded tense.

"I'm pretty wasted. Bryce and I just got back from visiting Lou in the hospital. They just removed a brain tumor a few days ago, and he looks pitiful right now."

"Oh God! I'm sorry. Is he going to be all right?"

"I don't know. He doesn't look very good right now."

"Well, maybe this isn't a good time to talk. I'll call you another time."

"No, no it's fine. How are you doing?"

"I'm clerking for a big law firm and learning a lot. It's hot as the dickens down here. But I haven't heard much from CJ."

"CJ wrote me a couple of short letters. He sounds all right. His NCOs are getting to him, but nothing he said he couldn't handle." David didn't want to share his own doubts about Wiz and CJ. He also didn't want to let her know about CJ's marksmanship recognition. They talked for awhile. David liked listening to the sonorous lull of her voice.

"I'm fine, except I broke up with my boyfriend. It wasn't meant to be, and we'd only been together five months. I'm actually enjoying my alone time, although I miss home. I would love to get away from this heat and get to the beach."

"Well, you'll have to come by and see my new place. I'm just a block from the water." David imagined seeing Veronica in her bathing suit. "I apologize for not staying in touch. I'll be sure to call you when I hear from CJ again. And you do the same."

"I will. I promise. Thanks again."

"No thank-you needed." David put the phone down and thought of Veronica sitting alone in her room. Bryce stayed for awhile and then headed back to his fraternity house.

On Saturday David and Bryce worked until 4:00 p.m. and then headed back to the hospital. They drove separately. David needed to get some things together at home and he wanted to see Melanie after their time with Lou. Lou was tired and slept through most of their visit.

David headed back home to change and pick up Melanie for dinner and a movie. The traffic was clear, and the wind off the ocean cooled the air. He powered down the windows and turned the radio to KRLA. They were playing "My Guy" by Mary Wells. Suddenly, Los Angeles and the Valley weren't so bad. He could smell the sea in the distance, and he hoped Melanie missed him as much as he missed her.

Nothing you could say
Could tear me away from my guy
Nothing you could do
'Cause I'm stuck like glue to my guy
I'm sticking to my guy like a stamp to a letter
Like birds of a feather, we stick together
I'm tellin' you from the start
I can't be torn apart from my guy

Lou was being torn apart. David thought about him being "my guy" in some crazy way. The soulful, bouncy song reminded him of how close they were at times. He turned left onto Ocean Ave. from Santa Monica Blvd., and he was home. After a quick shower, he changed and retraced his path. He got back on Santa Monica to pick up Melanie. There she sat on the stoop outside her house in tight white hip-huggers and gold-flecked sandals that looked to be straight from India. Her toes dangled and danced as he approached. He noticed that she had somehow managed to paint small white daisies atop her scarlet toenails. She looked fresh from the beach. David was entranced as he walked up and gave her a light kiss on her claret-colored lips.

"You look gorgeous!"

"You look great too. I've missed you."

"It feels like a long time."

"How's Lou?"

"The same. But let's not talk about him right now. I need a break. I want just to be with you, look at you, hear you, feel you."

"Sounds like a song." She laughed and David touched her arm. They went to dinner at Hamburger Hamlet in Westwood and then to the Village Theater to see Lee Marvin and Jane Fonda in *Cat Ballou*. Marvin provided the comedic relief David needed, and he found himself laughing to the point of tears, alternately squeezing Melanie's thigh and holding her hand, nibbling her ear between pounding down popcorn and occasionally diving in for a clandestine kiss. The movie acted like an elixir, so by the time they exited, David was ready to head straight to his apartment and jump into bed.

As they got closer to home, a dense fog set upon the streets. He flicked on the wipers as he turned down Ocean Ave., past the rows of beach bungalows painted in muted colors that now all looked gray. The mist swirled under the lamp posts, and the streets were wet with doubt.

David opened the door for Melanie. He turned on the lights, and they embraced. They sat up late and talked about Lou and what lay ahead for each of them. The lightness of the movie dissolved as the night's conversation moved into the tangle of the future. David took off his shirt and Melanie massaged his back, and then he did the same for her. After a joint and two glasses of wine, they fell asleep in each other's arms.

In the morning the fog had cleared, and they made love unconsciously, before their eyes could really see. David felt a deep comfort lift his despair for his friend.

When they finished breakfast, David drove Melanie home. She had promised her mother they'd have lunch together and then spend the afternoon shopping along the Miracle Mile.

It was fine with David, because he wanted a quiet day at the beach. The Dodgers were playing a double header against the Pirates at Forbes Field. Koufax was slated to pitch the first game. Back at the apartment, he filled his pack with a sandwich, a large jug of water, his book *The Dharma Bums* by Jack Kerouac (Rene had given it to him), his radio, a towel, a folding backrest, and a bamboo roll-up mat. He bolted out to the beach.

Nothing obstructed his view as he unfurled the mat and set up his spot for the afternoon. He poured himself a tall glass of ice water and turned on the game.

Koufax got behind right away. It looked like it was going to be a long afternoon. A thick layer of frustration and dread had accumulated over the last month. David didn't have the patience to keep listening. He turned off the radio and went for a swim. He bodysurfed on a couple of humpbacked waves, came back, and toweled off. When he flicked the transistor back on, the Dodgers had pulled within one run. By the time he finished his sandwich and opened *The Dharma Bums*, the Dodgers had jumped ahead by a run and Koufax had righted himself. The future looked a little brighter.

CHAPTER TWENTY-TWO

Friday, July 16, 1965

Oh my, what a line! No runs, four hits, and nine strikeouts. That's the story tonight from Dodger Stadium. The incomparable Koufax won his sixteenth game against the Chicago Cubs. Here's how the scoring went: in the second inning, Jim Lefebvre and Koufax both singled. Maury Wills followed with a ground ball to the Cubs' indefatigable shortstop Ernie Banks, who missed it, allowing Lefebvre to score. Junior Gilliam lined the single that brought Koufax home, and the Dodgers were up two to 0. Maury Wills singled home Lefebvre in the sixth to make the final score three to 0. It was another shutout for Koufax, who managed to get two singles, giving him four hits over the last two games. Maury Wills stole his fifty-seventh base as the statistical parade continues through this extraordinary season. The win tonight keeps the Dodgers tied for first place in their seesaw battle with Cincinnati.

David and Bryce visited Lou Wednesday night after work. He started to show steady signs of improvement. He told them that his surgeon and his oncologist talked with him daily, and they were encouraged by his strength and resilience. Lou sounded sharp and coherent for the first time since the operation.

"Cancer has this anaplasia quality, the malignant cells are like radical anarchists that try to destroy their own family of cells by procreating and mutating into monsters. So essentially, there's a revolution happening inside my brain. Hopefully, the surgery wiped out most of the alien forces," Lou said.

"I don't know how you are handling all this," David said.

"I don't have much choice. I just have to go with what happens now, try to stay positive and trust it will work out, because otherwise it's pretty terrifying."

Lou flicked on the TV. Adlai Stevenson had died earlier in the day. Walter Cronkite was documenting Stevenson's legacy, showing clips of his two runs at the presidency, and talked about how he was offered as a sacrificial goat by the party. Everyone knew that Eisenhower was unbeatable in both elections. When the program finished, Lou told them that Rene and Frank had called in the morning and said that they had planned on heading down over the weekend with a manuscript for him to check out.

"I think I'm done for the night," Lou said.

David and Bryce took off. Driving home, David talked about going back up to the Bay Area. He said he wanted to talk with Rene first. He also couldn't decide whether he wanted to go alone or bring Melanie along.

"If she were my girl, I'd definitely want to take her," Bryce said.

"I'm thinking that's what I'll do." He was definitely starting to fall in love with her. He was also in need of having some time alone.

A dense mist rolled through the streets, and the foghorns blasted as they drove toward the apartment. The beacon on the pier blinked on and off, guiding ships. David parked in the damp street, and they walked to the apartment.

David plucked two letters from the mailbox and unlocked the door. Bryce sat down on the couch while David opened the letters. The first was from CJ, and he read it out loud to Bryce.

Dear David,

Thanks again for writing, it really helps when mail call arrives and I get a hefty stack. Hitting the home stretch now, basic is almost over and it looks good for Wiz and me. The sergeant offered me an accelerated track in special weapons and sniper training. All that hunting has paid off. I told him I'd be interested only if Wiz was also accepted to the program. Since he's almost as good a shot as I am, they went for it. I'm getting pretty jumpy about getting over there and getting it done with. They're beating our butts over there and the Army is screaming to let us start kicking some ass. I'm not sure how long before we complete this last stage, but I can't wait. I'm itching to go. We all are.

I can't tell you much about the training, some of it involves classified information. It will be awhile before we deploy to Vietnam. The word is we'll have some leave time before we go, and hopefully, I'll see you and the guys. I pray Lou is doing better, thanks for keeping me in the loop.

Sorry this is so brief but we've got a special detail tonight and I've got to get ready.

Your solider friend,
CJ

P.S. Hey, I want to thank you for trying to talk me out of joining. I respect you for it and maybe I should have listened. But it's too late now. Say Hi to Bryce and Barn and let them read this letter if you don't mind.

The second letter was from Wiz. It didn't say much. He neglected to mention anything about the special training, probably because he thought it was classified. It was just a chatty note that he read in a flash and then handed it to Bryce. Bryce gave it back to him, and David put both letters in his top dresser drawer.

"Do you think I ought to call Veronica?" David asked.

"Why?" Bryce replied.

"Because I said I would."

"She'll just worry. Let CJ write her if he wants, or let her find out from her folks. You're just getting yourself overinvolved, trying to save her the same way you tried to save Wiz and CJ. Just let it go. What's the worst thing that could happen?"

"Veronica might find out I didn't tell her, and she wouldn't trust me again."

"So what?"

"You're right," David said, but it didn't feel right. Maybe he'd call her later.

David took out a couple of beers and rolled a joint. Bryce leaned back on the sofa and chugged the beer in two gulps. David lit the pot, took a good hit, passed it to Bryce, and got him another beer. Before long they were both high and loose. David turned on the stereo and put on *Another Side of Bob Dylan.*

"Does Lou remind of you Dylan?" David asked.

"What do you mean?"

"What do you mean, what do I mean? I mean does Lou remind you of Dylan?"

"That's kind of a stupid question, don't you think?"

"I think if it were a stupid question, I wouldn't have asked it. It's a simple question. You can answer yes or you can answer no."

"Well, I don't think I can answer either way because Dylan is Dylan and Lou is Lou," Bryce replied.

"That is profound," David laughed and swigged the last of his beer, leaned into the chair, and listened to the rest of the album.

There was something about Lou's surly, unrepentant way in the world; the way his words banged and exploded against each other that drew David close. Lou was born with a knack to take risks. He chased the butterfly over the fence and soared within his consciousness to places that David had never imagined. He claimed himself an artist before any of his friends dared to think about being anything.

Hopefully, Lou would make a full recovery and they'd be able to regain what had started on the trip to San Francisco; a new life, a new way of seeing. He wanted more time with his friend. There was so much to explore.

Thursday night Frank and Rene showed up at the hospital. Lou succeeded in running Molly and Chester out for the evening. When Bryce and David arrived, his room was decorated with flowers, balloons, and a large poster of rainbows with humpback whales jumping through the waves. Frank and Rene pinned the two-by-four poster behind Lou's bed, so he became the foreground of the action.

Bryce and David cracked up as they walked inside. Frank and Rene were dancing around to the Beatles' "A Hard Day's Night."

"Hey, David, come in. We're celebrating. Lou's manuscript was accepted for publication by Mermaid Press. Ferlinghetti couldn't fit it into his schedule, but he linked us with the Mermaid, another North Beach gem. Still, Larry thinks he's the new Rimbaud!"

"Rene, I think he's more like a young Hart Crane myself," Frank added.

"Hey, let's tone it down. I'm just a guy with a brain tumor and this little manuscript still isn't anything. But I'm grateful and definitely into celebrating."

Lou looked more animated and alive than anytime since the operation. Rene crowned Lou with a black beret and put a large bowl of grapes and a bag of fresh-baked chocolate chip cookies on the stand next to the bed.

"There now. You look beautiful! When are they releasing you anyway, you don't look like you need this place anymore." Rene beamed.

"Hopefully in the next day or two. The oncologist said I don't need any more chemo. They have a couple more tests they want to run, and if everything checks out I'll be home Friday or Saturday."

Rowena walked in with a broad smile on her soft lips, trying to act professional with a tray of medicine and her stethoscope dangling in front of her breasts.

"Looks like a party, but I didn't get an invitation."

Rene ran over and grabbed her hand and took a deep bow and said, "My dear, please allow me to introduce myself, I'm Rene Lacombe and this is my compadre Mr. Frank Whiting. We are literary advocates for Lou, whose poetry is about to grace the world. You are most cordially invited to celebrate in our soirée this evening." Rene reached over and delicately placed a large ruby grape between her lips. "Aha, a perfect fit."

"Well, the great poet has to take his meds." Rowena leaned over and gave Lou his cup of pills and a small plastic cup of water. After he swallowed the pills, Rowena reached down again and gave him a sloppy kiss on the cheek and a full-throttled squeeze.

"This is wonderful! I'll be back after I finish my rounds."

Bryce introduced himself to Frank and Rene and began to thumb through the manuscript that lay on an empty chair in the corner. The thin volume rattled in his hands as Frank talked to Lou.

"I want you and David to come back to Stinson as soon as you're able and spend some time on the beach with us. I've got plenty of room at my place, and if you want your own cabin, I can arrange that as well. And, of course, bring Bryce." Frank nodded toward the corner of the room where Bryce was still engaged in reading Lou's poems. Bryce looked up and offered a plaintive smile.

"Yes, you can definitely count on that, as soon as I'm able, we'll do it. But I'm starting to feel a little weak. I think Rowena slipped me a sleeping pill. I'm needing to close my eyes."

"No problem," Rene said. "We're out of here. But we'll be back tomorrow."

Rowena came back to say goodbye and make sure Lou didn't need anything else. As David walked out the door, he turned and saw Rowena sitting on the edge of the bed, smiling and looking up at the ceiling like she could see the stars and the moon and whatever was beyond.

As they rode down the elevator together, David confirmed that he wanted to visit Frank and Rene as soon as he could make arrangements. Hopefully, with Lou. As the door opened on the ground floor, Frank said, "What are you guys doing tonight?"

"Nothing as far as I know," Bryce said. "I thought I might see my girlfriend."

"How about you, David?"

"I was going to see Melanie."

"Rene and I are going to a coffee house in Venice to hear some music. Maybe you and your sweeties would like to join us?"

"Where is it?"

"It's a place called the Lighthouse on Washington. Do you know it?"

"Of course. What do you think, Bryce?" David asked.

"I'll check with Shanti, and if we're there, we're there. See you guys."

They all disappeared into the night. David called Melanie and asked her about going to the Lighthouse. She thought it was a great idea.

It was nine thirty by the time Melanie and David pulled up to the coffee house. Melanie wore a new pair of jeans and a purple blouse. She had her hair pulled back, so her tiny sapphire earrings darted out at David in the faint dome light of the Galaxy.

"I'm excited to meet your friends."

"The way you look, I'm sure they'll be excited to meet you as well."

"Stop it."

They walked inside. It was a vacuous old storefront, built in the early '50s as a large corner grocery store with floor-to-ceiling windows wrapped around the south and west sides of the building. Frank and Rene greeted Melanie and David as they walked inside. They sat down just as Bryce and Shanti arrived.

"Listen, you guys are going to dig this band," Rene said. They're called The Ravens and the keyboard player, a guy named Ray Manzarek, is a friend of mine. They've got a new lead singer tonight, Jim Morrison. He's wild. He's a buddy of Ray's from the UCLA film school. Maybe you'll see him on campus. Wait till you hear him."

Four dark-clad guys stepped onto the makeshift stage; bass, lead guitar, drummer, and keyboard. That was it. The keyboard player leaned into the microphone and said, "Hey, check this out. My friend Jim wrote this song for you, we call it "Moonlight Drive."

The room lit up with golden swirling lights, and the tall, thin guy with heart-shaped lips started to wail. David looked at Bryce, Shanti, and Melanie, then at Rene and Frank, who just nodded and rolled with the thrum and grind of the beat. Morrison's haunting, careening voice lofted them all into space.

"That guy's incredible," Rene said as they ended the set. "This band isn't long for the Lighthouse. I'll tell you that."

"That's for sure! So when do you head back up north? I'd like to come up there again," David said.

"Probably Saturday, after we visit Lou again and work out some details about the book," Rene said. "Frank has a trail project on the Marin Headlands, and I've got a big reading set up for Sunday night."

"You should come up again. Bring Melanie along. I'm sure we'd keep her entertained," Frank said.

"Oh, I'm sure you would," Melanie laughed and looked at David. "I'd love to go up there. I haven't been there since I was kid."

"That sounds great," David said as he wrapped his arm around Melanie. "I'll give you a call after we talk."

David and Melanie said their goodbyes and walked into the night. On the way back to Melanie's house, David said, "I hope this works out. I'd love to take you up there."

"I'm sure I can get away, but I've got to check our practice schedule first. Let's talk tomorrow."

That sounded good to David. The thought of a trip up north with Melanie excited him, but something didn't feel exactly right. He wasn't sure what. Maybe Rita?

Friday morning Melanie called and confirmed that she'd be free the following weekend.

"I'll check with Rene and Frank and make it happen," David said. "I might see them tonight at the hospital. I'm going over there after work, if not I'll call them when they get back to San Francisco."

"I'm so happy," Melanie said.

"Me too," David said as he hung up.

When David arrived at the hospital that evening, Rene and Frank were already there, along with Molly and Chester. It was definitely a festive evening, and Molly had snuck in a challah that David's mother had given her for the Sabbath. The good news was that Lou was scheduled to be released the next day.

"This is absolutely great," Rene beamed. "We'll make a kiddush together to celebrate Lou's exodus from this dismal place and bless him and his complete recovery."

"Rene, I didn't know you were Jewish."

"Molly, I'm a student of all religions. When I studied Theology at the University of Chicago, I lived with four Jews and we had Sabbath dinner every Friday night. So let's transfer this juice into wine and make the prayer. Then we'll make a *Motzi* over the bread."

Rene took over the evening and told stories about his adventures in Chicago and how he once played tennis with Saul Bellow. "He used to call my serves long every time I aced him, until finally I said, 'Saul, you know those serves are well inside the service box, why do you keep calling them long?' Bellow said, 'I write fiction, young man. I see my own lines. Now serve the ball and stop complaining.'"

Before Rene and Frank left for the evening, David asked if the following weekend would work for a visit. They were overjoyed and said it was perfect. "Call me this week and we'll put it all together," Frank said.

Lou looked good, and as David left the hospital, he allowed himself to imagine them living together again. He fantasized walks along the beach, talking about Gandhi, Martin Luther King, and the Greeks. He recalled their trip to Mount Vision and wondered what it would be like going there with Melanie.

It was a quick drive back to Santa Monica. David listened to the game as he drove. Baseball felt like a universe beyond the scattered stars, a place where he drifted alone without any baggage or regret. He parked at Ocean Beach and watched the surf. The moon still had plenty of life and cast its shimmering presence over the calm sea.

CHAPTER TWENTY-THREE

Tuesday, July 20, 1965

A little miracle happened here tonight, folks. Koufax won his own game by singling home the winning run. He's been on a hitting streak lately, and tonight Alston made a bold decision by allowing him to bat for himself in the ninth, with two outs, no less. It was quite a game. The Astros took an early lead against Koufax when Frank Thomas doubled, and the catcher, Gus Triandos, smashed his first home run of the season into the left-field stands. Koufax settled down after that, and it became a pitchers' duel. The Astros' left-hander, Mike Cuellar, matched Koufax inning after inning. Cuellar was spotting his fastball and curve with dazzling accuracy, keeping the Dodger hitters off balance. In the bottom of the seventh, the Dodgers finally broke through and tied the game at two to two when Jim Lefebvre singled home Lou Johnson.

It's the Dodgers' sixth straight win and gives them an almost 3.5-game lead over the rest of the pack. The win tonight gives Koufax a seventeen-three record. That's just unbelievable. At this pace he could become the first pitcher to win thirty games since Dizzy Dean. Wouldn't that be something?

Saturday morning David called Melanie and told her their visit to San Francisco was set. The details needed to be worked out, but that wouldn't be a problem. He told her about Lou's recovery and explained that he and Lou had made plans for Sunday. He was excited about the prospects. She encouraged him to have fun with Lou, and anyway, she was busy the next couple days with volleyball tournaments.

The next morning traffic was light, and David had a heavy foot. The Galaxy grooved through the open lanes and by nine o'clock, he was knocking on Lou's door.

Molly greeted him with a hug. Chester waved from his easy chair, the Sunday *Times* resting on his lap. The dining room table was littered with crusts of toast and plates still stained with egg yolks. Lou sat at the table, finishing a cup of coffee.

"Can I get you some breakfast? At least some coffee?" Molly asked.

"Coffee would be great."

David sat down across from Lou, who had a beatific smile. His high school baseball hat with the EV embossed on the front covered his shaved head. The hat looked a little big, but it held important memories. Molly came out of the kitchen and put the coffee in front of David.

"I really don't know if this is such a good idea." She frowned and looked at Lou.

"Mom, we've talked about this and checked with the doctor. He said it was fine to go out. In fact, he thought it would be good for me as long as I take easy."

"I know. I know. I just don't want you to overdo it."

"We're just going for a drive. That's it," Lou said. "Finish your coffee, Mandel, and let's go."

David swallowed the last of his caffeine and pushed back from the table.

"Nothing to worry about, Molly. We'll be careful," David said. He patted her on the shoulder and followed Lou out the door.

Lou got into the car and pumped his fist in the air. David started the engine and turned on the radio. Lou turned the volume to maximum as David put down the windows.

"You brought everything?" Lou asked.

"Everything. Just as you ordered."

The first stop was the old ball field. It had been two months since either of them was there. They parked in the lot and sat for a moment. David wasn't sure what Lou wanted, but he had brought his glove and borrowed one from Bryce. He had also thrown a couple of baseballs in his canvas sports bag.

"Now what?" David asked.

"Now we play ball. You remember how to do that?"

"Sure. But I still don't understand."

Lou got out of the car. David grabbed the gear and walked beside him. Lou walked slowly but with great deliberation, as if he were approaching a podium to deliver an important speech. The field had been cut recently. David smelled the scent of competition lingering around the diamond. Without thinking, he put his arm around Lou's shoulder and pulled him close for a second.

When they got to the field, Lou stopped at home plate. The morning sun had not started baking the day. A cool breeze blew mercifully down from the mountains. Perfect weather for baseball. David dropped the bag and looked at Lou.

"Where's the rest of the team?" David laughed.

"It's just you and me. I'll pitch and you'll catch."

Lou took the glove and two balls from the bag and wobbled to the mound. He looked a little weak, but there was determination in his stride. David put on his glove and waited for Lou to ascend the hill. Lou tossed one ball down to the right and clapped the other ball against the center of his glove. It was like a dance about to begin. The music came from the wind and the distant sound of cars speeding back and forth, going nowhere. Lou stared down at David, feigning that he was getting a sign from his catcher.

"So you want me to call balls and strikes?" David asked.

"Of course not. They are all strikes at this point," Lou said. "I just don't know how many I have left."

"Too many to count," David said.

Lou went into his windup. It was in slow motion; he looked like old man moving through a clouded memory. The ball sailed in a high arc, a rainbow, and settled into David's glove as if landing on a soft pillow.

"Way to fire. You are breaking the sound barrier," David said.

"Yeah, and that was just my slow curve," Lou replied.

They tossed the ball back and forth for another twenty minutes. Each pitch filled with a commentary communicating a shared affection, a history, and a kind of mutual absolution that did not need words. They played catch.

"I think that's enough. I'm probably wearing out your hand with my velocity," Lou said.

"Hey, I think I've had enough too. You've still got it, professor."

"Sure I do. I just need a little rehab upstairs and I'll be fine."

Lou looked exhausted as they threw the gloves and balls back in the bag. David pointed to the dugout where they had spent so many hours dallying between innings; planning strategies, catcalling opposing players, and on occasion, slandering umpires. They walked over and sat down on the bench. David pulled out a bottle of water and passed it to Lou.

"Better drink, big guy, you worked pretty hard out there."

"Right. I'm not sure how many more games I've got left. I know the doctors are optimistic, but I've got a bad feeling."

"Shit. You better recover. I'm not going to be able to pay the rent without you."

"That will be the least of your worries, Mandel," Lou laughed.

"Yeah. I don't want to think about it. You are going to be fine. So you still up for the other part of this adventure?"

"Absolutely. It's already starting to get hot. Let's head up there."

David drove straight east through the foothills and into the forest. As they climbed the steep roads, the air cooled and the shade of the thick conifers reminded David of the last time he and Lou had driven this road with Rita. A lot had changed in two months. Now it was just the two of them.

David pulled off at a spot where they had fished many times. There was an easy path to the creek, although it was not marked, and hence, didn't get a lot of use. The first fifteen feet, they had to push through scrub oak and manzanita bushes, but then it opened to an easy animal trail down to the water. David moved carefully and made sure Lou had good footing. From there they skirted around a couple of large boulders to a wide pool, completely surrounded by trees so the water rarely saw the sun. A perfect trout habitat.

"You only wanted me to bring one pole?" David asked.

"That's because you are going to fish and I'm going to watch."

"Because?"

"Oh fuck, Mandel. I'm spent. It was all I could do to just lob those balls to you. I can't get my brain to work fast enough to hook and land a trout. You just catch us some fish and I'll critique your technique."

Before he set up his line, David handed Lou a sandwich from his pack and grabbed one for himself. They sat at the shore and watched a couple of trout rise for flies near the opposite bank. Lou talked about his book and how excited he was. It was almost like old times, except when David looked at Lou, he saw someone he didn't quite recognize.

David threaded the monofilament through the eye hooks and reached down for his container of lures.

"Use the white-and-red super-duper I gave you last year," Lou said.

"I thought I'd use that silver spoon. It usually works here."

"Hey, dead man's choice. Just do it."

"That isn't funny."

"Super-duper. Use it."

David pulled out the lure Lou had given him and tied it to his line with a Rapala knot. He cast it toward the back part of the water where they had seen the fish rising earlier. He clicked down the reel and let the super-duper sink for a couple seconds, and then slowly started to reel it back. It didn't take long before the rod bent down hard, and as it did, David instinctively lifted up and set the hook. The fish cleared the water immediately, splashed down, and sped away. David tightened the drag slightly, but the fish kept running. As he reeled in, the line hummed as the fish struggled for freedom. David spun the reel faster, and the fish flashed close to where he stood.

"Bring him a little closer and I'll net him," Lou said.

David turned the reel a few more revolutions, and the twelve-incher was in the net.

"Nice fish," Lou said. "Two more and we'll call it a day."

In the next hour, David had several more strikes. He hooked two smaller fish and released them, and kept one more twelve-incher and a fat fourteen-inch beauty. Lou gleefully assisted with the netting. The day complete, David wet his creel and placed the fish inside. He pulled up a handful of tall grass from along the shore and placed it inside to help preserve the coolness.

"Guess you were right about the lure," David said as he started the car.

"I'm seeing some things pretty clearly right now," Lou said. "Good fishing." When they arrived at the Ash house Lou got out carrying the three trout. He turned and gave David a thumbs-up.

Once home David made dinner then decided to write. He had purchased an old Olympia typewriter from a pawn shop on Lincoln Ave. The keys were well-oiled, and it had a nice touch as he plied words onto the paper. Perhaps it had belonged to a local poet, someone like Lou, but older and more seasoned. He had started a story last week and thought he might work on it again. Maybe he was onto something. His mind was churning from the day's events. He opened all the windows, hoping to cool the apartment, except the breeze off the ocean never materialized. Instead, a hot wind gushed through the streets and rustled the curtains. He called Melanie and they talked for awhile. She said everything was arranged on her end. They agreed to talk again in the morning and confirm the details.

He didn't notice Rita's Chevy pull up beside the curb. He was startled when someone started hammering at the door. He flung it open. Rita Kano was standing in front of him, her smile split between excitement and embarrassment, her eyes lightly brushed with mascara, her lips frosted with a cherry tint. She looked good, very good, wearing cut-off shorts that ended at the middle of her tawny colored thighs and a simple ruffled white blouse. The first two buttons were open. She smelled like lavender and salt air.

"Well, are you going to ask me inside or just let me stand here till the moths start eating my hair?" Rita asked.

David stepped away from the door, and with a flourish of his hand, welcomed her inside, still wondering what she wanted and feeling apprehensive.

"You okay with me being here? You aren't worried about your girlfriend finding out?" she asked.

"I'm happy to see you," David said, ignoring the remark about his girlfriend. He was happy, but he was worried as well.

Rita looked around while he turned off the radio and picked up the dish and glass from the floor in the living room. He looked at her and tried to make sense of the feelings that sped through his body as she glared at him. But David noticed there was a hint of compassion in her eyes that betrayed the seriousness of her taut lips.

"I don't know where to start," she said.

"Would you like a beer? Or I have some pot if you want," he said.

"May I sit down?"

"Yeah, of course." He offered her a place on the couch and asked again, "Can I get you anything?"

"I want to talk with you," she said.

"That's fine. Let's talk," he replied.

First, I have to confess that I've been planning this for some time. I've known about your new friend almost since the beginning," she continued.

"Just as I've known about your friend. What's his name? Bobby. Bryce told me," David said.

"David, you don't need to get defensive. I'm just stating the obvious, and besides, my thing with Bobby isn't what you think," Rita pushed back.

"How do you know what I think? You can do whatever want. It's none of my business. I really don't care." He didn't like where this was going.

"Don't care? Then why even bother to talk with me now?" Rita countered.

The wind picked up outside and blew over an unlit candleholder sitting alone on the sill. David walked over and picked it up, then turned back to Rita.

"Why did you drive out here?" he asked.

"I'm not sure. I just know that the way I ended it was impulsive and hurtful and we never said goodbye, or said whatever it was we really needed to say. I didn't say anything to you about forgiveness," Rita said.

"Forgiveness? I would have thought that was something I was supposed to ask for."

"Well, maybe we each have amends to make? I don't know. It's not something I have much experience with."

David looked into her eyes. Was she feeling the same desire he was sensing?

"Do you want to walk along the beach? It might be a little cooler than sitting here."

"If that's what you want, as long as we can talk," Rita answered.

"Let me get something first."

He walked into the kitchen, opened the freezer and took out a small bundle wrapped in aluminum foil. Inside was a plastic bag with a couple of joints. David took one and held it up in Rita's direction. She nodded in agreement. He grabbed a book of matches. They headed out the door. As they crossed Ocean Avenue, the night air draped them in a warm mist. Without thinking, he found her hand as they walked onto the sand. Her skin felt familiar and strange at the same time. In bare feet, they darted toward the sea. He was raw and awake, and for a moment, his thoughts turned to Melanie and their still unresolved status. He wondered how the night would unfold.

Rita snuggled close as the sound of breakers amplified.

"What have you heard from Lou?" Rita asked.

"I saw him today. He's home, but they still don't know if they got all the cancer."

"It's awful," she said.

"Yeah. I'm worried," David said as Rita squeezed his arm.

David stopped, cupped his hands and lit the joint. They passed it back and forth, leaving a mini contrail of smoke above the distant surf. After walking to the pier, they turned back. When they got to where they had started, David stopped and kissed her. It was like falling off a cliff; floating, flailing, screaming as their tongues darted back and forth.

"So now what?" David said, coming up for air and releasing her. He stepped back and threw up his hands.

"Now we forgive each other and I get in the car and drive away. Almost like the movies, but it's real. It is over. You release me and I set you free, no looking back, no regrets," Rita said.

"Just like that, a few sentences and all those years just wash away?" David asked.

"They don't wash away, David. How can they? It's like allowing the sea to simply do what it does; it covers the rocks, it shapes them, and then when the tide goes out it exposes them. We're just another part of the landscape that runs up and down the coast. Our time together was just that. It will always be there, and as long as you don't pour acid on it, we'll always have it to share. That's why I came," she answered.

"I still don't understand why you need to make amends. Forgive you for being yourself? I'm the one who needs to be begging for your forgiveness, don't you think?"

"That's not anything I can control, David. It's not as if I didn't see any of this coming. I chose not to see what was obvious. Why would you want to rescue me and jeopardize your own future?"

"What are you talking about? Rescue? Jeopardize? If anything, I was just too scared to keep going. That's the truth."

"That's your stuff, David. I just want to leave with a clear conscience."

David reached for her and brought her close. "I don't think you ever did anything that warrants me needing to forgive you."

Rita stepped back from him. "David, I'm sorry for having believed that there was more than there really was between us. I'm sorry for having used Lou to provoke you. I'm sorry for being so righteous about my faith that I actually believed it would make a difference."

David shook his head and tried to embrace her again, but she put her arm out.

"Say it, David, please just say *I forgive you*! Goddamn it, say it. That's all you need to do. Is that too much for you?" she pleaded as they faced each other on the empty stretch of beach.

Whether the wind really shifted or the chill he felt was from the hand of fear, he could not discern. He stood there transfixed, incredulous, and astounded that Rita had come out tonight. This premeditated encounter wasn't about one final fling. He remembered that last night at her cousin's house. Then he looked at Rita and saw tears streaming down her cheeks. He gently touched her shoulders.

"Yes, I forgive you. I love you," he said finally.

"I love you too," she said, then turned away.

David watched as she dashed off, leaving puffs of sand in the moonlit air, each step offering a cloud of amends for nothing more than unpretentious passion. He thought about rushing after her in dramatic Cary Grant fashion, instead he walked to the edge of the shore. He continued south until he knew Rita was well on her way back to the Valley, back to Bobby, back to her expiation, back to whatever quest awaited her on the other side of the mountain. He finished the joint while he sat on the sand and listened to the sound of the water spilling over itself, again and again. It was almost enough to pacify his distress. Rita had torn him up pretty good.

Back at his apartment, he lit two candles and put on his *Joan Baez/5* album. Before he fell asleep, he pictured Lou and the last game they had played together. They had been tense and distant, and yet what he recalled about that day was how the ball snapped out of their hands like it was on fire. They were both on top of their game. The grass was thick. The sky was clear, and all their pitches were strikes.

He flipped on the radio. The Dodgers announcer was recapping the game. Koufax had won his seventeenth game of the season. David closed his eyes and imagined Koufax pitching in the World Series.

CHAPTER TWENTY-FOUR

Saturday, July 24, 1965

For those of you just tuning in, here's what happened. In the top of the tenth, the game was still tied two to two. Koufax had pitched a gem, but the Dodgers couldn't get that go-ahead run, so they went into extra innings. Koufax limited the Cardinals to just four hits and struck out eight batters. Of all things, Koufax gave up a home run to the most unlikely of hitters, Bob Uecker, the reserve catcher. A notorious non-hitter, "Uke" took Sandy deep in the fifth inning to put the Cardinals on the board.

Perranoski took over in the tenth and did his best to hold the Red Birds, but after Lou Brock singled, Willie Davis muffed a routine fly ball and Brock scooted home. The Dodgers couldn't get anything across in the bottom of the tenth, so our final tonight is Cardinals three, Dodgers two. It was a tough defeat. The only good news for Koufax is that he won't be pinned for the loss. What a crazy night. The Dodgers outhit the Cardinals ten to five, and then there was that home run by Bob Uecker.

David watched the news after work. It was Wednesday night and White House Press Secretary Bill Moyers, who was commenting on the accusation that President Johnson had already decided to drastically increase troop levels in Vietnam, said, "Such speculation is irresponsible, reckless, and grossly untrue." *Everyone knows what is about to happen*, David said to himself. *This is such bullshit.* CJ had been saying it in his letters, and the news anchors made no secret of the fact that the war was expanding, and expanding rapidly. David gazed at part of CJ's most recent letter during the commercial: "They're beating our butts over there and the Army is screaming to let us start kicking some ass. I'm not sure how long before we complete this last stage, but I can't wait. I'm itching to go. We all are."

After the news he phoned Melanie. They were set. He would pick her up after work tomorrow, then drive straight through to San Francisco.

David packed food for the trip. He told Melanie he'd take off early from work, and asked her to be ready around three o'clock. He was excited and anxious as he put the groceries in the fridge. It had been over a week since they'd seen each other except for a brief night of stress-relieving sex. Both of them had been busy.

When he arrived, Melanie bounded off the stoop with her soft travel bag embellished with little maps of the world. First thing, she scooted beside him and posted a big kiss, leaving a residue of velvety lipstick on his cheek. Aside from the exquisite visuals, Melanie had an uncanny genius for fragrance, the car immediately smelled as if it was saturated with some kind of fresh citrus, and it was all he could do to keep from nibbling her as they sped toward San Francisco. The ocean to the west, the costal range to the east, the radio blasted the Righteous Brothers, Sonny and Cher, and The Drifters.

After they filled up with gas and got coffee at a small roadside diner, the rest of the journey clicked along. David told Melanie he had taken Rene's advice and started writing as much as he could. He had filled a few notebooks with his commentaries, his inner fears, and his dreams. Occasionally, he tried a poem, and there was a short story. It involved a character like Rene who lived in a cave in northern New Mexico. It came to him in a dream when Lou first got diagnosed. The protagonist, Henry Laughing Horse, was half Cherokee and half Irish, and had been living in an abandoned cliff dwelling for seven years, farming and raising goats. Henry is a healer. In the story, a young woman named Naomi brings her nine-year-old son to Henry to cure him of an unknown disease. She has taken her son to every doctor in the Southwest, and no one has been able to heal him of morning blindness. He can't see anything until sunset, when his sight returns and then disappears again in the morning. David hadn't resolved the story and hoped to talk about it with Rene over the weekend.

When they entered the city, a dense fog rolled across the bay like a long-haired cat stalking its prey. The street lamps on Mission Street were fluttering, creating a muted damp light that poured onto the sidewalks. David parked outside the Garden of Light Café. He pulled their bags out of the trunk. Melanie jumped out of her seat, grabbed his hand, and kissed him.

"This is so unbelievable. I haven't been to San Francisco since I was a little girl. It is so, so magical!"

David silently shook his head and smiled. They walked up to the entrance. A few people sat around tables, talking, laughing, drinking tea and coffee. When David opened the door, Tibetan bells rang, and the patrons looked up at he and Melanie briefly, then continued their chatter. Rene quickly emerged from the kitchen and rushed toward them with open arms.

"Oh, I'm so glad you're here. Welcome, welcome." He hugged them both and ran his large ruddy hand through Melanie's hair. "So beautiful, even after the long drive, yes, come inside and sit down for a moment. I just baked some raspberry muffins. You must try them."

Neither of them was hungry, but they couldn't refuse Rene's enthusiasm, and the warm baked dough smelled sweet and enticing.

"Yes, sure, that would be fantastic," Melanie said.

In a flash Rene returned with the warm muffins and a mound of whipped sweet butter.

"Tea or coffee, what's your pleasure?"

"Tea," they both blurted.

"Yes, tea it is, if you don't mind I'll get you a pot of my favorite, Mu Tea. I think you'll love it."

"He's really a darling, isn't he? I'm so happy to be up here with you."

"Me too," David said, but he still wasn't sure about Melanie. Part of him wished he'd come with Lou, or even alone.

Rene returned with a steaming pot of tea in a large, delicately etched container with royal blue engravings of dragons spiraling out of the ground and an old Buddha figure laughing with his arms stretched toward the sky.

"There, now we're all set. How is Lou doing?" Rene inquired.

"Better, much better, he's home now and resting. He's starting to get some energy back," David said.

"Fantastic, his book will be ready next week—only fifty copies We wanted more, but figured we'd wait till we sell them all. We wanted to get it printed as quickly as possible, so the quality isn't as professional as we would have liked. Frank and I will take them down on our next visit. So what are your plans?"

"Frank has a place for us at Stinson Beach, and I want to take Melanie up to Mount Vision and do some hiking around Point Reyes."

"Sounds perfect. Your room here is ready anytime you like. How's your writing coming along?"

Before David could say anything, Melanie dashed into the conversation.

"He's writing a lot and has a short story going right now."

"Oh, really? That's great. Just keep it going, David."

"Well, I don't really know what I'm doing, but that's true about a lot of things right now. I had this dream and I turned it into a story about a boy and a healer. The kid has this disease that blinds him every morning, but when the sun sets, he's able to see again. The mother takes him to a healer."

He didn't want to tell Rene that the healer in the dream was based on him. He didn't know how to broach his need for help, yet he didn't know how to reconcile the story. So he went ahead and explained.

"In the dream the boy goes into a cave, and then I woke up. I don't know yet if he recovers or not. I'm not sure what is going to happen next."

"Sounds like a perfect place for Tiresias to appear," Rene laughed.

David had no idea who Rene was talking about, but he noticed Melanie smiling and nodding. He shuddered in embarrassment at his literary ineptitude.

"Tiresias?" David asked.

"Tiresias, the blind soothsayer of Thebes. Yes, maybe employ him somehow. You would be in good company. Homer, Sophocles, and even T. S. Eliot used him. Do a little research and see what evolves? Have fun with it, that's my only advice. Your story sounds like it has real potential."

"Thanks for the idea." He knew Rene would come up with something outrageous. They talked for another hour before Rene handed them the key for the guest cottage behind the café and took his leave. Sleep came surprisingly easy.

In the morning they said goodbye to Rene and started out of the city. At Van Ness David turned left. Then another left on Lombard Street, and finally to the Golden Gate Bridge.

David turned off at the exit to Stinson Beach that took them around the outskirts of Mill Valley to the junction of Highway 1, via Muir Woods and Muir Beach. This was the same route he and Lou had traveled only a month earlier. So much had changed in that brief time. He wanted to share the same trails and vistas with Melanie. For a moment he wished that Lou was the one sitting next to him. They passed the turnoff to Muir Woods where the ancient redwoods loomed over the dank valley floor like creatures from another planet. The road twisted around like a series of concentric pretzels. Long flat slabs of aquamarine swells roiled westward in what looked like endless watery universe.

It took most of an hour to travel fifteen miles. They were both drowsy by the time they arrived at the little market where Frank worked. David stumbled out of the car, stretched, and grabbed Melanie around the waist.

"Well, what do you think?"

"It's gorgeous, it's perfect."

The town consisted of a single street with a few restaurants, a flower shop, two book stores, and several trendy gift stores that sold local pottery, water colors, sculpture, and various assortments of shell, silver, and gold jewelry, as well as an endless variety of weavings, gift cards, and beach sundries. Straight across the street a three-mile strip of pristine beach beckoned. Before David could walk up the four railroad-tie steps to the market, Frank was down the stairs, greeting them.

"You made great time. Rene called me a couple hours ago and told me you'd be coming soon. Come, I'll show you the cottage. Just pull down that first street and drive to the end and park."

Frank jumped in the backseat and directed them to the little house. The place was idyllic, smack on the water. It was a faded-gray cedar-shingled bungalow with a gabled roof and a widow's deck outside the bedroom. A rickety picket fence defined the property. The tiny yard was profuse with poppies, begonias, nasturtiums, hibiscus, bougainvillea, and roses. Everything about it exuded comfort. Frank escorted them upstairs, where an oversized four-poster bed took up most of the little bedroom.

"Frank, this is just fantastic, thanks so much," Melanie said.

"Not a problem, I just hope Lou can get back up here soon. I think this place will speed his recovery."

David quickly agreed. "I'll drive him up here as soon as I can."

"Melanie, is there anything you need?" Frank asked.

David noticed that his hand lingered on her shoulder as he talked with her.

"No, I've got my bathing suit and my hiking boots. I'm all set. Although, I'd like to get a few things for the fridge."

"Of course. Just come over to the store once you unpack, we've got pretty much everything you could possibly need and then some. Tomorrow I want to take you somewhere special. It's a place I wanted to take you and Lou last month, David, but it didn't happen. Will that work for you? Say around nine o'clock? All you'll need is water. I'll take care of the rest."

"Sounds great," Melanie said. David nodded in agreement.

"Where should we meet?" David asked.

"I'll just knock on the door," Frank said.

Melanie and David put on their bathing suits and were on the beach ten minutes later, watching spinner dolphins cruise up and down, parallel to the shore. The water was frigid. Neither Melanie nor David wanted to swim out very far, since David had read that a surfer had his arm chewed off by a white shark just the week before. It wasn't that uncommon at Stinson Beach. Tomales Bay, just north of the beach, was a breeding ground for great whites.

By four o'clock they were hot, hungry, and tired. They walked back to the cottage and jumped in the shower. After lathering each other with the rose-scented soap, they made love. Stepping out of the shower, David wiped Melanie's back and thighs with the thick white towel, and embraced her in front of the full-length mirror. He could see his own arms wrap around her lower spine. She turned around. Tears were in her eyes. The doors and windows were open, so they could hear waves crashing outside.

"What's happening?" he whispered.

"Remember yesterday, when I said I wanted to tell you something and you asked if it could wait?" she said softly.

David nodded, recalling the moment on the road just before stopping for coffee.

"I can't wait any longer. David, I think I'm falling in love with you."

For a long set of seconds, he looked at her. Then he spoke. "I think I'm falling in love too." But he wasn't sure. He felt it was too soon, and yet here they were.

In the morning, Frank knocked on the door with a bagful of fresh pastries and a basket of strawberries. Melanie made a pot of coffee, and they sat around the breakfast table wolfing down the warm sweets and talking about shorebirds, seals, and sharks. Frank knew all the intricate details of wildlife around the bay.

After breakfast they piled into Frank's old station wagon and went north along the coastal highway. The herons and egrets were still feeding in the salt marshes that bordered Bolinas Lagoon. A couple of times David noticed that Frank's hand *slipped* onto Melanie's knee when he turned around sharp corners.

Frank drove beyond a long stretch of dark verdant land full of dairy farms. Then he turned off on a gravel road that arced back toward the coast and finally parked in an open space bordered by a manzanita thicket. A faint sign pointed toward a trail. Frank grabbed his old rucksack that looked stuffed with enough provisions for a couple of days in the wilderness.

"You'll love this trail. It follows the ocean for fifteen miles and ends up near Drakes Bay. I saw a set of mountain lion tracks last week that led me to a fresh kill. It was kind of unnerving, but I figure she had a full belly and probably sized me up as being too old and leathery to make a good meal anyway."

"Lou and I saw plenty of tracks when we were hiking around Mt. Vision," David said.

Melanie scowled. "Are you both trying to frighten me?"

"I'm just kidding with you. Not about the mountain lion, but the meal. We're perfectly safe," Frank laughed.

"You are sure about that? I'm happy staying back here." she said.

"Melanie, it will be fine," David assured her. "That big cat doesn't want anything to do with us. We ran into a park ranger who told Lou and me there are so many deer around here that a lion has a plateful all the time. She's not the least bit interested in us."

"Well, that makes me feel a little better," she said rather sarcastically. "Still, a lion is a lion."

David worried that anymore lion talk was going to end the hike for Melanie, so he changed the subject.

"Too bad Lou couldn't join us. I really hope he's getting better." David flashed back to the hike last month up Mt. Vision.

"Lou's fate is like everything else: wild and indiscriminate," Frank opined.

"That's a weird thing to say, Frank." Melanie stopped in the middle of the trail and looked at him.

"Nothing weird about it, Melanie. Look around. You didn't even see that snake right there." He pointed to the grey-and-brown tail of a small bull snake as it disappeared into a bramble of blackberry bushes. "By next year that thing will be able to consume a full-grown gopher and will push all the rattlesnakes around here out of its territory. If it makes it through this winter, it'll mate and pass on its progeny; if not, it becomes lunch for one of the hawks, or maybe it gets snagged by that lion I tracked."

Oh God, David thought. *Here he goes about the lion again.*

Frank continued, "You spend enough time out here, and you'll understand we aren't much different than that snake, wild and indiscriminate. The only significant distinction is art, and that's were Lou already made his mark. He wrote a good bit about the way things really are, as opposed to how they seem." Frank paused and reached into his pack. He looked at Melanie. "Do you want an apple?"

"Does it come with knowledge?" Melanie laughed.

"Nope, just hopefully without worms. How about you, David?" Frank extended the fruit toward David.

David took the apple and bit down hard and chewed for awhile. "Well, I still wish Lou could be up here with us. It doesn't seem right."

Melanie was smiling and taking little bites of her apple. She seemed charmed by the older guy. They walked along the old fire road for another half hour, then Frank stopped and said in his gravelly, deep voice, "Now we have a choice."

"Oh good, I like choices," Melanie bounced.

"Well, that's good," Frank said and stared out across the vast Pacific. "Here's the choice. We can continue strolling along the ocean trail or we can turn up here."

He slowly pivoted on the heels of his white high-top tennis shoes and pointed toward the dense wooded hillside. "This is where I followed the big cat's tracks the other day. It's not a real trail, but the elk, deer, and crazies like me have tramped it down enough, so it's easy to follow, and there is a little spring surrounded by a grove of redwoods just below the ridge."

"Walking along the ocean suits me just fine," David said. He figured he'd give Melanie an out, just in case she didn't want to venture off the main path.

"Come on, David, let's take a risk. You're not scared are you?" she teased.

"A little, but I know you'll protect me," David retorted. He hoped it was the right call. It was a long way from Beverly Hills.

"Okay, up we go," Frank said, and led the way.

The cool ocean draft disappeared quickly, and David stripped down to a T-shirt. Melanie pared down to a tank top. Frank didn't change anything. After thirty minutes of silent trudging, David smelled something rotting. Frank stopped and signaled with his finger over his lips. A flotilla of turkey vultures was cruising above them. They proceeded as if tiptoeing into a room with a sleeping infant. A deer carcass rested close to a small clearing beneath a tumble of rocks where a spring percolated out of the ground. Very little flesh remained on the bones. The shell of the rib cage bulged up from the ground, only one front leg was still attached to the skeleton.

"Pretty much finished it up yesterday," Frank whispered. "Nothing left for dessert."

Melanie looked at David in horror. He caressed her briefly. "It will be okay. Trust me," he said softly in her ear.

Frank walked to the spring and they followed. The sun was directly overhead. He climbed over the rocks above the water and called them over to a large flat serpentine ledge that rested above the clearing. Melanie and David sat down beside him. They could see the ocean in the distance, as well as a few ships steaming toward the Golden Gate. The westerly breeze blew away the scent of death.

"Are you hungry?" Frank took off his rucksack and pulled out a shopping bag heavy with food.

"Starved, what you got besides apples?" Melanie laughed.

"A real San Francisco lunch." Frank distributed turkey sandwiches on sourdough bread, drenched with mustard, tomato, and mayo.

Before they started eating, Frank twisted around and looked up to his right. He froze and gently returned his sandwich to the bag. He stood up, and as he did, he signaled for Melanie and David to do the same.

"What are you doing, Frank?" Melanie whispered.

"Look!" Frank pointed to a spot up the ridge. They saw the lion flash through the brush. In its brief appearance, David saw the muscular thickness of the animal. Its head was huge. It dashed away with an elegant leap over a large rock. They remained frozen until Frank finally sat down.

"Do you think it'll come back?" Melanie asked as she peeked around, making sure nothing was behind her. Frank got up. He walked around David and put his arm around Melanie. David stared at Frank, who was now holding his girlfriend.

"It's gone. She's done with this spot for now. She'll probably be cruising north and check the elk herd at Tomales Point. They cover a lot of ground very quickly," Frank said. He moved back to where he had been sitting.

They finished lunch and started down the trail. David tried to imagine what he might say to Melanie's mother if she told her about the mountain lion. After a few minutes, Melanie stopped to drink some water. Frank continued ahead. David watched the older man easily navigate the steep, rocky trail. He liked Frank but didn't trust him.

"Are you all right, Mel?" David asked, noticing a slight tremble in her hands as she put her water bottle back in her pack.

"Yes, I'm fine. I'm just a little shaky, and I do need to pee, but not here."

As he descended the trail, David imagined CJ and Wiz sharpening their wilderness skills as they trained behind scopes looking through crosshairs, not at lions or deer but at men who waited to die, across a sea that separated peace and war.

They caught up with Frank just as they reached the car.

"So, how did you know that we'd actually see the lion?" she asked him.

"I didn't. Some things are just meant to be," he said, with a wizardly grin.

David wasn't sure what he meant, but Melanie had a big smile on her face.

On Sunday David and Melanie got up early and walked the length of the beach where Bolinas Lagoon drained into the ocean. By the time they walked back to the diner for breakfast, they were both famished. David's thoughts turned to Koufax. He hadn't heard or thought about baseball since they left L.A. He bought a *San Francisco Chronicle* at the register and peeled it back to the green sports page. The headline heralded the Giants' four-to-two victory over the Braves, moving them to within two and a half games of the Dodgers, who had lost. He sat down across from Melanie and put the paper aside while he scanned the menu, all the while wondering about Koufax. Melanie ordered bacon and eggs, and David decided on buckwheat pancakes with fresh strawberries.

"What's up?" Melanie asked, seeing David was preoccupied.

"The Dodgers lost and the Giants won." David felt a surge of apprehension as he looked at Melanie.

"And?"

"And I think I'm very lucky to be with someone as beautiful as you," David answered.

"That's the right answer." She smiled.

"There is one thing that's bothering me." He paused.

"Yes?"

"You and Frank. Seems like every chance he gets, he puts his hands on you."

"It's nothing. Just something older guys do. Like dads and daughters."

"I don't like it," David said.

"Believe me, handsome, you've got nothing to worry about." She squeezed his hand.

David wasn't so sure. He picked up the sports section and thought of Koufax.

CHAPTER TWENTY-FIVE

Wednesday, July 28, 1965

As usual, the crowds came out to see Koufax. Over 53,000 tonight, all of them expecting to see him win his twelfth straight game. But it wasn't in the stars tonight. The Dodgers lost four to one. The Reds hitters got off a couple of early shots against our left-hander. In the top of the third, Leo Cardenas led off with a home run. With two outs, Koufax walked Tommy Harper. The speedy center fielder promptly stole second base. Pete Rose followed with a loopy single that scored Harper, and suddenly the Dodgers were down by two. Not to make excuses, but Koufax was having trouble warming up from the first inning onward. He kept going into the training room between innings to have his arm massaged. Cincinnati scored two more in the top of the fourth, and that was enough to seal the game. The Reds pitcher, Sammy Ellis, went the distance, surrendering just a single run in the bottom of the fifth. Koufax was lifted for a pinch hitter in the bottom of the eighth. He lost his fourth game of the season. And that's the story from Dodger Stadium tonight. Reds four, Dodgers one.

After finishing breakfast, David and Melanie drove back. Sunday traffic was heavy on the interstate, and David wanted to take his time. He wanted to bring up his discomfort with Frank again but didn't know what else to say. *Nothing to worry about,* she said. David dropped Melanie at home a little before 10:00 p.m. When he got home he was too tired to sleep. He rolled a joint, took a few tokes, and then opened his journal and started to write about the weekend. Things were moving quickly now. He recalled all that had happened. He wondered if Lou would ever recover enough to move in with him.

He got a call from Melanie late Wednesday afternoon. She didn't have time to be with him that night. She had started to train with a group from the USC team. It was voluntary and informal, according to NCAA rules, but her training still required a lot of time and dedication. She told David that if she had any chance of making the team, she would have to push herself with the same tenacity that earned her a scholarship.

Fuck it, he thought. *I'm going to the ballgame.* Koufax was pitching. He went to the refrigerator and took out a slab of cheese. He couldn't think of anyone who would join him on such short notice. Bryce was at practice. He cut off a hunk of the Swiss and chomped it down. Maybe Grace would want to go. She and David had become friendly over the past few weeks.

It was four thirty when David knocked on her door. Grace was wearing her pink-and-purple-flowered kimono, which she filled so that the material stretched to the limits. In her right hand she held a long dark cigarette. Her hair was wet. David could smell the shampoo.

"Hello, Mr. David. What's up?"

"Hey, Grace. You want to go to the Dodgers game tonight? Koufax is pitching, and I'd like some company. What do you say?"

Grace paused for a moment and then smiled. "Your treat, right?"

"My treat, including the snacks."

"Okay. That sounds terrific. I love the Dodgers."

David emphatically pumped his hand in the air. "All right. How long will it take you to be ready?"

"Give me twenty minutes to make myself beautiful," she laughed.

David ran back to the apartment and quickly gathered his jacket and checked his wallet. He had plenty of cash and didn't care how much it cost. He was about to walk out when he noticed his baseball glove on the chair next to the closet. Quickly, he scooped it up and put it in his pack. He ran to the car even though he knew Grace wasn't ready.

Grace squeezed into the front seat with a large plastic bag. David started the Galaxy and made for the Santa Monica Freeway. He figured the drive would take an hour, allowing for traffic, but that would still get them there by six thirty. It gave them plenty of time to park and get tickets. David nodded toward the plastic bag resting on the floor beside Grace.

"Extra sweaters. It's supposed to be cold. Didn't you check the weather?"

"Who cares?" David said. "Koufax is pitching, that's all that matters to me."

"You've got a thing for Koufax," Grace said as she lowered the window.

"There is something exceptional about him," David said.

"Just cause he's Jewish?" Grace laughed. "No offense. I like him too. He's cute. Like you."

David wished Lou was sitting next to him. He wanted to tell Grace about Koufax and the intricacies of baseball, especially pitching, but thought she wouldn't be interested.

Traffic started to slow down once they passed the interchange for the 101 freeway. David sighed and loosened his grip on the wheel. They'd get there in plenty of time. He remembered seeing Koufax pitch last year against the Giants. He struck out Willie Mays on two fastballs and then a slow curve. He turned to Grace.

"Pitching is art form, and Koufax is like a great painter, like Picasso."

"Hey, that's pretty brainy, David. You want some chips?" Grace tore open a bag and stretched it in David's direction. He reached for a handful. "No, really. That's interesting. Tell me more."

"You ever play baseball?" he asked.

"Oh, yeah. Look at me. I'm the perfect backstop, don't you think? Actually, I was the catcher for our high school softball team. It was a long time ago when I was in shape."

"So you know how important the pitcher is?"

"Of course. We had a real flamethrower. Her name was Curly Babcock. She used to make my hand throb by the end of the game. I even used extra padding inside my glove," Grace said.

Traffic had picked up, and David eased onto the accelerator. He could feel his heart start racing as they got closer to Chavez Ravine.

"Koufax. He's the pitcher's pitcher. Consistent, powerful, smart, astute; he's got it all," David said. As a hero, Koufax appealed to both his savage and human side, but he kept that to himself.

"Yeah, I get that," Grace said.

"We're making good time now. I think another twenty minutes and we'll be there."

Grace leaned the bag of chips in David's direction and he took another handful. There was more he wanted to tell Grace. He wanted to tell her what it felt like to hurl a little sphere at a man standing sixty feet away from you, holding a club in his hand. How on one hand, it didn't make any sense if you thought about it, but that for David and probably the rest of the pitchers in the world, climbing to the mound was like being onstage. You are exposed and in control, not only of your destiny, but of all those on your side.

"David, watch out!" Grace shouted. A white van suddenly cut in front of them, causing David to brake hard to avoid the wild driver.

"L.A. crazies," he said.

"That was close. You were talking about Koufax. Anything else I should know for tonight?"

"Just if he wins tonight it will be his eighteenth. He's already leading the league in about every category."

"All right then. I'm ready to see the best of the best. Go Dodgers. Go Koufax," Grace yelled.

The exit for Dodger Stadium was four miles ahead. David felt a surge of elation. He glanced at Grace and smiled. Her frumpy demeanor didn't appeal to him, and yet, she was a perfect companion for tonight. Easy, carefree, and completely enthused about the game and Koufax. Her only expectation was to have fun. But there was more he wanted to share. If Lou were here, he could tell him how he loved the way the world seemed to slow down as he imagined Koufax peering in for his sign. How Koufax would take a small breath, and then unfurl the wrath of his intense muscular energy in an effort to overpower a hitter. It was magical and beguiling.

David turned off in the direction of the stadium. He parked in a distant lot that still had lots of spaces. He didn't mind the walk, and they had plenty of time. As they approached the field, he saw throngs of people. Koufax always drew a larger-than-average crowd. The lines at the ticket booths were already deep. David noticed a couple of scalpers meandering around the back of the lines. Oftentimes, he had stood with his father as he bartered with these rascals, coming away with better than the available seats, albeit at times, at a slightly inflated price. So he knew how to handle the situation. After talking to a couple of sellers, he found one with seats and prices to his liking, and the exchange was made.

Tickets in hand, he led Grace into the world of major league baseball. The seats were halfway between first base and the right-field foul pole. David bought a couple bags of peanuts and a large Coke for Grace. They found their seats, and he opened the program with the lineups for both teams. He quickly scanned the matchups Koufax would be facing.

"The Reds are stacked with great hitters," David said as Grace ripped open the bag of peanuts. "Pete Rose, Frank Robinson, and Tony Perez are the three to key on tonight. They will be tough outs."

"Yeah, but Koufax will mow them down. Right?"

"That's what we are hoping," David laughed, appreciating her verve.

Grace took out a thick white wool sweater and wrestled it over her thick frame. "It's kind of cold tonight, don't you think?"

David nodded in agreement, digging into his pack for his jacket and pulling out his baseball glove. He wiggled his fingers into the mitt. His hand felt warm and comfortable.

"You going to wear that during the game?" Grace asked.

"No, I just wanted to get it ready. You never know when a foul ball might be coming our way."

They stood up for the national anthem. Koufax worked through the first inning without giving up a run, but David pointed out he was taking a lot of time between pitches. A few times Koufax swirled his arm in circles as if he were trying to loosen the muscles in his shoulder. "It seems like he is having trouble getting loose."

"Yeah, but he's still getting them out," Grace said.

Not much happened through the first couple innings. Together, David and Grace finished the first bag of peanuts. In the top of the third inning, David put on his glove. Koufax kept stretching his arm as he warmed up for the Reds hitters. Something didn't look right. Sure enough, he gave up two runs in the inning.

"They'll come back," Grace said.

"I hope so," David said, pounding his mitt.

The Dodgers couldn't score against Sammy Ellis, the Reds pitcher. He was looking like the dominant pitcher tonight.

Grace and David were halfway through the second bag of peanuts when Koufax gave up two more runs in the bottom of the fourth. David took off his glove and his jacket. This wasn't what he expected. Down four to zero, it didn't look like Koufax was going to get his eighteenth win tonight.

"He just doesn't have it tonight," David said.

"It's the cold," Grace said.

"Yeah, maybe so. But it's warming up now."

David bought one more bag of peanuts, and Grace got a hot dog. The game dribbled forward. In the fifth, they jumped up and Grace lost her hot dog when the Dodgers finally scored a run. Koufax settled into a groove and was no longer stretching his shoulder, but the damage was done. The Dodgers lost four to one.

"Are you disappointed?" Grace asked as they walked back to the car.

"Of course," he said. "I'm a pitcher. I always expect to win."

It was a little after eleven when David thanked Grace for the evening and said good night. He wasn't tired, so he started to write in his journal. He wrote about CJ and Wiz and how guilty he felt about them sticking their asses on the line, while he was sitting around watching the ball game with Grace Yamamoto. The late night news announced that LBJ approved 50,000 more troops for deployment to Vietnam. Effective immediately, monthly draft quotas were going to increase from 17,000 to 35,000.

Vietnam felt close. It filled his lungs and his brain. He worried about his friends and the world. "Great stakes are in the balance," LBJ drawled on. "We intend to convince the communists that we cannot be defeated."

"That 'we' that you referred to are me and my friends," David mumbled. As far as he was concerned, LBJ was full of shit.

The phone rang. David looked at the clock: eleven fifteen. He assumed it was Melanie, and he felt the touch of her skin. He picked up the phone. His mother was on the line.

"Lou's had a stroke, he's in the ICU. Molly just called me. It happened about two hours ago. It doesn't look good."

"What do you mean, 'It doesn't look good'?"

"I mean it's serious. If you're not too tired, you should go over there. Just go."

David grabbed his keys and wallet and was out the door. He had to restrain himself from speeding. His mind was already at the hospital, already in the room with Lou, already imagining the worst when the worst wasn't even imaginable. What did a stroke mean, except that he was going to die? He turned on the radio, and they were playing Miles Davis' "Stella By Starlight." It soothed him enough to realize he had passed the turnoff for the Ventura Freeway, the hospital exit was only another few minutes away, just enough time to hear Miles finish the cut. By the time he parked, he was in a calmer state of mind, but that deteriorated as he headed toward the double doors of the hospital. No one was at the gift shop or the greeting desk, so he followed the singular black arrows to the registration desk, where a redhead with pale-pink lipstick and large black-framed glasses greeted him. She told him the ICU was on the second floor. No visitors were allowed in the room, but there was a waiting lounge where he'd probably find any friends or relatives who might be there. Chester and Molly were sitting slumped on a small cushioned bench. No one else was around.

"It's awful," Molly started before David could speak. "He's had a massive stroke, a clot, probably from the surgery, but who knows? He's unconscious and on a respirator. Right now they're trying to check and see if he has any . . ."

Molly started to collapse. David and Chester grabbed her.

"Dr. Copeland, the hospital neurosurgeon, was just here. He said he'd be back as soon as he had a better idea of what options they had," Chester said.

"Can we see him?" David asked.

"Hopefully, soon," Molly said.

"Molly, I need a smoke," Chester said. "I'm going down the hall. Call me if the doctor comes back."

David sat across from Molly and felt an icy spike of fear run up his spine. The more he tried not to think about Lou dying, the more he obsessed about it. Molly looked like all the air had been sucked out of her.

"Is there anything I can get you?" David asked.

At first she didn't answer. Then, looking down, she said, "He was doing so good. This morning we took a walk around the block. He dressed himself, had a plate of scrambled eggs, home fries, and half a cantaloupe. After breakfast he even worked on some poems or something. I heard the typewriter clicking away for almost an hour."

"I'm so sorry," David said, wishing there was something to do other than listen to Molly.

She took a breath and continued. David listened helplessly. She told him that he had taken a nap in the afternoon and watched some television. After dinner, Lou had told Chester and Molly that he was feeling tired. He sat down in the living room and started reading a book. Then around eight, while Molly was putting away the dishes, she heard a crash in the living room, and there he was, slumped on the floor.

Molly started sobbing and wrapped her arms around David. He felt her thin muscular arms tense and release as she cried.

Dr. Copeland came out to talk with them about an hour later and said Lou had suffered a serious stroke. He would remain on life support, and there was still no telling how much damage had been caused. Lou was unresponsive. Dr. Copeland said it would be all right to see him, but they had to go one at a time. They all agreed. Molly went first.

A full hour passed before it was David's turn. He walked into what looked like a space capsule filled with monitors, tubes, machines that clicked and whirred, and several charts hung at the foot of the bed. Lou's head was tilted to one side. A thick vinyl tube was taped to his chin, running into his mouth and forcing air into his lungs. An IV was strapped inside his right forearm, his eyes were closed, and he was very, very still.

While David stood beside the bed, he remembered the day they had fought during lunch, when Lou started mouthing off about Rita. Lou had been so pissed off. Now, what David saw before him was a shadow, a skeleton of his best friend. He felt numb, locked up, and distant. Suddenly, he heard his name being called and turned to see Rowena.

"Hey."

"Hi," he said back.

"Sorry to intrude, but hospital policy is that only family can be in ICU alone. The head nurse sent me over. I'll just stand here and pretend to be invisible."

She leaned against the doorframe with tears in her eyes. Her light chocolate skin had tiny freckles. She was beautiful, with her large almond-shaped eyes and her lips that always looked moist and kissable.

"He's really bad, David, really bad. He's such a beautiful man, what a pity to see this happen. When I heard I just kept thinking it must be some mistake, the surgery went so well, and while he still had an uphill battle, I think he was ready for it. But now this! Damn! Sorry. I won't say anymore."

David walked over to the door where she stood. She threw her arms around him and squeezed. She smelled like tears, sweat, and medicine.

"It's okay," David said. "I'm just wanting to sit here for awhile and be with him."

"I understand," Rowena said.

David walked over to the chair next to Lou's bed. Nothing about his body moved except the slight heave of his chest as it pulsed up and down with the rhythm of the respirator. David touched his limp cool hand that was hungry for circulation. He couldn't fling a baseball or write a poem. Lou's eyes were sealed. He couldn't see the way Rowena's nipples pointed slightly out of her nurses uniform. His friend had become just a shell that encased soft organs as they pumped and squeezed and absorbed the fluids, without any executive function.

David looked back at Rowena. She nodded. Unsure what to do, David figured he'd just talk to Lou.

"So, here we are again. I wish it was different. I'm sure you wish the same. So how'd you ever think of writing a book anyway? It's fucking amazing." David glanced toward Rowena.

"It's okay, David. Maybe he can hear you. Keep talking. Say whatever you need to say."

David turned toward Lou and told him he didn't blame him for the way he had baited and cajoled him over the years. He said he didn't harbor any ill will for accusing him of being a jerk to Rita. He told Lou that he meant more to him that any friend he'd ever known and that, while he carped and complained about how obnoxious he could be and how he went out of his way to put him down at times, he appreciated how he challenged him with new ways of looking at the world. David stopped. He felt Rowena's hand on his shoulder. The machines hummed along.

"I wish I could have been a better friend," David whispered. Rowena stayed behind him. He could hear her breathing. After a few moments, he continued.

"You are not easy; you never claimed that as a trait, you never claimed anything other than your right to your perceptions and beliefs. I'm feeling a little lost right now. You were like a guidepost. It kills me to say that sometimes I craved your approval."

He looked at Lou's inert body and asked it: "What happens if you decide to die on me?" It sounded so trite that he hoped Lou wasn't lambasting him in his coma, but if he was, well that's just the way it was going to be. He asked Lou if he was in pain. Feeling so powerless tortured him.

"You must be getting sick of listening to all this. You probably just want to be left alone, but that's too bad because I still have more to say."

"That's good, David. Keep talking," Rowena said.

"Yeah. Okay," David said, touching Rowena's arm and then looking back at Lou.

"This is all so messed up. I keep thinking you'll just wake up and we'll walk out of here together. I'll pick you up in the morning and we'll start moving your stuff into the apartment." He reached over and took Lou's hand. "Hey, I know you can hear me. It's going to be all right, no matter what."

David got up and hugged Rowena. He walked down the corridor to where Chester and Molly were sitting. They looked worn and distant. Chester could barely keep his eyes open.

"How is he?" Molly asked.

"His hands are getting warmer," David said.

CHAPTER TWENTY-SIX

Sunday, August 1, 1965

There is a pop-up toward third base. Kennedy is going to glove it, and that's the game here at Busch Stadium in St. Louis. The Dodgers win and Koufax notches his eighteenth. Boy, oh boy, did they need this one after last night when Bob Gibson bested Don Drysdale in a tough four-to-three loss. The win tonight preserves a one-game lead over the Reds, and who else besides Koufax would be the one to save the day? He pitched a gem, striking out eleven, giving up only five hits, and offering no free passes. The Cards' young left-hander, Ray Sadecki, pitched a solid game, giving up only three hits and two earned runs. The game was scoreless through five, then in the top of the sixth, Wes Parker homered for the Dodgers. Koufax couldn't hold the lead, allowing doubles to Curt Flood and Dick Groat, tying the game at one to one. The Dodgers came right back in the top of the seventh and scored a pair on a home run by Jim Lefebvre and a sacrifice fly by Koufax. In the bottom of the ninth, Koufax started to tire and gave another run, but then he put the brakes on the Cards, preserving a three-to-two victory. And there you have it, Dodger fans.

David had trouble waking up. He hadn't gotten home until the early morning. Finally, he realized the phone was ringing. It was Melanie. He told her what happened with Lou. She asked if he wanted company. He couldn't get his brain to work and said he'd call her back after he showered. He ran the water for a long time and finally woke up. He dried off and called her back.

"Are you going back out there today?"

"I think so. I don't really know what else do. The doctor wasn't real hopeful," he said.

"I'll go with you if you want."

"Thanks, but I think I need to be alone out there."

"I understand."

"Maybe tomorrow night. It's Friday and we can do dinner and a movie. How does that sound?"

"It sounds great, but call me later today and let me know how things are going. Have you called Frank and Rene?"

"Shit, I totally forgot. I better call them right now and let them know what happened. Thanks."

He phoned Rene and gave him the bad news. All Rene said was, "That is terrible." David gave him as many details as possible, including the phone number of the hospital. Rene didn't stay on the line very long, he said he needed to call Frank. They'd discuss the situation and figure out a plan, but for now he imagined they'd still be arriving late Friday evening.

David shaved. He didn't look good, his eyes were drawn, red, and wrinkled. He felt the weight of Lou's life around his cheeks and across the muscles between his shoulders. He was nauseous. The thought of food didn't register, except his brain said he'd better eat something or he wouldn't make it through the day.

He put on a pair of shorts and a blue T-shirt and scooted over to Skip's Diner. What he needed first was a mug of strong coffee. A pretty new waitress—her name tag read Denise—came over to his table.

"Hi there, can I take your order?"

"Sure. I'll have the breakfast special, over easy, with a side of sausage and a fruit bowl."

"Wheat, rye, or white toast?"

"Rye. When did you start working here? I haven't seen you before."

"Monday was my first day. It's a great summer job until I start school."

"I'm a regular here, my name's David."

"Well, David, you look hungry, I better get this order in. Coffee?"

David nodded and Denise poured. He watched her shimmy toward the kitchen. She wore tight Levi jeans and a plain white blouse;

her backside was slim, almost skinny, although her ass had a perfect roundness to it, like a volleyball. He sighed. The last thing he needed at this moment was the complication of another girl. David watched Denise swerve around the locals crowding the stools at the counter, pouring coffee, smiling in a very genuine way that made her patrons feel relaxed and ready to offer a sizable tip.

Ten minutes later Denise was back with his breakfast in one hand and a pot of coffee in the other. "Warm up?" she said and nodded toward his half empty cup.

"Sure. By the way, where are you going to school?"

"UCLA, this fall."

"Me too."

"That makes about 22,000 of us."

"All the more reason to know someone."

"You're right. I've got to get back to work. We're done, right?"

"Right."

"Enjoy your breakfast," she said.

"That I will."

David finished eating and was out in the street, the sun beaming relentlessly. His face burned as he walked the short distance back to his apartment. It was a perfect beach day. He changed quickly at the apartment and was in the surf ten minutes later. The breakers were climbing tall and smooth, and he lost himself in the day, riding wave after wave.

By four o'clock he had showered, put on jeans and a fresh collared shirt, and made it onto the San Diego Freeway. He tuned in KRLA. They were playing "Wooly Bully" by Sam the Sham and the Pharaohs, a perfect refrain for the day's news that promulgated a brand of deceitful double talk. Make war to have peace, and kill communists to achieve freedom and liberty. It was all "Wooly Bully" to David as he climbed over Mulholland Drive and descended into the Valley. The closer he got to the hospital turnoff, the less concern he had for the news and the more he thought about Lou. He had no idea what to do other than to show up again. He had talked to Bryce and Barn earlier in the day. He suspected he'd run into them at the hospital.

Rowena greeted David with a furrowed brow outside the ICU lounge. She shook her head and moved close so she could keep her voice down.

"I'm so sorry, David. I really didn't think he'd go in this direction. Nothing has changed. He's still hooked up to all the life supports. There's nothing to be done."

"That's what I feared. Who's up there?"

"His folks, and your two buddies arrived about an hour ago."

"Anyone else?"

"Not that I've seen."

"Thanks, Rowena."

"David, he's not going to last long, you better prepare yourself. I hate to be the one to say it, but it's the truth. Please let me know if there is anything . . ."

"I will."

Rowena disappeared through another set of double doors. She was an angel with a fine figure.

David saw Barn and Bryce hunkered in front of a huge television. They were transfixed on *American Bandstand.* Dick Clark introduced a couple of dancers, then told the audience they were going to hear "My Girl" by the Temptations. The music started as David walked over. "What's going on?" David said.

Barn answered, "Hey, David. This really stinks, doesn't it? He's really messed up. Bryce and I went inside, he looks like a frozen ghost. It's awful, terrible. I'm not sure what we are supposed to do, except Bryce wanted to hang out for a bit. He said you'd show up and maybe the three of us could figure something out. You know that three-heads-better-than-one thing."

David loved and hated Barn's authenticity; part clown, part fool, part little boy. He blurted out life as he saw it; immediate, impulsive, and direct.

"Yeah, I can just see us as a three-headed monster trying to figure out where to go on a Friday night. What do you want to do? I don't know, what do you want to do? I don't know," David said.

Barn laughed. "You got that right. That's pretty funny, especially for the guy without a sense of humor."

David ignored his poke. "Are Molly and Chester inside?"

"They are. They've been here since early this morning. Chester is asleep around the corner. Can't you hear him? He's snoring like someone is trying to strangle him," Bryce said.

"I went in last night and said what I needed to say. I don't know what else to do," David said.

"Yeah, Barn and I did the same thing. It's pretty strange. It's like speaking to someone through a one-way mirror."

"I'm going inside for a little while. Can you guys hang out for a few more minutes?" David asked.

"Not a problem," Bryce said.

"Sure," Barn added.

Chester had stuffed himself into a pale-blue love seat, his jowls inflating and deflating the way a male frigate bird attracts its mates. Molly was busy knitting a scarf.

"Hello, David." Her exhaustion had squeezed all the emotion out of her like a used-up tube of tooth paste. She looked vacuous, almost drugged. "If you want to see Lou, just press the buzzer and the nurse will let you inside. Nothing has changed, nothing probably will, that's what the doctor told us early this morning around six, when we arrived."

"I'm sorry," David said.

Nothing had changed. He lay there inert, except for the sound of the machines that functioned for him. Like the day before, Rowena showed up in the room. They didn't talk. David looked at her and then back at Lou. He remembered Lou as he stood on the mound concentrating on his spot, the bottom of the strike zone on the outside corner. He looked back at Rowena.

"You know he was a great baseball player."

"I've heard that," she said.

"A pitcher."

"I like pitchers." She smiled.

"Lou liked to make eye contact with the batter before he started his windup. He treasured the mental duel that ensued once a hitter stepped into the box. He told me once that he never felt like he lost that psychic duel. Even if the guy whacked his pitch, he believed that he had gotten inside his mind, so the next time up he'd have a slight advantage."

"He's a real battler, isn't he?" Rowena said.

"You got that right. I guess it's natural to remember these kinds of things."

Rowena nodded. David continued, "I just can't think of him just lying there. How do we know if he's even still here? Maybe the real Lou already moved on, and what we're seeing is just an apparition."

"Could be," she said.

David became silent. The monitors, the lights, the tubes, the needles, and the smells that leeched through the bags draped beside his bed signaled a distress beyond anything David had ever known. The entire scene rattled like dry bones in the wind. Instinctively, David reached into his pockets, looking for something that would make a difference. He came up empty.

David said goodbye to Molly. He wished there was something he could offer other than an embrace. He walked over to where Barney and Bryce were watching television and sat down. *American Bandstand* was wrapping up. The crowd on the screen was dancing to the Miracles' "Tracks of My Tears." The three of them sat together until the program ended. David felt something shift inside. He knew Lou would like his plan.

"Hey guys, let's get out of here for awhile. I've got an idea."

"Sounds good to me, this place is giving me the creeps," Barn said.

"What do you have in mind?" Bryce asked.

"You'll see."

The Feel Good Batting Cages were located on Victory Blvd. a few blocks east of Woodman. Together, the friends had spent hundreds of dollars over the years smacking balls into the wire cages. It was a spot they all understood. It was dinnertime, so the place was deserted. David took a five-dollar bill out of his wallet and exchanged it for quarters and distributed them to Barn and Bryce. No instructions were necessary as they filled their palms with coins, grabbed helmets, and selected bats.

They took the three cages on the far end and set the speed to "major league setting," the one that had *80 mph plus* written underneath it. Simultaneously, the trio of machines started to whiz balls at the boys, and they swung together. After a few pitches, they were in a groove. David was in the middle cage, so he could hear the smack each time Barn and Bryce connected. The balls exploded off their bats, none of them missed or fouled any of the pitches, so when they finally walked away, they were drained of adrenaline, anger, and fear.

"Fuck yeah!" Barn screamed as he high-fived Bryce and David. "We kicked ass and batted the blues out into the night."

"For Lou, for Lou!" They all shouted. It was the best David could do for himself and his friends. It wasn't nearly enough. Nothing was. They went their separate ways.

That night he and Melanie ate at a little Chinese place on Santa Monica Blvd., the size of a railroad car. It was famous for its Szechwan dishes. After dinner they went to his place and made love, then showered together. With the water raining down, she kissed the back of his neck and stretched her muscular arms around him so her breasts squeezed tight against his bare back. She was very easy to love, and her loving made it easy to forget the world for a little while.

David wanted Melanie to spend the night, but she had an early practice at USC, so he dropped her home a little before midnight. Driving back to the apartment, he noticed the oil light on the Galaxy flashing on and off. Everything else seemed to be working all right, but the red warning light kept flickering. He made it home and figured he'd call his father in the morning to see what he thought.

First thing Saturday he called Jacob and explained the situation. David was relieved when his father told him that, unless he had a serious oil leak, he probably just needed to add oil and change the filter. It was an easy fix. After a quick trip to the auto store, he added oil and installed a new filter, and the warning light disappeared. He thought about Lou and wished there was a way to repair *his* warning light.

He was washing up when the phone rang. It was Rene. He'd totally forgotten that he said they'd be arriving late last night.

"How's Lou?" His voice sounded urgent.

"Not good. Where are you?"

"Just down the road from you. Frank and I are staying with some friends in Venice. We've got Lou's books and I have a plan."

"I'm listening," David said. Rene knew how to get things done in the world.

"First, Frank and I are going to see Lou. We'll drop off several copies of the books with Molly and Chester and do whatever we can for them. We've arranged a book release at the Lighthouse tonight at 5:00 p.m. Will you let Lou's friends know?"

David said he would, and he immediately made the calls. Everyone would show up, except he wasn't sure what to do about Rita. She was the last call. He told Melanie that he'd pick her up at four in order to have plenty of time to park and visit with Frank and Rene before the event. The image of Rita and Melanie together boggled his mind. It was a full count. He called Bryce to get advice. Lou would have been the better choice. He could hear Lou's voice, *Mandel, what's your problem? Let them work it out. You can't hide from reality. You need to dive in head first and feel the water.*

Bryce answered after the third ring. David quickly laid out the scenario. His dilemma was clear.

"What's the problem? Rita is Lou's friend. You need to invite her and let the chips fall. Melanie can handle herself. Can't she?"

"I suppose so," David said.

"Is there anything else? I've got to get to practice," Bryce said.

"No. I've got it."

"Just do it, David," Bryce said and hung up.

He dialed Rita's number and there was no answer. Then he called Melanie, thinking he'd let her know Rita was going to be there. No answer. Nobody home. He looked at his watch, it was eleven o'clock. There was still plenty of time to visit Lou, get back home, shower, change, and pick up Melanie.

Driving to the hospital, he figured he'd call Rita again when he got there. The call to Melanie could wait. Molly and Chester were sitting outside the ICU. They were smiling. David couldn't reconcile why unless Lou had made a miraculous turnaround. He got excited with that prospect as he approached.

"David, look!" Molly held up a small book with a stunning photo of Lou walking on an open stretch of beach on the cover. The title, in black letters within a white banner at the top, was *First Flames, Poems by Lou Ash*.

Molly took a copy from the small pile of books on the end table and handed it to David. He opened it and thumbed through the pages. It was a thin volume, with some of the selections Lou had read to him from his notebook.

"This is fantastic," David said.

"Those two guys just left. Boy, I sure misread them. They are great to have done this," Chester said, pointing to the books. "We'll be grateful forever."

David nodded and started to return the book to the pile.

"No, take it. It's for you. Rene said you'd probably be here shortly."

David shook his head and picked up the book. "How's he doing?"

"The same," Molly shrugged. "It's just a matter of waiting and praying now."

"Can I see him?" David asked.

"Yes, you know you just need to check in at the nurses' station."

David walked down the hall and talked to the nurse in charge. He asked if Rowena was working, but it turned out she had worked the night shift. David was allowed inside, but another nurse would need to be present. A small, lean woman followed him into Lou's room. She whispered, "I'm sorry we are short-staffed right now, I can only give you a few minutes."

David walked right up to Lou. Nothing had changed except his book was in the world. David held it up in front of Lou.

"Great job, big guy. Sorry you won't be there tonight, but I guess you will be."

He reached down and rested his hand on Lou's right arm. Words escaped him, but inside he asked for Lou's recovery. He closed his eyes and felt his fingers squeeze around the arm that saved his last game. The nurse tapped him on his back, and that was it.

Molly and Chester asked David to thank Frank and Rene again. They weren't going to the party. They needed to stay close to Lou. This was their vigil. David assured them he'd let them know and told them he'd be back tomorrow.

He got in the car and started to pull out of the parking space when he remembered that he hadn't called Rita. He turned off the engine and reentered the hospital. No one was around the bank of phones. He dialed. One ring, two rings, three, and on the fourth there was a click and Rita's mother was on the line.

"Hi, Mrs. Kano. It's David. Is Rita home?" David's could feel his hands began to sweat.

"No, she isn't. Is there anything wrong?"

"No. I just needed to let her know about a gathering for Lou tonight."

"Well, she won't be able to go. She and her sister left for San Diego a couple hours ago. They're spending the night and won't be back until tomorrow. Any message you want to leave?"

A great sense of relief zipped through his body.

"Just ask her to call me when she can. Tell her it's about Lou."

"I'll let her know."

David drove home. He worked on his story, and then walked along the beach until it was time to pick up Melanie. They arrived at the Lighthouse at four thirty. Rene and Frank were there, helping arrange chairs and talking with their friends. Frank rushed over and shook David's hand and clasped his shoulder.

"Great to see you," Frank said. "Melanie, you look beautiful." He draped his arms around her and pulled her close. David noticed the ease with which they enfolded one another. *Here we go again*, he whispered inside.

Rene sauntered over after finishing his conversation. "Have you seen the book?" he asked.

"Yes, it's terrific. I just missed you at the hospital."

"I figured you'd be right behind us. So here's the plan. Once everyone arrives, I'll step up to the front of the room and share Lou's story. Then I'll read a selection of his poems and talk about them. After that there'll be some music and time to hang out. Frank will be in the back at that table." Rene pointed toward the door. "People can buy the book for $1.25. How does that sound?"

"Sounds like you covered all the bases."

Rene winked and continued running around and setting up. Melanie and David took seats in the front. It wasn't a large venue. David figured thirty chairs. By the time Barn, Lydia, Shanti, Bryce, and the others arrived the place was almost full. Rene and Frank must have put the word out to their artist and literary friends.

The evening went just as Rene had predicted. His reading of Lou's work was inspiring. It was hard to imagine that Lou could have done much better. His style would have been more tense and provoking, though, daring his audience into the poems. Rene had a dramatic flair that helped the words fly off the page. The whole night was as fine as anyone could have expected under the circumstances.

David and Melanie stayed until the end. The twenty-five copies Rene had brought to the reading sold out. He told David he had received permission from Molly and Chester to distribute the remainder of the copies in bookstores. David figured Rene knew the literary market better than most. Everything was terrific, except Lou was still at death's doorstep.

Melanie had an early practice Sunday morning so David drove her straight home. It was fine with him. The past few days had drained him, and he looked forward to the quiet. The only person he wanted to spend time with was Lou.

Rita called late Sunday afternoon toward the end of the Dodgers game. David turned down the radio. She said her mother had given her a message to call. David told her about the book-release party and all that had transpired. He gave her an update on Lou.

"I'm sorry I missed the party. We had planned this trip for a couple weeks, but if I'd known . . ."

"It was real last minute. I called as soon as I knew," David said, though that wasn't exactly the truth. "I got you a book. I gave it to Shanti. She said she'd get it over to you."

Rita thanked him and they quickly ran out of words. He wasn't sure when he'd see her again. It felt inexplicable, like so many things in his life. After he hung up, he returned to the game. Koufax had just closed out the Cardinals. There was at least one thing that wasn't strange or unusual.

Chapter Twenty-Seven

Thursday, August 5, 1965

Here we are at County Stadium in Milwaukee. As you probably know, Hank Aaron has been on a home-run rampage. He hammered both Drysdale and Osteen the past two nights for numbers twenty-one and twenty-two. But tonight, Koufax held him to an 0-for-three evening. Before I go any further, let me recap the game for you. Things didn't start out too well for our left-hander. In the first inning, Joe Torre, the Braves' first baseman, powered a ball over the left-field fence, giving the Braves a one-to-0 lead. But Koufax didn't flinch. He kept the Braves in check for the next couple innings. In the top of the third, Jim Lefebvre nailed his eighth home run with Jim Gilliam aboard, and the Dodgers scratched out two additional runs on singles, walks, and force-outs. Their arsenal paled against the muscular Braves, but the runs counted just the same, and now Koufax had a three-run lead with his fast ball sizzling and his curve crashing down like a hammer. In the final frame, the Braves scored a couple more runs, but Koufax and the Dodgers prevailed six to three. Koufax secured his nineteenth victory of the year. His twelve strikeouts made it fifteen times that he'd struck out ten or more in a game, and it was the seventy-fifth time in his career. His numbers mean something, but it was his rhythm and dominance that held me throughout the night. I've never seen a pitcher quite like him.

Monday morning David was reading the last bits of the *Sunday Times* Opinion section, featuring the current mess in Vietnam, when the phone rang. He was sure it was Melanie. He had a momentary flash of excitement, the anticipation of her face and perhaps more, but it was his mother on the other end of the line.

"David."

"Yeah, Ma, is everything all right?"

"Lou passed away about an hour ago. I'm sorry."

What seemed like a long time went by while David absorbed the words. His body froze. His mind turned into a movie projector that filmed the hospital room, the ICU, the last place on the earth where he had witnessed what remained of Lou's life. He saw close-ups of his long fingers and the soft fuzz below his earlobe.

"What happened?"

"I'm not exactly sure. Everything just stopped. They think he had another stroke."

"Shit."

"It's unfair. He was so young," his mother said.

"Yeah I know. I just can't believe it."

"David, will you be okay? Do you want to come here for the night?"

"Ma, I think I just need to be alone."

"Okay. They don't know anything yet about the arrangements, but I'll call you as soon as I know."

David hung up and called Bryce and Barn. He talked to each of them for a long time. Then he called Melanie, but there was no answer. He walked into the kitchen. He started to do the dishes from a couple of days ago. When he finished that he cleaned the bathroom and vacuumed the living room, then he went outside and walked along the beach for an hour with nothing except Lou's face before him. When he returned he reached Melanie, and she came right over. She spent the night, but he didn't get much sleep.

Melanie left in the morning after trying to console him, but to no avail. He drove to work feeling restless and forlorn. Bryce was already putting gaskets and spark plugs in their proper bins when David arrived. They talked briefly about trying to reach Wiz and CJ. Bryce figured both their families already knew since Chester and Molly were close with Wiz's folks.

"I can't believe he's dead," David said.

"Me either. Not Lou. It was one thing to see him like that, but now? It's bizarre."

"I don't know what to do."

"Nothing to do. It's just depressing."

There wasn't anything more David had to say. It sickened him that Lou was dead. Lou's world was gone. What he might have done, what he might have written and said and touched and loved, now had a final period with THE END typed as the last sentence.

David smelled the Sunshine Cart before he heard the familiar honk. The boys looked at each other, then walked toward the food. They were both surprised that they had appetites. Simon and Rosy were too busy to talk, but the sizzle of fried eggs and bacon took the edge off the blues they both felt.

They sat down on the milk crates behind the storeroom and hunched down as the sun had its way with them. David peered around. Lou was dead. David looked at Bryce while he ate his food. His eyes were bloodshot and there was a heaviness about him. David swallowed the last of his sandwich. He wadded the wax-paper wrapping into a tight ball and made a free throw into the trash can.

"Hey, how's the team looking?" David asked. He needed to think about something other than Lou.

"We're tough. We have strong pitching, a couple of sluggers— one from Texas and another from back East. They're massive. Our infield defense is like a troupe of magicians. We stand up pretty good against the varsity, at least at this point, and that's saying a lot."

"I'd love to see you play."

"Well, the practices are open. You ought to drop by."

After work David dropped by Melanie's. He talked with her mother while Melanie showered and changed. Marilyn offered her condolences and wanted to know the details surrounding Lou's death. It didn't make for light conversation. He tried to change the subject several times, but she seemed perversely interested in the mournful details of Lou's demise.

"I'm sorry, David. Can I get you a Coke or some lemonade? Are you hungry, a piece of fruit perhaps?" She stood up and took a step in his direction. "What's your pleasure, David?"

"Water would be great, thanks, Marilyn."

"Here you are." She handed him a tall frosted glass filled with ice and water and returned to the soft chair across from him.

"You and Melanie get along quite well. I know she's becoming fond of you."

"It's mutual."

At last, Melanie emerged from the bedroom. He couldn't wait to zip out the door. Marilyn kissed Mel goodbye, squeezed David's arm gently, and said, "Have a good night."

They got in the car. David didn't have any ideas about the evening. Melanie was wonderful; she suggested they pick up sandwiches and drinks and walk out to the beach to catch the sunset. That sounded perfect. There was a little shop on the corner of Lincoln and Pico that sold dipped-beef sandwiches. They stopped and picked up the food and were on the beach twenty minutes later.

David called home when they got back from the ocean and found out that funeral arrangements were set for Friday morning. A service at Beth Shalom Temple would be followed by the interment at Mount Zion Cemetery. So there it was. The final map of Lou's life spread out across the Valley, a few more stops, then just memories. Melanie said she'd try to get out of practice on Friday but couldn't make any promises. David understood. It might be better for her not to be there. It felt too complicated.

It was just before midnight when David got to Melanie's house. They sat in the car and talked. Melanie sat close, and they hugged between sentences and silences. They ran out of things to say and finally kissed goodnight. David drove home through the wide empty streets.

Wednesday night Melanie called. She was crying.

"The coach scheduled a scrimmage at Redlands on Friday. I have to be there," she said.

"It's all right. I kind of figured that might happen."

After a few minutes, she calmed down and David reassured her that he'd be fine. He knew it would be better that she wasn't going to be there. Her presence would only encumber his freedom to be with his friends, his memories, and whatever else Lou's death held in store for him. And of course, Rita would be there.

There was good news Thursday morning. Bryce got a call from CJ. He and Wiz were coming in tonight. They were able to get a pass to attend the funeral. Bryce said that Tony and Dolores wanted everyone over for dinner tonight. It had been a couple of months since David had dropped them off at the processing depot downtown. A lot had changed in a short time.

Traffic was light, and David made it to the sprawling Agostino ranch house by six thirty. The street was filled with new cars and a few pickup trucks, probably belonging to friends of Tony. Dolores greeted David at the door. She beamed, her eyes moist and radiant. She wore a low-cut sailor blouse, white shorts, green sandals, gold loops on her lobes, and had overdone the makeup. She smelled thick with gin.

"Oh David, it's so good to see you. You look great. Come in, they're all in the backyard. I'm sorry about Lou, it's awful that we're getting our boys home on that account."

"It's all pretty crazy right now," David said and rushed through the house past the piano and the palatial kitchen. He saw their shaved heads first, then their pressed Army uniforms. They looked lean and strong, both of them had little caps tucked into their belts. Everything about them was starched, pressed, straight, and polished. They each had a beer in hand. Suddenly, a pair of hands covered his eyes.

"Guess who?"

David didn't need to guess. Veronica's warm breath blew across his neck. "Don't they look wonderful?"

"Yeah, I want to get a closer look."

"I just can't get enough of CJ, but he's changed."

David nodded and moved toward the throng surrounding CJ and Wiz.

"Hey guys!"

"Whoa, it's our 'savior-man.' How you doing, David?" Wiz said as he gave David a strong handshake and punch in the shoulder.

"Hi, David, it's good to see you." CJ wrapped David up in his arms. "Thanks for keeping in touch."

"No problem, you both look fantastic," David said.

"Amen to that, I've never worked so hard in my life. It feels good though," CJ said.

David didn't want to ask what was next. He figured they'd answered that too many times already. He kept looking at them. They were all ears and foreheads. Then Barn appeared, and after chugging a beer, he asked CJ and Wiz if they had heard anything about Rick Norris. CJ said he had asked his sergeant if he could find something out. The guy assured him he could, but it would take a little time. CJ slapped David on the back.

"Come on. There is a load of lasagna that my mom and my voluptuous sister made." He winked at David. "Then we drink till we can't walk. There's lots I want to tell you." He drew near to David's ear. "And I want to know more about Lou."

They ate and drank and talked about old times. After a couple of hours, David felt himself starting to get drunk. If Lou were here, he would have hated sitting around talking about the past like a bunch of losers. David got up. He needed to pee and wandered into the house. As he came out of the bathroom, CJ was waiting for him. He had a smile on his big ruddy face.

"Let's take a walk," CJ said. "Just around the block."

"You'll be missed," David said.

CJ stepped close to David. "I told everyone I'd be back in a little while. We need to talk, and they're too drunk to care right now. Come on."

He led David out the door and they walked side by side, following the sidewalk that was like an old friend.

"You must be messed up about Lou," CJ said.

"The worst part is that he seemed like he was getting better, and then he was dead."

"Fuck. I can't imagine how his parents are dealing with this."

David couldn't quite believe his ears, considering CJ was about to deploy sometime soon.

"Goddamn CJ, you better . . ."

"Don't even say it. Wiz and I are coming back. You can count on that."

CJ put his arm around David as they reached the end of the block. He smelled like beer and fear and Old Spice cologne.

"You're a good friend, David. I wish we'd done more stuff together. The hunting and shooting was great, but I don't know. I just wish maybe we could have been better friends, like you were with Lou."

"Well, when you come back we'll get all cuddly together," David said.

"Fuck you."

"Fuck you too," David said, and he stared at CJ for a long time.

They got back to the party and David said his goodbyes. Lydia and Claudia were enfolding their solider boys. It was time to leave.

On the way out, Veronica handed him a cup of coffee. David stood in the kitchen and drank it.

"David, I'm so happy that I can see him. He looks good. I'm starting to think that maybe he made the right choice after all, maybe this is what he needed to do to get things right with himself," Veronica said as she rinsed a few cups in the sink.

David finished the coffee. "Maybe you are right," he said, not believing it. "He needed to get out of here."

Veronica dried her hands and walked over to David, gave him a serious embrace, and kissed his cheek.

He pointed the Galaxy onto the road and climbed back over the mountains. He drove home, listening to the Dodgers game. Koufax was well on his way to winning his nineteenth game of the season. He was ahead six to one in the eighth. The game eased the stress of the night and the trepidation of the funeral. He wasn't sure why, but it did.

The next morning David stopped at the cemetery on the way to Temple Beth Shalom. The service was scheduled at 10:00 a.m. He woke up at seven, without an appetite. He had a liquid breakfast of vitamins, orange juice, and coffee, and was on the road by eight o'clock. When he rolled into the cemetery, there was a single white truck parked in the distance with a trailer attached. Two Black men dressed in gray shirts and pants sat under a lone pine tree, a yellow backhoe was parked next to the pavement. An empty hole stared out at the open sky. Beside it, six shovels stood out of a high mound of dirt like giant toothpicks. David walked up to the two guys who were talking quietly to each other. They were older, with graying flecks along the sides of their heads. One of them had a wispy beard with a silver shine.

"Good Morning," David said.

"Morning, sir," the guy with the beard said.

"Is that for Lou Ash?" David pointed toward the grave.

The bearded guy nodded. "He was my friend," David said.

"Sorry for your loss," the other gravedigger responded.

"Nice job you did, very clean."

"We try our best." The bearded guy stood up and brushed the back of his pants, he was a bit over six feet. Then the other man got up, he was six inches shorter, stocky like a wrestler. David extended his hand for a shake.

"I'm David Mandel. I just want to thank you."

"You're welcome. I'm Louis and this is Curly." Louis extended his hand, they shook, and then the short gravedigger did the same.

David didn't know what to say next. He wanted to say something profound or humorous, but all he could do was nod and say thank you again. The hole looked deeper than he imagined, like it could easily accommodate two or three caskets and still be the required six feet.

"It looks big," David said.

"It's the right size. Everyone has the same thoughts," Curly said softly. "It's because there isn't any light shining from below."

"Yeah, that makes sense."

"Not sure if it does or doesn't. It just is," said Louis.

"What made you want to come out here before the interment?" Curly asked. "Not many people do that. Most get here late and want to leave early, that's the pattern."

"I'm not sure. I guess I just wanted to see it before everyone was here."

"That's okay with me," Louis said.

"Maybe now that I've come out here, you'll remember this spot because I came early."

"Could be, you never know," Louis replied.

"I better get going," David said.

"Don't worry, we'll keep an eye on him," Louis said.

Jacob, Rose, and Alex met David in the temple parking lot. They walked in as a family. The front pews were filled with Lou's relatives. CJ, Wiz, Bryce, and Barn sat behind them. Rita was there with Claudia, Shanti, and Lydia. David walked over and briefly embraced each of them. His arms lingered around Rita. She whispered, "Sorry."

Rabbi Joseph Steinberg appeared through a side door and leaned his tall restrained body in the direction of Chester and Molly. He was cleanly shaved, his silver hair stroked straight back, his lips, nose, eyes, and ears were all exactly proportioned. A modern and appropriately spiritual man, but as far as David knew, Lou had never spent any time with Rabbi Steinberg. Chester and Molly were disinclined toward organized religion and had not sent Lou to Hebrew school.

"Shalom, family and friends of Lou Ash. Today finds us broken and crushed. Sorrow is not our friend, yet she is our companion, never far from our hearts. As we mourn the tragic loss of Lou Ash, we realize that often things happen to us that we simply cannot understand."

It wasn't clear how long this was going to last. Rabbi Steinberg transitioned into a traditional set of prayers. At some point, everyone would be heading to the cemetery, Lou's coffin leading the way. His body rested in front of the room. David looked toward Molly and Chester. They sat face to face with their son, inside the polished pine casket. It was the color of fresh-cut wheat and stood like an anchor, refusing to allow anyone the luxury of release or comfort. David recalled how Lou had saved his last game and how he had been so vibrant and alive hiking on Mount Vision.

The service moved forward. It was warm in the sanctuary, and David started to feel the full-body tackle of death; his hips, knees, and ankles buckled each time he raised himself in prayer. His mind wrestled with Lou's demise. He struggled with a specter mounting inside him. He needed to do something. It was a full count, and he needed to make a pitch. He looked at the box that held his friend. He wanted to scream, run, smash things, and fight against the reality in front of him.

The congregants of Temple Beth Shalom were now bowed low in the final refrain of the Alyenu prayer. There was a pause, and David rose out of his chair. He knew the concluding prayer was next.

"Rabbi, Rabbi Steinberg. May I say a few words before we finish?"

Steinberg froze and grabbed him with his dark eyes. He didn't recognize David.

"Excuse me, I don't believe I know you."

"David Mandel, I was a close friend of Lou."

The rabbi quickly glanced at Molly, who nodded assiduously and whispered something loud enough for Steinberg to hear the assertiveness of her response.

"Mr. Mandel, you have some words you'd like to share in regard to your friend?"

"I do."

"Please step up," the rabbi said as he took a seat to the side of the stage.

David cleared his throat. He didn't know what he was going to say. But he started anyway.

"I was a friend of Lou's, maybe his best friend. If you knew Lou even a little, you'd know that he was a one-of-a-kind type of person. He didn't withhold his opinions or judgments when it came to how people treated each other. He hated phoniness and hypocrisy. We had our disagreements, but we were close, really close."

David glanced at the rabbi. He was squirming, wringing his hands, staring at David, probably worried he'd go on and on.

"Lou was a poet. A good one. In fact, he just published a book of poems called *First Flames*. We can certainly celebrate that."

Steinberg elevated on his toes and made a move toward David.

"One last thing. Lou was an inspiration for me because he wasn't afraid to believe in himself. More than anything, that's what I'll miss about him. Thanks, Rabbi."

"You're welcome, David. Now please join the family as we conclude the service."

After the last prayer, everyone gathered at the gravesite. They recited the Mourner's Kaddish. David saw Curly and Louis sitting reverently behind a few trees. A stainless-steel lowering device ushered Lou into the large hole that didn't emit any light. David waited for his turn with the shovel. He stabbed deep into the mound, then pivoted and released his portion into the grave. His part was finished. Now Curly and Louis would take over. David raised his hand in their direction, they waved back as they walked toward the backhoe.

He drove slowly through the gates that separated the living from the dead. There was a reception at the Ash residence. David stayed just long enough to pay his respects to Molly and Chester. Driving home, he knew his life would never be the same.

CHAPTER TWENTY-EIGHT

Tuesday, August 10, 1965

We all like a good drama, and tonight was one of the best. A four- to-three victory for Koufax, giving him twenty for the season against only four losses, but it wasn't easy. No, sir. The Dodgers took an early lead, scoring once in the second and twice in the third, with Gilliam, Wills, and Roseboro doing most of the damage. Then, in the bottom of the sixth inning, Ron Fairly singled and Wes Parker launched a rocket into left field for a triple that easily drove Fairly home, giving Koufax a four-to-0 lead in the seventh. Koufax put the Mets down in order in the bottom of the seventh, and it looked like there wouldn't be any drama at all.

But excitement did start in the top of the eighth inning. Bobby Klaus and Roy McMillian led off with consecutive singles. It was impossible to discern whether Koufax was tiring or whether the Mets were finally seeing his fastball, but the next batter, Charlie Smith, the third baseman, doubled and scored Klaus from first, making the score four to two. The right fielder, Joe Christopher, followed with a sacrifice fly, and now the Mets were within two runs. Koufax terminated the threat by striking out Jim Hickman and walking off the mound, shaking his head and pounding his fist into his glove.

The Dodgers didn't score in the bottom of the eighth. In the ninth, Koufax slowly ascended the mound, hoping to bear witness to his twentieth triumph of the year, but Ron Swoboda clubbed his first pitch into the left-field bleachers, moving the Mets within a run of tying the game. The tension mounted. Koufax still had three outs to get. The fans were going crazy, and Sandy didn't disappoint. He struck out two of the last three batters, giving him fourteen for the game. He gets my academy award for tonight!

Before David got out of bed Saturday morning, there was a knock at the door. Melanie walked inside, holding a bag and a couple of paper cups of coffee.

"Surprise, surprise! I thought you might want some breakfast and coffee."

"Sounds wonderful!"

"Fresh coffee and a bagel with the works."

"Thanks."

"How are you? I'm so sorry I couldn't be there with you yesterday."

David got out of bed and started on the coffee. "I don't know how I am. Lou's gone, and now I'm not sure what to do."

"Do? What can you do?"

"I know. I saw him go in the ground and tried to imagine what's next. But nothing came. I just miss him."

"Of course."

Melanie moved next to him and put her arms around him. She turned his face toward hers and kissed him. He kissed her back. Still thinking about Lou, he got up and paced around the room.

"David."

"Yeah?"

"There isn't anything you can do."

"That's not all right with me," David said.

"It's not all right with me either, but Lou's gone."

"I've got an idea. Grab the bagels and the coffee while I get dressed," he said.

"Where are we going?"

"Just come on."

David took his keys and rushed out the door. Melanie trailed behind him. They got in the car and David sped toward the freeway.

"You are driving very fast, David."

"I know. I want to go fast."

"You're scaring me a little. Could you please slow down?"

David slowed down just enough for her to feel okay. He got on the 101 heading north. He turned on the radio and lowered all the windows. The air blasted through the car. "Dancing in the Streets" by Martha and the Vandellas was playing, and he felt Melanie's hand on his lap. Her grip was strong and tight at first, but then it loosened and he could feel her relax. The Galaxy cruised flawlessly at seventy-five and then at eighty. It was a smooth ride over Mulholland Drive. The songs kept changing, and they both sang along.

He took the turnoff to the Ventura Freeway heading east. The traffic was a little heavier, but not enough to slow them down. He passed the turnoff he used to take to Rita's cousin's house. It seemed like an eternity had passed since he had been with Rita.

"I know where you are going," Melanie whispered in his ear.

"Are you okay with it?"

"Yes. Absolutely." She kissed his earlobe.

David stepped down on the gas pedal just enough to surge in front of a car on his right that was going the same speed. His stop was still five or six exits ahead. He'd be there soon enough, although he imagined driving and driving for days.

He passed the turnoff for the zoo and then saw Barnham Blvd. He turned off and automatically steered toward his destination. It was a partly sunny day. The smog and fog had merged to form a soupy gray haze, and it was already pushing eighty degrees. David slowed down and rolled up the windows. He kicked on the AC and turned off the radio.

"Are we close?" Melanie said.

"Almost there. Another minute or two."

They passed through the gate. He was surprised that he wanted to return so soon. He hadn't planned it, but here he was. Maybe Lou had risen and the grave would be opened. Lou would be sitting on the ledge of the hole, throwing a baseball up and down and catching it in his mitt. Maybe he'd be writing a poem in his notebook. Maybe he'd just be standing, waiting for David to arrive.

"This is kind of weird, don't you think?" Melanie said.

"Yeah. But, I need to do this. You all right?"

"It's just weird, but I like weird sometimes. Like now. It's okay."

David parked on the road closest to Lou's grave. There weren't any other vehicles around. It was still early. He and Melanie got out of the car.

The burial site didn't have any markers except a white paper encased in plastic with the name Ash written in black ink. Curly and Louis had done a good job. The area around the place was clean and raked. There were no signs of Kleenex or footprints or life of any kind. The dark soil above the grave had a quiet, settled feeling, as if some bulbs or seeds had been recently planted. David imagined sprinkling it with a garden hose, and then thought of how the grounds keepers would always wet down the infield before games. He imagined two Lou's, one on the mound and one in this hole.

"Hey, what's going on?" Melanie said.

"Just thinking about flowers and baseball," David said.

"And Lou?"

"Yeah. Of course. I still don't know what to do."

"You are doing it," she said.

A white pickup truck drove up and parked behind the Galaxy. Louis and Curly closed the doors quietly and walked toward them. They each gave a little wave in David's direction.

"You're back so soon," Louis said.

"Yes, I guess I just couldn't keep away."

He introduced Melanie to the gravediggers. He said that Melanie wanted to see the spot because she couldn't attend yesterday. She didn't protest.

"Well, whatever the reason, it's okay by us," Curly said. "You're welcome to come visit your friend anytime. Anytime the gates are unlocked just come on through. But, we don't want no interlopers at night. You know crazy people wanting to see ghosts and such."

"Well, that's too bad," David said. "I was kind of wondering about Lou's ghost, now that you mention it."

Melanie poked him.

"Yeah, I figured you for one of those looney kinds," Louis laughed. "You need anything from us before we go? We got a service in another couple hours and have to get it ready."

David looked around. It was a very good question. Did he need anything from the gravediggers?

"Well, yeah, maybe one thing."

"Okay, what's that?" Curly said.

"What kind of birds come around here."

"That's a weird one. Nobody ever asked that before. You ever heard that one?" Curly asked his taller friend.

"Nope, that is a new one," Louis said.

Melanie poked David again. "Why are you asking about birds?"

David looked around. "Well, I don't know. I just was thinking it's such a quiet, peaceful place."

Curly started to laugh. "Oh, I get it now. You wondering about vultures circling around. Looking for their just desserts, so to speak?" Louis said.

"Hadn't thought of that," David said. "Just thinking about having company."

"Oh, yeah. Company. Well, me and Curly are here. We are his company."

"Sure are," said Curly. "And after we're gone, they'll be someone else. Always was and always will be. We got to go now. You take all the time you need."

David stood in front of Lou's grave. Melanie took his hand.

"I was thinking more about hawks and hummingbirds. Those birds remind me of Lou," David said.

"Yeah, hawks and hummingbirds would be good company," Melanie said.

David remembered the words of the Kaddish. He said them out loud and looked up for any birds in the sky.

They drove back to his apartment. He drove fast, but for a different reason. Melanie sat close. He loved the way she smelled, and he was finished with death for the moment. He wasn't in the ground and he wanted to punctuate that notion. It was obvious that Melanie felt the same way because her hand was moving inside his thigh.

Back at the apartment they tore off each other's clothes like they were on fire. The violence of the initial moments unnerved him, but she was even more keen than he to attack. She pulled him down hard and they were gone. Her body radiated like an inferno, and every shape looked perfect. Neither of them had ever experienced sex after death. They talked about it afterwards. The force felt otherworldly to David, like a reprieve or a redemption. The disappearance of hope and then it's sudden return was like an existential game of hide-and-seek. It was as if he had blasted through a stone wall, and now all he felt was the peaceful exhaustion of being on the other side. He knew it wouldn't last.

By Monday David had caved into the reality that his best friend was dead. He didn't have a roommate, and Wiz and CJ would soon be in Vietnam. He had still not heard about Rick. His grief was stunning. It had a peculiar grip, like tentacles wrapping around parts of him that he didn't know existed. His body worked, yet he felt constrained in even the simplest of tasks, like walking or making breakfast. Writing was impossible. He could not believe how much he had depended upon Lou for his compass readings. Where now?

He drove to work and was going through the paces of stocking and filling orders when he saw his father walking down the aisle with a slight grin on his face.

"Guess what?"

"What?" David said.

Jacob reached into his breast pocket and pulled out a pair of tickets. He wiggled them in front of David. "Koufax is pitching against the Mets tomorrow and going for his twentieth."

"No way!" David said.

"So you won't be too busy?"

"No, Tuesday is perfect."

The day zipped by quickly. He unpacked and catalogued the car parts and fantasized about watching Koufax pitch again. He told Bryce about the tickets, and they spent the day talking about baseball and commiserating about Lou. They deconstructed Koufax's delivery, so supple and elegant, and at the same time, designed for maximum power, as well as deception because the hitter never knew whether he was getting blinding heat or a rainbow curve ball. They exchanged statistics of past performances, made projections into the future of the season, all of which served to soften the misery of the past few days.

Tuesday-night traffic was light when David and his father left for the ballpark. David listened to the news—over fifteen hundred Viet Cong attacked a relief convoy between Duc Co and Pleiku near the Cambodian border. At least one F-100 jet fighter was shot down; the commentator said the pilot was presumed captured. According to military sources, the battle was the largest engagement to date, and the number of causalities sustained was still unknown. The fighting continued. He looked out at the Santa Monica Freeway; everything was moving smoothly, no accidents or stalled vehicles.

"Your friends are headed over there pretty soon, aren't they?" his father asked.

"Yeah. Any day actually."

"Terrible."

"Worse than that," David said.

They turned off at the Dodger Stadium exit and wound their way up Elysian Park Ave. to the giant plateaus of the parking areas. Outside the stadium, David bought a newspaper with the rosters, the starting lineups, and the current statistics of all the players. They climbed the stairs and wound through the tunnels and walkways, each with its own pop-up view of the field. The sound of the organ blasted away, and David glimpsed the movement of Dodger blue around the field. The seats were along the first baseline, about halfway up in the loge boxes, with a perfect view of the pitcher's mound and the infield.

The Mets dugout was directly below, and David saw Al Jackson, the Mets starting pitcher, warming up along the right-field line. Across the infield, Koufax threw his final warm-up tosses while talking with John Roseboro. Maury Wills and Jim Gilliam were playing catch; Ron Fairly, Wes Parker, and Lou Johnson were running leisurely across the outfield grass while the ground crew scurried around with rakes, brooms, and miniature tractors that smoothed and graded the infield. The flags rippled along the top edge of the stadium. Below the horizon the remaining stands of pine, eucalyptus, and recently transplanted palm trees provided respite to the urban sprawl that loomed over the basin.

David could feel his adrenaline boiling inside. He made himself comfortable in seat number 147. Koufax took the mound and everyone rose for the national anthem as the sky darkened and the lights illuminated the sharp distinctions between the red clay infield and the Kelly-green grass of the outfield. David looked at his father as they sat down to watch the game.

"This is just what I needed. Thanks, it's the best, the very best."

"I thought you'd appreciate it."

"Here we go."

Koufax went into his windup and let loose with a fastball David could barely see, and the game was under way. An older guy with curly white hair, wearing a Dodgers hat, and his chubby middle-aged son sat next to them. Before the game started, David noticed they had powered down two beers apiece and were starting on their third. The father had a nose that looked like it had lost every fight over the last fifty years; the rest of him was thin and muscular, like he had spent a lot of time working out or lifting bricks for a living.

"Goddamn that guy can pitch, don't you think?" The older guy said.

He turned to David as Koufax struck out another Met. David hesitated to engage with the guy, figuring that once he started he'd be committed for the next eight innings. But then he figured what the heck, it's a game, get in the spirit of it.

"Yeah, he's the best of the best, at least right now," David said.

"Right now and maybe ever. I've seen my share. Even better than Feller and Dizzy Dean. I've seen them both, great pitchers, incredible, but not even Feller dominated like this guy." He nodded toward Koufax as the Dodger pitcher slowly walked back to the dugout.

"Hey, I'm Jack Delaney, this is my son Bob."

"David Mandel and my father Jacob." They shook hands all around.

"Can I buy you gentlemen a beer?"

"No thanks," David said.

"Sure, you can buy me one," Jacob answered.

"Three more beers here," Jack shouted to the hawker a couple of rows above them. Bob grabbed the beers, his hands were the size of dinner plates. He dipped his thick tongue in one of them and licked the suds the way a cow licks a salt block, then passed the other two. That made four beers for the neighbors.

"Cheers," Jack and Bob yelled.

"Back to you," Jacob said.

Koufax took the mound for the second inning after the Dodgers went meekly in the first. Watching Koufax warm up, David remembered something Lou had told him about once when they were studying mythology: *A hero is driven by obedience to a secret impulse—* Emerson. Koufax reared back into his windup, and the ball disappeared into the night. The Mets batters swung and missed.

"Goddamn, that guy can pitch," Jack stammered again.

"Yeah, this could be his twentieth tonight," David said.

Koufax didn't display any visible emotion, his drive and competitive spirit came from some imponderable place. Maybe he simply loved playing baseball and wanted to be the best. But the notion of a *secret impulse* that enabled him to elevate beyond the pack? Was that inside Koufax?

"What we have right here, David, is undoubtedly the greatest left-handed pitcher, perhaps the greatest pitcher, in the history of baseball," Jack said, pausing to sip his beer.

"You'll get no argument from me," David said.

"Me either," Jacob said.

"And right now I think there are guys like Gibson, Whitey Ford, and even Drysdale—all of them almost as good as any of the other great ones. But Koufax is the best. And what's more, he's a Jew," Jack said.

Koufax struck out the Mets first baseman on a blazing fastball to end the inning.

"You guys want a hot dog? You need to eat something, makes the game more fun," Jack said.

David glared at his father, who shrugged his shoulders.

"Hot dogs?" Jack asked again. "I'm going to get another beer anyway. Come on. I'm buying."

"What do you mean, he's a Jew?" David said.

"He's a Jew, that's all. Not many Jews playing baseball, let alone pitching like he does."

"I'm a Jew," David said. "And I play baseball."

"Hey, no offense. I'm just saying."

"Saying what?" David said with a bite in his voice.

"David, calm down," his father said.

"You saying it's odd for Jews to be playing baseball?" David said.

"Look. I'm sorry. You don't need to get bent out of shape, kid. It's just a baseball game. Besides, I'm great fan of his. Don't matter to me what religion he is."

"Then why'd you say it in the first place?"

"I don't know. Everybody says it," Jack said.

"Says what?" David said.

"Hey, David, let it go," his father said.

"Yeah, kid. Listen to your dad. Let it go. I'm going get a hot dog. You want one?"

David glared at Jack as he slid out in front of him and disappeared through the tunnel that led to the food stands. Bob looked straight ahead at the game.

Jacob stood in front of his aisle seat. "We're trading seats," he said.

"No need. I'll drop it."

"No, you won't. I know you better than that."

Jack came back with four hot dogs. David shook his head, but Jacob took one so Bob took two. David and his father watched the rest of the game without any commentary from Jack or Bob. Koufax completely crushed the Mets after nine full innings. All 36,800 fans went crazy, cheering and screaming for Koufax, *the Jew.*

CHAPTER TWENTY-NINE

Saturday, August 14, 1965

To call tonight's game a classic pitchers' duel doesn't serve it justice. The Dodgers beat the Pirates one to zero behind Sandy Koufax. This was a ten-inning gem between two fine pitchers, each surrendering just five hits. Don Cardwell matched Koufax inning after inning. The only difference in the game was a fluke error by the great Roberto Clemente in the bottom of the tenth, otherwise they might still be out there. Their stuff was that good. Koufax struck out twelve, allowed no walks, and pitched his fourth shutout of the season while winning his twenty-first game of the year. The only glitch tonight was the attendance; only 29,327 fans showed up. There were about 15,000 no-shows due to the "situation" in Watts.

David watched the mayhem on television Thursday night. He could smell the fires that were burning just a couple miles from his apartment. Sirens blared throughout the night. He awoke around 4:00 a.m. in a sweat, then fell back to sleep. The alarm went off at eight o'clock. His apartment was sweltering because he had closed all the windows due to the smoke. He dressed quickly and drove to work.

David arrived at the store a little after eight. The heat was already unbearable, and the smog smelled like rotten eggs as it burned through the whites of his eyes. His energy was down. When the Sunshine Cart arrived, he ordered a large coffee and a cinnamon twist.

"How was that game with your dad the other night?" Simon asked.

"The best, he's at twenty wins. It was a monster game." David left out the details about the altercation.

"Well, I wish he could do something about this weather, man, it's brutal."

"It's disgusting. I don't remember it ever being like this."

"Yeah, all this smoke doesn't help anything. It's all pretty sad," Simon said, his voice trailing into a somber tone.

"Sad? That hardly touches what's happening. Despicable, vile, shameful, it's as bad as I've ever seen," Rosy said.

David remembered the morning headlines, *Negro Riots Rage On, Death Toll 25.*

"I could see the smoke driving in this morning."

"Man, it gets worse and worse, more cars, more smog, more heat, more oppression. Everyone gets more tense and there doesn't seem to be any escape from it all," Simon moaned.

"This place won't or can't change," David said.

"Maybe so," Simon said. "But this is home for me."

"I'm not sure where home is anymore," David murmured. With Lou gone, he wasn't sure about very much. He chomped down on the thick sweet roll Rosy had made.

"David, you take care of yourself this weekend. It's really crazy out there right now. No telling how long this will last and how far it's going to spread."

"Thanks, Simon. I will see you Monday," David said. He felt something tugging. The city was burning, and the violence was swirling in every direction. The city was plugged with fear.

After work the traffic moved quickly. David figured people were staying home with their doors locked and their weapons loaded. He was fine having the empty lanes. Smoke billowed from both sides of the road. He wondered if the Dodgers game would be cancelled. They had already nixed the football game at the Los Angeles Coliseum. Emergency vehicles passed every few minutes, headed both east and west. He had a date with Melanie, and he was going to be right on time.

He picked up Melanie, and they quickly decided to go to the Hamburger Hamlet in Westwood. It took a long time to get served, but neither of them was in a hurry. After they finally ordered their food, David gazed across the booth to Melanie. He reached over and softly touched her cheek.

After dinner they headed over to the High Note just as the band started to play. They had the dance floor almost to themselves and just let their bodies rip and glide till they were both soaked with sweat. It was a new band from San Francisco called The Jefferson Airplane. The music rocked inside his head and his body. He and Melanie swirled around each other, touching occasionally, but mostly they let the sweltering beat push and pull them like a riptide, undulating and pulsating into another realm of consciousness. Everything that had happened to David over the past few weeks evaporated into the night. By ten o'clock they were exhausted and waddled out the door with a couple of large paper cups filled with iced tea and lots of lemon. Before getting back into the car, Melanie turned to David.

"David, I know this sounds weird, but would you mind taking me over to my dad's place? He's leaving for New York tomorrow morning, and I haven't had time to pick up a check from him for school. It's really all right if you don't want to go. I'll go."

"No, it's fine as long we don't have to stay around."

"I promise. In fact, you can stay in the car if you want, and I'll run up."

"It's okay."

In the distance, they heard sirens roar. They headed east on Wilshire where Melanie's father lived and worked. David wasn't looking forward to the encounter. He believed Melanie meant what she said about it being a quick visit. He wanted to get back home with her and sort out the events of the day, and more importantly, get her into bed.

Benjamin Saltzman greeted them at the door. David had met him a few weeks earlier. Benjamin's face was pale, his eyes glossed over. He was trembling.

"My God, it's so good that you're here and safe. I was sick with worry. I called your mother, and she didn't have a clue about your whereabouts."

"Daddy, what are you talking about?"

"What? Don't you know what's going on?"

"Yes, but I'm not going to stop my life."

David walked past Benjamin into the living room. The large television was blasting live footage from the riots.

"Mel, they're burning down the city, the schvartses—they've gone crazy, they're burning stores, homes, fire trucks, they've gone mad! Look."

Out of the polished walnut case where Benjamin Saltzman housed his state-of-the-art RCA television, a screeching newscaster told the story for probably the hundredth time.

This all started Wednesday night when officer Lee Minikus made a routine stop of a vehicle in the Watts district of South Central Los Angeles. Office Minikus pulled over a car driven by Mr. Marquette Frye, whom he had observed driving erratically. Frye failed to pass a field sobriety test, and as he was arrested, Mr. Frye, Frye's mother, and brother Ronald assaulted Officer Minikus. All three were arrested. A crowd of onlookers began throwing rocks and bottles. More people gathered, and soon fires were started, followed by looting and assaults on police and fire personnel. The situation is now clearly out of control. There are accounts of some white motorists being dragged from their cars and beaten.

The television cameras panned the streets, showing buildings ablaze and raging mobs dashing from block to block, looting stores and then torching them.

"I don't understand," Melanie said.

"They're savages, that's what it's about, these people are animals. Burning their own homes and stores, hurting their own people. Even the police chief called them 'monkeys in a zoo.' Animals, that's what they are."

"Daddy, that's disgusting!"

"Disgusting, you want disgusting? Look at what they're doing. They're destroying the whole city."

"People are frustrated." David said.

"No excuses, David. None. They should all be locked up," Benjamin blared.

"Daddy, we've got to go."

Benjamin Saltzman walked over to his bureau and picked up an envelope. Without saying a word to David, he handed it to Melanie.

"You be safe, darling," he said and walked into his bedroom and closed the door.

Melanie and David bolted from the apartment. They didn't say anything for the first few miles. Then David said, "That didn't go so well."

"He'll get over it. He always does. Nothing I can do to change who he is."

"Yeah, well, he's not the only one. That's the problem," David said.

"What problem is that?"

"The one in the streets right now. It's awful."

"That's for sure, but let's not talk about it anymore."

"Fine with me." He turned off the freeway and pointed the car toward his apartment.

Melanie agreed to sleep over after she called her mother and assured her that she was safe. The sound of strife howled through the darkness like urban coyotes heralding more new kills. They smoked a joint and played the Myles Davis album *My Funny Valentine*. It helped drown out the cacophony. After the album ended, David looked at Melanie and could tell the pot had hit her brain too. They climbed into bed and held each other, naked and frightened, aware that parts of the world were in chaos and bleeding. They couldn't ignore or deny it, and at the same time, they had to find a tender corner to rest.

In the morning they made love again and went for a long run on the beach before the sun started another doleful, unbearable day. They ran until their sides started to unravel. The sand felt fresh and forgiving. They collapsed on the wet shoreline, laughing for no apparent reason other than it was all that remained. After dragging themselves back to the apartment, they showered and held each other as the water cascaded over their shoulders.

After getting dressed, they walked over to Skip's Diner for breakfast. David bought a copy of the *Times*, tucked it under his arm, and followed Melanie inside. The news was all bad except for the sports page. Big news; not only had Drysdale shut out the Mets one to nothing to maintain first place, but Koufax had signed a new contract for next year worth a hundred thousand. He became the highest-paid pitcher in baseball. There had been rumors that he might not sign next year, but now he was delivered for at least one more season.

Koufax was set to pitch against the Pirates and go for his twenty-first win. Already, the sports writers were calculating the possibility of a thirty-win season for him. If he continued to pitch every fourth game, he'd have twelve more starts, so thirty was not out of the question but meant winning almost every game. David mused about the possibility of this being the greatest season a major league pitcher had ever attained, considering his shutouts, strikeouts, and complete game accomplishments.

"David," Melanie said.

He looked up and her lips were cupped into a frothy smile. "Yes?"

"Are you going to eat? Your food is just sitting there. What's so interesting in the paper?"

"Nothing really, just an article about Koufax signing a new contract."

"That's not nothing, David, that's fantastic."

"Yeah, I think so. But I haven't gotten to the front page yet."

"Well, let's have breakfast before page one gives us indigestion."

"Look at this!" David pointed to it. "They've imposed martial law!" He read the article to Melanie. There was to be a community meeting scheduled that morning between Negro businessmen, preachers, and teachers to try and restore order in the Watts area. Meanwhile, police told residents they needed to remain inside their homes. "It sounds more hopeful than the Vietnam news," he said.

"Yeah, but it's still a war zone, and it's just a few miles down the road," Melanie said.

David paid the bill and took Melanie by the hand. They walked into the sunshine and headed for the beach. He felt rotten about sitting in front of the Pacific while the city was in flames just a few miles away.

"Maybe I should join the Peace Corps or Vista," he said.

"You could. But it sounds kind of drastic to give up college before you even start."

"The truth is I don't know what I want to do. Maybe I'll move up to San Francisco and find work with Rene or Frank. I can write."

"And get drafted?"

"Maybe go to school up there."

"David, I'd like to go home. I've got to get ready for practice and I need some time for myself."

As he drove back home, L.A. burned and screamed for redemption, but this Saturday offered nothing except a surreal display of smoky orange and crimson colors. David knew that in the distant western horizon, bikini-clad girls were still giggling on the beach. There had been talk of cancelling the Dodgers game. Traffic was congested from the Wilshire exit all the way to the airport, and the announcer suggested using alternate routes. It sounded like a good idea to David. What he needed was to find some alternate routes in his life.

At Venice Blvd. he turned left and headed east until Sepulveda, then he veered north toward the airport and reached Manchester Blvd. There was no direct way home. He could see billows of smoke wafting upward where the San Bernardino Mountains were supposed to be. After a couple of blocks, he noticed police cars parked along the side streets, then he saw armored personnel carriers moving right down the street, and suddenly traffic stopped. Straight ahead was a roadblock with police and soldiers in full-camouflage battle regalia. Total gridlock prevailed. Everyone was Black or in uniform. Some of the motorists were taken out of their vehicles and interrogated. One young guy started yelling and was immediately squashed to the ground, cuffed, and thrown in the back of a patrol car. A helmeted L.A.P.D. officer climbed atop his cruiser with a bull horn and shouted that all roads going east were closed. Cars were directed back toward the airport and the San Diego Freeway. All traffic into the Watts and South Central L.A. area was halted until further notice. A steady stream of trucks with National Guard troops poured through the street that paralleled Manchester; it had been opened strictly for the military.

David didn't notice the uniformed officer approach. His windows were sealed tight, the air conditioning blasting away as he gaped at the scene. The cop tapped his baton on the window. David lowered it and met his white helmet with its dark sun visor pulled ominously over his eyes.

"What the fuck you doing here? You crazy or are you looking to start trouble?"

"Neither, just trying to get home," David said. The cop looked pissed and impatient.

"Get this rig turned around and get the hell out of here. You aren't getting anywhere in this direction. You understand me?"

"Sure, officer, thanks for the information." David powered the window up in defiance before the guy could utter another word. The war had come home; the terror, the insanity, the hatred sizzled in the streets. In the distance, an occasional shot echoed against the suffocating haze, the smoke twisted up as if offering a sacrifice. He made a U-turn into the traffic heading west. It took thirty minutes to move the two miles back to Sepulveda Blvd. He continued another couple miles until he reached the San Diego Freeway and disappeared into the southbound traffic, which had almost returned to the normal rush to the beach and shopping centers.

He was a useless observer, at best a witness, a chronicler of something for the future. Before long he was back at Venice Blvd., and it was still early afternoon. The whole mess gnawed at him, but he wasn't sure what to do.

When he got home he decided to take a walk. He needed to clear his head. Just as he was closing the door behind him, he saw Bryce walking up the sidewalk.

"Hey, where you going?" Bryce said.

"Just stretching my legs. What's up with you?"

"I thought you could use some company. Sounded like the riots were getting kind of close."

"Yeah, good to see you. I might need your protection," David laughed. "Want to walk?"

They crossed Main Street and moved in a southerly direction. The sound of sirens grew louder, and there was a strong scent of flames in the air. By the time they reached Rose Ave., people were on the street, talking and shouting. Police cars were howling in pursuit of the fire engines. David asked a couple who were standing outside their home holding their baby if they knew what was happening. The guy had long yellow hair and a handlebar moustache; soft doe, bloodshot eyes; and wore a black T-shirt and cut-off jeans smudged with a panoply of oil paints.

"Yeah, man, I know what's happening. They just showed it on the tube. There's a riot just down the street at 7th and Broadway. A bunch of rioters are trying to burn that little Chinese grocery store. The police and fire department have closed Broadway between 4th and Lincoln. It's like a war zone."

"Jesus, are you kidding me?" Bryce said.

"No, they just showed it on the tube, I'm telling you the truth. I wouldn't go any further south. The cops are pretty freaked right now. They're getting hit with rocks and Molotov cocktails."

David kept walking south.

"Hey, what are doing?" Bryce said.

"I want to get closer."

"Didn't you hear what that guy said?"

"You don't have to come if you don't want."

Bryce threw his hands up and kept pace with David, all the while shaking his head. The sounds grew louder, and the sky grew darker. David picked up the tempo, and as he did, he remembered the story he'd been writing—the boy with morning blindness and Tiresias, the blind prophet. The writing was going slow, but he felt he had something. He looked around. There was smoke and chaos everywhere. What was he supposed to see? Let alone supposed to do?

"For Christ's sake, slow down. I'm with you," Bryce said. "I just don't know what you are doing, that's all."

"I just want to see the fire with my own eyes." David said.

CHAPTER THIRTY

Wednesday, August 18, 1965

It's been a long night. The Dodgers and Koufax look worn down. At the end of twelve hot, grueling innings, the Phillies have come away with a six-to-three win. The loss knocks the Dodgers out of first place and keeps Koufax from running his win total to twenty-two. Who knows how long this would have gone on if Maury Wills had not made an error in the twelfth leading to the Phillies' win. Koufax pitched a strong seven innings, giving up just five hits, but his control was off, and after walking the first two batters in the eighth inning, he was finished for the night. It's been a tough week for everyone in this city, and I can't help but think the riots took their toll on this team just like everyone else. It's not an excuse. It's just an honest observation. For once, I believe the Dodgers will be looking forward to leaving the City of the Angels when they head up to San Francisco tomorrow for a series against the Giants.

When David got to work on Monday, his father told him a cousin of Rosy and Simon's had been killed in the riots. They wouldn't be back until Tuesday. He asked his father about the details, but there weren't any. All Simon had said was that his cousin was killed and that he and Rosy needed some time. The riots were over, but the lingering sense of tragedy, both personal and communal, remained like an open festering wound.

David worked through the usual ten o'clock coffee break. He tended to his boredom stocking shelves and filling orders.

Bryce came to work Tuesday morning and greeted David with a punch to the shoulder. "How you doing?" he asked.

"Dragging and angry."

"Whoa."

"You heard about Simon and Rosie's nephew?"

"Yeah, it's awful."

"I'm thinking about getting out of here. I'm needing to rethink what I want to do this fall."

They walked to the front of the store where customers were lining up to place orders and ask questions. To the left of the counter was a small lunch room. David went in and Bryce followed. They sat across the table from each other.

"You ought to just let things settle down before making any decisions," Bryce said.

"Haven't you noticed life doesn't *settle down*? It just keeps ramping up. Besides that, I've pretty much had it with this place."

David wanted to talk with Lou. Bryce was a good friend. He was solid, smart, and would be successful in whatever he desired. And he still had his baseball career. He had a path, but he wasn't Lou.

The next day David heard the long blast from the Sunshine Cart and headed out to see Simon and Rosy. Bryce met him in the parking lot. David wasn't sure what to expect. Business as usual? Somber withdrawal? Anger and despair? His heart sped up as he approached the cart and saw everyone lined up as usual, barking food orders, and there was Simon laughing and joking as he always did. He hung back and waited until things slowed down. He liked to have uninterrupted time with Simon, so he plopped down and waited. Simon glanced over, nodded his head and raised his eyebrows, but he was too busy to say anything. Within ten minutes Simon and Rosy had served everyone. There was a low hum of satisfaction among the customs as they gulped their last ounce of coffee and downed the final bite of a sandwich or a sweet roll. David approached the counter.

"What will you have, son?" Simon asked in his bass, matter-of-fact voice.

David shivered, fearing that something had shifted between them. For a few seconds, Simon held his cool distance, his face stoic and controlled, but when David ordered a fried egg sandwich, he broke into smile.

"It's good to see you," Simon said. His warm eyes shattered any doubt David had about their connection.

"I'm so sorry to hear about your cousin."

"Thanks. Horrible, should have never happened."

Rosy handed David his order. She always poured an extra dose of pepper and sliced tomatoes on his egg sandwich, so when it came out in its hot wax paper it sizzled and dripped. The crowd had now totally cleared. Rosy popped her head over from the grill and reached out her hand to make contact with the boys.

"Hi, Rosy," David said. "I'm sorry." Bryce added his condolences.

"He was just at the wrong place at the wrong time. Poor soul. He was only sixteen and a good student," Rosy said.

"Nathan Ezekiel Jones. My sister's boy," Simon said. "A baseball player just like you guys. He would have had quite a future. Big kid, like me. He could hit just like Willie McCovey."

"Terrible," said Bryce.

"A lot of people died. Friends of friends, kids of friends. The cops shot without any warning. They fired and asked no questions. Police and National Guard running around like crazy men," Simon said.

"It's a sad state of affairs," Rosy added. "What good is going to come from this? If I lived on those streets, I'd have no compunction but to riot and tear it down, it stinks. Who wouldn't want to destroy it?"

"Now what?" David asked.

"Now we get back to our lives. Funeral is Saturday, and I'll need to be spending some extra time with my sister. Then we roll along and hope there won't be a next time, but we all know it's just a matter of time," Simon said.

"Well, I hope it's a real long time," Bryce said.

Bryce walked back into the shop, leaving David with Simon and Rosy. David stayed and commiserated with them. They were such solid folks. Simon had told David about their life. They owned a small house in Manhattan Beach just a block from the water. They had photos of it on the back wall of the cart that David saw every time he stood at the counter. One picture always grabbed David. It was of them with their chocolate brown Labrador Clara standing in the front yard with the sunset in the background. "Our pride and joy," Rosy always said. David wondered if there was a photo like that waiting for him somewhere in the future.

"So what about you, Mister David?" Simon said. "What's next on your plate?"

"Right now, I'm not sure. I'd like to go up north again. I like it there."

"And school?"

"I don't know. I'm going to eat this egg sandwich right now. Maybe I'll have more information tomorrow."

"Amen to that," Simon said. "See you tomorrow."

They drove off down the narrow street between two large soot-stained brick buildings; the van waddled from side to side. Simon tooted his horn as he turned right onto Flower Street.

When David got home he called Rene.

"David, it's so great to hear from you. You've survived the maelstrom. My god, the footage of the war down there looks like Vietnam. It's insane!"

"That it is. I want to make plans as soon as possible to get up north. Is that trip to the Sierras still in the works?"

"Absolutely, in fact you should be getting a letter today with a list of supplies and equipment you'll need to bring. Is Melanie still planning to join us?"

"I'm not sure."

"Well, we can't figure the food out until we know whether we're three or four, so let me know as soon as you can."

"I'm thinking of driving up this Friday after work. That would give me till the next Sunday to get back and give us seven or eight days to be up there. Is that too long?"

"God no, that's just about perfect. I'll tell Frank and we'll get on it. You check with that lady of yours. I hope she joins us. I know Frank thinks she's got a lot of potential."

David hoped Melanie would join him as well but still had some reservations. He wondered what kind of *potential* Frank had in mind.

Sure enough, Rene's letter arrived. It was in a thin envelope, addressed in small perfectly crafted letters. There was also a letter from CJ. David opened the one from Rene first and laid it on the kitchen table in front of him.

Dear David,

Please pay careful attention to the details below as your survival (and Melanie's) depends on it. Here is what you'll need for the trip . . .

David had almost everything except the sleeping pad, and that would be easy to score at the local mountaineering store in Santa Monica. The biggest question was whether Melanie was going to make it or not. He doubted she'd break away for a full week with classes starting and the season looming.

That night Melanie came over and surprised him with the news that practice had been suspended for that week for some technical NCAA reason, so she could go on the trip. It made his night. They celebrated with fried seafood at the Seaside Bar and Grill in Venice. It had an upstairs deck where you could watch the surf and get a good view of the sunset. They talked incessantly about the trip. He showed her the list Rene had sent.

"I don't have any of this stuff, except the socks."

"Don't worry," he said. "It'll be a small investment for the future."

"Future? I like the sound of that word," she chortled.

She gazed at David. Her eyes glistened with a keen mixture of matrimonial glee and ferocious intent until he blinked, and she laughed hysterically. "I got you worried, didn't I?"

"I suppose you did. It's not easy for me to think much about the future."

"David, it's really a shame that sometimes you take yourself so damned seriously. Lighten up." She splashed him with water from her glass. "Get over it."

"You've got a point," he said, getting up.

"Of course I do. Just don't get yourself all worked up about it. Come on, I need to get up early for practice."

David drove her home and was back at the apartment in less than an hour. Before going to sleep, he opened CJ's letter. It was the first lengthy missive he'd received from his friend.

Dear David,

I hope this letter finds you safe and out of harm's way. I wanted to write you as soon as I heard about the riots. Things got tense for a time on the base. We've got a lot of negroes in our battalion, so you can imagine the bullshit that went on between everyone as we watched what was going down. There were a couple of fights, but the sergeant got things under control. He let us know that if we wanted to survive in Nam, we better learn to "love one another" or we'd all be dead meat. The captain ordered all televisions turned off for the next two days.

Everyone is pretty agitated around here. We keep hearing about the big battles in Nam, the same stuff you must be seeing on the news. Wiz and I can't wait to get over there and do our thing. No one is telling us anything about our deployment, and even if I knew I couldn't tell you. I'm sorry about Lou, it's hard to believe he's really dead. One thing about being in the Army, it gives me plenty of time to think. I've been having dreams about my father and remembering all the hunting and camping trips we did together. He tried his best to straighten me out, and all that ever happened was I came up a loser. Not that I'm feeling sorry for myself, cause I'm not. Especially now after these past couple months, I realize that I'm really all right. I mean I hold my own against all these guys from around the country, in fact they respect me and that's a new experience. Now that I have a little more time I'm starting to play the piano a little bit. They've got this funky old upright in the recreation room, and I go over there in the evenings and play some blues and old Hank Williams tunes.

Wiz is chasing tail as usual. For a little guy, he's got an insatiable appetite for the foxes. I'm less inclined, although he insists we go to the pick-up bars, and I have to admit I've had a couple of tastes myself. There really is something about wearing a uniform that brings the girls right up to your door. It's just another thing that marks the days until we get shipped out.

Maybe you've been in touch with Veronica? She's writes me a lot. You know how she worries all the time. There's not anything I can do or say that will quiet her fears, that's just the way she is. We're hearing that it's getting worse over there. I just know I've got to go and do this. Just tell Veronica not to worry. I'll be fine.

It was great to see all of you, even though the circumstances sucked. Say hi to everyone and keep out of trouble.

> *Your friend in arms,*
> *CJ*

Wednesday morning David got up early, wanting to avoid the traffic. Before leaving for work he turned on the TV. Mayor Yorty criticized Governor Brown for withdrawing the troops too soon. Statistics were still being crunched. Funerals were being planned.

He could only take a few minutes of news, and then he started out for work. It was a quiet, gritty morning. The smell of fresh dough baking and coffee roasting, mixed with the industrial aromas of steam and sweat, invigorated him. *Everyone is back at work*, he mused. It was like a momentary ceasefire, but the sound of sirens still echoed in the distance.

He left work early in order to meet Melanie and check out her equipment. She was beaming when she opened the door. Strewn across the living floor was everything from the list.

"What do you think?"

"Way to go!" He said.

She had bought top-of-the-line equipment; a feather-light down sleeping bag rated to 0 degrees, a state-of-the-art Kelty frame pack, and the thickest Ensolite pad they had in the store. She was excited and proud. After checking all the equipment, he kissed her goodbye. They decided to get together Thursday night to make final plans for the trip. He felt like he had just thrown strike three. He was busting out.

David got home just as the game started. Koufax was scheduled to pitch against the Phillies and Jim Bunning who was always a tenacious opponent. The pennant race was tight between the Dodgers, the Giants, and the Braves, with all three separated by a single game. The Phillies' Richie Allen and Dick Stuart were two of the strongest hitters in the National League. Both were capable of taking Koufax down. The air outside was hot and smoky, and David had a bad feeling about tonight's game.

CHAPTER THIRTY-ONE

Sunday, August 22, 1965

The Dodgers lost four to three today, but that isn't the story. What we saw today will stay embedded in baseball history as a sad and infamous event. The game had been tense from the start. Maury Wills led off the game with a bunt single. Ron Fairly doubled him home. In the top of the third, the Giants pitcher, Juan Marichal, knocked down both Wills and Fairly with high inside pitches. Between innings it was reported that the umpires warned both dugouts that anymore knockdowns would result in ejections and probable suspensions. When Marichal came to the plate in the bottom of the inning, the Dodger catcher John Roseboro returned one of Koufax's pitches very close to Marichal's ear. Marichal responded by cracking Roseboro's skull with his bat. He then took a step back and looked like he was going to club Roseboro again, who had blood streaming down his face and was furiously going toward his assailant. Koufax ran into the fray, trying to disarm Maraichal, while Willie Mays grabbed Roseboro in an effort to avert another whack of the bat from the Giants pitcher. The home-plate umpire, Shag Crawford, finally tackled Marichal from behind and quelled the danger. The whole scene was just crazy! After order was restored, Marichal was tossed out of the game. Roseboro left to receive medical attention. Fortunately, it looks like he'll be okay.

Koufax was clearly shaken by the attack, because he walked the next two batters and then gave up a home run to Willie Mays. After that inning he settled down, but the damage was done. The Dodgers scored once more in the top of the ninth but came up short. Whatever enmity existed between these teams before today, it just got a lot worse.

As planned, David went to Melanie's house Thursday night, and they loaded her gear for the trip. David's stuff was already in the car. They kissed good night and David drove home. He was still thinking about Koufax's loss the previous night. He wondered if he would win his twenty-second game on Sunday.

The next day David took off work early and avoided the Friday rush out of the city. He picked up Melanie at two, and they were just south of Fresno by 6:00 p.m. Melanie looked beautiful as she sang along with the radio. She knew all the lyrics from The Drifters, Mary Wells, The Righteous Brothers, and every tune that popped out of the speaker.

By the time they pulled into the Mission District it was half past nine. David drove around, trying to find a parking place close to Rene's. On the second pass, someone in an old black Ford truck pulled out and he grabbed the spot before it disappeared. They each shouldered their backpacks and lumbered down the street to the café. The place was packed, and when David opened the door he saw Richard Brautigan standing at the podium, his long straw-colored hair resting on a black denim jacket. Rene had mentioned that he would be reading this night. Lou had loaned David one of his books last year. Rene waved to them as they shuffled through the crowd, waddling like a couple of upright turtles, bumping into people and causing Brautigan to cease reading. The author glared at David while Rene cleared a spot for them to sit next to him.

The reading ended, and Rene asked David if he wanted to meet Brautigan, who was busy lapping up praise from the crowd and signing copies of *A Confederate General from Big Sur*.

David declined. Lou would have said yes, but David didn't care.

"Good decision. He's so full of himself," Rene said as he whisked them into his back-room office and studio. "Now, how are you two? Is there anything else you need for the trip?"

"We are set," David said.

"Okay, Frank is coming over in the morning, and we figured you two could just hang in the city tomorrow and then we'd leave at the crack of dawn on Sunday. That way we'll be heading against the weekend traffic."

"Perfect. I wanted to spend some time in the city anyway," Melanie said.

By Saturday afternoon David and Melanie were back at the café. Melanie had seen what she needed to see. Frank had set out several maps on a large table so they could get the general idea for the trip. After giving Melanie a long hug and shaking David's hand, Frank suggested they take two vehicles so that David and Melanie could just continue south down 395 instead of backtracking all the way north to get home.

They crossed the Bay Bridge early Sunday with Frank and Rene in the lead. It was before dawn as they headed south and then east toward Livermore and Tracy. Melanie slept, and David pondered the current pennant race. Thinking about baseball kept him alert. He remembered that the Dodgers were playing the Giants at Candlestick Park. Koufax was set to go against the indomitable ace of the Giants, Juan Marichal. He knew it was the final game of the series and the Dodgers had taken two of the first three. A win today would put them two and a half games ahead of the Giants and give them some breathing room for the upcoming fourteen games on the road. Koufax was attempting to win his twenty-second game, and if he succeeded, he would be in position to make a run for an incomparable thirty-win season. He still had at least ten, or perhaps eleven, more starts.

The sun started to climb over the low foothills. There weren't many cars on the road. David looked over at Melanie as she slept. She was beautiful but as unpredictable as a whirlwind.

When they got to Manteca they stopped for coffee and pancakes at the Gateway Roadside Inn. Frank smeared three tabs of butter on his buckwheat cakes, swirled his spoon around in his coffee, and looked up at the three of them. "Emerson said, 'Cities give not the human senses room enough.' Anyone want more syrup?" Frank raised the stainless-steel container.

"I'll have some more." Mel instinctively raised her hand.

"Me too," David said. "I remember Lou saying something like that when we hiked up Mount Vision."

"Well, he probably heard it from Frank. My friend can't quote enough Emerson." Rene stood up and nodded toward the road.

David disagreed, but didn't say anything.

"We've still got a few hours till we get to Tuolumne Meadows. I want David and Melanie to hike the high country before we camp tonight. Frank, you can spout Emerson all week if you want, but it's time to get back on the road."

At Big Oak Flat there was a sign: Last cheap gas before the park. They stopped. Rene asked Melanie if she wanted to ride with Frank awhile so he could tell her about the landscape as they approached Yosemite. It sounded good to her. She glanced at David, and he just shrugged and said, "Why not?" She hopped out and Rene got into the Galaxy.

David didn't like the idea but couldn't come up with a reason to prevent the switch. What was he doing with these two hippies twice his age? He was overmatched, yet he trusted his instincts to keep moving forward. Rene looked at him with a dreamy smile; his eyes glowed, his thin red lips turned up in a grin as he hummed the French national anthem, and then he turned away.

David tried to think about baseball or walking along the beach but couldn't shake his thoughts about Frank and Melanie driving alone through the tall trees and deep canyons.

"Do you think Frank is interested in Melanie?" he asked.

"Interested? You mean does he want to get in her pants?" Rene said.

"Yeah."

"Well, she's a very beautiful woman, and Frank's a virile kind of guy."

"I'll kick his ass," David said.

"I suppose you could, but calm down. Frank's too honorable to pull any shenanigans like that. He's quoting Emerson, not D. H. Lawrence. Besides, he likes you as much as her."

"What's that supposed to mean?"

"Just what I said. He respects you."

"I don't get it."

"Let me change the subject for a minute. How is your story going? The boy with morning blindness and the old healer."

"I haven't had much time to write, but it's coming along."

"Good," Rene said. "See that sign up there? Tuolumne Grove?"

"Yes."

"Pull over. It's time to take a little break and walk through the redwoods."

David pulled over. Frank and Melanie were right behind them. Soon they were all walking down a fern-lined path profuse with dogwood.

"These trees aren't as tall as the coastal redwoods, but when it comes to shear volume and bulk, there isn't anything on the earth that compares with the giant sequoia," Rene said.

He led the group as they meandered along the soft velvety floor and entered the dark primordial forest. David felt microscopic as he dodged through the bracken ferns and tiny white flowers that poked through the loam. Melanie marched along in front of him, her firm, muscular thighs pulsed and pumped like pistons. Her skin, the color of cinnamon, started to reveal tiny balls of sweat.

Frank and Rene were up ahead, laughing about something. He heard them jabbering about the last time they had come through this stand of redwoods.

"The botany professor from Berkeley, what was her name?" Rene said.

"Abigail, Professor Abigail Meadowcraft," Frank said.

"Great name," Rene replied.

"She was so manic. Couldn't stop naming all the plants with their proper scientific names and talking about the environmental relationships, the web of life she called it."

"Yeah, then you got overzealous and surprised her with a juicy kiss on her lips, out of nowhere," Rene said.

"It's rapture," I said to her. "Now just enjoy it."

"She stopped talking the rest of the hike."

"That was the idea," Frank said.

David and Melanie just caught the last bits of the conversation.

"Who did you kiss?" Melanie asked.

Frank replayed the story. David didn't think it was funny.

"Do you often kiss women unexpectedly?" she asked.

"Never before or after, as I recall. It just seemed like the right thing to do at the time," Frank said.

David looked around. Everyone was feeling so jolly. He had nothing to add to the conversation. His throat was parched. He thought about CJ and Wiz running around in a different kind of wilderness. He wished Lou were here. Lou's perspective usually gave him a lift. He had a way of perceiving life from a reasonable distance; the bigger picture, he used to say.

David stopped to take a drink and offered his water bottle to Melanie. She gulped down a third of the liquid.

"Good, do you want anymore?" he asked.

"No, I'm really fine now. You've been so quiet, you hardly said a word. Are you all right?"

"Yes, of course. What's not all right?" he lied. "I'm just thinking about all this—it's so pristine."

"Thanks for making this happen. I love it. I love being here with you."

They kept walking. Frank and Rene were ahead again. He thought about his choices. Everything suddenly felt wide open. Too open. Frank was laughing about something again. Maybe another woman?

"Look up." Melanie pointed to the distant canopy above. The trees stood straight like guided missiles, three hundred feet into the air. At the tops were knobby green tassels of lacey fir. They stood for a minute, necks craned back so they witnessed the tunnels of light that flashed up between the trees. It had an unnerving effect, a kind of spiritual vertigo, a sensation of spinning or whirling as if they were actually standing in a cathedral and looking out through the cavernous vaulted ceiling into the heavens.

"I'm getting dizzy," David said. He grabbed Melanie around the waist and pulled her close, nuzzled the back of her neck, and dared his right hand to brush across the front of her blouse. She swung herself around and kissed him quickly.

"These trees make me feel clean and holy." Melanie turned back around. "I want to catch up with Frank and Rene and see what else they have to say about this place. Don't you?"

"Kind of. Although I was also thinking of finding a giant hollowed-out tree and taking a little nap with you."

"Forget it, nature boy. There's too much to see, and we've only just got into the park."

At the bottom of the trail they all sat on the stump of a giant redwood, green with moss, spongy with age, moldy with memory. Frank unpacked some treats from his daypack. People quietly meandered around the grove. David counted fourteen Japanese tourists with floral shirts, dark shorts, and high-top hiking boots. They were being led by a guide, a thin woman with an animated red mouth and long fingers, who pointed at the bark of the redwoods, then jumped up and reached toward the clouds as all fourteen heads followed her fingers. None of them said a word. They looked awestruck.

"This is sacred ground right here, kids. I'm just sorry Lou isn't here with us. Before we partake of these goodies, let's just meditate on him for a couple minutes," Frank said.

David felt his stomach twist into knots. He didn't like sitting in the quiet. He wanted to shout and run through the trees. The idea of meditating, even about Lou, made him uneasy. He wanted to get back to the car and speed into the thin air that swirled around Tioga Pass. Lou was dead and gone. Hopefully, Louis and Curly were there watching over his site. He opened his eyes and looked at Frank sitting there like a stone Buddha from a galaxy he didn't understand. He wanted to punch him and then he closed his eyes again.

"David," Frank said. "You still on the planet?"

"Yes," he said.

"Here are the snacks." Frank passed around granola bars, peaches, apricots, and almonds. "Let's eat up. We need to get going if we're going to make camp before sunset."

David reached around and squeezed Melanie tight.

"Frank, this is amazing. I just can't thank you enough," Melanie said.

Frank nodded and sauntered up the trail with Rene, talking about where they planned to camp for the night.

They agreed to skip the valley floor with its exotic views of Half Dome and Yosemite Falls as well as crowds of people, and instead, continue up Highway 120. They stopped at Tuolumne Meadows and took a short jaunt toward Glen Aulin. The profuse wildflowers were audacious in color, especially the shooting stars, monkshood, and columbines.

They stood in the meadow where mounds of white-and-black speckled granite poked through the grass like bulging eyes glaring at the unrelenting sun. David watched trout dart from bank to bank. They walked an easy mile to the grassy meadows where the Pacific Crest Trail bisected the Tuolumne River, scrambled around bare granite, and stretched up to Wild Cat Point. None of them wanted to leave. Frank and Rene struck out along the river and returned a few minutes later.

"It's too damn beautiful up here, and who knows when you'll be back again? There's a couple hours of light left. We've got all the gear we need to make a quick bivouac for the night. Only thing is we don't have a permit," Frank said and looked over at Rene. "Screw the permit!"

"I agree," Rene said. "Here's the plan, we hustle back to the car; that shouldn't take more than an hour and a half. Grab our gear and some food, just enough for an early dinner, but no cooking, no fire, just our bags and tents. We'll camp off the trial far enough so the rangers won't notice. We'll bed down somewhere close enough to the river to get fresh water, then we head out at the crack of dawn for Rock Creek and avoid having to mess with paying for a camping site for tonight. What do you think?" He looked at David and Melanie.

Melanie immediately launched her fist in the air.

"Sounds great to me," David said. He stared around at the magnificence of Yosemite Valley, with peaks splayed in every direction.

Rene and Frank started to jog down the trail. Melanie and David followed. Once they arrived back at the cars, Rene and Frank efficiently packed the sleeping bags, tents, food, and water bottles and they were ready to go in fifteen minutes. They walked until it was agreed they'd be out of sight of hikers and rangers.

David and Frank quickly erected the two tents, securing the guidelines with large boulders in case strong winds kicked up in the night. Rene and Melanie filled water bottles in the creek and found a bright spot of waning sunshine near the river to eat and review the day's events. Rene passed out apples and turkey-and-cheese sandwiches on sourdough rolls, still soft and fresh.

They watched the sunset from a narrow spine of granite that jetted north of the campsite. It was an easy climb to the top and offered views along the drainage of the Tuolumne. Frank broke out a joint and passed it around in silence. David took a toke, then walked out toward the edge of the escarpment to get a better look. When he turned back, Frank had his arm around Melanie. They were laughing. Full count, David thought, fastball high and inside. He rushed toward Frank.

"What the fuck are you doing?" David yelled. He ripped Frank's arm from Melanie's shoulder.

"Easy, David, we were just cracking up over that marmot. See it?" Frank pointed toward a pile of rocks. "There, standing at attention like an old English sentry."

"David, what's wrong with you?" Melanie said.

"What's wrong is that Frank has been coming on to you right from the start!"

"Well, of course I have," Frank said. "She's a beautiful woman. But I wouldn't violate what you have together. You want to hit me? Go ahead. It's all right."

"You're an asshole," David said.

"You're probably right, but I mean you or Melanie no harm."

"It's true, David. Frank is a kind of asshole, but of the mystical variety," Rene said. "Really, he's only trying to guide you."

"Okay, it's agreed Frank is an asshole. I don't need a guide. And he needs to back off Melanie."

"I'm not your property, David," Melanie said.

"Well, I think we'd all better take another toke and get some sleep," Rene said. "It's been a long day."

They sat on fallen logs and rocks and passed a joint around. Frank stepped over to David and reached out his hand. "Are we good?" David shook his hand and nodded, feeling foolish and a bit overmatched.

David climbed into the tent with Melanie. She took off her clothes and slid into her sleeping bag.

"What's gotten into you?" she said with her back to him.

"Are you blind? He was all over you."

"You've got nothing to worry about. I promise. Take your clothes off."

She unzipped her bag and opened it, creating a down mattress, then unzipped David's bag while he shimmied out of his clothes.

"Come on top," she said, "and don't say a word, don't say anything. Don't make any noise," she whispered. "Not a sound. Nothing, nothing, nothing."

CHAPTER THIRTY-TWO

Thursday, August 26, 1965

Tonight was the first game back for Koufax since the Marichal incident at Candlestick Park. Roseboro played half the game yesterday but took tonight off. It's hard to say whether it would have mattered since the Mets won five to two. Koufax got nicked for two runs in the first and another in the seventh. He didn't look himself, even though he only gave up four hits. He walked two batters and only struck out five. At times he seemed distracted, maybe thinking back to the last start when his good friend and catcher walked away with fourteen stitches. Marichal received an eight-game suspension and a record fine of $1,750. That's a lot of money, but if you ask me, it's not enough. What he did was criminal and an eight-game suspension is just a slap on the arm.

The loss leaves Koufax with a twenty-one–six record. This was his third attempt to get that next win, but to no avail. Hopefully, once he gets his favorite catcher back behind the plate his fortunes will change. That's all I've got for you tonight from Shea Stadium in New York.

Monday morning they broke camp early and were driving over Tioga Pass by eight o'clock. David felt renewed. He wanted to get into the high country and hoped that his enmity with Frank was over, although he wasn't certain. They would need to trust each other in the wilderness. Rene and Frank had a lot more experience in the mountains than he did. He didn't like feeling dependent, especially on Frank.

They reached the Rock Creek store and campground after a couple of hours. It was the last chance to buy supplies. Melanie bought everyone coffee and pastries. David nabbed a copy of the *San Francisco Chronicle*, dated Monday, August 23. He was stunned to read of the debacle that had taken place at Candlestick Park on Sunday.

"Holy shit. Look at this," David said. He opened the paper so the others could see. There was a photo of Juan Marichal with a bat cocked in his right hand, standing over Roseboro, and Koufax trying to reach across the catcher's body and grab the bat.

"It doesn't look like the friendly national pastime I used to know," Frank said.

Rene shook his head. "The whole country is falling apart. First Watts. Now this. It's good we're getting away from it all. At least for a little while."

David stuffed the sports section in his pack. *Fire starter after I read it*, he thought.

The trailhead at Mosquito Flats above Rock Creek Lake was at 10,000 ft. The air was thin and crisp. By the time they loaded their packs, secured the cars, and started to hike it was midmorning. The trail was clear; a bit narrow with light pulverized granite covering the ground. The packs were heavy with five days' worth of food and gear, but for David it felt good to be harnessed into life at its most basic level. At first he strained against the elevation, then found his rhythm as they hiked toward Mono Pass, looming a couple thousand feet above. He climbed up the switchbacks, struggling to keep up with Melanie who was clearly in the best physical condition of the four. Rene and Frank kept a steady pace behind them. Everything looked sculpted, perfectly edged; the smoky-white granite boulders, the cloudless sky, the alpine meadow dashed with wildflowers. David knew the flowers from his trips with Bryce. The meadows were profuse with blue columbine, shooting stars, lupine, blue-eyed grass, and buttercups. He pointed them out to Melanie, who was mildly impressed.

After an hour they stopped. Melanie propped herself up on a giant chunk of granite and tapped at a spot beside her, beckoning David. He climbed up beside her. They had gained enough elevation to see the valley far below as well as get a good glimpse of Mount Starr to the northeast.

"David, this is so incredible. I've never seen anything like it."

"I'm amazed. I've never been in from this eastern side. It's really wild. I'm glad you like it. Hey, look at that." He pointed to a marmot that had positioned itself as a guard on the boulder directly behind them. The animal started shrieking to his brethren, alerting them to their presence."

Frank and Rene joined them on the rock. They were beaming, looking fresh and excited. Neither appeared the least bit fazed from the climb.

Frank noticed the marmot and grinned at Melanie, who started to laugh. David couldn't understand what was so funny. Their inside joke irritated him. Why couldn't Frank just let it go. *Or maybe it's me who can't let go*, he thought.

"Quite a site," Rene said. "At this rate we'll be at the top in another hour. We can have lunch on the pass. This country is just magnificent. Did you see that eagle soaring back there over the lake?"

Melanie and David shook their heads.

"It was quite a treat. I haven't seen one up here before." Rene paused. "Last time I saw a bald eagle was up in Alaska about ten years ago, they're all over the place up there. But here it's a different story. Frank and I think that somehow Lou transformed his spirit into that bald eagle."

They started up the last steep pitch toward the top of the pass. Frank settled in close behind David and Melanie, while Rene traversed in front. David didn't like the sound of Frank's boots behind him, but he got used to the thumping.

Rene seemed to glide over the trail at a pace David had not seen before. "What's got into him?" he asked.

"It's his trance walking," Frank said. "Something he learned from a lama when he traveled in Tibet as a kid. It's really something, isn't it?"

Rene was far in the distance. He was lunging up the mountain, covering a few yards with each step, his head bobbing up and down as if he were on a pogo stick.

"He can't keep going too much longer, but I'm sure he'll make it up to the pass before we do," Melanie said. "Who was the lama?"

"Govinda, Lama Govinda. He's actually a German, but made his name as a Tibetan monk, poet, and writer. Rene met him in France. Lou was just starting to read Govinda's books before he got sick," Frank said.

Lou is dead, David thought. Lama Govinda and his books aren't going to change that. The jagged smoky-gray peaks of the Sierra cut puzzle pieces into the pure sky. Maybe Lou's spirit is here or maybe it's not. This place was filled with wonder that was for sure.

David's breath constricted as he approached the top of Mono Pass and stepped up to the sign that read 12,045 feet. Rene was already there. Melanie dropped her backpack and put her arms around David.

"I've never imagined anything quite like this," she said.

"It's amazing," David said. The majestic Sierras rose in every direction.

Rene dangled his legs over the west side of the ridge, his back to the rest of them. He played his harmonica softly while the dry wind evaporated the sweat on his back. Melanie and David leaned their packs against the sign. Frank sat down next to Rene. Melanie broke out a large bag of dried fruit, almonds, and bits of chocolate she had bought at the stand on the drive up from Los Angeles and passed it around.

There were deep emerald lakes in every direction, sculpted rock formations, forests folded tight against cascading glacier-fed creeks. David thought of Lou again. He remembered standing at his gravesite feeling helpless. Maybe Lou was flying around within the feathered corpus of that eagle. With regards to death, there was the inevitable and there was the unknown. That's all he knew.

He thought about Koufax for an instant and then, just as quickly, he imagined Lou on the pitching mound—his lips tipped up to the right, his eyes full of anger and contempt, his hands set still above his belt buckle, muscles tensed and inflamed, so full of life and angst and hope. David gazed around at the high peaks. He felt a pair of cool hands on the back of his neck.

"Are you all right?" Melanie asked.

"Oh yeah, I'm just trying to digest the immensity of it all."

"Good luck with that."

"Well, I've got a big appetite," he said.

"Frank says you spend too much time up there in that big room of yours."

"Maybe he's right." *Frank, Frank, Frank. Here we go again.* It was beginning to feel like a full count.

David turned away and gazed around again. The sky at 12,000 feet offered more questions than answers. The entire western horizon erupted with forests, lakes, rivers, and glacial basins, all of a magnificence beyond anything he'd ever imagined. David wished Lou was there at that moment; they would have smoked a joint and talked about writers or God or truth. They would have sat for a long time in silence, feeling everything until the tension was insurmountable. The wilderness offered endless possibility, pleasure, mystery, and a good bit of danger. Lou would have found ways to translate all this into his poetry. He reached over and put his arm around Melanie.

"Awesome, isn't it?" he said.

They made camp at Fourth Recess Lake. The air was still and sweet as they shed their packs and scurried around looking for flat land to pitch the tents. Melanie and David chose a spot on a little bluff, protected on three sides by dwarf pines and junipers. It had a view of the lake to the southeast and was far enough from where Rene and Frank set up that they could make love without being heard. They cleared the rocks and branches, set down the ground cloth, and unfurled the tent.

Frank had located the tallest tree in the vicinity and flung a couple of lines over a high limb, about fifteen feet above the ground.

"I think we're far enough from Yosemite so those people-friendly bears won't bother us, but I don't want to take any chances, so we'll tree our food just in case. Make sure you don't leave any snacks in your tents either, you don't want them nosing around you in the middle of the night."

Frank secured the ropes around the base of the tree, and they sat down to lunch and to look at the maps. David appreciated Frank for his thoroughness and generosity but still didn't trust him. Something wasn't right; he didn't know what. Sure, he was jealous and insecure. He'd never known anyone like Frank. Maybe he was making more of Frank's interest in Melanie than was there. He wasn't sure.

He and Melanie arranged their belongings inside their shelter. Then they huddled with Frank and Rene to hear the plan.

"We can basecamp here or move one more time, it's up to you guys," Frank said. "From here we're an easy day hike to Pioneer Basin. There are six lakes up there under Mount Crocker. South of that we can get up to the Grinell Lakes, Rosy Finch Lake, and Little Laurel Lake and climb up Red and White Mountain, that's almost 13,000 feet."

Frank's long dark index finger scratched along the map where the confluence of Mono and Second Recess Creek joined. "That could be a good spot for a second camp. The only thing is that it would make our hike back to the car a long day, but our packs would be lighter and the trail would be mostly downhill. Anyway, you two think about it. Rene and I are cool with whatever you decide."

Early Tuesday morning David made a fire before anyone else woke up. There was plenty of downed, dry wood on the forest floor. The air still had a bite, so he moved quickly to stay warm. He put the kindling into the fire ring and lit it. The flames jumped up on the first wooden match, and David began to layer larger and larger pieces.

Within a couple minutes the scent of pine and juniper wafted through the camp.

"I smell a fire," Melanie said as she poked her head out of the tent.

"Yeah, you do. Come see this gorgeous sunrise."

"I'll be right out."

"Nice work, David, looks like you've got yourself a job," Frank said as he stretched and approached the fire. "You want some help?"

"No, I think I've got this part under control. You want tea?" It was a new day. David could feel himself softening a little toward Frank.

"You bet," Frank said.

"You can make some for me as well," Rene shouted as he followed right behind Frank.

David untied the rope that held the food, grabbed the tea bags and a sack of brown sugar, and headed back to the flames where the water was boiling over and spitting into the fire. Melanie stood next to him, yawning and wiping sleep from her face. She looked beautiful with her long chestnut hair flying in every direction and her green-blue eyes still sandy and unawake.

David poured the boiled water into the cups, added the tea bags and let them steep. He stood next to Melanie's smoky body. She leaned into him. Her nose was cold. He pulled back so he could find her lips and they kissed till their knees bumped and buckled. When David opened his eyes, he saw Frank looking furtively at them.

David wanted to fish along Golden Creek and end up at Golden Lake for the rest of the day, or at least until he had enough trout for dinner. He remembered the taste of golden trout from his experiences with Bryce and his family, and the thought whet his appetite. Fishing calmed and excited him at the same time.

He loaded his daypack with his fishing gear and lunch. Frank and Rene had already set out on their hike. Melanie gathered what she needed for the day and was closing up the tent. David thought about Hemingway's short story "Big Two-Hearted River." Its protagonist,

Nick Adams, had the need to leave everything behind and fish in the wilderness. Like so many things, it was Lou who introduced him to the story. He paused and recalled his last fishing episode when he caught the trout for Lou. Fishing would be good today. He could feel it.

They started out toward the creek. Melanie looked tantalizing as she walked beside him, her hair flying wild in the morning breeze. David felt invigorated. He was aware of a lightness of being that transcended Vietnam, Lou, and all dread of the future. The stress of the last couple weeks dropped away as they made their way along the trail.

Time passed quickly, and when they reached Golden Lake, they were both famished. They found a spot with a perfect view of Mount Huntington and unpacked their lunches. The sunlight reflected off the granite and snow. They stripped away layers of clothing; first jackets, then shirts caked with sweat, so that finally they were both down to T-shirts and shorts. David set his shirt in the sun to dry. Melanie followed his lead, leaving just her bra, which she quickly abandoned, baring her breasts to the bold Sierra sunshine. She turned to kiss David and rub herself against his skin. Food no longer seemed important. They slid off the flat stone onto a grassy spot beneath. They swished and swam against each other at a fevered pitch, hidden from the rest of the human world, and at the same time, exposed in the rarified glacial air. Breathless, exhausted, laughing, and swooning, they coupled like the wild creatures that inhabited this range, responding only to the instincts of the earth. Afterward, they rested and talked, with crusts of rock and blades of grass clinging to their backs and hips.

"You still worried about Frank?" Melanie asked.

"That's a hell of thing to ask after what just happened," he said.

"Is it? I just want to make sure you know it's you I love," she said.

"I know that. But there are always circumstances."

"Oh, David, come on."

A large trout splashed down ten feet from the shore. Without saying a word, David poured himself back into his clothes. He glanced quickly at Melanie, who seemed perfectly comfortable with him dashing off. She remained naked as he set up his fishing gear.

"Aren't you getting cold?" he asked as he quickly tied a small dry black gnat on the end of his line.

"Not at all, the sun feels great on my skin. Are you worried that someone will come by and see me?" she said.

"I suppose so."

"You weren't so worried a little while ago," she mused.

"I wasn't thinking about it then."

"You weren't thinking at all. Don't worry, my clothes are right here. If I hear anyone, I'll get dressed. You just go off and catch our dinner."

The fishing kept David engaged for a couple of hours. The little gnat conspired against the hungry trout, so that each cast produced an array of splashes and pirouettes, some producing a catch and others just foreplay. Most of the fish were between twelve and fourteen inches, the largest a sixteen-inch beauty. By three o'clock he had seven keepers—more than sufficient for a great feast.

Melanie was dressed and ready to go by the time he circumvented the lake. A chill started to grip the air, and a large hammer of dark clouds was building on the western horizon. David knew that being vertical on a hard rock surface would make them perfect targets to unyielding bolts of lightning. They beat it down the trail.

Frank and Rene were feeding a large fire when David and Melanie arrived in camp. "Beautiful campsites all up and down Mono Creek," Rene said. "We found a perfect spot near the trail to Pioneer Basin. There's plenty of wood, water, and shelter, and it gives a further reach into the high lakes and more peaks. We're thinking to pack it up tomorrow morning. Would that work for you two?"

"Sounds fine with me," Melanie said.

"What about you, David?"

"I like the idea of getting deeper into the wilderness," David said as he pulled the stringer out and displayed the line of golden trout, now stiff, but still handsome with red spots along their sides. "I'm glad you've got the fire going. I'm going to need a strong bed of coals for all these fish."

"That's one hell of a string. Are they all from the lake?" Frank asked.

"Yeah, I caught a bunch in the creek, but I threw them back."

The skies were gathering fistfuls of anger and torment; it looked like one large bruised cloud that swelled and flexed above them. In the distance, somewhere beyond the western horizon, they heard the dull acrimonious sounds of thunder, as if a marauding army was stomping forward, ready to pillage.

"We'd better get them cooking quickly. We're in for a serious bit of weather. Frank, make sure the tents are secured, and I'll rake these coals over for the fish," Rene said while he filled the kettle with water.

Frank stacked heavy rocks on the tent pegs and stretched out the rain flies so they were taut and secure. A stiff raw wind ripped through the camp, awakening the coals; the sizzle of fish stirred the air. When Rene turned the fish, the rain started; just a few drops at first, not even enough to dampen their parkas. It teased like that until they finished their meal.

Hastily, they made for the tents. Melanie burrowed into her bag as the drizzle turned to rain. David dug out a small flask of brandy he had stowed away for such a night. A couple of sips relaxed them enough so they collapsed into sleep.

David woke after a couple of hours, his mouth as dry as the desert, dehydrated from the sun, the hiking, and the brandy. After drinking a few gulps of water, he tried to get back to sleep but couldn't. The storm was in stasis, like an enemy planning its final assault to the besieged castle. An uneasy stillness abounded; just a slight breeze fraught with the acrid fumes of impending mayhem. He partially unzipped the tent and peeked out. There wasn't a star to be seen. Off in the distance, he saw sparks of light in the clouds but no sounds, no moisture, just the promise of a storm. It was a full count, but his arm felt listless. A bolt of lightning cracked a hundred yards north. Then came the crash of thunder.

"Holy Christ," Melanie screamed. She grabbed David's arm.

"That was close," he said.

"David, I'm scared."

"Just hold me tighter. It will pass."

"I hate this. It's like a war zone."

Suddenly everything lit up and shook. The light was so intense David was blinded for a second.

"David, that hit right next to the tent! I can't stand this!" Melanie screamed and put her arms around him.

"There isn't anything we can do. Keep holding me."

Another blast erupted and lit up the campsite.

"Rene! Frank!" Melanie screamed. "Do something!"

"Just stay in your tent," a distant voice shouted back.

"I wish we were closer to them," she said. "This is all your fault."

"Come on, Melanie," David said. "Calm down, we'll be fine. I know it's scary, but we'll be all right."

"We need to get down to lower ground, we're too exposed up here. We need to move right now," she said and started to unzip the tent.

David grabbed her and pulled her back. "Melanie, we are *not* moving from this spot."

"I'm getting out of here," she said.

Before she could say another word a dagger of lightning struck close to the tent again. Melanie jumped into his arms and trembled. He held her and stroked her hair.

"It's going to pass soon. I promise. Everything is going to be all right," David said. He hoped that was the truth. He'd heard that heat from a bolt of lightning was hotter than the surface of the sun. They would fry fast. Melanie cried and shivered in his arms, terrified and hysterical.

"David, please do something. I need to get out of here, please! Let's just run back down to the car, we'll be safe there. We can use our flashlights to see the trail, please let's go. I don't want to be here."

"We can't leave," David consoled. The rain beat down on the tent, but they stayed dry. The thunder was like a relentless interrogation by a divine being, but the questions were incomprehensible. Melanie tried to break away from David again and run outside, but he held her tight.

The wind amped up and streaked through the trees like jet planes, creating a shrill screaming whistle, an inexorable howling that added to their torment and helplessness. *Enough already*, David thought. Finally, Melanie buried herself deep into her sleeping bag and put all of her clothing inside making herself into a chrysalis, cut off from the dread outside. She started to hum and rock slowly as if she were transforming herself into another being.

An hour later David unzipped the tent and peered out at the night; the lightening was moving east across the lake. He remembered something about the negative and positive charges within the clouds and how they were like stepladders that made their way toward the ground, like angels creating a staircase between heaven and earth. He was awed by the process as the lightning and thunder faded north and east. There was an equanimity here between the trees, the trout, the river, the storm, and them. *We're all the same trembling pulses of life.* He climbed back into his bag and fell asleep.

David awoke to the smell of something cooking. He poked Melanie.

"You all right?" he asked.

"Exhausted. But, I'm good," she said and kissed him. "It was horrible. I can't believe I almost ran off. You really saved me."

"It was terrifying," David said.

When Melanie and David emerged, Frank already had a kettle of boiling water for tea, and Rene stirred a large pot of oatmeal mixed with raisins, cinnamon, and powdered milk.

"That was one wild deluge. I can't remember a fiercer storm and I've seen quite a few. A couple of those strikes were pretty close. You two must have had quite a time of it." Frank smiled, looking straight at Melanie.

"I thought you'd come over and rescue us," she said as she wiped a bit of hair from in front of her bloodshot eyes.

"Not me, I was too scared," Frank said.

"David kept me from trying to bolt and run down the trail."

"That would have definitely been the end; signed, sealed, and delivered back to your maker. It's good you listened to your hero," Frank said.

David cringed and stirred his oatmeal. Frank guided Melanie to a large rock, close enough to the fire to feel the warmth, and poured a generous glob of honey into her cup and filled it with hot water and an English Breakfast tea bag. The sun squirted up through the cragged peaks, and long rays of light beamed down upon them all. It covered the camp with its generosity, drying their tents, their clothes, and their wood. The muddy ground started to harden. It was all good, except Frank lingered beside Melanie, and the count was full again.

CHAPTER THIRTY-THREE

Wednesday, September 1, 1965

It's been a long day. A double header that couldn't have been more improbable. Koufax pitched the first game. He had beaten the Pirates seven consecutive times over two seasons. Drysdale had won his last two games and has been pitching almost as well as Koufax. They played twenty innings of baseball, and the Pirates only scored five runs, but the Dodgers only managed three and lost both games.

In the fifth inning of the first game, Jim Pagliaroni smashed a double and scored when Bob Baily singled. It was the first run the Pirates had scored off Koufax in twenty-two innings. An inning later, Bill Mazeroski singled to left and Willie Stargell followed with a triple to deep right-center. The game remained tied until the top of the eleventh. Koufax looked strong through the ninth and even into the tenth, so Alston gave him the green light in the bottom of the eleventh. It looked like the game was going to keep going because the first two batters hit easy grounders right back to Koufax. But Koufax walked Stargell, and Pagliaroni pulled an 0-two fastball off the scoreboard in left, and that was it for game one.

Vernon Law bested Drysdale in the nightcap two to one. With the double losses, the Dodgers lead over Cincinnati is a minuscule .001. San Francisco is one game back in third, and Milwaukee is a mere two games behind in fourth. And for their hard work tonight, the Pirates are only two and a half games back. Can a pennant race be any closer? I hope not.

By the time everything dried out, it was almost noon. They decided they would stay one more night where they were and then move camp on Thursday. They spent the rest of the week near the confluence of Mono Creek and Second Recess Lake. David fished the high lakes that sat just below Mt. Mills and found them plugged with hefty golden trout. He only kept the ones that were over sixteen inches.

The storms subsided, save for an occasional afternoon sprinkle that was just enough to cool off the day. Frank kept a respectful distance from Melanie.

David woke early on Sunday. It was the beginning of a new month. He opened the journal he had started at the beginning of the trip and added another entry. It was the only way he was able to keep track of the days that melted into one another in the wilderness. He ended his entry with this: *Much has changed, although I can't name exactly what has transformed. I feel different. I love Melanie and yet the relationship feels tenuous. I felt close to Lou up here. It's not going to be easy without him. Going back today. And what's next?*

The hike back took five and a half hours, but it was mostly downhill. They reached the cars by two thirty, and that gave David and Melanie plenty of daylight to make a dent on their drive back. Exhausted and elated, David said goodbye to Rene and Frank. Melanie hugged them both. David didn't notice any amorous moves from Frank. Maybe Frank was really all right. They flung their packs into the Galaxy and rambled down the gravel road.

Melanie slept between Bishop and Little Lake as they snaked along the California Aqueduct, occasionally catching glimpses of the southern Sierra peaks that terminated at Mount Whitney. David turned on the radio and listened to a recap of the news and sports.

The first stars bled through the eastern horizon as David carried Melanie's backpack to her front door. He wrapped her in his arms and remembered how it had been for the past week, being so near, touching, laughing, and hiking as if it would stay like that forever. But forever ended as she closed the door.

David climbed back into the car and headed home. There was a pile of mail waiting; registration information for school, a slew of bills, and a thin letter from CJ that he read after taking off his pack.

Dear David,

We're shipping out. Wiz and I are together, we're part of a team. I can't say anything more than that, but just don't believe what you read in the papers. There are more metal boxes than ever coming home. I'm resolved to do what I can and feel proud having a chance. There isn't any way of knowing when I'll be able to write or call again, so don't worry if you don't hear from me. I'll be thinking of you and all the guys.

I know you'll stay in touch with Veronica. I'm sure she is going to be a basket case. Believe it or not, the one thing I'm missing is the piano, but I decided that when this is all over, I'm going to get back into it, maybe even enroll in a conservatory. Can you believe it? Meanwhile I have taken up the harmonica, it's about the only instrument that makes sense as a solider. I'm pretty good, they call me the "hummer" in our platoon. You might check out a blues guy by the name of Sonny Terry, a blind guy from Greensboro, North Carolina. He plays with Brownie McGee. What a wild pair! You'd like their stuff. The blues fit what it's like around here, waiting, wondering, listening to the stories that the lifers tell about the action and the suffering.

I can't say that I'm not scared because I am. Who wouldn't be? You feel your nerves and then shine your weapon, iron the uniform, polish your shoes, and fall in for mess or physical training. That doesn't leave you any time to ponder the fear. I suppose if we did, we'd all go crazy. But for now, we're all revved up to do our duty for father, flag, and country.

Dad sends me post cards two or three times a week. He's so stoked that I'm doing this, it's almost like he is here with me. I wish he'd back off a little, but you know how he is. So I write him back and keep the correspondence sketchy and lighthearted. What a joke, as if anything around here is lighthearted. The humor is like a grade B horror movie, straight out of the graveyard. You made the right choice for yourself going to college. It just wouldn't have worked for me. I know I've said all this before, maybe I'm still trying to convince myself that I made the right choice. How do you ever know that kind of shit?

I'll contact you as soon as I can. Meanwhile keep your nose clean and your powder dry.

     Your buddy,
     CJ

David put the letter in his top drawer. His stomach started to grind. CJ and Wiz were probably already in Vietnam; the postmark was August 25. He stepped into the darkness of the courtyard and smelled the salted air. Instinctively, he headed for the ocean. He imagined a thick jungle, the sound of helicopters, a cacophony of shouting, and the *tat-tat-tat* of gunfire. He'd seen it all on the evening news.

Monday morning the phone woke him. It was Alex.

"It's nine o'clock. I hope I didn't wake you. Are you alone?"

"You did and that's a hell of question for you to be asking, don't you think?"

"Not really. I just thought that you might want to spend some time with your bloodline before you disappear into college. How is Melanie anyway?"

"Thanks for asking. We had a great trip and Melanie is fine and, no, she isn't here. And it's only been two weeks since I've seen you."

"I'm glad you're keeping track," Alex said.

David didn't have any plans for the day and welcomed her company.

"I'll tell you what, get yourself packed up and I'll pick you up at ten thirty. Just be ready because I don't want to wait around the house."

"It won't be a problem."

Traffic was light. David made it to the freeway quickly and found himself cresting over Mulholland Drive, singing along with Eric Burton, windows down, the dry Pacific air sailing through his hair, forgetting everything but the music and the wind.

Baby, do you understand me now?
If sometimes, you see that I'm mad
Don't you know that no one alive can always be an angel
When everything goes wrong, I seem bad.
Well I'm just a soul whose intentions are good
Oh Lord! please don't let me be misunderstood.

It was a perfect California day; the mountains were clear, the sky nothing but blue all the way to the end of the universe—exquisite. He almost passed the Nordoff exit while listening to the Beach Boys pouring it out in "Do You Wanna Dance?" He couldn't wait to pick up Alex and beat it back to the beach. The Sierras were fantastic for their beauty and vision, but nothing could match a beach day like today. Hang out, ride the surf, smell the briny fragrance, and watch the muscular oiled bodies stroll back and forth.

Still humming to the Beach Boys, David walked in the door and found Alex sitting on the large green chair in the living room with her legs crossed, her beach bag beside her feet. She was chewing gum and popping with inward suction, looking very uneasy.

"What's wrong? You look like you're about to be booked for grand larceny."

"I don't know what's going on, but Bryce called here a few minutes ago wondering where you were. He said he'd been trying to reach you, and he sounded very concerned. He wouldn't tell me anything, except that he had to talk with you as soon as possible. I told him you'd be here shortly and he made me promise I'd make sure you called as soon as you walked in the door. So I imagine we're not going to the beach?"

"Alex, just don't go psycho on me, all right? I don't know what's going on. Let me call Bryce and then we'll go. So just relax."

Bryce answered the phone after just a single ring. There was pause, and then he said, "David, I'm sorry to have tell you this."

"Tell me what?"

"I got a call from Rick Norris's mother this morning. He was killed two days ago, his PT boat hit a mine, and a couple of sailors came to the house and told his folks. They are hysterical. The Navy promised to have him back here by Wednesday. His mom said they'd have the funeral Friday at the Baptist church on Van Nuys. She wanted me to call everyone. I've already talked to Barn, Shanti, Lydia, and Rita. Can't call Wiz or CJ, but someone needs to call their families. I didn't want to take on that job."

"Shit! Ricky is dead, oh man! I can't believe it."

"Believe what?" Alex shouted from the living room.

"Hold on, I need to tell Alex." David set the phone down. He met Alex as she posted herself against the doorway between the kitchen and the hallway, her arms locked against the wood so he couldn't pass.

"Yes?" Her owlish eyes penetrated his defenses. "Yes? What can't you believe?"

"Rick Norris was killed in Vietnam. His PT boat hit a mine," David said.

Alex walked back to the chair and crumbled like a rag doll. She huddled within herself while David finished talking with Bryce. He agreed to contact the D'Agostinos and the Levin family. They'd be able to get the information to CJ and Wiz faster than he could.

Rick was dead, and there wasn't anything to do about it. A wave of nausea slammed below David's ribcage. He drank a glass of water. It settled him for the moment. He walked over to Alex and gave her a hug. "I'm sorry," he said.

"You see, it's like I told you. Everyone is going to die. This war is going to take all of us one way or another."

"Look, this is awful. Poor Ricky," David said. He didn't know what else to say. He looked into his sister's eyes. "Not everyone is doing to die. I'm not going to die and you are not going to die. I have to make some calls, but then we are going to the beach."

"How? How are you going to go to the beach?" Alex asked, holding back tears.

David didn't know the answer.

"We're going, that's all. I just hope you made enough food."

David made the calls and they were on their way twenty minutes later. He turned on the radio, hoping they'd be playing something good. It was Smokey Robinson singing "The Tracks of My Tears."

Alex and David joined Smokey. KRLA kept playing hit after hit. They sang all the way to the apartment.

David parked and within five minutes they were on the beach, unwrapping the tuna sandwiches Alex had made. David bought lemonade, and they settled down for serious beach time. He knew that the dam holding back the shock and grief was about to explode, but he kept pretending he'd be all right. But Rick Norris' demise lassoed him again and again as the Southern California beach world frolicked in every direction. Everything around him was detached from Vietnam, but as he looked across the Pacific, he imagined Rick's body being loaded into a plane.

David and Alex swam past the first set of breakers to a spot where they couldn't touch the bottom, where the real waves started to form. Alex was a strong swimmer. She was agile and instinctive in the water. It was one place where they were equals, and she was fearless when it came to bodysurfing. They exhausted themselves until their arms and legs were like gnarled pieces of kelp.

They collapsed on the blanket. The image of Rick's corpse popped into David's mind. His body was floating face-up in his whites through a pool of bloody water, a sardonic smile across his thin lips, a smoldering cigarette tucked on the side of his mouth, his eyes open blanks riled against the annulment of his life.

"Oh God, David, look who's walking down the beach. Those two guys again!"

"What is it with you, Alex? The only time I see those guys is when I'm with you."

"Thanks a lot, but maybe this time you can just let them pass without making a scene."

"I didn't make any scene. All I did was keep them from hassling you."

"You could have just walked away," Alex said.

"Let's just leave it."

The two drunken surfers stumbled through the tide. They didn't notice David. Alex burrowed her head down against David's shoulder. He felt her breath and her fear on his arm. He didn't particularly care if the two interlopers started anything or not, getting into a brawl might be just what he needed. It might break the barrier of grief, but he didn't want to upset Alex, so it was just as well that the two kept walking.

"You can open your eyes now. They're gone."

Alex didn't move for a few seconds. She slowly uncoiled and rubbed her eyes like she was waking up from a deep dream. "You're not going to die like Lou and Rick, are you?"

"Like I told you before, I'm not dying anytime soon."

"You already have two dead friends and two more that just sailed off to Vietnam. I worry about being left alone."

"Please get a grip on yourself," David said. He realized he didn't have a "grip" on anything at the moment.

"You just can't deal with me, can you?" Alex asked.

"Yes I can," He said and gave her a hug. "I'm going to get some snow cones. That's how I'm going to deal with you. You still like strawberry?"

"That sounds good, sorry."

The line inside the snack bar was eight deep. The scent of frying corn dogs and french fries, mixed with splashes of popcorn and cotton candy, wound through him while he dug around for some cash. Just then he felt someone poke him hard in the back. He turned quickly and saw the two drunks. They stared at him with wretched smiles on their prickled faces. The chunkier one stood further back, while the guy who had started the first fisticuffs planted himself two feet away. Obviously, he was the instigator of the shove.

"So we meet again, but now there isn't any lifeguard to save you."

"Bug off," David said. He didn't want to start anything right in the middle of the food line, so he turned away, hoping that if he just ignored them, they'd leave. He bought two snow cones; one orange, one strawberry.

Just as he walked out the door, he felt another thump against his back, harder than the first one. He almost dropped the snow cones sheltered in a cardboard tray. Full count, he thought. He set the tray down on a table, then turned and ducked at the same time, allowing the instigator's fist to catch air as he stumbled forward into the crowd heading into the restaurant. The oaf staggered to his feet, his face distorted. He lunged again. This time David smashed his fist deep into the guy's solar plexus. The guy's eyes glassed over like a rabid animal lost in the world. When the drunk caught his breath, he charged once more. David feigned with his right hand and smacked the guy with a left cross on the side of his face. He went down and stayed down. His big friend ran off and disappeared along the shore. David heard someone yell, "Call the lifeguard."

He bolted before any life guard or police showed up. He was shaken, but somehow remembered to pick up the tray with the snow cones. He rushed over to Alex and put the treats on the blanket.

"I got into it with those thugs again. I'm going to disappear in the water for awhile just in case. Everything is okay. They won't be bothering us anymore."

"God, David, are you all right?"

"I'm fine. Enjoy the snow cone. Don't worry if mine melts."

He disappeared under the water and swam straight out for as long as he could. When he resurfaced he looked back toward the shore to see if anyone was in pursuit, but all he saw were the rollers breaking onto the shoreline. After few minutes of paddling around he headed back.

"Where's my snow cone?" he asked.

"I ate it. It was melting. You want me to get you another one?" Alex asked.

"I'm good," he said, but he wasn't *good*, because his friend Rick Norris was in a box somewhere between Vietnam and the San

Fernando Valley. Rick's accommodations were not spacious or intriguing. There was no more sunshine, blue sky, or snow cones for Ricky.

After taking Alex home, David returned to his apartment. First he called Melanie and told her about Rick. She couldn't believe it and asked if he wanted company. He said he needed to be alone tonight, but maybe tomorrow. Then he showered and turned on the Dodgers game. Koufax had given up the winning run in the top of the eleventh and failed again to win his twenty-second game. His world appeared to be on a losing streak. The Dodgers were no longer in first place. David needed some lightness in his life, but all he had to look forward to was the funeral on Friday.

CHAPTER THIRTY-FOUR

Sunday, September 5, 1965

We're winding down fans. There is less than a month left in the season, and today the Dodgers won their seventy-ninth game. Koufax pitched a gem but didn't get the win. He went seven strong innings. Through the first six, he shut out the Astros on just one hit. But in the seventh, he gave up three singles that translated into two runs, because Willie Davis misplayed one of the hits. I'm sure Sandy is stewing just a little bit, since two of the four hits came off the bat of his legendary rival Robin Roberts. These two are probably going into the Hall of Fame but, today, neither one got the win. Baseball isn't always fair.

Koufax was taken out for a pinch hitter in the top of the eighth inning. Thirty-eight-year-old Roberts held a two-to-one lead going into the bottom of the ninth. Up to that point, the only Dodger run had been in the top of the third when the third baseman, Don LeJohn, doubled home John Roseboro.

In the top of the ninth, Jim Gilliam tripled home two runs and then scored on a single by Jim Lefebvre to give Los Angeles a four-two lead. Ron Reed closed out the Astros in the ninth. Today was the sixth time Koufax has tried in vain to get his twenty-second win. It isn't for any lack of effort. No sir. Sandy looked good, and the important thing is the Dodgers won. That's it from the Houston Astrodome. The Dodgers beat Houston four to two.

Melanie came over Thursday night. David hadn't seen her since the trip to the Sierras. She had been preoccupied with school. His mind was on the funeral.

"I'm sorry," she said.

"For what?" he asked.

"I don't know exactly. I'm having trouble seeing what's around the corner." She kissed him and wrapped her warm body around him. "Do you want me to go to the funeral with you?"

David paused for a moment. "No. I think I need to just be with my friends."

"I understand, but if you change your mind, I'll come with you."

"I'll let you know. That's kind of you." The thought of Melanie at the funeral made him apprehensive. It would be hard enough if Rita showed up, and it was likely she would be there. He fell asleep recalling their Sierras trip.

In the morning Melanie asked him if Rita would be at the funeral, and he said he wasn't sure but that probably she would. There was a long silence while she dressed and finally said, "Do you still love her?"

"I don't think so."

"If you have to think about it, then you probably do."

"Why is that? The point is I don't think about her anymore," David said, knowing that wasn't quite the truth. Rita did pop into his consciousness more than he wanted to admit.

"David, it isn't that complicated of a question. Either you still love her or you don't. You're about to see her in a couple of hours with all your old friends, everyone's going to be emotional and vulnerable, and I think I have a right to know what the hell you are feeling."

"Rita is history, it's over, and no, I don't love her anymore," he said, still unsure of his answer. "You don't have to worry about her. I love you. It's all going to be fine."

"I wish I could believe you," she said and kissed him and walked out the door.

He dressed for the funeral and started driving north toward the San Fernando Valley. KRLA was playing a series of Rolling Stones songs. As he went over Mulholland, the DJ started playing "Time Is on My Side." Mick Jagger howling and flailing, singing:

Time is on my side, yes it is
Time is on my side, yes it is

Now you always say
That you want to be free
But you'll come running back
You'll come running back
You'll come running back to me

He turned off the radio but kept singing the lyrics all the way to Bryce's house. He had told him he'd pick him up and they'd drive to the church together. David wanted to believe that time was on his side. He wanted to trust that everything would be running back to him; Lou and Rick and maybe Rita as well. Time was on the side of the Rolling Stones, and he wanted to be wherever they were at the moment as opposed to sitting in Bryce's driveway, waiting to see his dead friend lying alone, awaiting his last moments above ground. His mouth was dry and his brain felt fractured with grief. The second funeral in less than two months. Time? How can it be on anyone's side?

David sat in the car waiting for Bryce. He was wearing his gray slacks, button-down blue oxford shirt, and his blue blazer with a milky-white stain below the right elbow. He had forgotten to get it cleaned after Lou's funeral. He was getting antsy and was about to get out of the car when he saw Bryce hop out the door. His parents, Brent and Shelia, waved to David. They didn't look dressed for the funeral. Brent was clothed in faded tight Levi's and a white T-shirt, and Shelia wore orange shorts and a flowered blouse.

"They're not coming?" he asked as Bryce slid into the front seat.

"No. Mom said it was just too much for her. The thought of him lying there, she said it was just too much. And, of course, my Dad said, 'Well, if you're not going, neither am I,' and that was the end of it. How about your folks?"

"No, they didn't even consider going. They didn't know Rick that well and never met his folks."

KRLA was broadcasting The Lovin' Spoonful's new hit "Do You Believe in Magic?"

It was weird lead-in music for a funeral, but somehow it fit and it kept David buoyant until he walked into the Holy Grail Tabernacle of the Southern Baptist Union.

Standing above the open casket was Leonard Marston, Claudia's father, draped in white satin robes, with an enormous black lacquered cross dangling from his neck. His long gray hair was slicked back. His hands were folded together, his eyes closed in pensive prayer, head tilted toward the muted colored fresco of Jesus Christ on the ceiling, directly above the supine remains of Rick Norris. David approached the casket. From his line of sight, he could see the sheen of Rick's forehead, the tip of his nose, and his perfectly polished black shoes that glimmered in the stark spotlight.

The front two pews held the Norris clan. The extended family clustered around Rick's parents, Merle and Thelma. The family was lined up directly in front of Rick, so close that they must have smelled the embalming fluid. David suddenly wanted to leave. He bumped into Bryce as his body unconsciously convulsed and started to retreat.

"David, watch out! Come on, let's find a seat before this place fills up," Bryce said.

"There's Rita, Claudia, and Shanti." David pointed to the left side of the room, about half way up from where the casket rested. There was an aisle seat directly behind them that looked perfect. He wanted an exit strategy, just in case.

The girls turned around as Bryce and David sat down. David looked at them. They were beautiful. Their carnality permeated the air. Each girl, in turn, touched David and Bryce on the knee and whispered something about how awful it was. There wasn't anything any of them could do or say, except maybe keen at the top of their lungs that this just wasn't right, but then Leonard started to preach.

"I greet you on this blessed and afflicted day, this time of great sorrow and great joy and ask that you join me in praying for the soul of our beloved Rick, our hero, our child who did not die in vain. This is a young man at peace, for he is with our Lord Jesus Christ, and I assure you that he is not suffering, he is rejoicing in the bosom of our Savior. Amen!"

And the congregants shouted, "Amen!"

"I will read from the scripture of Matthew, Chapter 11, as he shares the wisdom of our master, John the Baptist. Matthew says of those times and perhaps of these times:

And from the days of John the Baptist until now the kingdom of heaven suffereth violence, and the violent take it by force. For all the prophets and the law prophesied until John.

And if ye will receive it, this is Elijah, which was for to come. He that hath ears to hear, let him hear. But whereunto shall I liken this generation? It is like unto children sitting in the markets, and calling unto their fellows, and saying, we have piped unto you, and ye have not danced, we have mourned unto you, and ye have not lamented.

Leonard paused. David peered through the crowd. The supplicants were enthralled with the preacher's words and images. Jesus came to the rescue. But Ricky didn't look rescued. He looked very dead. David tightened his fists.

Leonard continued:

We are a torn generation, there are those who would not lament this loss, there are those who would celebrate this loss, there are those who dare to defile, not only the heroism of this country, but even question the majesty of our Lord. To them I say, "Be certain. You will have your judgment day." Now it is time to ingather our departed soul, for he is at rest and at one with the Lord. He does not want, he has served and he is bound up with the angels in the Kingdom of God. Amen.

Rita turned around and faced David. She was crying, her makeup started to puddle around the bottom of her eyes, her face was wet with tears. David handed her some tissue and touched the side of her face. She stretched over her seat and kissed him briefly on the lips. His emotions were frothing over. He started to doubt all the decisions he'd made about leaving her.

Leonard finished preaching. The family paraded around the casket, and Leonard laid hands upon them as they filed out into the glaring sunshine. David debated whether he wanted to see anymore of Rick than what was visible from his seat, but before he could decide he felt Rita's hand in his.

"Walk with me," she said.

Together, they moved forward through the line of mourners to Rick's open coffin. She released his hand the moment they stopped in front. Rick's creased white dress uniform was the only authentic part of what rested in front of David's eyes. The rest of him looked like a waxed replica. His small perfect nose and high cheekbones were the same, but his face looked like it had been glossed over with some kind of furniture polish. He looked ghoulish and perverse. Rita took his hand again. She'd seen enough, but David resisted her pull and took a great inhalation while he stared at Ricky one last time, thinking about the end of things. The termination. He looked hard at the satin lining of Rick's final bed.

After the service everyone was invited to the Norris home for refreshments. None of the friends wanted to go, but they did. David and Bryce drove over. Rita, Claudia, and Shanti followed, and so did Barn and Maxine. While they were all standing around, drinking ginger ale and eating small tuna-fish sandwiches, David pulled Rita aside.

"Want to get together later?" he asked.

"When?"

"Now. I'll drop Bryce off at his parents' house and meet you at our old spot."

"Library?"

"Yes. I'll be there in twenty minutes," he said. *Full count and I'm putting it right down the heart of the plate*, he thought.

"Yes," she said, "twenty minutes.

Thirty minutes later, Rita was following him back to the apartment. A cool fog romped across the coast, sealing the sun from its normal work. David unlocked the door, and Rita followed him inside. He could feel the tension running down his spine as he turned on the lights. Sometimes Melanie just decided to show up, but he'd already made up his mind.

Rita sat down on the couch. "I don't know if we should be doing this," she said.

"Neither do I," David replied.

"Then let's stop now. I'll say good night and go home, say a prayer for Rick, and go to bed."

"That sounds like the right thing to do," David said. "You always know the right thing to do."

He leaned toward her and she met him. They kissed. They kissed again. Then they made love while listening to a jazz station play a lot of John Coltrane and Myles Davis. It wasn't the best sex they had ever had, but it took away the pain. He held her close and tight for a long time feeling down, exhausted but liberated. It was the only way to claw out of darkness.

They cried for Rick and Lou. They cried for Wiz and CJ, and they cried because the world had broken apart and neither of them could imagine what was coming next.

"We can't do this anymore," Rita said.

"I know. It's over." David knew it in his bones and he could see it in her eyes. Their love was buried, just like his friends.

Rita left, and David wasn't sure what to do. For a moment, he tried to decide if he was going to tell Melanie about what had happened. It didn't take long to conclude that it wouldn't be a good idea. He went to sleep feeling exhausted and confused.

Saturday morning arrived. It was Labor Day weekend, and David had no plans. Melanie was busy with her volleyball team and had a family event in Malibu. She invited David, but he declined, saying he was still too upset about Rick's death. That was partially true.

Sunday he listened to the entire Dodgers game. Koufax was pitching against the legendry Robin Roberts. David lost himself in the game. He didn't think about Rick or Lou or Melanie, just Koufax. Koufax didn't finish the game. He didn't get the win, but he didn't get the loss either.

CHAPTER THIRTY-FIVE

Thursday, September 9, 1965

Swung on and missed, a perfect game! (Thirty-eight seconds of cheering by the crowd.)

On the scoreboard in right field it is 9:46 p.m. in the City of the Angels, Los Angeles, California. And a crowd of 29,139 just saw the only pitcher in baseball history to hurl four no-hit, no-run games. He has done it three straight years, and now he caps it off with his fourth, a perfect game. And Sandy Koufax, whose name will always remind you of strikeouts, did it with a flurry. He struck out the last six consecutive batters. So when he writes his name in capital letters in the record books, that "K" (for strikeouts) stands out even more than the O-U-F-A-X.

Wednesday started out with the usual low costal fog and more bad news about Vietnam. From David's perspective, bad or good news about the war became more difficult to discern. There were always losers; the vanquished were either Americans or Vietnamese, either way the conflict only intensified because both sides were intractable. The battles fed the insatiable evening news, the thirst for violence and acrimony never slaked. The U.S. Marines destroyed a band of thirty-eight Viet Cong on the Batangan Peninsula. The box score read seventeen dead and twenty-one captured; the Marines suffered only "light" causalities. Meanwhile, the Air Force attacked North Vietnamese sites only seventeen miles from the Chinese border, bridges and railroad stations were destroyed in an attempt to disrupt the supply line between China and Vietnam.

David had breakfast and read CJ's recent letter.

Dear David,

Finally, we've arrived. Eighteen grueling hours crammed on a jet, bored out of my mind, I couldn't sleep, there was nowhere to get comfortable. Everyone around snored louder than the engines, but now we're here in Nam. By the time you get this I'll be deployed. I'm not sure where, but it doesn't really matter. It is all a war zone. It's hot and insane here. Everyone is drunk or stoned as soon as they are off duty, and then they evolve into various states of fear, anger, or mania, all of which makes for a kind of pandemonium that is funny in the darkest sort of way. Wiz and I have befriended the guys from our outfit. It's a split group, half are from Georgia and South Carolina, and the rest are all from New York. We get along surprisingly well, play a lot of poker and spend our days off in the strip clubs in Saigon. None of it seems very real right now, but I suppose that'll change.

I've had a lot of time to think about my life back home; I miss everyone and sometimes I do wonder what I might be doing if I was still there. College sounds more appealing from my new perspective, and I think that I might want to explore my music a little more. Even working at some dumb job would beat what I'm faced with at the moment, and at the same time, being here with these guys, I'm needed and respected, and that wasn't always the case back home. One thing I've learned is that you have to trust yourself in situations where you don't have time to second guess. You have to act first and think afterwards, that's what's drilled into you again and again. We'll be in the bush before too long. It all depends on how active the North Vietnamese are along the border.

I see these guys coming back from the field. They look dazed and they don't want to talk about what it's like or what happened, so I stopped asking. Wiz and I talk about how we could be sitting on the beach in Santa Monica, and instead we're in this sweaty city getting ready to go into the jungle. Honestly, we're both a little scared, but who wouldn't be in our situation? There's nothing we can do about it now. We made our choices and now we have to roll the dice. I'm confident we'll get through it all right. I don't know why, but I just am. Wiz feels the same. We joke

about being the survivors, coming home and telling all you cowards how
great it was and how we saved the world from the commies just for you.

I've got to get this finished and head for a special briefing. It could be
about our deployment. Keep writing.

As ever,

CJ

He folded the letter and put it down on the table. He moved it around in different positions, as if trying to discover how it fit into the greater scope of his life. He decided to mark the letter with small compass points: *N,S,E,W.* He left the letter facing north, gathered his lunch, and headed off to work.

When he got home he took his usual walk along the beach and ate a quick dinner. It was Thursday, and Koufax was slated to start against the Cubs at seven. He was still in search of his twenty-second win, and the way the news was going, it didn't appear that tonight would be any different from his previous starts. Koufax was ossified in the midst of a fabulous season and nothing was moving forward but bombs and the rush of bullets. Lou dead and gone, Rick six feet under, CJ and Wiz about to march into the jungle with their sniper rifles. How long would they last? He and Bryce were set to begin classes on Monday. He considered running off to San Francisco; maybe he could work for Rene or just bum around the coast for a period of time.

Just before the start of the Dodgers game, Melanie called and wanted to stop by, but he didn't want to see her and have to talk about Rick's funeral or what happened afterward. "How about tomorrow?" he said. "I think I'll feel better after a good night's sleep. I'll call you in the morning." She seemed fine with that and, hopefully, didn't suspect a thing.

He turned on the radio. Koufax breezed through the first inning. The Dodgers trailed the Giants by half a game and were tied with Cincinnati for second place. Bob Hendley, the young pitcher for the Cubs, brought a two-win-two-loss record against the Dodgers. Statistically, he looked overmatched against Koufax, but he retired the

Dodgers easily in the first inning. David had one joint left in his stash and lit up as Koufax took the mound in the second inning. Slowly he inhaled as the first stirring of the sea breeze wafted through his open windows.

There was a knock at the door. It was Grace.

"Just in time," he said.

"Well, that's sweet," Grace said as she sniffed the pot fumes. "I saw the light on and wondered if you wanted some company."

"That would be great, if you don't mind sharing a joint and listening to the game."

Grace laughed. "Pass it over."

They sat next to each other on the couch David had covered with an east Indian bedspread printed with elephants, bells, and women carrying water pitchers on their heads. They passed the joint back and forth.

"What's been going on? I haven't seen you in a bit," Grace said during the commercial between innings.

"It's been a tough week. A good friend died in Vietnam. His funeral was last Friday," David said as an image of Rita passed through his mind.

"Oh, I'm sorry."

"Thanks."

"Are you hungry?" Grace asked.

"I could eat something," he said.

"Be right back."

She returned fifteen minutes later and planted a bowl of dip on the table, opened a bag of chips, and spread out sliced carrots and pieces of celery. She glanced at the letter from CJ and looked up at David.

"Do you want to move that?" She pointed with her chin to the letter. "It might get messed up with the dip and all."

David nodded and picked up the letter and put it in his bedroom.

As he walked back to the couch, he said, "It's from one of my friends in Vietnam."

"I thought it might be."

"He's about to be deployed. He and another friend."

"Must be hard for you and for them. Especially because you just lost a friend. I'm sorry." She reached for a piece of celery and looked at David.

The joint had gone out. David relit it, took a puff, and passed it to Grace. She inhaled and passed it back.

"You want to go for a walk?" he asked.

"Sure. Where to?"

"Just down to the water. I need some air."

The evening sky was clear, and there was a bite of cold in the air. They walked along Pacific Avenue and then ducked down Breeze Way to the beach. They walked for a long time without saying anything.

Finally, Grace said, "This war, it's going to keep getting worse. Isn't it?"

"Looks that way. We're certainly not going to back down."

"Your friend who writes the letters, did he play baseball with you?"

David stopped walking and looked out at the inky water. "He did, but it wasn't his thing."

She instinctively touched David's shoulder. "Maybe we should go back and finish listening to the game."

David nodded, and they turned around. By the time they got back to the apartment it was the sixth inning and Koufax still had not surrendered a hit. They were both hungry and jumped right into the snacks.

"You know, he's already done it three times," David said.

"What's that?" she said, putting a chip in her mouth.

"Thrown a no-hitter. He's done it three times."

"Pretty good," she said.

"No, excellent," David said. "Remarkable." He reached for a chip as the game resumed.

In the bottom of the seventh inning, with two outs, Lou Johnson ended Hendley's bid for a no-hitter by hitting a double. He was left stranded at second base, and the score remained one to 0. In the top of the eighth, Koufax walked to the mound and began his warm-up tosses, his fastball still blazing in the night.

"Seven perfect innings," David said. "In high school, that would be it. A perfect game."

"Yeah, but there are still two more innings. You think he will do it?" Grace asked.

The joint had gone out, and David relit and inhaled. He passed it to Grace. She took a long drag.

"I think so," he said. "But, it's baseball."

"So what's that supposed to mean?"

"You played, you know how it goes. You win. You lose. You never know," he said.

"Oh," she said. "Very philosophical." She passed the joint back.

As the top of the eighth inning started, David wondered if Koufax would be able to pull it off. A perfect game? What had mattered to David over the course of this season was Koufax's capacity to elevate and find something deep inside himself that seemed to transcend the confusion and despair of the times.

With two out in the eighth, twenty-two-year-old Bryon Browne stepped in against Koufax. This was his first major league game and, ironically and miraculously, he had hit Koufax pretty good his first time up in the second inning. It was an odd, overwhelming match-up between the recent University of Missouri graduate and Sandy Koufax, who was already being touted as one of the supreme pitchers in baseball history and was having, perhaps, the most dominating performance of his career.

"It doesn't seem fair," Grace said.

"What?"

"Koufax against Bryon Browne,"

"It doesn't. But sometimes that happens in baseball. Sometimes in life," he said.

The Pacific night remained placid, the air moving just enough off the ocean to keep the apartment comfortable. David thought about the distance between where he now sat and Dodger Stadium, perhaps twenty miles. It was easy to envision the lights, the smell of beer and peanuts, the glistening outfield grass, and the crisp white-and-blue uniforms of the Dodgers. The infield had a tinge of red clay, and the same stars that loomed above David were shinning down upon the pitcher's mound, illuminating the rubber, and the rosin bag, and the four bases that remained empty of Cubs base runners.

Gone was the grief from the funeral, gone were his thoughts about CJ and Wiz, gone were his thoughts about the war. Every ounce of his being was riveted to the radio, the play-by-play, the pitch, the swing, the sonorous throat of Vin Scully as he waxed through the innings about the unfolding drama. Byron Browne became the eleventh strikeout victim. He went heroically, swinging with force and, maybe, imagining that he could have been the one that made history.

When Koufax took the mound in the ninth, Scully could barely contain his commentary. "He's done it three times before, no one has ever thrown four no-hitters, and this is more than just a no-hitter. Koufax has been perfect through eight innings. Twenty-four up and twenty-four down."

Koufax made quick work of the first two batters. David opened two beers and handed one to Grace. "Here we go," he said.

"Where are we going?" Grace said.

"We are going to listen to perfection," he said and clinked his beer against her bottle. "To perfection."

A gigantic moth crawled across the lampshade and edged its way toward the bulb. David watched for a second, deciding whether to swat it or try to grasp it in his fist. Outside, an ambulance rushed down Pacific Avenue. He leaned out the window unconsciously as the emergency vehicle zipped out of sight. The next batter was Harvey Kuenn. Scully described Kuenn as a professional batsman, a fourteen-year veteran. He had started the year with the San Francisco Giants but had been traded to the Cubs in midseason. A lanky, wily hitter; at six foot two, Kuenn had both power and control. Not known for hitting home runs, he was a doubles machine. Making contact and getting on base was his expertise. Throughout his years of play in Detroit, Cleveland, and San Francisco he averaged well over .300.

Scully was counting the minutes.

The time on the scoreboard is 9:44. The date September 9, 1965. Sandy into his windup and the pitch, a fastball for a strike. He has struck out, by the way, five consecutive batters, and that's gone unnoticed. Sandy is ready and the strike-one pitch is very high, and he lost his hat. He really forced that one. That's only the second time tonight where I have had the feeling that Sandy threw instead of pitched. Torborg had to go up and get it.

One and one to Harvey Kuenn. Now he's ready: fastball, high ball two. You can't blame a man for pushing just a little bit now. Sandy backs off, mops his forehead, runs his left index finger along his forehead, dries it off on his left pants leg. All the while Kuenn is just waiting. Now Sandy looks in. Into his windup and the two-one pitch to Kuenn: swung on and missed, strike two. It is 9:46 p.m.

Two and two to Harvey Kuenn, one strike away. Sandy into his windup, here's the pitch. Swung on and missed, a perfect game!

They sat awestruck, the lamp dribbled light around the room. The moth had disappeared. Grace looked giddy and wasted.

"Hey, thanks for hanging with me. And for the food," he said.

"You kidding me? This was great."

"You are a good person, Grace."

"Yeah, you just think I'm sexy."

"Yeah, I do," he said.

Grace kissed him on the cheek and waddled back to her place. David looked through the doorway into the night, it was quiet and empty. Grace turned back to him.

"Perfection. What could be better?" she said.

"Yes, what could be better?"

CHAPTER THIRTY-SIX

Tuesday, September 14, 1965

Justice was served here today at beautiful Wrigley Field in Chicago, or maybe you could call it irony. Five days after Sandy Koufax outdueled Bob Hendley in an epic battle that resulted in Koufax hurling a perfect game, Hendley turned the tables and bested Koufax two to one. How could it have been scripted more perfectly? Bob Hendley, the Macon, Georgia boy who almost matched Koufax last time out, somehow found a way to beat him today.

There was plenty of optimism in the Dodger dugout at the start. Koufax was literally un-hittable last time he pitched. He had dominated the Cubs all season. But Koufax gave up a blooper double to Glen Beckert, the second Cubs batter, and that immediately ended his streak of hitless innings. Hendley held off the Dodgers until the third inning when Wes Parker singled, but he was left stranded at first.

By the bottom of the sixth inning, the score was still 0 to 0. Jim Lefebvre miffed an easy ground ball by the Cubs center fielder, Don Young. Glenn Beckert hit a grounder that forced Young out at second, and that brought up Billy Williams, who was already 0 for two against Koufax. Koufax threw a fastball low and outside, but Williams crushed it over ivy in Wrigley field. Both runs are unearned, which is the same thing that happened to Hendley last week. So as I said earlier, justice was served.

The Dodgers scored once in the top of the seventh as Don Drysdale pinch hit for Koufax and drove in Wes Parker for the Dodgers' only run. The loss brought Koufax's record to twenty-two wins against eight losses. He gave up just one earned run and struck out three batters. He didn't walk a batter, and it was a performance that could have earned him a win, but the Dodger bats were feeble, and Hendley won the battle this time around. That's it from Wrigley Field.

Sunday morning David woke up to pounding. It took a few seconds for him to focus. He had been dreaming that CJ arrived home and they were driving to Tijuana to celebrate his return. He walked slowly to the door. Barn stood in front of him, smoking a small cigar, his sunglasses tipped up over his hair. He wore a pair of yellow swim trunks, a sleeveless white T-shirt, and a pair of well-worn black thongs. He had a broad, uncanny grin like he had just discovered the secret to getting any woman he wanted into bed with him.

"What the hell are you doing here?"

"It's a perfect beach day, and you've been dodging me all summer. It's time we had some fun together before you disappear into academia. I'm worried about you, David. There's no snap or crackle in your voice. You look like shit, and even though you've got that babe, it doesn't seem to matter. You need to loosen up and party. Want a cigar?"

Barney reached into the pocket of his baggy trunks.

"No, I'm fine, thanks for the offer."

"See what I mean? You don't know how to enjoy yourself anymore. Is she here?"

Barn poked his thick head inside the apartment, hoping to sneak a glimpse of Melanie, but all he got was a dank wisp of dinner from last night.

"So I got a joke for you, David. When was the last time you told a joke? Can you even remember?"

David shook his head. He was horrible at telling jokes. His timing always a trifle behind. He laughed before the punch line and that always made him feel inept and self-conscious. That combination killed the joke.

He grinned at Barn. He wanted to hear the joke, but his mind kept racing around his desire to be with Melanie and his doubts about starting college the next day.

"So where is she?" Barn asked as he stepped past David into the living room. "Bathroom?"

"She's not here," David said, wishing that she was in the bathroom so he could push Barn back out the door. Barn walked around the small apartment like a TV detective, picking up things, examining them as he held them up to the light. One of CJ's letters was on the kitchen table. He picked it up.

"He writes to you?" he said as he started to read it. "He really writes you?"

"Of course he does," David said a little miffed. "I've told you that and offered to share the letters with you."

"Why does he write you?" Barn asked as he continued to peruse the letter.

"He writes me because I write him."

"CJ writes pretty good. He must have learned it in the Army."

"Barn, why are you here?"

"I told you. It's our last chance. Come on David, get your beach stuff and let's go."

Barn kept walking around the room, puffing on his little cigar.

"Okay, okay, give me a minute," David said.

"Wait, you got to hear my joke first. So there is this woman shaking out a rug on the 15th floor of her apartment building when a gust of wind, probably the Santa Anas, blows her the fuck off and over the railing. *Damn, that was stupid*, she thought as she fell. *What a way to die.*

"As she passed the 12th floor, a man standing at his railing caught her in his arms. While she looked at him in disbelieving gratitude, he asked, 'Do you suck?' 'No!' she shrieked, insulted. So he dropped her.

"As she passed the 10th floor, another man reached out and caught her. 'Do you screw?' 'No!' she protested before she could stop herself. So he dropped her.

"The poor woman prayed to God for one more chance. As luck would have it, she was caught a third time, by a man on the 7th floor. 'I suck! I screw,' she screamed in panic. 'Slut!' he said, and dropped her."

Barney drew a deep breath on his skinny cigar, chuckled to himself and gazed at David, who just sat there. "Don't think it's funny, do you, David?"

"Not really," he said. "But I laughed, didn't I? You know how to tell it."

"You don't think it's funny because you've forgotten how to laugh. You think just because your buddy Lou is gone, life is over for you too? Fuck it, David. You need to pick it up and run with it, man. You've still got that thumper between your legs. You've got your whole life ahead of you, and if you can't laugh, shit, I don't know, you're just real messed up."

David couldn't believe it. He sat down on the couch and started laughing. Something cracked open and he gazed up at Barn.

"Yeah, man, that's it, let it all hang out," Barn said.

David liked Barn's husky voice. His eyes were warm, but biting and provocative. He guffawed with David, and as he did, his chest and stomach heaved up and down like everything in his being was connected. For the first time David realized that Barn, in his own flippant, carnival style, knew how to defy death. Spoof it. Smoke another cigar. Tell another joke, fuck another beach bunny. Barn was in synch with himself, and no God or syllabus or great novel was going to change that.

"Hey, I'm hungry. You got any food in this place?" Barn queried.

"Not much. I think we can stop at the diner before we hit the beach."

Barn kept telling jokes. David kept laughing.

They had a quick breakfast and set up at the beach. The crowds were just starting to arrive, but they found a perfect spot midway between the breakers and the snack bar. They laid out their chairs and towels and sat down to take in the sights before going into the water.

"So you think CJ and Wiz are going to make it back?" Barn asked as he lathered himself with suntan lotion.

"I try not to think about it," David said.

"What's the matter with you? Of course you try not to think about it. You think I try to think about that? I'm asking you what you think. I think one of them or both will get nailed. They're reckless. You know that."

"Shit, Barn. I thought you wanted to laugh and ride the waves."

"I do, but I saw that letter and it got me thinking, that's all."

"Well, someone once told me hope for the best, plan for the worst. I guess that's what I think," David said.

"Always the psychologist. You still didn't answer my fucking question," Barn said as he stood up. "Never mind," he said. "Let's catch some waves."

The water temperature was perfect. The rollers were slow and easy. Time escaped them both as they glided and raced through the surf. Exhausted, they hauled back to the chairs and were silent for a few minutes. David surveyed the landscape, recalling the summers when life was uncomplicated. Today was like one of those perfectly glorious days. Barn fascinated him. David looked at him and wished he could laugh and cavort his way through life the way his friend did. Barn was as genuine as the seaweed that washed ashore.

Barn lit one of his small cigars. "You see those two sitting to our left. The blond and the redhead?" Barn said.

David turned his head slightly. "Yeah, they are hard to miss."

"Let's go make our move."

"I thought you just wanted to talk about old times and be with your old buddy," David said.

"What better way to reminisce than with a couple of beauties like those two. Look at the rack on the redhead. I'll take her and you can have the blond. Let's go."

"No way," David said.

"All right, all right. So tell me true. What do you think about CJ and Wiz?"

"I think they are going to be all right. I know CJ has a plan. I know he wants to come back and make things right. Wiz? Who knows? He always lands on his feet. They'll be back. That's what I think."

"I hope you're right," Barn said. "But, I have to say, I have a bad feeling."

By three o'clock they were both thoroughly baked. Barn had acquired phone numbers for both the blond and the redhead. He offered to copy them for David, but he declined. They packed their stuff. David glanced at Barn as he scrambled ahead of him toward the snack bar, his towel under one arm, his chair under the other. They walked back to the apartment. Barn showered, lit another cigar, and got ready to leave.

"David, you take care of yourself. You think too much for your own good. You are letting the world crush you instead of grabbing it by the balls. It's time just to be a stud."

Barn feinted a right punch to David's midsection, and David pretended to return it with a right cross to his chin. Barn punched David in the shoulder and headed out to his car. David wasn't sure when he'd see him again. He tried to make sense of what was rumbling around inside of him. It was dread mixed with elation. He watched Barn drive off in his blue VW beetle.

On Monday David started UCLA. His greatest challenge turned out to be trying to find a parking space. Classes lasted just long enough to pick up the syllabus and meet the teaching assistants who actually ran things. By two o'clock he'd purchased most of the books he needed. He and Bryce had met briefly for coffee in the courtyard outside the lunch room. Bryce had conditioning drills in the afternoon, but they spoke about getting together later in the week. Fortunately, they had the same English and History classes.

The sterling event of the day was discovering Lew Alcindor in his history class. David knew about Alcindor, the new seven-foot-two basketball star. Everyone in Westwood knew about him. Alcindor didn't look at anyone during class. He just stared straight ahead, and when the professor dismissed the class, he stood up and strolled out the door.

Tuesday David had only two morning classes. He was home by noon and on the beach by twelve thirty. He took his copy of *The Sun Also Rises*, the first book required in his English class. There was an essay assigned for the following Tuesday on the meaning of the "Lost Generation" and its relevance to today's society.

Koufax and the Dodgers were in Chicago and, ironically, he was scheduled against Bob Hendley again. The Dodgers were two and a half games behind the Giants, in second place, tied with Cincinnati. This late in the season, dropping back more than three games, especially in a tight three-way race, was dangerous.

David sat on the beach, listening to the game as he rifled through Hemingway's classic for the third time; he'd read it twice in high school. Jake Barns was not his favorite character. David prized the crispness of Hemingway's style; the clean sentences, the restraint, and the space he left in your mind after a terse descriptive sentence. What disturbed David each time he read the book was Hemingway's blatant anti-Semitism. Robert Cohen, the antagonist and a Jew, is characterized as wormy and untrustworthy. He's far less the man than Jake. He is not enduring, not muscular or heroic. Cohen, the whiner, the wimp, fit all the negative stereotypes of Jews.

David put down the book and gazed across the water, the waves crested high and slow. *Perfect rides*, he thought. He ran into the surf, cooled himself, rode a few waves and slumped back onto the blanket. By the bottom of the sixth inning the score was still 0 to 0. That didn't last long. Billy Williams took Koufax deep with a man onboard. The Dodgers couldn't catch up. That was it. Koufax lost his eighth game by a score of two to one.

Later that night David heard the Giants had won and it meant the Dodgers were now three and a half games behind. He wondered if Koufax felt abandoned or discouraged or if he just took his shower, iced his arm, drank a beer, and flicked on the tube. He put down *The Sun Also Rises* and thought about Koufax and Jake Barns.

CHAPTER THIRTY-SEVEN

Saturday, September 18, 1965

It doesn't get any better than this. Another Koufax special. He won his twenty-third game of the season, a one-to-0 victory over the St. Louis Cardinals. It all happened right here in Busch Stadium. These Koufax events are becoming legendary. The Dodgers managed just three hits, and it wasn't until the sixth inning when they broke through. Up to that point, Ray Washburn, the journeyman pitcher for the Cardinals, held the Dodgers to a big goose egg. In the Dodgers' half of the sixth inning, third baseman John LeJohn walked and was replaced by a pinch runner, John Kennedy. Koufax bunted him to second, and Maury Wills got him to third on an infield out. That brought up first baseman Wes Parker, who took two quick strikes before lining a single to center to score Kennedy. And that was all the scoring for the game.

It got dicey in the ninth. Curt Flood led off with a single, and Busch Stadium started to rock when Dick Groat sacrificed him to second. That brought Alston out to talk with Koufax. Koufax nodded. Alston nodded. John Roseboro patted Koufax on the shoulder, and they all returned to their respective positions. Koufax bore down, and before you could take a couple of deep breaths, he got the last two batters to pop out and he gained his twenty-third win. What's more, it's his third one-to-0 victory in a row and his sixth shutout of the season. That's my report for tonight. At least the Dodgers won't lose any ground to the Giants. We've only got a dozen games left. Stay tuned.

Thursday David stopped in Westwood Village after classes to buy the new Beatles album *Help*. KRLA had played it all summer. When he got home he sliced open the cellophane wrapper and slowly admired the disc. His record collection was pretty thin. He sat transfixed with the album squarely between his paws. He put it on and rolled a joint. The first two cuts, "Help" and "The Night Before," were just fine, they guided him into a euphoria he craved. By the time "You've Got to Hide Your Love Away" slipped into the groove, he had forgotten about all that had transpired over the summer.

The first side ended, and he flipped it over. The second side wasn't as powerful, except for the one cut "Yesterday."

Yesterday, all my troubles seemed so far away
Now it looks as though they're here to stay
Oh, I believe in yesterday
Suddenly, I'm not half the man I used to be
There's a shadow hanging over me . . .

He lifted the arm of the record player and slipped it back to the beginning. He listened to the track again. "There's a shadow hanging over me." Yeah man, this was pure unfiltered nostalgia, and he loved it. He loved the soulful, melancholy crooning.

He made a sandwich for dinner and got down to his books. The phone rang. He glanced at the clock: 10:25. It was probably Melanie calling to say good night.

"David, I hope I didn't wake you." It took only a second to recognize Veronica's voice.

"No, I'm just listening to some music and doing a little reading. It's great to hear your voice."

"David, can I come over?"

"You're here? Sure, of course."

"I was on my way to see the folks, but I just can't deal with them tonight. I called them and said I'd be there tomorrow. I was driving through the desert and started to panic. I don't know why. I just can't stop thinking about CJ. I'll be over in about twenty minutes. You're sure it's all right?"

"Yes. Don't worry. Just come over," he said.

David sat for a moment on the couch. He was excited that Veronica was on her way. He pictured CJ and Wiz smothered inside a thick jungle canopy, sharing a smoke and preparing for battle. His thoughts moved back to Veronica and the fantasies he'd carried for years. Five minutes passed, and David opened the drawer where he kept CJ's letters. He took out the most recent one, which had arrived Tuesday, and read it again.

Dear David,

This will definitely be the last letter before we go on patrol. Our mission was delayed. No surprise there. I'm discovering that everything runs behind in this war. We're the first full Army division to arrive, so it's taken awhile to get untracked, but now we're definitely ready. I'm getting familiar with the names of places, Da Nang, Ah Khe, Pleku, and Chu Lai, where the Marines are based. When I try to pronounce their language it's like my mouth is full of marbles.

We're set to go search and destroy. That's what they call it here. It's been raining a lot. I hope it stops before we leave. I never liked camping in the rain. Wherever they send us, it will be courtesy of a big CH-47 Chinook helicopter. I'm ready, and so is Wiz. Once there is a break in the weather, we'll set out. Meantime, I'm staying dry, sleeping on my little cot, and listening to a lot of music.

You wouldn't believe the birds here. I suppose it's because of all the water. I never thought I'd be interested in bird watching, but with all the time on my hands right now, it gives me another thing to do. There are all kinds of ponds and rivers. It is an ideal habitat for water fowl: cranes, storks, spoonbills, and even swans.

I'll write once we get back. Don't worry. I'm coming back. You are probably starting classes soon. I sure hope college works out for you. You're a bright guy and I do appreciate you keeping in touch. You are the only one who writes besides Mom and Dad and, of course, Veronica. I can't be as honest with them as I am with you. Thanks for keeping me up with all the guys. Everyone sounds good. Well, almost everyone. Sorry about Lou. What a raw deal that was. They are calling us for chow. You enjoy yourself, Mr. David.

Your buddy,

CJ

He checked the clock: 10:38. He put the letter back in the drawer. He debated whether to show Veronica any of them. He decided he wouldn't unless she asked to see them, and even then, he wasn't sure. CJ wouldn't have wanted her to see what he wrote.

Veronica walked in the door without knocking. Her red hair was disheveled. She looked exhausted, but still ravishing. David rushed over to greet her. She dropped her purse and threw herself around him, every part of her felt warm and moist. Her tears smothered his cheeks. She stepped back and looked at him.

"It's great to see you," he said.

"There can't be anything great about the way I look. I've been crying on and off the last hundred miles. Jesus Christ, have you been following the news? David, can I use your bathroom? I've got to freshen up. I'm just a mess."

"Sure, what news?"

"I'll tell you in a second." She closed the bathroom door, and he heard the pipes clank and rattle as hot water throttled through the walls. When she came out, she had pulled back her mane of red hair and tied it off with a yellow scarf that exposed the fullness of her face. Everything about Veronica was voluptuous. She walked over and kissed David on the cheek.

"It's so sweet of you to let me come over on such short notice. You must think I'm really crazy."

"Never, not you, you're, you're my . . ." He couldn't find the word.

"Friend, right?" she said.

"Yes, a good friend. Can I make you some tea?" he asked.

"That would be divine."

"Sit down and I'll get it started."

David took down a blue teapot that Melanie had given him. He felt guilty and noticed trepidation searing up his spine. He put two bags of jasmine tea into the boiled water and grabbed a couple of cups and spoons. "You want some honey for your tea?"

"Yes."

He wondered what he would say if Melanie suddenly appeared? Unlikely as it was, it was still a possibility. Thursday's practice often ran late, and it was a long drive from USC across town. He set the tray down in front of Veronica and began to pour the tea.

"So what news?"

"They're calling it the 'Winter Campaign,' because it was so quiet during the monsoon season. The generals are now certain that a major escalation is about to take place. No more defensive actions, 'We're taking the offensive this coming season.' It means more intense fighting." Veronica paused and took a sip of tea.

"I read that too. Hopefully, it won't involve CJ," David said. He knew they would be very involved. They might be engaged with the "enemy" right now.

"And where does that leave CJ and Wiz? It leaves them with a slim-to-none chance of surviving. Every time they go out they have targets on their chests." Veronica started to weep.

"I'm sorry," he said.

"I don't want to burden you."

"No burden. I'm your friend, remember?"

Veronica smiled and moved a little closer. "Friends?"

"Yes, friends," he replied.

"Any word from CJ?"

"Not since he landed in Vietnam," he lied.

"That's what concerns me."

David paused, not sure what to say next. Finally, he asked, "Are you hungry?"

"No, not in the least." She looked at him. Her eyes were enormous, sad and swollen, and yet, she looked so beautiful. *What next?*

"How about a walk on the beach? Clear your head, stretch your legs."

"Yes, that's perfect," she said.

They got to the beach and took off their shoes. The sand was cool as they made their way toward the tide. The moon waned in the western sky. Veronica looked up and David instinctively took her hand. Her palm was soft and deep with comfort. She didn't flinch or hesitate, it felt natural to hold her hand. She relaxed and swung his arm as they walked toward the pier.

They meandered along the beach until, finally, she said, "I'm getting a little tired, why don't we head back to your place."

"Sure," he said.

They arrived back at the apartment. Veronica slipped into the bathroom and David poured a couple of glasses of ice water and set them on the table in front of the couch just as she came out of the bathroom.

"David, I'm really too tired to drive. Would you mind if I slept here?"

"Of course not. You can sleep in the bed and I'll take the couch. I wind up falling asleep on it half the time anyway, it's totally fine."

"That's ridiculous, I'm not going to put you out like that. I thought we'd just sleep together."

David stared at her. Her smile conveyed complete mastery over the situation, anything she wanted already belonged to her. The only reservation that roared through his mind was the idea that she wanted to "sleep." He'd know plenty of girls who compartmentalized fucking and snoozing, it was just a platonic deal.

"David, is there a problem?"

"Veronica, I can't just sleep with you."

She laughed, "Don't you think I know that? Just get into bed and I'll join you in a minute." She disappeared again into the bathroom. David stripped to his briefs. Full count, he thought, and started to fantasize.

Veronica walked out of the bathroom wearing a lacy short nightgown, white and sheer enough to leave nothing to his imagination.

She pulled back the sheets and stared at him. "I'm flattered," she mused.

Shamelessly, she slid beside him. They kissed for a long, long time, squeezing and moaning, running hands along each other's bodies, then dove together and finally reached what had been building up for years. Every pleasure he bestowed she replied to with greater fervor, her expertise displayed a delicacy and precision that was beyond anything he'd experienced. Then they started over until they were exhausted and finally fell asleep.

Veronica was still out when he woke up. He felt euphoria and panic chasing around the bases in his mind. He imagined Melanie walking through the doorway and looked back at Veronica. He was definitely playing fast and loose.

He didn't have any classes today. He wasn't sure of his next move. Veronica looked luscious. He wanted to remain friends, whatever that meant. He went into the kitchen and started to make coffee. He heard the shower running. By the time it brewed, Veronica had emerged fully clothed, her hair still dripping. She vigorously dried her mane with his largest bath towel.

"I hope you don't mind? I've got to bolt. The folks will get worried. You were wonderful last night. I won't ever forget it. I just hope you understand."

"Of course I understand," he said, even though he didn't.

"We're just friends, David. That's all, that's it, it was inevitable, it was astonishing, and it's over."

"Right," he said.

Veronica ran up to him and kissed him spryly on the lips. It was finished before the second hand could click again. She was out the door saying, "You'll call me as soon as you hear from CJ?"

"Absolutely," he shouted as she drove off.

Melanie called just after high noon. David was making notes for his small discussion group in English scheduled for Tuesday morning.

"David, I'm so sorry I didn't call sooner. I hope you weren't worried."

"Just a little," he said, feeling completely guilt-ridden.

"You know I'm swamped. If it's okay with you, I think we should just forget this weekend, but maybe you can come over Sunday night?"

"Sounds like a good plan," he said. "I'm a little slammed with school stuff."

"It's a deal, thanks for being so understanding."

"I'll call Sunday and we'll make plans," he said.

Saturday David listened to the Dodgers game. Koufax was poised to win his twenty-third game. They played the Cardinals, and the Dodgers were still in second place, three and a half games behind the Giants. Returning to the rhythm of the game was enough of a distraction to ease his conscience. When Koufax was on the mound, every pitch broke or tied another record. With 335 strikeouts already in the books, Koufax needed only fourteen more to break Bob Feller's major-league record of strikeouts in a single season. David, along with every other fan, knew Koufax was capable of accomplishing that in a single game. He had already fanned fourteen batters twice that season.

David lost himself in the balls and strikes. Koufax mowed down the Cardinals inning after inning, scattering four hits along the way. He didn't break Feller's record, but he secured his twenty-third victory, beating the Red Birds one to 0. Koufax had four more starts before the season ended, and unless they caught the Giants, that would be it. David leaned back on the couch and wondered how it would go with Melanie on Sunday. The count was definitely full.

CHAPTER THIRTY-EIGHT

Wednesday, September 22, 1965

It was a wild one tonight at County Stadium in Milwaukee. The Dodgers squeaked out a seven-to-six win over the Braves. It took eleven innings and a lot of drama, but they got the mission accomplished. I don't know any other way to say it, Koufax got shelled tonight. It was one of those rare performances when he just didn't have his best stuff. The fireworks started early for the Braves; Frank Bolling connected for a grand slam in the second inning. Mack Jones led off the third inning with a home run followed by another four-bagger by Gene Oliver. It was six to 0 in the bottom of the third with no outs when Hank Aaron pounced on Koufax for a screaming line-drive single, and that was it for Sandy. Hello and goodbye, Mr. Koufax. Even the great ones have their off days.

Fortunately, the Dodgers inched their way back into the game. Miraculously, Howie Reed, Ron Perranoski, and Bob Miller held the Braves scoreless through the next six innings, and the Dodgers clawed back in the game by scoring two in the fourth and three in the fifth to add to their run in the first inning, and the game remained tied after nine. Lou Johnson drove in Maury Wills in the eleventh inning after Wills stole second. With the win tonight, the Dodgers have won six straight. The Dodgers leave Milwaukee and head back home just two games behind the Giants. It's getting down to the wire, with just ten games left in the season. It can't get any more exciting than this. See you back at Dodger Stadium.

David walked over to Skip's Diner for breakfast. His anxiety about Melanie curbed his appetite, but he knew he'd better eat. It was Sunday, and he felt forsaken and lazy, but he still wanted to be around people.

His memory of Veronica lingered, and he tried to focus on Melanie, unsuccessfully. It was foggy as he crossed the street, and it served to accentuate the dreaminess of what had happened. As much as he wanted to let it go, his thoughts of Veronica got more intense, so by the time he arrived at Skip's, she loomed like a siren, slithering and vamping across a movie screen. In the theater of his mind, Melanie was sitting alone in the back.

David sat down at the counter. All the tables and booths were filled with old timers and surfers. Out of the corner of his eye, he spotted Denise taking an order from a four-top at the other end of the restaurant. She shifted her weight back and forth and bobbed her head as she jotted the order, offering her delicious smile that ensured weighty tips and indelible fantasies. Although there were thousands of students at school, David assumed he'd run into Denise at some point during the first weeks. He recalled, earlier in the summer, their conversation about UCLA, but maybe she'd changed her mind and didn't enroll this semester. Maybe she'd fallen in love and decided to get married. David kept making up excuses until Denise rushed over and flipped her order pad to a fresh page.

"Morning, what can I bring you this morning?" Denise said, without making eye contact. He was just another plate, with coinage waiting at the end. He hesitated for a second, assuming Denise would lower her gaze and, at least, give him one of her patented spicy smiles. That's what he wanted for breakfast, along with a couple of fried eggs and hash browns. The pause worked. But instead of the smooth curved lips, he received a frozen glare from a pair of ice-blue eyes.

"Are you ready to order? We're busy and I'll come back if can't decide."

"Two eggs over easy and a pile of hash browns, coffee, and orange juice. How was your first week at college?"

"Fine, anything else?"

"No, that will do it."

The traffic in the diner calmed down, but the smell of fried bacon and fresh coffee lingered. By the time he finished two glasses of water and thumbed through the paper, Denise apologetically delivered his breakfast and sat down beside him.

"Sorry, it's been a terrible morning. I dropped a plate of biscuits and grits at six thirty, and it's been downhill since then. I didn't mean to growl at you."

"I probably had it coming."

"You didn't do anything."

"Well anyway, I'm sorry about your morning. How about you meeting me for lunch sometime next week at the Campus Grill? I don't really know anybody except my friend Bryce at school. It would be great to see a familiar face."

"I guess that would be all right. You need to know that I'm seeing someone."

"So am I. Colleagues, that's all."

"All right. Maybe next week. How are the eggs?"

"Never better," he said.

When David got home, Melanie called to cancel their dinner plans. He was relieved. It wasn't just the guilt, it was the weight of his life at the moment, an inexplicable inertia loomed inside him. He imagined dropping everything and heading up to San Francisco.

After writing most of the afternoon, David thought he'd drive over to Lincoln Blvd. and get some food. He saw Grace Yamamoto sitting under a pale-yellow light, reading and eating a large dish of ice cream. He tried to ignore her, but it was like disavowing a sneeze. There she was.

"David, you can ignore me if you want. I know you could care less about socializing. A simple hello will suffice. It's pretty difficult to ignore your corpulent landlady, especially as she reads Dostoevsky, with her doleful sighs, while munching ice cream. You want some? It's chocolate mint."

"No, thanks. How's the book?"

"You don't really want to know. It's called *Notes from Underground.* It's kind of depressing. Have you read it?"

"No, I haven't."

"Well, you might like it. It's dense but short. It is full of all sorts of angst and questions about the meaninglessness of life. The kind of thing you can relate to," she said.

"What do you mean?" he asked, knowing exactly what she meant.

"Come on. You and I have talked. Remember?"

He smiled and sat down in the chair beside her. "Tell me more," he said.

"Ice cream? It's melting fast."

"No, really. I'll pass."

"See, that's what I mean," she said.

"What are you talking about?"

"Suffering. Like the guy in the book. You'd rather suffer than eat ice cream. The hero, or antihero as the critics call him, rants about the complications of living in a society where you don't have control. You sure you don't want some ice cream?"

"Okay, maybe a little.

Grace passed the bowl over to him and he took two large spoonfuls. "Pretty good, isn't it?"

He nodded and handed the bowl back to her. "It is melting, thanks for the taste."

"Your welcome. Anytime you want ice cream or Dostoevsky just let me know."

"You are a good *friend* Grace," he said, realizing the word had a lexicon of different meanings in his recent life.

Monday morning, Melanie appeared at David's door. It was seven thirty, and she was hysterical.

"Can I come in?" She slobbered her words.

"Calm down, of course you can come in. What's wrong?"

Melanie sat down and David put on some coffee and returned to the couch. Her face looked worn and stretched like she had been crying for a long time. Her head slumped down.

"What is it?" he said.

She sat down close to him. She looked as if all her strength had been drained. Her cheeks were warm and clammy. She moved away from him and placed her hands between her knees.

"This isn't easy." She took a deep breath and looked straight into his eyes.

"I cheated on you. I'm sorry. It just happened. I still don't understand. I've never behaved this way, it's not me, and yet, still it happened. I'm sorry. There wasn't anything you did or didn't do. I love you, but I just don't know anymore."

"What happened?" David asked. He felt an icy stream surge through his body.

"There was a party with the team, and a bunch of guys from the football and basketball teams showed up. We were all drinking and dancing, and I met this guy. It doesn't matter who it is because it's not about him, it's me."

"Who was it?" he asked. The ice turned to fire, his anger ignited. "Football or basketball?"

"What difference does it make? It was just a *one-nighter* and I was drunk. I don't care about him."

"If you don't care about him, how could you sleep with him?"

"David, I feel awful. I'm sorry. I don't think I can be in a relationship right now. It's all too complicated. I love you, I really do. These past months have been the best of my life, but we're at different schools, we're both busy. I'm traveling with the team next week. It's too much."

"Tell me again what happened." He had already heard what happened. "Tell me it was basketball. I can't imagine you with a football monster."

"David, please stop it. It doesn't matter, I just can't do this anymore. Neither of us are ready for this, and we're only going to collide again and again."

"Goddamn it. Just tell me what happened."

"Jesus Christ, David, you know what happened. I told you I was unfaithful. What more is there to say?"

"A lot more," he said, wondering if this might be the time to come clean about Veronica, while Melanie was going down for the count. The adrenaline intoxicated him. He wanted to detonate the situation and watch their love splash across the walls in variegated hues.

"David, there's just nothing else to say. It's over, I'm sorry."

"You're sorry that you fucked him or you're sorry that it's over or you're sorry that we ever got together?" He regretted the words as soon as they came out. He was just as culpable as Melanie.

"Please don't make this any harder than it already is."

She collapsed on the floor, and pounded her fists against the couch. He could smell the musk of her sorrow and remorse. He stood over her, feeling trapped and inert. She got up and disappeared into the day.

He noticed circles of her tears on his shirt. The room suddenly caved in. He ached and wailed until it was time for his class. When he saw Bryce later that day, he told him what had happened. Bryce responded with appropriate empathy and kind words, but it didn't make any difference. He was alone.

Tuesday he ran into Denise and they had lunch together, but he couldn't remember what they shared or if he felt any attraction.

After Denise left David sat alone in the lunch room. The odd thing about the breakup was that he felt the same way Melanie did. What had shocked him was his own indiscretions with Veronica and Rita. Unlike Melanie, he couldn't own up to it. It felt like an existential punch in the gut. He had failed to admit that he had his own desires and couldn't face the truth that he sought to be as free as she did. He had swung and missed. It was another one of life's curveballs.

School kept him busy through Wednesday. He didn't think about Melanie all day until he came home and started to feel loneliness in his body. There was a dull ache inside his rib cage. He smoked a joint and listened to the Dodgers game, his usual default.

Koufax was knocked out in the third inning, after giving up six runs on the three home runs. It was a disaster, but the Dodgers managed to squeak out a win in extra innings. Strange how things work out sometimes, David mused. All his friends were busy in their lives. He had no girlfriend. His baseball-playing days were over. The only thing he wanted to do was visit Rene and Frank. So he called. When Rene answered he said, "Get in the car and drive up immediately."

He still had school on Thursday, but he told Rene he'd leave right after class and he hoped to be up there before midnight.

Before going to sleep, he thought about CJ and Wiz. He prayed they'd make it back. He didn't want to attend any more funerals for a long while.

CHAPTER THIRTY-NINE

Saturday, September 25, 1965

What a night! The Dodgers won their eighth straight game and trail the Giants by just one game. After getting bombed in his last outing, Koufax came back with a fury, dominating the Cardinals in a two-to-0 victory. Koufax broke Bob Feller's all-time strikeout record. He struck out twelve Cardinals and now had 356 strikeouts with two starts remaining. He gave up only five hits and recorded his seventh shutout of the season. It was the eightieth time in his career that he struck out ten or more batters and the nineteenth this season. There had been some controversy about breaking Feller's record of 348 strikeouts in 154 games, but since this was the 154th game, the dispute is now irrelevant. You might say Koufax is king tonight. Hold on tight, we're coming down the stretch and the Dodgers are playing their best baseball of the season. That's it tonight from Dodger stadium. Dodgers two, Cardinals zero.

Thursday, after class, David came home to find another letter from CJ.

Dear David,

I'm back from the bush for a few days. Life happens fast out here. It feels like I've already been in Nam for months and it's only been a few weeks. It's hard to explain so I won't even try to tell you what happened. It's rough. Wiz and I made it through. We did good. We held our space; protected our guys. We were lucky. Everyone was lucky. Luck is the most valued commodity here. It's just a giant wheel of fortune for all of us. I'm covered with bites: spiders, mosquitoes, and whatever else they have out here. I had to stay quiet for long stretches, one movement and it's all over, so I learned to just play music in my head. I imagined my hands combing the piano keys, playing Mozart's Sonata 16, the easy one. I know it by heart and can lose myself in it. I'm not sure what Wiz does. He probably thinks about getting laid again and again. That's not a problem here, because everything is for sale.

I got your last letter. Thanks, it makes quite a difference, and mail call is a big deal. Veronica and the folks write, but it isn't quite the same. Have you seen Veronica lately? She seems to be doing better. At least that's what she writes, maybe she's just trying to keep me from worrying about her. I wish she'd just find something for herself and not obsess and worry about me, it's always been like that. She's always been like a second mother.

Still, no regrets, I know this was my choice and I had other options, although they didn't seem viable for me at the time. Maybe that's hard for you to understand, but like I've said before, I needed to get away from the whole scene, especially the family, specifically my dad. I hate to admit it, but that is the truth. Nothing else would have pleased him, and it isn't as if I'm doing this for him, or even because of him. I understand, at least I think I understand, why I made this decision. What I know for sure is I'll never be the same once I get home and that's a good thing. The old CJ is already dead.

> *As ever,*
>
> *CJ*

David folded the letter, placed it back in the envelope, and buried it under the maps and repair receipts in the glove box of the Galaxy. With some clean underwear, his toothbrush, a Levi jacket, a red wool sweater Rita had given him, one change of socks, and two T-shirts packed, he started the car. Ten minutes later, he was in the left lane of the San Diego Freeway. He turned the radio on, powered down the windows, and headed north. KRLA was featuring the top albums of the summer. They were playing the Rolling Stones' "Out of Our Heads."

They played "The Last Time" as he connected onto the Golden State Freeway and climbed out of the Valley. They were playing "The Spider and the Fly" when he cruised through the north Valley. He kept singing the Stones' songs, slurring and harping his syllables like Mick Jagger.

As he headed out of Bakersfield, he remembered Ginger and the trip he and Lou had taken only months ago, but it seemed like a whole lifetime had passed. He recalled how easily it had been, Lou driving, the smell of the sea wafting through the windows, the heat of Ginger's tongue in his mouth. Ginger was a guidepost, a marker of time during this season of release. He was finally feeling a sense of liberation. His thoughts turned to the Garden of Light Café. He was making good time.

The lights in San Francisco lingered and the streets were alive. It was eleven fifteen. There was still a dozen or more cars parked in front of the café. A sweet fog washed across the sidewalks. He grabbed his pack and trundled toward the entrance; it felt like home. The weight of his belongings were light, a few simple things were easily transported.

Rene sat among a small cadre of friends. David could see he was telling a story by the way his hands swept across the table as he gestured. David moved into the light and Rene saw him.

"I've been waiting for you. Great you're here. Let me get you something to eat and a pot of Mu tea. But first, the introductions." He swung around the table and rattled off the names, none of which David remembered, but they all generously welcomed him and began to riddle him with questions while Rene prepared a plate. Within a couple of minutes, Rene returned and rescued him from the throng.

"So, how are you doing? The split-up with Melanie must have cracked you open pretty good."

"I think so. It's still rattling around. It hasn't really landed yet."

"Well, it will soon enough. It's good you came up here. There isn't much in L.A. as far as refuge is concerned. I planned a few things, I hope you don't mind, but I took the liberty anyway."

David nodded has approval.

"Tomorrow morning we're going to the Zen Center on Bush Street. I want you to meet Kanto Nashami, he's a friend, and we're going to sit for a couple of hours. You won't understand it, but that's part of the magic of the process. He's a roshi, a priest from Japan. He's going to get you emptied out and then fill you up again."

"It sounds like surgery," David said.

"An excellent analogy. Very perceptive of you. I think you'll appreciate the process, especially given your psychological state. Don't worry, I'll be right there with you," Rene said.

"Okay, I'll give it a try."

"Wonderful. After sitting, we're heading across the bridge and we'll walk the Dipsea Trail to Stinson Beach. I've arranged for a friend to meet us there, and he'll drive us back to our car. Then we're off to Berkeley for dinner and music."

"Music?"

"Yes, a folk singer named Phil Ochs," Rene said.

"Sounds like I better get some sleep."

"Follow me." Rene led David to his usual room.

Rene woke David up with a steaming cup of chai tea and a muffin. "Drink up, we have a seven o'clock appointment with the roshi."

Rene turned onto Bush Street and stopped at an unassuming large building with small oriental characters across the door. He knocked and a tiny woman opened the door. She bowed, smiled at Rene, and said something in a language David didn't understand. Rene replied in the same tongue. She looked at David and bowed as well. He nodded while she gestured toward a large sitting room filled with black cushions. The space was sober, clean, and filled with morning light from the eastern window. Rene said that the place had once been a Jewish temple. The walls were painted a sandy color, and the ornate crown molding was highlighted with new white paint. Otherwise, the room was empty, except for a large bronze statue of the Buddha. A small man dressed in black robes emerged from a door on the south wall. He bowed, and Rene did the same in his direction. David nodded again. He wasn't sure what he was supposed to do. After the bowing, the roshi stood silently with his eyes closed, his hair a purified white. He had a wispy beard and very radiant, tan skin. When he opened his eyes, he shouted, "Aha Rene-san, yes welcome, you brought the young man, very good. I am so happy to see you!"

"Yes, it's wonderful to see you again as well. It's been too long," Rene said.

"When are you taking me out to the mountains again? I miss our hiking and talking. I need to get out of the city like everyone else, so you will make plans for us?" Roshi asked.

"Absolutely, next week if you like," Rene replied.

"Next week it is. So now for your friend, what is your name?"

"David."

"Very good. David, a biblical name, a fine title for you. I suppose that Rene has told you nothing about Zen Buddhist practice and meditation? I'm sure that's correct." Roshi smiled and nodded toward Rene. "There isn't much to explain. You will simply sit," Roshi said.

The roshi pointed to a thick black tufted pillow. "You will reside here." His tiny finger pointed down like a beam of light. "Close your eyes gently, imagine a welcoming smile on your face, try to open your heart."

David had lots of questions, but he silently followed Roshi's instructions.

"Very good. Don't worry about your thoughts. Just observe them. Notice your breath. Follow it as it goes in and out. If it helps, count your breaths, but only up to ten and then start again."

David wanted more of an explanation, but it wasn't coming. He heard Rene sit beside him and could hear his breathing.

Roshi continued. "You might feel uncomfortable. Don't worry. It's all right to move a little, but don't stand up. If you need to stretch, it's all right. Just do your best to remain still and follow your breath.

No right. No wrong. Just observe with compassion." Then he went silent.

David tried to remember what the roshi said. He felt an urge to stand up and walk around, but he concentrated on his breathing, focused on the inhalation and exhalation, and soon noticed a relaxation in his body. His mind was quiet and blank for a few seconds, then CJ appeared with a rifle, and Wiz was walking beside him. The landscape was thick with tropical vegetation. David followed the image, but it disappeared. His back started to hurt and he straightened his spine. It helped relieve the stiffness. He inhaled slowly and released. He focused on his breath for what seemed like a long time and felt a measure of serenity. An image of Koufax came into his mind. Koufax was standing on the mound, breathing slowly, his eyes spellbound, motionless, and then he rocked into his rhythmic windup. David felt calm and connected. He had no sense of time. Suddenly everything in his body constricted, tightened, clamored, and he panicked. He had to stand up, but he couldn't will himself to move. Then he felt a crisp tap on his shoulder and heard the sound of a bell.

"David, stand up slowly, but remember to open your eyes first." The sound of Roshi's voice was deep and hollow. He wasn't aware that his eyes were closed. "Slowly feel your feet back on the ground, raise your shoulders and lower them, feel the flow of your energy coming back into your limbs."

David looked around. Rene stood a few feet away and smiled like he had just won the daily double. Roshi hovered directly in front of him.

"What time is it? How long did I sit?" David asked.

"What difference does it make?" Roshi laughed.

"I was just wondering."

"That is a good thing, *wondering*, you should continue that practice. The other questions you have, feed them to the sea gulls and see if they provide nourishment. You had a real Jewish experience."

"What?"

"It was a pleasure meeting you, David. Enjoy your hike with Rene." Roshi dissolved through the same door he had entered from. David thought of the white rabbit in Alice's wonderland, rushing back down the hole for a very important date! He tried to get Rene to explain what had happened and what Roshi meant by a "Jewish experience," but he only laughed, saying he was clueless. One thing David knew for sure, Rene was never clueless.

When they got back into the car it was nine fifteen, so he figured that he'd sat for thirty or forty minutes. Rene would neither confirm nor deny the assessment. He drove across the Golden Gate Bridge and took the Mill Valley exit that wound up to the top of Mount Tamalpais. David had an insatiable need for explanation and deconstruction of the meditation and the meaning of what Roshi said. Rene wasn't interested in explaining anything as they wound up the mountain.

Rene parked his car at the top and hopped out. David followed. The landscape was familiar. The same mix of oak, pine, and redwood forest that he and Lou explored several months ago. The coolness of the trail hovered as they darted in and out of shadows.

"David?"

"Yes?"

"What are you going to do now?"

"Now?"

"When you get back to L.A. What's your plan? Do you imagine yourself staying there?"

"No plans, just a lot of reactions and confusion. I feel truly alone for the first time in my life, and I'm not sure what to make of it. That's why I drove up here, I don't feel so isolated when I'm here. Something is different."

"Yes, but you could say that about anyplace."

David held the thought. They walked in silence, crunching leaves and twigs. The sounds of wrens and chickadees flittered through the thick canopy. They broke out into open space again, and the path became dusty and weedy and twisted back. When they reentered the trees, Rene pointed to a gray fox that stood looking at them about twenty-five yards down the trail.

The fox darted off. David said, "I can't stop thinking about what Roshi said."

"The Jewish experience?" Rene asked.

"Yes. Why do you think he said it?"

"I'm not sure. What do you think?"

"I think it's auspicious, especially since Rosh Hashanah starts Sunday night."

"Synchronicity," said Rene. "Roshi has a way of opening drawers inside your mind. It gets you wondering."

"But why?" David asked.

"It's a great question, and you have the answer, not me."

They finished hiking and were back at the car in the late afternoon. The traffic across the San Rafael bridge was light, and they arrived in Berkeley with plenty of time to cruise the bookstores and coffee houses that lined Telegraph Avenue. There were fliers about the Phil Ochs concert stapled to telephone poles and on bulletin boards everywhere. Phil Ochs was a songwriter David had heard of. He remembered that he wrote "There but for Fortune," covered by Joan Baez and Marianne Faithful, but David hadn't heard of any of his other songs.

"There'll be quite a crowd tonight. We'll need to get there early," Rene said, after sipping the last of his espresso at the Mediterranean Café where they had stopped for a snack.

"Not a problem, you are the guy in charge," David said.

"Not really," Rene said with his sagacious smile.

They arrived at Aladdin's, a sprawling coffee house near the intersection of Ashby and Telegraph at 7:00 p.m. The music started at eight. Rene sidled over to a small two-top near the window; it was as if the table was just waiting for them. They ordered more espresso. David sized up the room, mostly college kids, with a few longhairs and several overweight professor types in tweed sports coats with elbow patches.

Phil Ochs came out right at eight, dressed in blue jeans and a long-sleeved green shirt, his dark wavy hair looked combed, but only as an afterthought. He didn't introduce himself, just started to play "Draft Dodger Rag" in his sweet, twangy Texas voice. He looked edgy and handsome, with brooding brown eyes. His head bobbed with his guitar as he blasted his opening song.

When he finished Draft Dodger Rag, he said, "There's 130,000 troops already over there and no end in sight. The insanity has to stop now, it's only going to get worse, like it always does, and it's up to us to make sure it stops. We've all got to sing this song together." He set down the microphone and started to sing:

Oh I marched to the battle of New Orleans
At the end of the early British War
The young land started growing
The young blood started flowing
But I ain't marchin' anymore

Rene told David that in May, thousands of people had gathered in Oakland to hear Ochs and others urge an end to the war. Young men had started burning their draft cards and screaming at the police. David hadn't heard anything about it. Nothing like that was happening in Los Angeles as far as he knew. Ochs played until eleven, mixing traditional folk with his protest songs, talking about the war and about the music. David slipped into a trance. Time vanished, and then suddenly, the lights came back on. The final lines of Och's song sounded through David's head as they drove back into the city:

Call it peace or call it treason
Call it love or call it reason
But I ain't marchin' any more
No I ain't marchin' any more

They didn't get back to Rene's place until after midnight.

370

"I probably won't see you in the morning," Rene said. "I give a lecture once a month in Mill Valley, so I'll be on road before seven."

"Well, thanks for the weekend," David said. "It was just what I needed."

"David, you need to be here," Rene said.

David smoked a small pipe full of hash Rene had left next to his bed and fell asleep reading *The Doors of Perception*.

It was after nine when he woke up. The café already had customers noisily milling around. He stumbled into his clothes and drifted in. He sat down at a table and noticed someone had left a crumpled copy of the Sunday *Chronicle* sports section. He ordered a large orange juice and a triple espresso, some eggs and toast. He picked up the sports page. The Dodgers had won their eighth game in a row and remained a game behind the Giants, who also had won. Willie Mays had clubbed his fiftieth home run, and Koufax broke Bob Feller's all-time strikeout record. There was Koufax, and there was Roshi and the Jewish question to ponder. He finished his eggs. It was already midmorning, and he had a long drive back home.

CHAPTER FORTY

Wednesday, September 29, 1965

Oh my! Oh my! What a game. Koufax was just stellar from start to finish. Impeccable, really. He operated tonight like a surgeon, removing any speck of hope from the Cincinnati batters. The usually invincible Reds hitters: Pete Rose, Vida Pinson, Frank Robinson, Deron Johnson, and Tony Perez collaborated for merely two hits and one walk. All the rest were outs. An almost-perfect game. He barely even needed any fielders since thirteen of the outs were strikeouts. What made it even smoother was the Dodgers produced five runs, three of them courtesy of a Maury Wills' bases-loaded triple in the bottom of the seventh inning. Koufax faced only thirty batters, just three above the minimum. He secured his twenty-fifth win, his eighth shutout of the season, and his fifth consecutive victory, without allowing any runs. Could anyone pitch better than that? He truly is the man with a golden arm!

Meanwhile the Cardinals beat the Giants as Bob Gibson not only throttled San Francisco with his arm, he also clobbered them with his bat, belting a grand-slam home run in the top of the eighth inning. With the Giants' loss and Dodgers' twelfth win in a row, we have a two-game lead with only four games remaining in the season. Koufax will have one more start on October 2 against the Milwaukee Braves. Everything is coming down to the wire.

Driving back from San Francisco, Phil Ochs' voice and words echoed inside David as he threaded his way home. He speculated about Melanie and tried to imagine how a life with her might have been. He seriously wondered if he would be able to sustain another few years of living in Los Angeles. He figured he wouldn't.

He arrived at his parents' house with just enough time to take a shower and put on a clean set of clothes for the evening Rosh

Hashanah service. He had missed dinner, but that was fine. He disliked the feeling of being gorged while trying to follow the liturgy.

"You didn't eat," his mother said.

"No, I snacked all the way back. I'm fine," David said.

"That isn't any way to start the holiday," she said.

"You are right, but that's how it is for now. God will forgive or he won't. I don't have any control," David said.

"So smart after just a couple of weeks in college," she said.

David let the remark pass. It was the beginning of the Days of Awe. He liked the fact that Jewish holidays revolved around the cycle of the moon. It was ancient and tribal.

"You missed a great brisket," Alex said.

"I'll have some when we get back from temple," David said.

"It's not the same," his mother interrupted.

"I know that," he said.

The services were mercifully quick. The sermon focused on what it meant to be an "authentic Jew." The rabbi talked about the importance of following the precepts of the Torah as well as the importance of social justice. But the words rang hollow for David. He'd heard it all before and couldn't wait to get back to his apartment. He was tired, but he couldn't stop thinking about Roshi's words, "a Jewish experience." As the congregation walked out the doors, they were greeted by police sirens and quickly erupting pandemonium. Across the street from the synagogue, there were seven or eight brown-shirted American Nazis, complete with swastika arm bands and signs saying "Jews deserve to die" and "No Jews in America." The police had cordoned them off from the families leaving the temple, but the shouts and haranguing penetrated the air.

"This is disgusting. How can they let those animals stand there?" Rose said.

"The police have it under control," Jacob said. "Let's get in the car and get home." He started to shepherd Alex and Rose toward the car.

David stood mesmerized. He'd heard about the *party*, whose headquarters was in Glendale, a little south and east of the Valley, but he had never thought much of it. Just some crazies. Now they were right in front of him.

"David, come on, let's go home. Nothing to do here. The police will take care of it."

"Dirty Jews! Dirty Jews!" the Nazis were shouting. David's blood boiled. Full count. *I need to do something.*

"David, let's go," Jacob said. "Mother and Alex are waiting."

"David, come on," Alex called.

"Give me a minute," he said. "I'll be right there."

"No, there isn't anything to do. The police are here," Jacob said.

David turned away from his father and walked toward the mayhem across the street. There were four police cars parked in front of the Nazis, and they had put up crime-scene tape to block them off. David approached them.

"Back off, young man," a Black L.A.P.D. officer said. "They aren't going to cause any harm. Unfortunately, they have the right to be here."

"So do I," said David.

He stared at the Nazis. There were seven. All of them older than him. All of them with a blind fury in their eyes. *No harm?* he thought. *Who is he kidding?* He wanted to break through the tape and smash them one by one. He wanted to feel his fist go deep into their lives. He wanted to make the reality disappear.

"You need to move back across the street, sir," said the policeman. "We'll handle this."

David turned and walked back to the car where his family was waiting.

"What's wrong with you?" his mother said. "We need to get home."

"Yes we do," David said. "We most certainly need to get home."

"What were you trying to do?" Alex said.

"I just needed to get a little closer. That's all. I wanted to see their faces."

They had honey cake and tea when they got home. His father forbad any further talk about the Nazis. It was awful, and that was it. After dinner and dessert, David kissed them all goodbye and said he'd see them again in the morning for services.

Driving home, he thought again about Roshi's words. He wondered about the synchronicity of meeting Roshi and the night's events. Something was amiss. Buddhist monk? Now these Nazis? And of course, there was Koufax. The pitcher for the Los Angeles Dodgers could throw a hard object very fast. If he needed to, Koufax could inflict a lot of damage. He was strong and determined. Koufax once said, "Pitching is the art of instilling fear." That's what David wanted to do when he looked at the Nazis. He wanted to instill fear. He craved to let them know he'd had his *Jewish moment*, and it translated to *I'd kill you if I had the chance*. The rawness of his enmity terrified and calmed him at the same time.

For David, the episode with the Nazis wasn't over. Something had clicked inside and that had been all he needed. He was pretty sure of what he had to do, but there were still some loose ends.

His apartment felt welcoming and safe. It was *home*. He sat down and started to write. Nothing in particular came through, just a bunch of jumbled thoughts; streams of consciousness. But after an hour, the rivulets started to flow together into a river. He wanted to get away. That much was certain, but what else? He returned to his story about the boy with morning blindness and wrote for another hour before he slept.

Wednesday he was five minutes late to a lecture about Aristotle. He tried to follow the professor's words but was having trouble making sense of what he was saying. Before finishing the lecture, the professor wrote a couple of quotes from the great Greek. David copied them down. The class was to "think" about the citations and discuss them next time.

The actuality of thought is life. The search for truth is in one way hard and in another way easy, for it is evident that no one can master it fully or miss it wholly. But each adds a little to our knowledge of nature, and from all the facts assembled there arises a certain grandeur.

Bryce was waiting for him at a little coffee stand outside the student center. His clothes neatly pressed, Bryce wore a light-yellow long-sleeved shirt, with some kind of little creature on the pocket, and penny loafers. David knew Bryce had found his element, "his truth" as Aristotle would have said. Bryce had the grace and stamina for the long haul, success and certainty surrounded his lithe muscular frame; the athlete, pure and profound, an Adonis sculpted in balance, beyond reproach, his last lingering friend.

"You look trashed," Bryce said.

"Why thank you, I'm barely awake and don't need any compliments at the moment," David said.

"How was your weekend in protest land?"

"Pretty amazing. We heard Phil Ochs at a café in Berkeley. Quite an experience. It's not like anything that happens around here. I'm getting into that place more and more."

"Well, you better be careful, don't go burning your draft card. You've got at least four years of deferment left on it."

"I'm not stupid."

"No, but I can see you getting caught up in the drama of it all. I'm against the war, but I don't think marching in the streets is going to change anything," Bryce said.

"Maybe, maybe not. People are pissed off, and we keep sending more troops. Shit, Wiz and CJ are over there. It's insane, and for what?"

"For nothing. It's all bullshit. They talk about a commie takeover, the domino theory, like it's all just a game of checkers or something," Bryce said. "But what can you do but save your own ass? You're too damn smart to get hooked into any of that stuff that's going on up in Berkeley."

"I'm already involved," David said, not really knowing what he meant. He recalled the experience with Roshi and realized there wasn't any way to explain that to Bryce. His frustration started to burn inside. He didn't want to be having this conversation. What Bryce was saying made sense, but it also sounded self-serving and void of any passion or belief, except for simple survival. Cover your ass, that's all that mattered. CJ and Wiz wanted to go. David knew Bryce cared, but they were suddenly on opposite sides.

"Involved how? Did you join some protest group?" he sneered.

"That's not what I mean."

"What do you mean? You sound as messed up as you look. I think you ought to reconsider trying out for the team again. Even if you don't play much, it will help keep your head straight."

"My head is straight," David said. "All I'm saying it that things are different up there and it makes me think that maybe this isn't the right place for me. I know it sounds nuts, and maybe it does have to do with Lou dying, or Rita, or Melanie. I'm not sure anymore." David paused and looked away. Then he continued.

"Sunday night there were a bunch of Nazis outside the temple. It pissed me off and I wanted to do something."

"Nazis? Are you kidding me?"

"The police were there. All I could do was stare them down. I've got to do more than just *think* about this stuff," he said.

"Right! I wish I'd been there with you," Bryce said.

"Me too. I've got an idea, let's go find those assholes."

"And how do we do that?"

"I have the address. They broadcasted it on television. 233 East Montana Street, Glendale. I've got a detailed street map in the car. A gift from my father."

"Okay. And then what?"

"Then we just see what happens."

Bryce hesitated for a second. "All right then. Let's go pay those Nazis a visit."

David picked up Bryce a little after eight o'clock. They drove toward the very white community of Glendale. David was not sure what he would do once they arrived. His plan wasn't so precise. He knew that he wanted to get close to them without anyone getting in his way, and he also knew that whatever happened Bryce would have his back.

Following the map, they arrived at the house in less than thirty minutes. It was a nondescript frame home in a rundown neighborhood dotted with liquor stores, Laundromats, and small grocery stores. There was a small wrought iron gate around the house, and it had a porch with a shade partially drawn down, but you could still see in the window. David cruised by once and noticed that lights were on inside. He parked halfway down the block.

"Now what?" Bryce asked.

"We get out and take a walk," David said, feeling a surge of excitement and fear as he slammed the door. They walked side by side toward the unassuming white bungalow-style house. There were two small windows and one large one exposed to the street. A small air conditioning unit was thrumming in one of the smaller windows. David could make out a couple of figures moving around inside.

"Okay. Have you gotten close enough?" Bryce said.

"Let's circle the block once more and see what happens," David said.

"Fine. It's your party."

They walked around the block. All the homes were small and worn. Nothing violent or terrifying loomed, in fact, it was the banality of the surroundings that gave David a sickening sense of fright, like a deadly virus hiding in your bedroom. Approaching the Nazi den for the second time, they instinctively slowed down. David thought he saw someone stepping off the porch. He put his hand in front of Bryce and they halted. A second figure descended from the porch, and then a third.

The first guy opened the gate, and the other two walked onto the sidewalk. After closing the gate, the first Nazi joined the other two and started walking directly toward Bryce and David.

There were street lights every ten yards, so David was able to recognize two of the three as the members he had confronted. Certainly they'd remember his face. The guy who opened the gate was tall, maybe six two. He had been the leader. The other two were shorter, one thin and spindly, the other thick and spongey with long blond hair. He was the one David hadn't seen at the synagogue. They were about twenty feet away.

"I'll take the tall guy. You take the other two. You okay with that?" David said.

"Sounds good."

David knew he could count on Bryce. Last year they had run into some trouble after a football game. A few toughs from one of the local car clubs had jumped them. Bryce was strong, quick, and accurate with his fists and his feet. In addition to teaching the boys boxing, his father Brent had trained them in effective street fighting. Together they had made short work of the car club hoodlums. David knew he could hold his own.

When they were face to face, Bryce and David stood in the middle of the sidewalk. The tall guy looked straight at David.

"Son of a bitch. It's the Jew boy from the other night. What the hell are you doing here, you piece of scum?"

"Just wanted to get a better look at your pathetic troop with no one around to protect you," David said.

"You can't be serious," the tall guy laughed. "We are going to kick your Jew ass right here and now. And your buddy here, is he a Jew boy too?"

"No, I'm a redskin, and you're going to wish you never met me," Bryce said.

With that, David and Bryce exploded at their targets. One thing Brent always stressed about street fighting was never pass up the element of surprise. David took one small step back with his left foot and then pushed off with all the force he could generate and smashed his fist squarely under the right eye socket of the tall guy. At the same time Bryce rushed the guy with long hair and put a quick knee to his groin, spinning him around, and swiftly kicked him to the ground. Seeing the devastation, the skinny Nazi ran back down the street, shouting for reinforcements.

"Times have changed," David said glaring down at the two Nazi's on the ground.

Instinctively, they sped back to the Galaxy. David had the car in gear and moving before Bryce closed the door. They were on the freeway zooming back home within a couple of minutes. Both of them breathing heavily and laughing.

"Hell of a left, David," Bryce said. "It's that *mystery* punch."

"Thanks. I loved your line about the redskin."

"Well, I am part Cherokee."

David's hand throbbed as he drove Bryce back to campus.

The night didn't change the reality of a Nazi presence in his backyard, but it did transform something inside him. He replayed the evening in his mind. What had just happened? An authentic moment; Jew vs. Nazi. It was stunning. Thinking like Aristotle was one thing, but taking action, that was something else again. He smiled as he parked the car.

He walked inside his apartment, grabbed some ice and a towel, and sat down on his bed. It had been a long day. After wrapping his hand, he flipped on the Dodgers game. He put an extra pillow under his head and listened to end of the game. Koufax had been in control from start to finish. A strong Jew, David said to himself. He would have understood what had happened tonight. The game ended with a five-to-0 victory. David rested easy, knowing Koufax had one more start and then there was the World Series. He hoped.

CHAPTER FORTY-ONE

Saturday, October 2, 1965

The Dodgers are going to the World Series! It's been a real nail biter, but Sandy Koufax just made it official; the Dodgers have secured the National League pennant. He did it with his usual panache and power. He tossed a three-to-one gem, striking out thirteen Braves and allowing just four hits. He did walk four, but that was easily overshadowed by the fact that not only did he establish a career-high twenty-six-win season, but he set a new major league record with 382 strikeouts. What a year it's been for Mr. Koufax.

Pitching on just two days' rest, Koufax didn't have his usual resolute control. What he did have was his fastball, and the Braves were going down swinging from the start. In the fifth inning Cloninger, who already had won twenty-four games, walked Lou Johnson to start the inning. Jim Lefebvre followed with a single for the first hit off the Braves pitcher. With two men on base, Wes Parker hit a grounder to Joe Torre who was playing first base for the Braves. Torre fired home, but Lou Johnson had already returned to third. The bases were loaded and Cloninger was obviously rattled by the previous play because he walked John Roseboro on just five pitches to force in the go-ahead run, and then proceeded to award Koufax a free pass on just four pitches. With a three-to-one lead, Koufax could see the pennant waving in the floodlights, he dug down and pounded his way to the finish line. The Braves got base hits in each of the last three innings, but Koufax would not yield. Next stop is the World Series!

David's hand was still sore on Thursday, but the swelling was gone. He was disinclined to do any studying. School was irrelevant at the moment. He turned on the radio. Frankie Lymon was singing "Why Do Fools Fall in Love." He tried to figure out how anyone could write a song like that when he was only thirteen. KRLA had featured him because of the news that Frankie had been drafted and was assigned to basic training at Fort Gordon, Georgia. The kid who wrote and sang "Goody Goody" would soon be carrying an M-1 rifle and digging foxholes beside some forgotten swamp in the Deep South. The music had him moving and swaying around the room, but after a few minutes the walls started to feel too confining.

A letter from CJ had arrived that afternoon. It sat on the table, calling to him, but he wasn't ready to open it. He wasn't sure why he was resistant. He stared at it. Finally, he said, "What the fuck," and carefully opened and unfolded the letter.

Dear David,

I'm counting. Days, bugs, stars, helicopters, fucks, bodies, it keeps me going. The notion of sequence, the way the digits follow each other, the order gives me something that isn't here. There might be a better way to explain it, but I'm not aware of it. I need limits and boundaries in this place that is so full of shadows and spider webs. There is a lack of predictability, except that guys are getting shot and killed. The calendar becomes the bible, the hours and seconds become the chapter and verse. Does any of this make sense? I'm not cracking up. You don't have to worry about that, it's quite the opposite. Finally, I realize that this is only about one simple thing, survival. It's all about getting my ass back in one piece, counting the time, making that indelible X for one more morning, one more cigarette, one more song. It's the only gospel that works here. In the bush, losing your focus can cost you your life. I make lists and dwell on the numerals one to ten again and again. I assign value and make records of everything. We've lost a couple of guys already, and that's a low number, hopefully it will stay down.

The census helps me keep order in my head: the number of meals, the spent shells, the cigarettes, the names of the guys, the alleys, the patrols. I keep everything in a series of small notebooks that I get from a little store in Saigon. What I think about between the counting is being back home. I imagine the Valley, the citrus smell down the block, the lights of Van Nuys and the ocean—the cool Pacific. Everything here sticks to everything else; the mud, the bugs, even the people cling to each other. It's as if there is a tacky layer of blood and sweat that clings to everything else.

Wiz is fine, he gets along with everyone. He has always been a good poker player and that makes quite a difference out here. He keeps me laughing and everyday reminds me what we're going to do when we get back home—buy a couple of huge cheeseburgers and a bottle of tequila and drive out to the dam to watch the sunset like old times. None of this seems to faze him. He's durable and keeps his sense of humor. Time to go. I'll write again soon. Say hi to everyone and give Veronica a call when you can.

    Your buddy,
    CJ

He put the letter down and walked to the beach. CJ enumerated everything that was around him to keep his sanity. David could understand. He had counted balls and strikes. He was always looking for the right pitch. Now his selection felt limited, no future, no lover, no real ideas, except to keep walking. He was a fool who wasn't in love. He was lost in the middle of a decade that was strangling itself to death. He needed a fastball low and on the outside corner for a call *strike three.*

Friday morning David turned onto Westwood Blvd. He was already late for his ten o'clock Philosophy class and he didn't really care. He walked past a brunette with thick wavy hair and a tight tan skirt. She carried a couple of heavy tomes: physics and chemistry. He did a double take as the fragrance of her perfume lingered. He tried following her to class. Maybe he could make some contact, but she disappeared like a specter when she entered a throng of students. He hurried around the group, hoping to get another glance, but she evaporated into the autumn morning.

CJ's letter lingered during the Philosophy class. His friend was likely sitting in a large tent as he wavered between being disconsolate and resolute. David figured his writing kept him centered and sane. *Counting, just keep counting, CJ.*

After classes David walked over to the ball field where Bryce and the team stretched and warmed up. David sat at the top of the bleachers and watched Bryce and his new friend Samuel toss the ball back and forth from center to right field. He missed the camaraderie of being on a team. It wasn't so long ago when he savored the sweetness of the leather on his hand and the surety and density of the ball as he cupped it in his palm. When he pitched he gripped the ball across or with the seams, depending on whether he wanted it to rise or sink, sunrise or sunset. Bryce grabbed a bat and started to play a game of pepper, using the center-field wall as a backstop. Samuel tossed underhand, and Bryce bunted right and left as Samuel glided to each pitch and tossed it back. It was the same way he and Lou had warmed up before pitching.

Counting? CJ counted bugs and bodies. David counted memories. As much as he wanted to thunder down onto the field, he knew his census had to start again in a different kind of arena.

When the practice ended David walked down to the dugout and hung out with the team. He waited until Bryce and he were alone and then handed him CJ's letter.

"Hey, thanks again for the other night. I couldn't have done that without you," David said.

"My pleasure. It's a night we'll never forget. Isn't that one of your themes?" Bryce said.

"Huh?"

"Never forget."

David nodded. Bryce took the letter quietly, as if he were a choirboy receiving communion, and sat down on the bench. The dugout was a couple of feet below the earth, where the perspective was altered. David had never considered the buried-ness of the place. It was like a grave, a foxhole, a purgatory of sorts. Bryce cleared his throat a couple of times and spit a gob of saliva onto the trampled grass that bordered the dugout. Bryce shook his head, folded the letter carefully, and handed it back to David.

"I think he's pretty messed up. Sitting around making lists of things; it sounds a bit loony to me. Why isn't he out poking those gorgeous whores that everyone talks about or getting stoned or drunk?" Bryce said.

"I imagine he's done some of that as well. He's thinking about things and keeping track of it all. It helps him stay straight," David said. Not long ago he was counting his breaths with the roshi. Counting meant focus.

"Maybe so. He sounds pretty gloomy if you ask me."

"Why wouldn't he be?"

"How the hell do I know? It's just such a fucking mess, I can't imagine how anyone gets through a day of it. If you read between the lines, it's obvious that he's already killed some people," Bryce pointed out.

"I think that's true," David said.

"Well, how the hell do you live with that? I know that my old man did it. He told me so. I think that's why he's so packed inside himself. His whole body cringes up whenever he talks about his time in the Pacific and how he used to take out the Jap snipers."

"Damn, Bryce, you never told me that about your dad. That's harsh," David said.

"And that's why when I read this letter it makes me sick inside. Poor CJ, he'll never be the same," Bryce said. He had to leave for a team meeting, so David drove home.

Grace Yamamoto sat outside her apartment, smoking her favorite thin black cigarettes while she sipped coffee from a bright yellow mug. David knew she'd start a conversation. He had planned to stay home and do some reading and listen to the game.

"Hi, David, you doing anything tonight?" Grace asked.

"Home alone with my books and my good intentions," David said.

"Want a drink? I've got a decent bottle of white wine."

"It's a start," he said.

"I'm surprised. You're usually busy on the weekends."

"That's true, but tonight is different."

"Outside, or would you rather come in?" Grace asked.

David looked at her. She wore her usual one-piece tent. Tonight it was forest green with small white slaps of lightning bolts up and down the sides. She looked a little thinner, her face had some definition that he hadn't noticed before, and she sported a pair of shell earrings.

"How about outside?" David said.

Grace came out with an open bottle of white wine and two plastic tumblers. She put them down on the metal table and pulled out a chair for David.

"You hungry?" she asked.

"I'm okay for now. How about you?"

"I'm always hungry," she said, "but I'm trying to lose some weight. It's a preoccupation I have" She laughed.

"Well, you look good," he said.

"Thanks," she said. "By the way, I finished that book."

"What book?" he asked.

Notes from Underground, she said. "Remember Dostoevsky? The guy who is just like you. You want to read it?"

"Sometime soon," he said.

David hoped all this talk wasn't giving her the wrong idea. Grace poured the tumbler half full of wine and he took a long pull that finished half the glass. It was cold with just a little sweetness to it. He liked the taste. He smiled at Grace.

"It's a Riesling. I usually drink Chardonnay, but this looked pretty interesting."

"I like it." He raised his glass and drank half of what was left. "To a good Riesling among friends."

"I'll drink to that," Grace said and filled his glass again.

He got a little buzz while he watched the cars whiz up and down Pacific Avenue. Grace and he held the silence for a few minutes. They looked at each other and broke into smiles. The hibiscus still had some bloom and the jasmine started to unfold, so the fragrance of the night began to deepen and swirl. Grace disappeared inside and returned with a box of Ritz crackers and some soft French cheese.

"This really goes well with wine. Don't be shy." She set the cheese and crackers in front of him and touched his shoulder as she sauntered back to her chair. David spread the cheese on a couple of crackers, took another slug of the wine, then devoured two more crackers and set up three more. They finished the rest of the wine. Without a word, Grace disappeared and returned with another bottle of white wine, this time it was Chardonnay. She filled his glass again, and he tried the new wine. It wasn't as sweet. Grace poured more in her glass and smiled at him.

"You've never allowed yourself to relax around me, except at the baseball game. I thought maybe you didn't like me or were afraid of me. I can put people off sometimes."

"Maybe that's true."

"Which one?"

"I don't know, both I suppose."

Grace put her hand on top of David's and looked out toward the flowers that poked up under her window. Her hand was warm and clammy. David didn't care that her hand was on his as long as he could drink the Chardonnay with the other. Grace moved her hand away and looked at David. Her eyes were puffy and he could sense her neediness start to creep closer.

"What happened to your girlfriends?"

"They found greener pastures."

"No new prospects?"

"I guess not. It doesn't seem like the right time to get involved," he said.

"Are you thinking of moving?"

"I'm thinking of all sorts of things. But right now I'm not able to focus on anything, thanks to you."

"I hope that's all right," she said.

"Very much all right. How about you?"

"What do you mean?" Grace asked.

"What about you? Your life?" David asked, realizing he had never asked her anything personal.

Grace laughed and flipped her straight raven-colored hair back over her shoulder. She turned away for a second as if to gather herself for a discourse of great importance. David watched as she stood up and straightened her dress and then sat back down. She started to take a cigarette out of her case but changed her mind and stuck it back.

"Simple. My father died ten years ago, and my mother lives alone. She's sixty-six and lives in San Pedro. She likes living near the water, she fishes off the pier and actually catches enough to make dinner four or five times a week. I take care of paying her bills and making sure she gets to her appointments. We're close. It's just the two of us. That's my life."

Grace poured herself more wine and moved her chair closer to David. He leaned over and kissed her on the cheek.

"Thanks for the wine, and thanks for the cheese and crackers, and thanks for being here."

"Don't mention it," she said.

He wasn't going to make a play for her and she knew it. But as he walked back to his apartment, he had an epiphany. It was nothing like rockets blasting or a song that burst out from his heart, but he realized that as he was sitting there with his self-effacing neighbor, a woman who would probably never leave this little block of Santa Monica, she had found her own piece of mind and her own terra firma. He knew his days in L.A. were numbered. He started counting just like CJ. It was a full count and it wasn't going to take long before he made his final pitch.

He was surprised to wake up Saturday morning without a hangover. It was the Sabbath between Rosh Hashanah and Yom

Kipper. He washed his face and noticed his hand was just about healed. Whatever small pain lingered, it was worth it.

After breakfast, he went to the beach. The water was warm and the waves caressed him all afternoon. All that was left was the ball game. It was the penultimate game of the season.

David got home and showered for a long time. He thought he might go and visit Grace again, but she wasn't home. He recalled she had said she was going to her mother's for dinner. He cooked up spaghetti and made garlic bread and a salad. The game was going to start soon, and he felt content with the evening just the way it was unfolding.

Koufax mowed down the Braves. The Dodgers were going to the World Series. David knew that Koufax would not pitch the first game. It was Yom Kipper. It had been in the papers that Drysdale was scheduled for the first game and Koufax the second. It made sense to David.

The regular season ended the next day with another victory over the Braves. David had followed it from start to finish, and what remained was the clash between the National and American League champions, along with his future. Melanie never called again. She disappeared into the world of Wilshire Blvd. David knew his future in L.A. was over. The one inexplicable thread that held him all year was Koufax—however perplexing it was, it remained the truth.

That evening, he wrote CJ a long letter. Then he worked on the story about the boy with morning blindness. Morning blindness, he mused, it's the malady of youth. Of course, he was the boy as well as the healer. When the sun rose, he found himself still writing effortlessly as if the story was already written and he was just the scribe scribbling down the words.

EPILOGUE

Many years have passed since that Yom Kippur day in 1965. Looking back, I remember sitting in temple next to Alex, hunger roiling in my stomach, and it was only noon. Naturally, my thoughts turned to Koufax. Jim Murray, the *Los Angeles Times* sports writer, once called Koufax "a captive of baseball trapped by his talents and his instincts." In some ways, we were all captives of something back then.

Koufax sat somewhere in Minneapolis, a city surrounded by cornfields. Maybe he was alone in a hotel room, out of the glare of the news media. Wherever he decided to fast and pray, or not pray, the decision was at once simple and astonishing. He had his private burdens and transgressions, and in that way, he was not any different from other Jews on this particular day. But while his choice not to pitch contained no grandeur or self-aggrandizement, it remains an extraordinary moment in the long narrative of his people. On that day, the confluence of time, space, and sports converged on a baseball player whose simple decision cried out in the face of all things profane.

It was the last full count of the season. My deal with God and with the city had come to a final reckoning; another kind of accounting, not so dissimilar to what CJ had done. As to God, it was always about the same. I'd make my best effort. History had thrown my generation and me a giant curve ball, but I could have been born a leper in Bombay. My complaints weren't with God. My belief was that whatever force put everything into motion, it had one hell of an imagination along with a great sense of humor and pathos. I missed Lou and Rick, and that took a long time to heal.

My memory is that the morning service ended in the usual way: a couple of traditional songs, a plea for money, a blessing for an easy fast, and we were done. I walked out under the L.A. sky. The chants of atonement echoed within me. I felt humbled and eager to move down the road. I smelled hamburgers and fries sizzling along the fast food joints that were busy serving lunch—a perfume of enticement up and down Van Nuys Blvd. The sun hit my forehead and warmed me as Alex gathered my hand in hers. My father put his arm around my shoulder, and we headed to the parking lot together. The Angeles Crest mountains were clear on the eastern horizon.

I looked around for the Nazis, but they hadn't shown. Whether that had anything to do with my encounter with them or not, I'll never know. For my family's sake, I felt relieved because, if they were there again, I'm not sure what would have happened. As it was, the case was closed and that was fine with me.

My father and I watched Drysdale self-destruct that day. He didn't mind watching the World Series on Yom Kipper. The game started all right with Ron Fairly connecting for a home run off Mudcat Grant in the top of the second inning, giving the Dodgers the first run and first lead of the series. But in the bottom of the inning, Don Mincher, the Twins first baseman, knotted the game with a solo shot off Drysdale. Then it unraveled. Zolio Versalles blasted a three-run homer in the bottom of the third, and Drysdale couldn't finish the inning. He gave up seven runs and seven hits in just two and two-thirds innings. Not only was it depressing, but there was a whisper of culpability in the press the next day against Koufax for letting down the boys in blue.

Thursday I watched the game at school with Bryce and the guys from the team. They had a great television at the sports complex.

"He's got to get a win or it's all over." Bryce uttered the common wisdom that losing the first two games in the World Series usually equaled doom. The way Minnesota came out slugging against Drysdale, the prognosis wasn't encouraging, but Koufax had the ball today.

It had been cold and damp all week in Minneapolis. The papers had speculated as to Koufax's whereabouts during Yom Kipper. For his part Koufax ignored it all, and his choice of venue and method of observance remained private. All that mattered was that he was taking the mound for the second game of the World Series. Everyone knew where he'd be today.

Bryce and I watched as he matched Jim Kaat inning for inning for five frames.

"He's got his fastball, but he's having trouble with the curve," Bryce said. "Usually that's enough, but he's missing his spots, and they're getting some good wood on the ball."

"If they'd just score some runs it might give him some traction," I replied. "Kaat has the Dodgers tied up in knots."

In the bottom of the sixth, Zolio Versalles hit a line drive off Jim Gilliam's glove that skipped into left and allowed him to reach second base. Tony Oliva hit a blooper down the right field line for a double, scoring Zolio to give the Twins the lead. Harmon Killebrew followed with a single to left driving in Oliva, and suddenly the Twins had two runs and acres of confidence. For some inexplicable reason, Alston lifted Koufax for a pinch hitter in the top of the seventh. He was finished for the day and left as the veritable scapegoat for the seeming demise of the Dodgers. Ron Perranoski proceeded to give up three hits and three runs in less than two innings, giving the Twins a sweep at home and a five-to-one victory.

Bryce and I followed the World Series through the redemption and the hallelujah of the last games. Claude Osteen did save the day on Saturday. He pitched a gem, a five-hit shutout that placed a gargantuan stumbling block in front of the Twins hitters. Now to have a chance at the championship, the Twins would have to beat Koufax and Drysdale again. Down two games to one, Drysdale confronted the Twins on Sunday and held them to a couple of home runs while pitching a complete game and striking out eleven. The Dodgers came out swinging, scoring seven runs on ten hits, including a couple of boomers by Lou Johnson and Wes Parker. They tied the series at two games each, and Koufax was set go on Monday.

The Dodgers and Koufax roared out early and never looked back. By the end of the day, they had pounded out fourteen hits; four by Maury Wills. They stole four bases, three by Willie Davis who set a World Series record. They knocked out Jim Kaat in the third inning. Koufax mowed down the Twins like dry stalks of corn in a lonely field. They managed only four weak hits and went down swinging ten times. A near-perfect game, a shutout, a giant exclamation point. The Dodgers were now up three games to two. The series moved back to Minneapolis where Claude Osteen would try and finish up what he started in the third game.

Osteen lost steam after five innings in the frigid Minnesota air. The Twins weren't about to capitulate on their home turf. The Dodgers returned to their puny batting ways and were upstaged when the Minnesota pitcher, Mudcat Grant, hit a three-run homer to finalize the verdict against Los Angeles. That set the stage for the final game, and there was a lot of suspense about whether Alston would go with Drysdale or Koufax. He finally made his decision with his infamous remark, "I'm going with the *left-hander*." Later Koufax would comment that after all he'd done for the organization, the long, lean years of development and the final years of glory that he brought to the club, the least that Alston could have done was call him by his name, first or last, it didn't matter.

Koufax took the ball on two days' rest, his arm decimated by the 400 innings he had accrued over the season. His swollen joints were already a familiar story, yet his will, his muscular resolve, and his steely nerves still made him an indomitable force for the Dodgers. Later, he revealed that as he warmed up, he realized his curve ball wasn't sharp, the torque and twist wasn't there, so he challenged the Twins, power to power, no guessing, no finesse, simply white lightning from start to finish. Lou Johnson, who had been a favorite of Koufax all year, spotted Sandy a homer in the fourth inning and Wes Parker drove in Ron Fairly in the same frame to give *the left-hander* a two-to-nothing lead. Relentlessly, Koufax attacked the Twins hitters, allowing just three hits, a walk, and no runs while striking out ten and finishing what he started six months earlier, by winning the final game. He was the World Series MVP.

The season ended. Koufax received a plethora of honors, including a second Cy Young Award as the best pitcher in baseball. But there was a hidden darkness, a sobering pain, both physical and emotional, that labored within him. There would never be another season like this one.

As the days rolled by, I realized the connection that held me was gone. The tension of the games, the veracity and authenticity that carried me through, was over. Koufax disappeared after the next season with his own burden, contradictions and ironies, eschewing the crowds and the publicity. His story came and went in a single span of time, a parade of games that climaxed with a simple act on a sacred day. Holiness and humility are always rare commodities. I wasn't looking for either one, but found myself wedded to the distraction, the drama, and exhilaration that flew off the pitcher's mound, the grit and steadfastness, the refusal of defeat and the sheer joy of the game. What endured through all my losses and confusion was a portrait of grace, a shaft of hope that radiated the possibility that sometimes the good guys win.

Two days before Thanksgiving, CJ's body arrived in a hearse with a military escort. Viewing was impossible—the mortar had detonated just below his position, his remains were strewn around the jungle. The casket remained sealed. Wiz returned—lean, broken, and tearless. His uniform pressed with indelible creases, his polished medals illuminated the disease of war. Wiz had shared the story with us before the funeral. He was positioned thirty yards from CJ when the shell exploded. The rest of the platoon had scattered in the bush. Wiz was alone as he viewed the obscenity of what happened to CJ. He radioed for retaliation. Within minutes, gunships seared through the jungle and incinerated the source of CJ's departed soul. That unequal exchange was etched in Wiz's face that day. CJ's death, he later confided to me, would never make any sense. It only created a deeper canyon of pain where the blood ran and ran like a flood raging to the sea.

Veronica and Dolores wailed throughout the mass, keening and shivering. Tony sat erect, directly in front of the casket, unflinching, stoic and self-absorbed. I sat in the back of the church next to Bryce and Barn. Rita and Shanti sat with the other girls in front of us. I remembered CJ's letter about the *counting*, the census, the way everything added up, his attention to enumeration and the details that afford sensibility to life, despite distress and heartbreak. How many hours till the next meal, the number of sunsets, his accumulation of new songs, lists and lists that measured the impossibility of his destiny that now equaled the sum of one minus one. The City of Angels had lost another soul.

I observed the nape of Rita's neck as the priest recited the final psalm. Her presence, once so familiar, now felt distant and remote, the passionate sweetness of youth had vanished with the wisps of incense that emanated from the altar. We all wept with inevitable remorse, not only for CJ, but for all of us and our conflicted, unresolved place in history.

After the service I went to the D'Agostino house to pay my respects. The air inside the home was thick with futility. I didn't know what I was going to say. Veronica approached me. We hugged, her face wet, gaunt, and without reproach. Despite the events of the day, her beauty remained unabated in a classic portrayal of tragedy. It was the final scene of what was an inexorable and fated drama.

"David, I'm so grateful. It's awful and it's impossible, but I knew this would happen. You were really the only one who understood," Veronica said.

"I didn't understand. I'll miss him, I really will."

We said goodbye and that was it. It was almost Thanksgiving, and I decided I'd had enough. There was no need for discussion or reflection. The season was over. I dropped out of UCLA at the end of the semester and moved up to San Francisco. Los Angeles no longer held me captive. Rene had already found a small apartment for me on Potrero Hill, overlooking the Mission District. I applied and received acceptance to San Francisco State. They had a decent English department. I wanted to start the new year in a place where I could breathe. I became a Giants fan after Koufax retired in 1966. Several years later I started writing a book about Lou and Koufax and all that had happened that season. I still hike through the Sierras, sometimes with Frank and Rene, sometimes alone.

ACKNOWLEDGEMENTS

I started writing The Captive in 2012 when it was called "The Season." Through its many iterations the one constant has been the presence of my beloved wife Cindy Grossman. She patiently buoyed me as I moved from first person to third person narrators. Over the years I added and deleted characters, changed names and locations and cut scenes and had bucket loads of doubt. Her assiduous support and optimism gave me the energy to continue the project year after year. I will always be grateful for her confidence in my writing.

I express my sincere appreciation to Jim Levy. A friend for more than forty years and author of more books than I can keep track of, he has always been someone who I could and did call when I had writing or publishing questions. From the beginning, he accentuated what he found positive and exciting in my characters. As the book moved toward completion, Jim was invaluable in directing me through the maze of publishing. His organizational expertise matches his creative talents, a rare combination. Jim has always been truthful, available and generous with his advice.

Rich Farrell and the "read and critique," group at San Diego Writer's Ink provided a solid platform to help complete the book. I gained a great deal of craft and understanding from the feedback of Rich and the other writers in the group. I must give credit to Rich whose idea it was to have the radio announcer introduce each chapter in the book.

It was so helpful to have readers plow through the novel and provide an honest assessment. My friend and colleague Karl Halpert offered recommendations and encouragement. "Wow you really did it." I thank my journalist, friend Andy Dennison for his honest appraisal of "my first novel." His suggestions gave me ideas about how I could improve the work. I have deep appreciation for my other readers including my friends Steve Neirman and Nancy Tetenbaum who took the time to read the work and give me their comments. Tammy Greenwood of San Diego Writers Ink also gave me substantial editorial advice on how to refine the narrative of the book.

Thank you to Helen Rynaski who did an excellent job of copy editing the book. It was her suggestion to end the book with the "Epilogue," in order to create a separation for the switch to the first-person narrative.

I offer special gratitude to Emily Sadow for her artistic design talents and patience in helping me create the "Pacoima Press," imprint. I would still be floating in the cyber wilderness without her guiding light to help me define the image and font of that creation.

The book would never have been printed without the expertise of Christina Hass of Zenith Publishing Solutions who put it all together in a neat professional package. Her encouragement and positive feedback allowed me to bring the project home.

ABOUT THE AUTHOR

Born in Chicago but raised in Los Angeles, Bruce Grossman traveled in Europe after graduating from UCLA in 1969. He worked as a  teacher and photographer in San Francisco until moving to Taos in 1976, where he continues to live and work as a psychotherapist. *The Captive* is his first novel. *We Go On Living*, his book of poetry about the death of his father, was published in 2007. *No One Came To Taos To Be Jewish*, a memoir and history of Jewish life in Taos was published in 2022. He is married to the pastel artist Cindy Grossman and has two sons, both born in Taos.

www.ingramcontent.com/pod-product-compliance
Lightning Source LLC
Chambersburg PA
CBHW030550020726
47494CB00005B/1561